"I need you," Miranda said.

"Or rather, a man like you," she amended.

"You need a thief and a murderer?"

A flicker of a smile almost warmed the cool look she gave him. "I was lucky they didn't hang you before I had a chance at you."

"We were both lucky," he said dryly.

The smile vanished, and he saw sadness and apology in her eyes. "Perhaps," she said, thinking of the dangers of life on the Silver Tejo, dangers he could have no way of predicting. "It remains to be seen how lucky you were, Mr. McClintock."

Dear Reader:

Thank you for all your letters and encouragement. Our New Year's resolution is to keep our focus on quality—to publish the kinds of involving, character-oriented stories you want to read.

We have two terrific books for you this month: Karen Keast's *China Star* and Patty Gardner Evans's *Silver Noose*. Though both authors have written numerous award-winning contemporary romances, these books mark their debuts in historicals. *China Star* is suspense filled as the heroine seeks to avenge her mother's murder and finds more than she bargained for. *Silver Noose* is an emotional, heart-warming story of a man who learns to love more deeply than he ever thought possible.

Next month, look for *Between the Thunder* by Patricia Potter and *Promises* by Pamela Wallace. And in coming months we have books by Jeanne Stephens and a new Cassie Edwards; Pat Potter's sequel to the popular *Swampfire* and the second book of Heather Graham Pozzessere's trilogy.

I look forward to receiving all your comments and suggestions—these books are for you. Please write to me at the address below.

Karen Solem
Editorial Director
Harlequin Historical
P.O. Box 7372
Grand Central Station
New York, New York 10017

Silver Noose

Patricia Gardner Evans

Harlequin Books

TORONTO • NEW YORK • LONDON
AMSTERDAM • PARIS • SYDNEY • HAMBURG
STOCKHOLM • ATHENS • TOKYO • MILAN

*To my father—who wanted a book about
deer hunters, lost treasure and loose women.
Sorry, Dad—this isn't it.*

Harlequin Historical first edition January 1989

ISBN 0-373-28614-7

PATRICIA GARDNER EVANS

a New Mexico native and bestselling author of contemporary romance, has traveled extensively throughout the West, exploring old ghost towns, Indian ruins and abandoned homesteads, and drawing inspiration for her stories from the land and people around her. Although this is her first historical romance, she feels a special kinship with the heroic pioneer women of the old West because she practices some of their homecrafts, such as collecting and using natural dyes, food preservation and quilting.

Chapter One

September 1883—Silver City, New Mexico Territory

God, he didn't want to die like this. He had seen a man hang once in Laredo. It was a ghastly way to die, doing a macabre dance at the end of a rope, slowly strangling to death, unable to control the intimate functions of your body, not allowed the least dignity as you died. And he would die like that, in agony, shamed.

There would be no clean, quick, merciful snap of his neck. His hands tightened around the rough iron bars in the window, not feeling the rusty slivers of metal embedding themselves in his fingers. For the past half hour he had been watching two deputies test the gallows, which was set a convenient distance away from the jail. Obviously the men believed it would see action tomorrow, and he had no reason to think they might be wrong. Time after time they released the trap that would open beneath his feet in a few short hours. Time after time he saw that the drop would not be enough to break his neck.

At last the men were satisfied that everything was working smoothly and left. The black skeleton of the gallows was silhouetted against the sunset as he turned away from the window. Did all condemned men share such a perverse fascination with the preparations for their own executions? Probably not, not if they were waiting out their last hours in this jail. A man of more normal height would have had to stretch his neck uncomfortably to see out the window, and since it was going to be stretched soon enough, he likely wouldn't be too eager to get in any practice. The man in the tiny cell laughed blackly to himself. It was yet another instance when he couldn't decide if his height was a blessing or a curse.

He sat on the cot and stared at the solid iron door across the floor from him, exactly three and one-half paces away. As jails went, he supposed it wasn't bad. The jailer had told him proudly that it was new, not the flimsy structure Billy the Kid had escaped from back in '78. He glanced around the cell sourly. As far as he was concerned, that wasn't an improvement. Escape had proved impossible.

Solid stone walls and a cement floor kept most of the varmints out and prisoners in. There was an iron cot—no mattress or blanket—but someone had tossed his bedroll in after him last night. He'd managed to spread it before he'd passed out. The slop bucket had been emptied once, and someone had left a cracked pitcher of mostly clean water while he had been unconscious.

There was a rusty ring in the middle of the cement floor to which his leg iron was locked. The chain was just long enough to let him pace from the window to the door and back again, five paces. He dimly remembered a heated argument among his captors last night about hobbles; he guessed the men favoring hobbles had been in the minority, a small favor.

Carefully he stretched out again on the cot, wincing as the action pulled the muscles along his ribs. He was sure a couple were cracked, if not broken. He bet he had a beaut of a shiner, too. His right eye was nearly swollen shut, and one front tooth was loose. He had put up one hell of a fight, but there had been too many of them, and he'd been sound asleep when they had jumped him. Sound asleep, hell, he admitted to himself disgustedly; he'd been sleeping off a drunk. That was what had gotten him into this whole damn mess in the first place. Already flush with a few shots and the pleasure of finding a couple of the boys he used to run with, he had followed the tall stranger agreeably enough to look at the horse he had for sale. The whiskey and his greed had clinched the deal as soon as he had seen the big Appaloosa stallion. The horse was superb, a ghost gray with black splattered over his rump. He had a white face with dark intelligent eyes, a black mane and long white tail, and long, elegant charcoal legs. The stranger had said he was down on his luck, or he would never have been willing to sell ol' Lucky.

The stranger had certainly looked down and out, with grimy, rough clothing and a poor saddle. The only thing outstanding about him was his height—almost equal to his own, the prisoner thought—and that magnificent horse. He had immediately handed over the three twenty-dollar gold pieces the stranger had shamefacedly demanded, along with his own ordinary bay gelding. A transfer of saddles and the deal was complete. Only later had he realized that the stranger had about as much need of those gold pieces as he had of any more dirt on his clothes; what he had needed was a plain, forgettable horse.

It was a wonder that after leaving Rusty and Tyree in the saloon a few hours later he had been able to ride to his camp in a grove of cottonwoods along a creek outside of town. That was where the posse had found him, blissfully snoring his life away. And that was where he had learned that ol' Lucky was lucky, all right, lucky for his former owner.

He supposed he ought to be grateful to the old man in the buggy accompanying the posse. He had turned out to be the territorial judge, and it was he who had persuaded the others not to beat him to death or string him up right there on one of the cottonwoods. It was also the old man who had found the money in the belt around his waist.

He might have been able to convince them that they had the wrong man, despite the horse and his height, but the money had damned him. They didn't want to believe his story that he was down from Montana, looking to buy longhorns to drive back to the ranch he and his brother owned at Big Hole. It was too late for a drive to be starting, and they didn't see any cattle. All they saw was a stranger who fit the right description, riding a one-of-a-kind horse and who had, almost to the dollar, the same amount of money as the mine payroll that had been stolen just that morning. They figured he'd spent the missing money on whiskey and the gals in Shady Lane.

The trial was held in the small Silver City courthouse, the Honorable Willis Hart, presiding. His only defense had been the truth; they had all the damning circumstantial evidence. The only character witnesses he might have called, Rusty and Tyree, had evidently sobered up and ridden out of town before they'd heard about the robbery and the capture of the thief. Even if they had heard, it was unlikely they would have connected him with it.

The first witness against him had been the payroll guard, who'd been carried into the packed courtroom on his bed, where he was recuperating from a bullet from the robber's Colt. The wounded man had positively identified him as the highwayman who had held up the paymaster's wagon, shot him, then ridden off with the monthly payroll for the Santa Rita copper mine. The guard's groans were especially convincing. After the guard's performance, the paymaster's dry corroborating testimony had been anticlimactic.

The old judge had kept the proceedings orderly and legal; he obviously knew the law. He admonished the jury to remember that the robber's face had been hidden by a bandanna and that neither witness remembered what he had been wearing. All they were sure of was his size and his horse. The evidence was all circumstantial, and the money had been recovered, but it made little difference to the eight men. There was a basic principle to be upheld there in the stuffy courtroom. A man had been shot, a Mexican, to be sure, but still a man, and someone had to pay, if only as an example to others contemplating similar acts. The jury had deliberated only as long as it took the foreman to call for a show of hands. Eight hands went up, agreeing that the tall stranger was guilty of robbery and mayhem. The judge would pronounce his sentence the following morning, but the prisoner held out small hope that it would be a lenient one. The judge had a duty to preserve law and order, and a legal hanging was preferable to a lynching.

He had been led, heavily manacled, back to the one-room jail. He had considered making a break for it, knowing he would get a bullet in the back for his efforts. Quick and clean, it was a preferable way to die—except that then everyone would be assured of his guilt, and, stupid as it might seem, that rankled. Still, the whole town was probably already convinced he was guilty, so he was still considering the idea, for tomorrow.

He had asked Elias Baca, the elderly jailer, for some writing paper and a pot of ink and a pen. To his surprise, Baca had fulfilled his request. The guard he was supposed to have shot was Baca's wife's cousin, but the old man seemed to bear him no rancor. He had even stayed to talk a bit, chattily recounting the history of the town and other hangings. For a town that had been in existence less than a decade and a half, there had been a remarkable number. The formality of a trial had been dispensed with in most instances until the arrival of Willis Hart. Baca had told him of one hanging, a few years before, where the victim's capital crime had been that of being "a damned nuisance." The jailer's milky brown eyes had looked at him sadly, seeming to imply that in his case, the town had far more justification.

He had talked, too, rambling on about his life cowboying and mining, pathetically grateful not to be left alone with his thoughts.

After Baca left, he wrote a hate-filled, impassioned plea for revenge to his brother, Josh, who was busy adding on to their log cabin and building corrals for the cattle that were never going to arrive. He felt almost as bad about losing the money they had both worked so hard for as he did about losing his life. Josh still carried a bullet in his chest from the claim jumpers who had tried to steal their placer mine near Bannock. They had worked like coolies on that damn mine, living like animals until they had a big enough stake to start the cattle ranch they had both dreamed about. That dream had been the only thing that made the filth and the exhaustion and the back-busting labor tolerable.

He and Josh had had the spot picked out for months, holding their breath, afraid someone else would file on it first. There was rolling natural pasture, a year-round stream, even a small lake and a few scattered groves of pine. It was only a day's ride from Wisdom, with its railhead for shipping beef to fill the hungry bellies back East.

The day they figured they had the gold they needed to start the ranch, he and Josh had sold the mine, adding that money to their stake, too. They'd ridden into Wisdom, filed adjoining homestead claims and bought up as much additional acreage as they could afford. Earlier this summer they had built a large comfortable cabin by one of the pine groves so it would be protected from the winter blizzards that swept down from Canada. Then he had come south.

He had brought nearly all their remaining money with him. He and Josh had debated waiting until the following spring, but decided against it. He had come early, with plenty of time to look over stock, contract for delivery and hire drovers, and then planned to winter over and be ready to start north as soon as the snows melted next spring. The grass would be fresh, water plentiful and the long drive from New Mexico to Montana relatively easy.

He had come to New Mexico Territory instead of Texas because he knew the area and thought he'd find better prices and just as good stock. Ten years ago, when things had gotten a little hot for him in West Texas, he had meandered over here. Not that he had done anything that wrong, although if a man could be hanged for being a damned nuisance, he guessed he hadn't done anything that right, either. It certainly wasn't anything he was proud of.

At twenty-three, he had been one of the youngest men ever to boss a cattle drive up the Goodnight-Loving Trail to Abilene. After he'd come back to Texas, he'd still been feeling a little woolly and full of himself. He had gotten into a fight over a whore at Rosina's in Pecos. He had paid for the damages and the man's burial and thought the nasty little episode was closed, but the man he had killed had two brothers and a number of friends, so he'd decided to try New Mexico for a while.

He tore up the letter and tossed it in the slop bucket. He couldn't send it. He had no wife, no family to miss him, but Josh did. His brother would come down here to try to avenge his death and might end up in this jail—or worse. Then what would happen to his sweet little Ellen and his newborn son, Gabriel? No, he had enough on his conscience already. He had let Josh and his family down badly enough already by losing their stake; he wouldn't make it any worse.

He yelled for Elias Baca. The jailer answered through the door and agreed to tell Judge Hart that the condemned man wanted to see him.

It was hours until the judge showed up, past sundown. He spent the time considering what he knew to be useless escape plans and trying to ignore a terrifying sense of helplessness. He also prayed that he wouldn't disgrace himself, that he would die like a man.

The iron door swung open at last, then shut behind Willis Hart. "Good evening, McClintock. What can I do for you?" the judge rumbled jovially.

He answered without preamble. "I want you to write a letter to my brother and send him this watch." He pulled a gold pocket watch from his black leather vest. He had been surprised when he had woken up this morning to find he still had it, but the men who had captured him were interested in revenge, not thievery. The heavy gold chain anchoring it to his vest had broken during the fight, the gold nugget fob lost. "It was our father's. As the eldest son, it was passed on to me. Since I don't have a son, it should go to Josh, my brother." He handed the watch and a sheet of paper with Josh's address to Judge Hart. The judge seemed reluctant to take them, finally shoving the watch and paper in a coat pocket without looking at them. "I can't give you anything to pay for sending it, unless you want to take it out of the money I didn't steal." His mouth turned down bitterly. "Or you can sell the horse."

Willis Hart relaxed back on the bunk and regarded the man standing before him. McClintock clearly expected that he was going to serve a long prison sentence for his crime—if not worse—yet he handled himself with dignity. He was a good-looking man, not a youth anymore, but still young, with the years he'd spent on cattle ranges weathered into his handsome face. Dark haired, blue-eyed, he was much taller than most, several inches over six feet, yet he had the lean wiriness of the best cowboys. The judge sighed inaudibly. No doubt he'd had more than his share of women. Despite his clothing and the heavy mustache, he was no common cowboy. There was too much intelligence in that face; his speech was too refined, hinting at a good family somewhere.

"Do you have any more family, Jesse?" he asked. "A wife, perhaps?" He added in an aside, "You don't mind if I call you 'Jesse,' do you?"

If he minded he gave no sign. "No wife. My mother and sister are back in Kansas. My brother will notify them." He met the judge's direct gaze squarely. "I would count it a favor if you would tell him I was found dead, bushwhacked, no money on the body."

The judge eyed him reflectively for several long seconds. "You don't want him to know the truth. Why not? If you're innocent, as you say . . ." He purposely let his voice trail off.

Jesse's lips curled in a cold, humorless smile under his mustache. "The truth hasn't done me much good, Judge, and it would do my brother even less. He'd just come down here and try to prove I was innocent. That would hardly bring me or the money back, would it?"

Judge Hart nodded his agreement. "How am I supposed to know your brother's name and address?"

Jesse had thought out all the details. "A letter I was going to mail him was found on my body, along with the watch the bushwhackers missed. They were given to you to dispose of. You didn't send the letter because there was blood all over it, but you were able to read the address on the envelope." He smiled fleetingly. "You might also tell him the bushwhackers were caught and hanged, but the money was already gone."

Willis Hart was silent for a long moment. Intuitively, he'd been certain that Jesse McClintock had no more stolen that payroll than he had himself, and his concern for his brother instead of himself was just more evidence of his innocence. If it had been possible, Hart would have delayed the trial, but he hadn't been given the luxury of time. The posse who had found McClintock had been hot for "justice" and only too eager to become a lynch mob. He'd been able to avert a hanging on the spot only by promising a fast trial.

The judge sighed again. He wished he didn't have to do what he was going to, but sometimes justice had little to do with guilt or innocence. Still, McClintock was getting a chance that ten years in the hellhole the territory called a prison or a rope wouldn't give him, and, if he'd read him right, the tall young man would think a fighting chance was certainly better than none.

"I have a proposition for you, Jesse," he said finally. "My brother Thomas, my half brother, actually, was killed by a few of Geronimo's braves several months ago." The Apache chieftain and a band of Chiricahuas had escaped from the White Mountain reservation in Arizona the year before and were again wandering their homeland in Chihuahua and Sonora, with occasional raids into the United States, where the pickings were better. "He left my sister-in-law saddled with a ranch, and she's having a hard time by herself. Her last two foremen were ambushed by the Apaches, too, and the rest of the hands have drifted away. The ranch is down along the Mexican border, and it gets raided regularly, both by the Apaches and Mexican bandits. She's been up here the past few days trying to find a good man willing to take the job of foreman and run the ranch for her. Elias Baca told me about your ranching experience.'' Willis Hart glanced casually at the man who was standing so motionless, seemingly not even breathing. ''I think you might just be the man she needs.''

Jesse felt his heart leap almost out of his chest, but his face showed nothing. ''After being convicted of robbery and attempted murder, you're letting me go, to run a ranch?''

Willis Hart knew what the young man was seeing: a portly, almost elderly man with a white fringe around his shiny pink scalp, wearing a rumpled black suit and string tie, with a tomato soup stain on his white shirt. He was especially seeing that bulbous, brilliantly purple, enormous nose that reposed in the middle of his face. It overshadowed all his other features, rather nice ones, if he did say so himself. Even so, someone staring—and everyone stared—at him for an hour wouldn't be able to say later what color his eyes were or if he had a beard. They were brown, and he didn't. Judge Hart knew Jesse McClintock thought he was looking at a rummy old sot, listening to some craziness he'd found at the bottom of a bottle. The fact was that he was a strict teetotaller and had been all his life. McClintock seemed to find his height a curse; he should have to live with this nose, the judge thought sourly.

''I'm not letting you go, Jesse,'' he said quietly. ''I'm sentencing you to one year on the Silver Tejo, my sister-in-law's ranch, and before you get to feeling too happy about that, remember what happened to the last two foremen. One only lasted nine days, and I hear he didn't die right away, after the Apaches took him.'' He let Jesse consider that for a moment. ''You'll be in her custody. Her men will carry out any order you give them, as long as it has to do with the operation of the ranch. They will report immediately any sign that you are planning to escape. They will shoot you if you try. At the end of a year, I'll review your case. If you've done a good job—and,'' he added sardonically, ''if you're still alive, I'll commute the rest of your sentence. Then you'll be free.''

Jesse gave a curt nod. He wondered what these men who were going to shoot him were, since they apparently weren't cowhands, but he quickly dropped the thought. He had more immediate concerns at the moment. Losing his money and a year out of his life for something he hadn't done was hardly fair, and he was filled with useless rage against fate, but he bore the old judge no ill will. The man was offering him a better chance than he had dared hope for. The tide of elation was rising higher inside him, but still he refused to let himself get his hopes up. His mouth took a cynical turn. "Won't the good citizens of Silver City be annoyed with the sentence?"

"Some of them will be," Judge Hart agreed matter-of-factly. "But then they'll remember that no one was killed and the money was recovered, and they'll remember what Silver City was like before I was appointed. The townspeople are willing to forgive me a few eccentricities in return for the law and order I brought them." He made the statement without any false modesty, then added with an almost cheerful note, "Then, too, they'll remember where I'm sending you and figure it's a pretty good joke on you. Prison would be a hell of a lot safer. They'll probably start a betting pool on how long it will take the Apaches or the bandits to get you."

Jesse gave the judge a measured look. "If it's so dangerous, why does your brother's widow stay on?"

"You'll see why when you get there," he answered shortly, then stood. "You're leaving tonight. Unless," he added in dry question, "you have a hankering to see the inside of the territorial prison in Santa Fe?"

Jesse shook his head mutely. He'd take his chances with the Apaches, yet he still couldn't quite believe that what the judge was saying was true. It sounded too easy. Perhaps it was some macabre joke, or a transparent excuse to shoot him during a faked escape attempt.

The judge called for Elias Baca. The jailer unlocked the door and shuffled into the cell. He was half carrying, half dragging the heavy iron manacles Jesse had had to wear during the trial. They were locked around his wrists once again, and he was freed from the floor ring, his leg shackle left lying empty on the cement.

Jesse crossed the dark-shadowed, hard-packed dirt street. His back muscles bunched, ready for the shouts and the burn of hot lead. They never came. Aside from the three of them, no one else was even out. Jesse followed Judge Hart up three steps to the porch of a good-sized red brick house. Lucky was tied to the hitching rail beside two other horses, a buckskin and a gray. Jesse's quick glance told him the buckskin was a tough little cow pony and the gray was an Arabian, a rare, costly animal.

His eyebrows arched at the interior of the judge's home. It was surprisingly elegant and well kept. Maybe the old man wasn't as much of a rummy as he appeared to be. He had certainly been stone cold sober each time Jesse had seen him.

Jesse was brought up short at the door to the parlor. A nudge in his back from Elias Baca pushed him into the room, and he moved to stand before the cold black iron-and-chrome parlor stove. He knew he was staring, but he couldn't help himself. If this was the judge's sister-in-law, her husband had likely died willingly, grateful never to have to wake up in bed next to her again. She sat on a sofa across the room, and much of her face was hidden by her hair and the stained and shapeless floppy hat she wore, but what he could see looked like a piece of rawhide left out in the desert sun to dry and shrivel. She had a large wart on her chin, and her gray hair looked like an unshaken dustmop. She wore a man's coat over her dress, both of them some indefinable dark color. The old woman shifted on the elegant, green velvet sofa. Lord, Jesse thought in disgust, she even had a big potbelly and no doubt a tongue that would peel the hide off a man. She had to be the ugliest old woman he had ever seen.

Chapter Two

The woman never looked at him. Her companion, a middle-aged, stocky Mexican, had pulled his armchair nearly up to her knees, and from the tension he felt in the room, Jesse knew his and the judge's arrival had interrupted an argument between the two of them.

The Mexican gave him a long, hard look. He had a carefully clipped salt-and-pepper mustache and thick graying hair, clean and neatly brushed, in contrast to the slovenliness of the woman. His clothes were those of a horseman, denim pants tucked into the tops of good boots, spurs with large Mexican rowels, a collarless shirt with a red kerchief around his neck and a dark vest. His hat, flat brimmed and high crowned like a sombrero, with a band of silver conchos, lay with his gloves on the carpet beside his chair. The man's eyes were black and opaque, giving away nothing. The years had eroded his face into a landscape as harsh as the desert land he lived in. Cut him, Jesse thought, and he'd bleed sand.

He leaned back against the stove and tried to ease the weight of the manacles chafing his wrists. The judge sat down beside the woman, and a low-voiced discussion began. The Mexican joined in, but his gaze still occasionally drifted back to Jesse, who ignored him and occupied himself with the judge's parlor. The polished plank floor was almost covered by a Persian carpet, the rose and green colors soft with age. Heavy velvet and airy lace draped the two tall windows. There were two more overstuffed velvet chairs with footrests, and several spindly tables overloaded with knickknacks. A collection of china shepherdesses herded their invisible flock across an ornately carved mantel.

Several large, sepia-toned photographs in oval gilt frames hung on the wall over the sofa. One was of the judge, ten to fifteen years younger, seated stiffly in a chair with a plain middle-aged woman standing behind him. His nose had photographed prominently, Jesse noted with an unconscious grin. Below it was a family portrait, the judge and his wife again, and three young adults. Jesse's grin widened. The two girls and their brother were no doubt eternally thankful they had not inherited their father's most outstanding feature.

Flanking these photographs were two more of a man Jesse assumed to be another of the judge's brothers or his wife's. In the first photograph the man was with a woman about his own age, late thirties, early forties. Both the man and woman were handsome people. In the second he was several years older, the new woman many years younger. His hand rested possessively on her waist. Jesse couldn't blame him.

The woman was beautiful. As tall as the man at her side, she had dark hair, a finely boned elegant face and a slender figure. Her mere photograph in the same room made the old hag on the sofa look even worse, if possible. The man had been lucky, Jesse reflected; he had had two fine-looking women. There were no photographs of Judge Hart's late half brother and his wife. The old bitch probably broke the camera, Jesse laughed to himself.

He felt eyes on him again. The judge and the Mexican were now engrossed in conversation, and the old woman was looking at him, staring so intently, Jesse realized, that she didn't see he was staring back just as hard. The coal oil chandelier shone fully on her upturned face, and he was so startled by her eyes that he took no notice of the rest of it. They were the most unusual eyes he'd ever seen, inexplicably beautiful in that hard-favored face. Long thick lashes fringed them, black, not gray like her hair. Her eyes were the color of twilight, Jesse decided, allowing himself a rare touch of whimsy, that brief time between dusk and dark when the light is a misty lavender. But her eyes weren't misty; they were clear as glass, as if he could see down to her soul. As if anyone would want to see into the soul of that old harridan, Jesse snorted silently. Around the iris was a band of darker color, maybe black, maybe blue. He leaned closer in spite of himself, trying to see. There couldn't be another pair of eyes like that on earth.

Her eyes widened abruptly, then fell. Staring, Miranda! You were staring, she scolded herself, and he caught you. His clothes were filthy from the fight Willis had told her he put up when he was captured. Except for his once white shirt, he was dressed all in black—hat, boots, vest and pants. Unconsciously her eyes strayed back to him. His pants looked as if they must stretch somehow to go over his powerful thighs before they molded themselves to his lean hips and flat belly. She forced her attention down to his boots.

They reached almost to his knees and looked expensive, custom-made. His pants were tucked into the tops, and she could see that his long legs were straight, not bowed as so many cowboys' were.

He should look out of place in this elegant room as she did, Miranda thought, yet, despite his clothes and the iron cuffs on his wrists, he looked right at home. Standing at his ease in Willis's fancy parlor as if he had every right to be there, the man didn't look like a cold-blooded murderous thief, although Willis had told her that he'd been convicted of being exactly that only this morning. Then, in the next breath, he had told her that this criminal was just the man she needed to run the Silver Tejo and he was sentencing him to be her foreman. Willis was convinced that the tall stranger was innocent, and he was equally convinced that his plan would solve her problem as well as save a man from being unjustly imprisoned—or hung. Miranda stared at her hands in her lap. She wished she could be as certain that Willis's plan might not turn out to be a much harsher sentence.

From under her lashes, she slanted a cautious look up at his face, passing over the broad chest covered by his ripped and bloodied shirt and open vest. His wide-brimmed hat was pushed back on his head, revealing curly dark hair long enough to brush the scarf at the back of his neck. A thick sweep of mustache covered his upper lip, while his lower lip was well defined and surprisingly full. His dark eyebrows were naturally arched, giving his face a sardonic, almost wicked expression.

At the moment the mustache and his mouth were curled slightly in disgust. She couldn't blame him. She knew only too well what she looked like. Oddly, though, his eyes were soft, almost sympathetic, as he studied her, unaware that she was studying him, too. They were deep set, shadowed by girlishly long, thick lashes, and a smoky dark blue, like the storm clouds that built up over the mountains at home on summer evenings.

Despite his eyelashes, his features had more than enough masculinity to save him from prettiness, but she would bet that he caused more than his share of feminine heart flutters and swooning. He wouldn't be causing any tonight. Underneath the dark stubble of his beard, his skin had a sickly pallor that made his bruises all the more painful to see. His left eye was a vivid purple and red, and swollen nearly shut. The right eye was puffy and discolored, too, and there was a nasty scrape on his cheek. His bottom lip had been split, and his left ear was swollen away from his skull, as if someone had tried to tear it off. Miraculously his fine, straight nose hadn't been broken.

His body had been damaged, too. From the way he was holding his left elbow to his side, Miranda suspected he was trying to support hurt ribs. Willis touched her hand, and she turned to him.

Jesse was beginning to wonder if the judge had forgotten him, when the old man called him over to introduce him to his sister-in-law. He crossed the carpet and stood in front of the woman.

"Miranda, this is Jesse McClintock, your new foreman. Mr. McClintock, Mrs. Hart, my late brother's widow." The judge's hand indicated the other man. "And Manolo Rivera, the...ranch manager."

Rivera nodded silently, and Miranda Hart looked up for one very brief moment. Finally Jesse remembered to take off his hat, the chain connecting the shackles of his wrists clinking softly. He had been so taken aback at her appearance that he had forgotten to remove it when he'd entered the room. "Ma'am," he said expressionlessly. "Rivera." He wondered what the Mexican really did for her. The judge had said she had no ranch hands, yet he had also warned him that her men would be guarding him to see that he didn't escape. Since they weren't hands, what were they?

Miranda Hart said something too low for him to hear, and the judge patted her hand where it rested on the dark, dirty stuff of her dress. "All right, Miranda, dear. In a few minutes." He glanced up and gave Jesse a cool, steady look. "I'm sure you understand the realities of your situation. You may have been entertaining the notion that once you're clear of Silver City you can hightail it for Montana. Let me assure you that both Miranda and Manolo are excellent shots. I've also wired the sheriff in Deming. If he doesn't see the three of you the day after tomorrow—" Hart emphasized the word three "—he'll be sending out a posse to find you. So will I, and I'm sure you'll remember that posses don't worry about bringing escaped prisoners back alive."

Jesse gave him a brief nod indicating his understanding that he was still very much a prisoner. He had underestimated the old man. That was exactly what he had planned, to slip away from the Mexican and the old woman at the first opportunity. Escape might be more difficult than he had thought, but there wasn't the slightest chance in hell that he would spend one second longer than he had to in this godforsaken country.

Miranda Hart, the judge and Rivera rose, and Jesse saw that the widow was taller than she had looked sitting down, as tall for a woman as he was for a man. Judge Hart indicated that Jesse was to follow him. They went down a short hall into the kitchen.

After opening a cupboard, the judge took out a roll of linen bandage. "My sister-in-law noticed you were holding your side and

thought maybe your ribs had been hurt in the fight last night."
When McClintock's shirt came off, Willis Hart drew in his breath
sharply. The left side of Jesse's chest, from the nipple down past
his belt, was one ugly bruise. The purpled imprint of a boot heel
was clearly visible over his upper ribs. It was a wonder they weren't
staved in.

Deftly the judge wound the bandage tight around his ribs. After the first excruciating stab of fire, Jesse breathed easier. Riding
would not be pleasant, but now, at least, it would be bearable.

Willis Hart secured the end of the bandage, patting Jesse's
shoulder in an oddly paternal gesture. "There. You'll survive."
While Jesse eased back into his shirt, the judge reached into a
pocket of his baggy suit. For the first time, Jesse saw a genuine
smile on Judge Hart's face as he handed back his watch. "You may
yet have a son to give this to, Jesse."

The widow Hart and Rivera were already mounted, Mrs. Hart
on the gray and Rivera on the buckskin, when the judge led him
back to the front porch. As Jesse swung into the saddle, Willis Hart
stepped down from the porch and took his sister-in-law's hand.

Miranda Hart smiled and leaned down from her saddle to kiss
her brother-in-law's plump cheek. "Thank you, Willis," she said
softly, her smile fading as she darted a glance at the tall, stoic man
on the Appaloosa beside her. "I just hope we're doing the right
thing."

Her brother-in-law squeezed her hand reassuringly. "We are,
Miranda. Trust me."

Jesse watched the byplay, more than a little impatient to be on
his way. A few seconds later, he got his wish as the three of them
rode down the quiet street out of town, unnoticed.

Willis Hart entered his big, empty house, feeling suddenly like
the tired old man he pretended he wasn't. He shambled back into
the parlor and crossed the room to stand before the photographs
on the wall. Reaching out, he straightened one of the frames.

"Well, I've done what you would have wanted, Thomas, may
God forgive us both, but it may not work out the way you wanted.
You and I both know she doesn't cotton much to being looked af-
ter." A dry chuckle escaped him as he turned away to lower the
chandelier and extinguish it. "I expect Miranda and Jesse Mc-
Clintock are going to have their hands full with each other."

Jesse hadn't had a meal in twenty-four hours, and the last one
had been mostly whiskey. His empty belly was growling for food,
but he ignored it. The desire to put as much distance as possible
between himself and the citizens of Silver City as soon as possible

was stronger than his wish for food. He wasn't as confident as the judge seemed to be that they would approve of his unorthodox punishment.

Manolo Rivera set a satisfyingly fast pace, with Jesse close behind and Miranda Hart riding drag. He had to suffer the indignity of holding on to the saddle horn to stay in the saddle, because Rivera had kept the reins of his horse, but he accepted the situation philosophically. Compared to the indignities he had feared, it was nothing.

A cloudy moon lit the stage road, giving enough light for Jesse to see the country they were riding through. There wasn't much to look at. Nothing could thrive in the alkali soil but mesquite, cactus and yucca. The cactus grew low, its soft pads spiked with long vicious spines to catch the careless. The leaves of the yucca were longer, broader spikes with razor sharp tips that could slash even a horse's tough hide. Even the ferny mesquite, which looked like huge hairy spiders crouching in the moonlight, had wicked thorns. Nothing about this land was friendly.

Dawn was breaking over the peaks of the Black Range when Rivera turned east on a side trail. The sunrise, which Jesse had thought only a short while ago might well be his last, was a glory of pinks and golds and oranges. After a couple of miles, Rivera turned back north, following a faint track toward a jumble of huge, shadowy shapes. As they rode closer, Jesse could see that the shapes were massive boulders, rising out of the flat desert like a city of rocks, turned to pure gold by the rising sun's alchemy. Some stood alone, silent sentinels guarding the city, while others leaned on each other like sloppy drunks.

Rivera led the way into the center of a ring of towering rocks. Following his example, Jesse dismounted and watched as Rivera hurried over to help Mrs. Hart down from her horse. She fell heavily against him, then straightened with obvious effort.

Together, he and Rivera picketed the horses inside a neighboring ring of rocks. Watered by a natural spring, there was plenty of lush grass, along with several large oaks to shade the natural corral. Apparently they would continue to travel at night, a plan Jesse heartily approved of.

Back in the clearing where they were to camp, Jesse kicked a shallow trough for his hips in the soft sand, then knelt to lay out his bedroll for later. He swore under his breath as the heavy chain of his manacles caught in the blankets, making a hopeless tangle. He sensed a movement next to him, and a pair of slim, graceful hands appeared beside his own and began to efficiently untangle the chain from the wool. Jesse glanced sideways, but, her face hidden by her hat and her messy hair, the widow Hart was intent on his bed, not him. Sitting back on his heels, he waited awhile until she finished spreading the blankets into a smooth bed. "Thank you, ma'am," he said quietly.

She nodded wordlessly and began rising clumsily to her feet. Automatically Jesse slipped a hand beneath her elbow to help her up. Despite her bulk, she didn't weigh as much as he expected. They stood up together, and as soon as he was sure she was steady, he dropped his hand. The widow turned away without acknowledging his help in any way.

An hour later, unable to sleep, Miranda rose from her blankets. She stirred up a pot of beans she'd set to cook while they slept and fed the low flames a couple more fat dry sticks. Jesse McClintock had built the small, smokeless fire, virtually invisible in daylight. Sitting down in the soft sand, she braced her aching back against a boulder. She should have listened to Leola, she decided with a weary sigh, and come by wagon, even if it was slower.

She stared at the long shape wrapped in a dark blanket on the other side of the fire. She was sure he'd been asleep before his head had hit the folded saddle blanket he was using for a pillow. He had wolfed down the jerky and tough biscuits Manolo had given him, and she knew he had gone to sleep hungry. She should have given him her share, she thought guiltily; she wasn't hungry, anyway. Laying her cheek on the boulder's cool, rough surface, she closed her eyes. One night, almost as if he'd had a premonition of his death, Thomas had told her that he counted on her to do whatever was necessary to keep the Silver Tejo secure for Tommy in case something happened to him, and she had assured him that she would. Oh, Thomas, she cried silently, why did I make you that terrible promise? Will this man have to die, too, to help me keep it? Tears of exhaustion and despair tracked through the dust on her cheeks.

Eyes closed, Jesse lay still, waiting to hear the sound that had wakened him again. Rivera snored, and one of the horses whinnied, but those normal sounds wouldn't have alerted him. To have penetrated his nearly unconscious state of exhaustion, the noise would have to have been out of place, unexpected. He heard it again, a faint sound even in the still desert air, and he opened his eyes to find the source.

The huddled figure scant yards away from him was shaking, and he realized Miranda Hart was crying, sobbing quietly. Strangely, he felt moved by the stricken old woman. He had the curious urge to take her in his arms, to promise her that everything would be all right. He drifted back into sleep, instead, his last thought the sur-

prising realization that even a woman who looked like the end of
a long hard winter could have truly loved her husband and still
missed him.

They set off again at dusk after a hasty supper of beans and more
biscuits, even harder and drier than those they'd had for breakfast. He felt every fist and boot that had connected during the
fight, but at least his belly was full, Jesse thought ruefully. He noticed that Miranda Hart did not eat until he'd set his tin plate aside.

The ride was fast and silent again. The setting sun had bleached
most of the blue from the sky and tinted the scattered clouds an
orangy pink. The land flattened out, the vegetation getting spars-
er as the patches of white alkali became more numerous. The air
was so clear he could see for miles to the blue peaks of the Florida
mountains on the southern horizon. The mountains straddled the
U.S.-Mexican border, and the widow's ranch lay in the middle of
them. Silver Tejo. Jesse rolled the name softly on his tongue. He
gave the second word the throat-clearing h sound that he knew it
should have for the J. Tejo was a Spanish bastardization of an
Apache word meaning well, or spring.

The moon rose, full and very bright. Jesse passed the time trying
to pick out landmarks he remembered from his last trip through
here, nearly eight years earlier. Cook's Peak to the east was easy.
It was visible for miles, but he wasn't looking for the easy landmarks. He was looking for the smaller, more personal ones.
Whenever he traveled through new country, he stored away in his
memory likely spots for campsites, places to hole up from the
weather or hostiles. Automatically he rated them against his needs.
Was there adequate water, protection, fuel and game? He didn't
find much in his memory from this desolate country.

Near midnight they stopped for a brief rest. The night wind was
cold, and leaning against her horse, Miranda absorbed the patient
mare's heat gratefully. Absently she watched Jesse McClintock
fumble with his cigarette fixings, his manacles making him clumsy.
She doubted that he was often clumsy. He spilled a bit of tobacco
into the thin paper and tightened the string on the muslin tobacco
pouch with his even white teeth. The tip of his tongue flicked along
an edge of the paper, and she felt an odd tingling in her upper lip,
almost as if his tongue had touched there, instead. Unconsciously, her tongue mimicked the motion of his, trying to lick the
tingle away. He rolled the cigarette with an expert twist of his fingers and struck a match, protecting the sputtering flame in his
cupped hands. The brief yellow flare illuminated his face and his
wrists, and Miranda stifled a gasp of horror. The matchlight re-

vealed streaks of bright red where the iron manacles had rubbed his wrists raw.

"Give me your hands, Mr. McClintock."

Jesse's head snapped up at a voice that sounded like grains of sand ground against glass. They were the first words Miranda Hart had ever spoken to him. He saw a key clutched in her fingers, and grinding out his cigarette under his boot heel, he slowly held out his hands.

The key hovered over the lock on his handcuffs. "Do you promise not to try to escape, Mr. McClintock?"

He almost laughed in her face, but she sounded so serious and was looking up at him so solemnly. "I promise," he answered gruffly, feeling ridiculously guilty at the lie. Well, he justified it to himself as she unlocked the iron bands, he wouldn't exactly be breaking his promise. While they'd been riding, he'd decided that perhaps it would be best to delay his escape until after he reached the Silver Tejo. He could use a few days to heal up, and another horse and a few supplies wouldn't hurt, either, since they had taken all his money.

After looping the heavy shackles over her forearm, Miranda dug around in a pocket of her voluminous coat. "Here." She slapped a flat tin into his palm. "Rub this on your wrists. I use it on my hands."

He'd wondered at the incongruously soft and delicate look of her hands when she'd made his bed up for him. What the hell, he'd laughed silently, imagining her slathering her hands with some kind of cream every night; even homely old gals deserved a vanity or two. He slid back the top on the tin and dipped out a little of the pale unguent inside on one blunt forefinger. He sniffed it, but couldn't identify the faint, clean scent. Gingerly he rubbed it on the raw flesh on one wrist, expecting it to sting. Instead the salve immediately cooled and soothed his abraded skin. After he'd treated both wrists, he closed the tin and handed it back.

"You may keep it." She glanced up before she turned away, allowing him another brief glimpse of those absurdly beautiful eyes. "I have another."

He was remounting, when Rivera rushed over. From atop Lucky, Jesse affected disinterest in the intense argument that ensued between the Mexican and the widow. The argument was in Spanish, and his was rusty from years of disuse, but he got most of it. Rivera argued impassionately that the murdering thief couldn't be trusted and, forgive his disrespect, but why had she done such a *loco* thing as to let him loose?

Miranda Hart replied calmly that the thief's—Jesse appreciated the fact that she left out "murdering"—wrists were bleeding, and besides, he had promised not to escape. Her Spanish, although fluent, had an odd accent that Jesse couldn't quite place. The Mexican stared at her, speechless, then sent Jesse a menacing look as he turned away, muttering maledictions under his breath.

As soon as Rivera was out of earshot, Jesse decided to push his luck a bit further. "How about giving me back the reins to my horse? I've already promised not to escape," he reminded her with a straight face.

Miranda stared up at him for a moment, then at the stiff back of Manolo, chewing her bottom lip in an oddly childish gesture. "Well, I don't know," she began. "It might be too much of a temptation for you."

He leaned down from the saddle, very close to her, as he argued with soft persuasion. "Now just where would I go, ma'am, with no gun, no money and no food?"

She didn't jump back, appalled by the possibility of contact with him, as he'd cynically anticipated. Instead she held her ground, their heads so close he could feel the warmth of her breath on his cheek and smell her unexpected flower-sweet scent. Her eyes searched his for several long moments; then she nodded gravely and stepped to Rivera's horse to unwind Lucky's reins from the saddle horn. Silently she handed them up to him.

"Thank you, ma'am," Jesse said softly. Rivera glared at her with hopeless disapproval when he saw what new craziness she had done, but Jesse noticed that she carefully avoided looking at the Mexican.

They rode into the dusty railroad town of Deming just after sunup. Jesse was wondering if they would stop or push on to the ranch, when Miranda Hart halted her mare in front of the Harvey Hotel. Rivera began another argument about the wisdom of stopping, but she won it with two words—"I'm tired."

Late in the afternoon they met again in the hotel dining room. As Jesse approached the table, he saw a man with a silver star on his chest leaving it. The man gave him a brief glance, and Jesse thought sardonically that the judge had indeed wired the Deming sheriff. Despite her long rest, Miranda Hart looked worse than ever. She wore the dusty, shapeless hat to dinner, and wiry gray wisps of hair straggled out from under the brim, nearly hiding her face. She was the recipient of numerous looks, mostly disparaging ones, and the small blond woman who seemed to be in charge of the Harvey girls waiting tables stared especially hard. Probably trying to decide if she should ask the old woman to leave before the other diners lost their appetites, Jesse thought in disgust.

As if she were acutely embarrassed, Mrs. Hart avoided looking at anyone, especially the blonde. She kept her head down and picked at her food. Despite his impatience with her draggle-tailed look when, with just a little effort, she could have been at least presentable, Jesse felt sorry for her. She couldn't have many treats in her hard life, and he found himself inexplicably wanting her to enjoy the good meal and fancy surroundings.

They ate in silence, and Jesse eavesdropped on the conversations at the other tables around them. The topic of all of them was the Apaches' latest outrage. He learned that a few months earlier Chatto, one of Geronimo's lieutenants, and a few braves had killed a judge and his wife near Lordsburg, about sixty miles west of Deming, and kidnapped their five-year-old son. Now word had reached Deming just that morning that Chatto had been raiding in the area again. One of the few survivors had identified him from his distinctive flattened nose. The reports coming by telegraph from eastern Arizona and western New Mexico indicated that he and the twenty-six men with him had ridden an incredible four hundred miles in just six days, slaughtering and looting as they went. Twenty-six whites had been found dead so far, and General Crook himself was leading the force against him, but the consensus in the dining room was that pursuit was futile. The U.S. Army had no hope of catching the Apaches. Always they managed to slip back across the border into Mexico, disappearing like shadows in the night.

An hour later they were back in the saddle, still heading south. A couple of miles out of town, Rivera pulled up and turned around in his saddle to open one of the saddle bags across the buckskin's rump. Within seconds he was heavily armed, *bandoleras* fully loaded with bullets crossed over his chest and a gun belt with two pistols buckled around his waist. The only arms Jesse had seen up to then were the rifles in saddle scabbards that both the widow and Rivera carried. He felt naked without his Colt and Winchester; he didn't, he realized, even know what had happened to them.

Out of the corner of his eye he watched Miranda Hart belt a six-gun around her potbelly. She was looking at him as if she were trying to make up her mind about something.

"Give Mr. McClintock his rifle, Manolo."

"*¡Señora!*" Rivera's response was a furious burst of Spanish that dealt mainly with Jesse's proved lack of character and general untrustworthiness.

Miranda suppressed a sigh. Manolo had already made it more than clear that he didn't share Willis's opinion of Jesse Mc-Clintock's innocence. "Give him the rifle," she repeated implacably, "or I'll give him mine. It's not right that he be without a weapon in this country."

With obvious reluctance, Rivera handed the Winchester over, and Jesse didn't miss the silent warning as the older man patted the gun on his left hip. After checking to see that the rifle was loaded, he slipped it into its scabbard, then caught Miranda Hart's eyes. "How about my Colt?"

Wordlessly she signaled Rivera to return his pistol. The Mexican jerked Jesse's rolled up gun belt out of the saddle bag and shoved it across the narrow gap between their horses. Rapidly Jesse buckled it on, then drew his gun and snapped it open. The bottom of a brass shell showed in all six cylinders.

They started off again, and Jesse casually dropped back until he was riding even with Miranda Hart. For no reason that he could think of, he felt compelled to watch over her. Slumped and swaying in the saddle, the old girl was obviously near the end of her strength.

From the desert around them came the usual night sounds—an occasional furtive scurrying in the bushes as they passed, whistles and disturbances in the air from swooping nighthawks, the slow heavy wing beats of a horned owl cruising for dinner and a hopeful howl from a lonely coyote. The higher the full moon rose in the clear, star-sprinkled sky, the darker and lonelier the desert became. Nowhere in the solid blackness was there the warmth and welcome of a light shining through a window, or even the friendly flicker of a campfire.

They had been riding for an hour, when Miranda stopped without warning. The mare tossed her head and stamped impatiently while Miranda, silent and unmoving, stared ahead at the sawtoothed mountains rising from the flat desert. Moonlight on the dark jagged peaks made them glow with an eerie phosphorescence against the black sky. Home.

The road crossed the northern boundary of the Silver Tejo here, and she always stopped, a little ritual that comforted her because she knew she was on her own land and would soon be in her own house. She shifted in the saddle, trying to relieve the ache in the small of her back, and her glance fell on Jesse McClintock. He was standing in his stirrups, stretching his long legs and flexing his wide shoulders, the automatic reflex of a man who had spent years in a saddle and learned to take any opportunity to ease cramped muscles. His head tilted back, as if he were tasting the air, and Miranda thought suddenly of the mountain lion she had seen last spring.

Suddenly a figure appeared on the canyon rim, silhouetted against the full moon. Jesse's rifle was halfway to his shoulder, when he saw the figure raise an arm and wave. A two-note whistle echoed down from the top of the canyon, and Rivera whistled back. They rode deeper into the canyon, a watchman showing himself every fifty yards or so to silently wave them on. The widow Hart rode with her head down, taking no notice of the sentries. Jesse suspected that stubbornness alone was keeping her in the saddle, and he nudged Lucky closer until they were riding stirrup to stirrup.

The trail ended abruptly at a massive iron-and-wood gate. It swung open on well-oiled hinges to admit them single file into a large compound lit by a small bonfire. Jesse followed Miranda Hart automatically toward the shadowy hulk of a building at the edge of the firelight. She tried to dismount, but she had finally reached the end of her strength. Jesse leaped off his stallion as he saw her waver, then begin to topple out of the saddle toward the iron-hard earth below. A short, wide woman materialized out of the darkness and reached her first. Catching her, the woman half carried the widow toward the building, scolding her gently in Spanish.

Jesse was staring after the women, when he felt a touch on his arm. Rivera was at his side with his saddle bags and bedroll. He handed them over, then escorted Jesse to a low, long building on the opposite side of the yard. The older man threw open a door and gestured Jesse inside.

The door closed behind him, and Jesse found himself alone in the dark. "Welcome to the Silver Tejo," he murmured dryly to himself.

Jesse arched his back and settled deeper into the bed with an unconscious sigh. Last night he'd been too tired to appreciate that it was soft, fresh smelling and, surprisingly, not too short. From the angle of the sun shining through the small room's sole window onto the whitewashed wall, it was well past daybreak, yet no one had disturbed him. Jesse chuckled wryly to himself. Letting a man sleep late on his first day was not the way most new jobs started.

Tucking his hands under his head, he contemplated his future. He didn't see anything keeping him from leaving anytime he wanted. The hard part would be going back to Montana and explaining to Josh how he had lost their stake. Still, it might be wise to lie low for a while, and in the meantime, he would see what he could do about solving some of Miranda Hart's problems. He owed the old girl that much for saving his life.

Deciding he'd lazed in bed long enough, he sat up and swung his feet to the bare plank floor. A few minutes later, he'd determined that his room was in a bunkhouse large enough for twenty men and that he seemed to be the sole occupant. He saw no one in the compound, and there was no sound disturbing the hot, still air to indicate that anyone was working in the nearby barn or corrals. The place seemed deserted. Opening the last door in the long, low adobe bunkhouse, he found a closet with a tin bathtub and a handy water pump, and abruptly Jesse remembered that it had been almost a week since he'd been clean or even shaved.

Half an hour later he was back in his room, shrugging into a clean shirt from his saddle bag, when it suddenly sounded like all hell was breaking loose outside. Loud yelps, high-pitched shrieks and several animallike howls shattered the peaceful quiet of the morning. After grabbing his gun, Jesse jerked open his door and, forgetting caution, sprinted across the empty yard. The hullaba-loo seemed to be coming from the main house. What the hell was going on? Were they under attack?

He crashed through an iron gate and ran through a courtyard to the house. As he leaped onto the porch, a woman came flying around the corner, brandishing a broom, and slammed into him. Reflexively, Jesse's arms went around her, crushing the woman against him as he scrambled frantically to keep them both from falling off the porch.

The unholy din stopped as abruptly as it had started, and their raspy breathing was unnaturally loud in the sudden quiet. For long moments they couldn't do more than lean on each other, chests heaving together while they tried to catch their breath. Gradually Jesse became aware of the body in his arms. Soft, full breasts rubbed against his naked chest each time warm, moist breath fanned the hollow of his throat. Wisps of silky hair tickled his cheek and neck, and he smelled a hauntingly familiar scent. Long, slender legs were trapped between his, and a curiously large belly pressed against his hard flat one. He looked down into the wide eyes of a beautiful dark-haired young woman. He'd guessed wrong, he thought dazedly. The band of color around Miranda Hart's twilight eyes was deep green, not blue or black.

Chapter Three

W ho are you?'' He knew the answer before he demanded it, yet he had to hear her say it, as if he needed the reassurance that he could believe his eyes, believe that the woman in his arms was the one in the photograph he'd stared at so long and so hard in the judge's parlor—as well as the old hag he'd tried not to look at at all.

"Miranda Hart."

Her answer was an unsteady whisper. Her arms were still under his open shirt, wrapped tight around his waist, and Jesse's hands slipped up her back, subtly easing her closer. She relaxed against him, her ragged breathing slowing and growing more even. For a few moments longer Jesse enjoyed the soft feel of her and the sweet scent surrounding him; then, as if she finally realized the intimacy of their position, he felt her body stiffen under his hands. Her arms jerked loose, and she pushed against his chest, silently demanding release.

Jesse didn't let her go. Sliding his hands around to her arms, he held her with careful restraint, allowing her to retreat only far enough to break the contact between their bodies. How she had affected her remarkable transformation didn't concern him at the moment. Suddenly he was angry, angry with himself that he hadn't seen through her disguise, angry with circumstances that made her beauty a danger she was forced to hide in ugliness, and, most of all he was angry with Miranda Hart herself, for risking her life and that of her unborn child.

What he'd thought was a potbelly was a pregnancy, perhaps six months along. He couldn't be sure because her extreme thinness exaggerated the swell of her belly, making her body seem too fragile to carry her child. His fingers met around arms that felt like nothing more than bones with skin stretched over them, and her face was thin and white, except for the violet bruises of long-term fatigue under her eyes. The fine aristocratic bones he had admired in her photograph were now too sharp, her eyes too large. She was still beautiful, but it was an ethereal, almost ghostly beauty that haunted her face now, not the glow of good health. She hadn't needed the added hardship of the trip to Silver City.

"Why?"

Miranda knew what he was asking—not why had she used the disguise, but why had she taken the risk? "I needed you. Or rather, a man like you," she amended, her voice still thready. "And the only way to find one was to fetch him myself."

The skinny arms in his grasp had muscles, surprisingly strong ones. Jesse felt them bunch as she made another, more determined effort to free herself. He would have to hurt her if he tried to stop her this time. His hands dropped, and she stepped back instantly, putting several feet between them. His smile was sardonic. "You needed a thief and a murderer?"

A flicker of a smile almost warmed the cool look she gave him. "I was lucky they didn't hang you before I had a chance at you."

"We were both lucky," he said dryly.

The smile vanished, and he saw sadness and apology in her lavender eyes. "Perhaps. It remains to be seen how lucky you were, Mr. McClintock."

The ruckus that had brought him on the run abruptly erupted again. A pack of hounds came racing around the corner of the portal straight toward them. The lead dog had a half-eaten ham in his mouth, and the rest were right on his heels, baying and snapping. Awkwardly the widow started to bend down for the broom she'd dropped. Taking her by the arms again, Jesse set her out of the way with gentle firmness, then snatched up the broom and swung it, sweeping the dogs off the porch. The bone of contention forgotten in the dirt, the half-dozen hounds untangled themselves and leaped to their feet. The largest and boldest bared his teeth at Jesse in a low growl.

"Go on! Get!" Jesse commanded sharply. Why the hell were the dogs running loose? he wondered furiously. Broom or no broom, they would have run right over her and she would have taken a nasty fall.

The lead dog turned tail and slunk off, and the rest of the pack followed him out through the courtyard gate. Jesse felt the broom being taken from his hand and turned to look at the woman behind him.

"Please come inside, Mr. McClintock."

She'd said "please," but there was an unmistakable note of command in her tone. She inclined her head with just the right touch of superiority, mistress to servant, and Jesse nodded back with not quite the right amount of servility. Bending, he scooped up his dropped gun and tucked it into his pants along with his shirt as he followed her through the door.

She paused at the first room leading off the entrance hall and gestured him inside. "Sit down, please. I'll be back directly."

Without waiting to see if he obeyed her command—no doubt because she was used to being obeyed, Jesse decided wryly—she continued on down the hall. His eyes followed her until she turned the corner. He heard her speak to someone in Spanish, telling the unseen person that the dogs must have dug their way into the smokehouse again.

Standing in the doorway, he glanced around the large room. Although it was clearly the "front room," it didn't have the usual formal, feminine fussiness that made a man feel oversized and clumsy. Despite the expensive furnishings, the room had a homey, comfortable feel. A man could relax here and not worry about breaking anything.

Mounted on the whitewashed chimney of a fireplace large enough to roast a steer in was a collection of Indian lances and shields. Another wall was taken up entirely with books. They weren't the usual sets of expensive leather-bound volumes with gold-stamped titles bought only to impress visitors and never opened, much less read. These books were all sizes, crammed onto the shelves haphazardly, some of them tattered, all of them obviously used and well loved.

Hanging over a walnut grand piano that the newness still hadn't worn off of was a twin of the photograph he'd seen in the judge's parlor. Although he could recall every detail with his eyes shut, Jesse studied the picture again. Where had Hart found her? Not in the dust of Deming, of that he was absolutely certain. That sandpaper rasp of a voice had been another part of her disguise. Her true voice was low pitched and bell clear, with a trace of a British accent that made his English sound almost slovenly.

His eyes wandered the room absently for a few seconds, stopping, then focusing sharply on the wide window overlooking the portal and courtyard. Going to the window, he pushed aside the drapes and wasn't surprised to find a solid wooden shutter folded up underneath. In contrast to the elegant civility of velvet and lace, the shutter was made of rough unfinished boards thick enough to stop a bullet, but it unfolded at a touch on smooth hinges to cover half the window. Jesse saw the gun ports cut into the planks. The impression of a fortress he had gotten the night before was confirmed. The walls of the house were adobe, at least three feet thick, as was the ten-foot wall surrounding the flower-filled courtyard. The wall offered the additional protection of jagged shards of iron spiking the top. His mouth flattening into a thin line, he refolded the shutter and let the drapes drop back into place. Velvet and lace, flowers and fine furniture couldn't hide the fact that the house was first and foremost a stronghold against enemies determined to destroy it. Why hadn't Miranda Hart sold out when her husband had died? What did the Silver Tejo have that was worth risking her life for?

Moving back through the room, he paused by a high-backed wing chair with a small footrest. Tossed over one arm was a dark blue shawl, and on the seat was a small embroidered silk pillow the right size to fit behind an achy back or under a sleepy head. On the floor beside the chair was a basket of knitting. Jesse reached down and pulled out a ball of kitten-soft yellow yarn with two needles stuck in it. From one dangled a half-finished sock so tiny he could hardly imagine a foot small enough to fit it. In spite of himself he grinned at the rows of uneven stitches. Whatever else she was, Miranda Hart wasn't much of a knitter.

After replacing the wool in the basket, he picked up the book lying on the table next to the chair. A green satin ribbon marked her place, and he looped it around his fingers as he took a look at what she was reading. Keeping her place with a finger, he flipped through the book, unconsciously rubbing the cool slick satin between his fingers.

Miranda set a filled kettle on top of the kitchen stove and added a shovelful of coal from the scuttle to the glowing ashes. She had planned to inform Mr. Jesse McClintock of her expectations in a calm cool manner. Now she was too hot, and she felt the need to...settle herself before she faced him. A nice strong cup of tea was exactly what she needed.

While she waited for the kettle to boil, she prepared a tray. His face didn't look so hurt this morning. The bruises were more colorful, but the eye that had been swollen shut was open a little now and seemed undamaged. The terrible bruising on his chest had shocked her. She hadn't realized the extent of his injuries; they should not have asked him to ride, and yet she had had no choice. Willis had said they had to leave that night.

She added a plate of sugar cookies to the tray. He had certainly come running to see what the commotion was all about. He hadn't even taken time to finish dressing. His hair had still been damp from his bath, too. Clean and shining, it was very thick, almost like long fur. Her fingers unconsciously caressed the pattern stamped in the tin tray. His hair would feel soft, silky . . .

The kettle whistled her out of her daydream. Don't have any illusions about the man, she reminded herself sharply as she filled a porcelain teapot with the boiling water. He was here only because it was preferable to prison or the hangman, and it was imperative that he go on believing he was here solely at her pleasure. She only hoped he would not realize how desperately she needed him to stay.

Miranda added a generous measure of Earl Grey from a tin canister to the pot. He wouldn't like it; American men never did. By serving tea instead of the coffee he would undoubtedly prefer, she would show him that his preferences mattered nothing to her, she decided with an almost vicious satisfaction that would have startled her if she had been aware of it. Automatically she placed the pot on the tray. Americans never made tea strong enough, she thought absently. Properly made, tea could put hair on a man's chest. A vision of Jesse McClintock's chest flashed unbidden into her mind, and her palms suddenly itched at the remembered feel of that smooth, nearly hairless skin.

She snapped two fragile Spode teacups down on the stamped tin. Jesse McClintock's chest was no concern of hers. Her concern was to establish who was boss of this . . . outfit. Miranda nodded determinedly as she repeated the word aloud softly to herself. Outfit. She loved American English. The very words were full of energy and excitement, just like the country and its people. The second her foot had touched the dock in New York, she had fallen in love with the honest, lively speech around her, which the others traveling with her had just as instantly deplored. Suddenly her own speech had sounded stilted and stuffy to her ears.

Frowning at the rather sparse assortment on the tray, she added a plate of buttered bread. She needed him strong and healthy, not weak from hunger. After another look, she piled several thick slices of ham on the bread plate. He was a large man, she rationalized as she picked up the tray; it would take a lot of food to fill him up.

Jesse laid the book back on the table facedown, stuffing the satin ribbon in his pants pocket without thinking as Miranda entered the room. He took a seat on one of the two matching plush-covered sofas while she set the tea tray on the table in between the couches and sat down on the other one, facing him. With an absolutely straight back, she began pouring tea.

"Do you enjoy Mark Twain, Mr. McClintock?"

Jesse glanced toward the book he had been scanning. From the too casual tone in her voice, he knew she hoped he would mumble he couldn't read, that he'd only been looking at the pictures, and she would regain the advantage she'd lost in his arms out on the porch. It was a fair assumption for her to make. Most cowboys did well to trace their names, much less read. Highwaymen were probably even more illiterate. But still it annoyed him, almost as much as her conviction that he was a thief.

"Even thieves and murderers read, Mrs. Hart. I particularly enjoyed Twain's *Life on the Mississippi*." He saw consternation in her eyes as he gave her a bland smile, but she recovered quickly. She might be surprised to know, he thought as he accepted a cup of tea, that he always packed a few books with him even on the roughest trails. Jesse tipped in a little cream, stirred in a lump of sugar and took a long swallow of the tea. Like the question about his tastes in literature, the tea was meant to put him in his place and keep him there. He drained the small cup and held it out to her. It might also surprise her to know that he genuinely liked tea.

Silently Miranda refilled his cup, then passed him the plate of ham and buttered bread. It appeared he actually liked tea. The delicate china cup was all but invisible in his big hand, yet, oddly enough, he didn't look like the foolish bumpkin that he should have. He handled the cup and saucer as naturally as if he'd been born with them in his hands. He hardly had the rude social skills she'd have expected of a common cowboy. His graceful manners, refined speech and reading habits hinted at an educated, cultured background, and she realized that whatever else he was, Jesse McClintock was a most uncommon man.

He made a substantial sandwich out of the bread and meat, and she watched as his even, very white teeth bit a good-sized chunk out of it. He chewed, then washed down the bite with more tea. What other surprises did Jesse McClintock have in store for her? After *Life on the Mississippi* and the tea, she wasn't too sure she wanted to find out. Perhaps she should tell him a few of hers now, and she took a deep breath.

"That was quite a disguise."

His voice was low and a little raspy, rather like a soft growl. She let out the breath and took a long drink of her tea instead, while she considered whether she ought to just ignore his comment. Finally, with an almost imperceptible lift of her shoulders, she answered his implied question. "Not that much of one, actually. It was mostly the wig and the clothes, with a bit of greasepaint and putty." Unconsciously she touched the point of her chin where the wart had been, thinking for a moment of the small case in her bedroom that had been her father's stock in trade. The dried-up pots of paint, crumbling putty, tatty wigs and cracked leather case hadn't been worth enough to sell. She laughed soundlessly to herself. Her sole inheritance. "My parents were actors," she said aloud.

"Where?"

His tone held only idle curiosity, but his storm cloud eyes were intent on her. Again she considered whether she would answer. She didn't owe him any answers, yet she felt oddly compelled to give him some. "In London. In England," she added, and his raised eyebrow told her that he was well aware of where London was. "We immigrated to the United States when I was a child. My parents spent several years with a traveling company before finally settling in San Francisco. They formed their own company and opened a theater."

"Did you perform with them?"

"When I was a child," she confirmed shortly, then went on in a brisk tone before he could ask anything else, "I don't know how much my brother-in-law told you about our situation here, Mr. McClintock. The Apaches have killed over five hundred people in the New Mexico and Arizona territories during the past seven years. Twenty-one of those people were from the Silver Tejo, including my husband."

The little bit she'd told him about herself hadn't satisfied his curiosity about her, only intensified it. How had Hart ever convinced her to leave the civilization of San Francisco to live with rattlesnakes and murderous Indians? He finished his sandwich, and when she paused to raise the teapot with a questioning look, he nodded. She refilled his cup once more, then continued.

"We had approximately three thousand head of cattle at roundup time this spring, and twenty riders. Now I have three riders—a boy of fourteen, the boy's grandfather, who is sixty if he's a day... and you. I have no idea how many cattle are left. We weren't able to finish the roundup, and the Apaches and bandits from across the border have been stealing them for months." Her bad news finished, Miranda sat quietly with her hands clasped together in the lap of her neat blue calico dress, waiting for his response.

His face expressionless, Jesse studied her over the rim of the delicate china cup as he took a sip. She was looking at him with such trusting hopefulness—ironic under the circumstances. He knew what she wanted to hear: how he was going to solve her problems. There had been no surprises in her matter-of-fact recital. The surprise had been the difficulty he'd had concentrating on what she was telling him. Sunlight from the window behind her shone on her hair. Wound into a smooth knot at her nape, it had appeared to be a plain brown in the shade of the porch, but now he could see that it was rich, dark chestnut. She moved slightly, and the sun lit small flames of bright fire in it.

Her hair wasn't all that was distracting him. Her teeth were white and straight, except for one eyetooth. It was just a little crooked, and she had touched her tongue to it each time she'd seemed to be considering how much to tell him. He had become fascinated with that tooth, with watching the tip of her pink tongue flicking at it. He'd waited for it, eagerly anticipating its next appearance.

He focused on her hands in her lap, but that didn't help his concentration. Looking at her long slim fingers, folded demurely now in her lap, made him remember how soft and cool those hands had felt on the bare skin of his waist and chest a few minutes ago... made him wonder how they would feel on other places on his body.... He set his empty cup back on the tray with too much force and stood up. He was disgustingly close to lusting after a woman, and a respectable, pregnant woman at that. "I'll ride over the ranch the next few days, look over the cattle, then decide how many men I'll need," he told her brusquely.

"As you wish, Mr. McClintock," she said quietly, rising to her feet also. "Manolo will accompany you."

Jesse acknowledged her acquiescence with an abrupt nod. If she was disturbed that he hadn't asked her permission to leave, or for her approval of his plans, she kept it to herself. The sooner she understood that he wasn't going to ask her permission or approval for anything, the better. There could be only one boss on a cattle ranch. And the first thing he was going to do, he decided as he strode for the door, was pen up those damn dogs.

Jesse found he was "accompanied" from the moment he stepped out of the bunkhouse in the morning until he closed the door behind him at night. The boundaries of the Silver Tejo extended from the flat desert a few miles outside of Deming to the peaks of the Floridas, which formed the border between the United States and Mexico, and with Rivera as his shadow, he rode over virtually the entire ranch. Their long hours in the saddle passed mostly in silence, their only verbal exchanges Rivera's terse answers to his equally terse, infrequent questions about some aspect of the ranch's operation. The foothills were wrinkled with dry, sandy, shallow draws and steep narrow canyons, unexpectedly lush with grass watered by sweet springs. The ranch was indeed capable of supporting several thousand head of cattle, but the Apaches and rustlers had taken more than their share. He came upon numerous piles of bones and rotting hides that indicated a cow had been slaughtered and butchered on the spot, by Apaches, no doubt. One carcass had been no more than a few days old. He also found a narrow trail cut by hundreds of hooves leading over a pass into Mexico that showed the route the bandits had taken. He estimated that of the three thousand cattle Miranda Hart had said she'd had in the spring, there was no more than a third that number left now. A thousand head, he'd realized, the number he'd planned to buy and drive north to his and Josh's spread.

There was one canyon Rivera had kept him away from, telling him on one of the few occasions when he initiated conversation that there were no cattle there. Jesse had made it a point to ride past the mouth of the canyon several times anyway. A road led into it, the width and ruts indicating that it was well used, and he wondered what was back there that Manolo Rivera didn't want him to see. Black smoke drifted over it continually, but, just beyond the mouth of the canyon, the walls made a sharp turn, and Jesse could neither see nor hear any sign of human activity.

This morning he pulled up Lucky and dismounted at the mouth of the canyon. Rivera sat silent on his buckskin a few yards behind him, and Jesse knew with a sudden, unshakable conviction that Rivera wouldn't hesitate to kill him if he tried to enter the canyon. He stood beside Lucky for a few seconds, as if studying the foothills to the west. It was little more than an hour past sunup and already getting hot, yet he could taste fall's sweet crispness in the clean dry air. As if he had nothing more on his mind than a drink of water, he ambled over to the silver ribbon of a stream that ran out of the canyon. He heard the creak of stiff leather as Rivera shifted in his saddle—no doubt wanting to be sure he had a clear shot, Jesse thought dryly. As he knelt and scooped up a handful of the clear, ice cold water, a bright flash caught his eye. Pretending to scoop up another drink, he palmed the bright bit of rock. Rubbing his hand down his pants to dry it as he stood up, he slipped the rock in his pocket.

It was late that evening before he had a chance to look at it again, in the privacy of his room. He saw immediately that the rock was a piece of float, ore that had washed downstream from the canyon. The float's bright luster caught the lamplight, and the blade of his jackknife cut it almost as easily as butter. Although he and Josh had mined gold, he knew silver when he saw it, and the float was almost pure silver bromide. The smoke continually hanging over the canyon would be from a smelter. At least the mystery of how Hart had persuaded Miranda to marry him and why, despite the dangers and hardships, she'd stayed on after his death was solved. His faint smile was sardonic as he tucked the nugget without thinking into his vest pocket on top of the green satin ribbon. Greed could be very persuasive.

The mine also explained the presence of the other men he'd seen on the Silver Tejo. There were always two different men on guard duty at the main gate, which was never left open. None of them were cowmen, either by dress or mode of transportation. When they traveled they went by wagon, and they generally wore sombreros and loose cotton trousers and shirts under heavy serapes. All Mexican, they were short and stocky, with overdeveloped arm and shoulder muscles. Miners, he realized now, and Rivera had probably been their superintendent until he'd been pressed into guard duty.

He'd seen at least a dozen different men, but the widow Hart and Leola Rivera, Manolo's wife, were the only women on the ranch. He had gathered that there had been more, along with children, the families of the miners, but after the raid that had killed Thomas Hart, the men had relocated their women to the safety of a village near Deming.

Now Miranda Hart, who was undoubtedly wealthy enough never to have to do anything more arduous than raise a teacup, worked like the lowliest peon. Between them, she and Leola Rivera handled all the chores not considered "man's" work, and despite her condition and position, he noticed that she did her fair share, too. She boiled laundry, cooked, cleaned, and wearing a floppy straw sombrero and with her skirts tucked up, he'd seen her weeding and irrigating the large kitchen garden behind the main house.

In addition to their normal household chores, both women seemed intent on preserving everything the garden and orchard produced. Split pears, peaches, melons and squash dried in the hot sun on bleached boards; fat red chiles hung in long *ristras* suspended from the roof, and one evening he'd found thin strips of fresh beef hanging from the bunkhouse portal, drying into jerky.

After a week, Jesse had seen enough. As he and his warder were unsaddling their horses at the end of the day, he broke the usual silence between them. "Are you still going to town tomorrow?" That morning he had overheard Miranda Hart telling Rivera that they needed supplies.

Manolo heaved his saddle over the partition separating their horses' respective stalls. "Tomorrow," he affirmed stolidly.

Jesse slipped Lucky's bridle free and hung it on a handy nail. "Spread the word that I'll be in town the day after tomorrow, hiring hands. Pay will be sixty dollars a month. Anyone interested in a job can find me at the livery stable around noon." He sensed the eyes boring a hole in his back and turned to meet the Mexican's hard stare with one of his own. He hadn't asked the widow Hart's leave to go into town or to offer ten dollars a month more than the going rate, and he was certain Rivera knew it. She was going to have to give him a free hand to run her ranch or she would lose it. And he told himself that he didn't give a damn either way.

The silence stretched until Manolo Rivera abruptly nodded. "I will spread the word, *señor*."

From the wide doorway of the barn the next morning, Jesse watched the older man drive off in a buckboard, accompanied by three outriders. He knew the men weren't going along to protect the beans and flour Rivera was supposed to bring back. They were protecting the contents of the large wooden chest they thought he hadn't seen under the tarp in the back of the wagon. It had taken all four of them to load it the night before, its weight making them strain with the effort. Given his supposedly criminal nature, Jesse could understand why everyone on the Silver Tejo was taking such care to see that he remain ignorant of the mine and the shiny silver ingots he knew were in the chest.

If he hadn't already found the float, he would have learned the secret then, anyway. Confident that he couldn't understand them, the men had talked freely in Spanish among themselves. From their conversation he learned that his supposition that Rivera normally bossed the operation of the mine and smelter was correct, and that he wasn't particularly happy about pulling guard duty.

The heavy gates swung closed behind the wagon and riders, and Jesse turned to glance idly around the large two-story barn. It was empty except for him, Lucky, one milch cow, a couple of half-wild cats and a cocky leghorn rooster and his harem of hens. A dozen or so horses, most of them mares in foal, were stabled in the barn at night, but allowed the relative freedom of the corrals during the day.

After giving Lucky a good currying and an extra ration of oats, he turned him out into the same corral with Miranda Hart's Arabian mare. He was coming to appreciate the Appaloosa more each time he rode him. The stallion was tireless, as surefooted as a mule and just as smart, but with a much better nature.

Leaning against the top rail of the corral, he watched Lucky sidle over to the mare, looking hopeful. The mare sniffed, tossed her long silky mane and stalked off, her nose in the air. "As snooty as her mistress," Jesse said, laughing to himself as he turned away.

The corrals were the only structures made of wood he'd seen on the ranch. All the buildings, including the barn, were adobe. Jesse knew the reason wasn't that the mud bricks were all Hart could afford; he could have afforded anything he'd wanted. He'd used adobe because it didn't burn.

The Silver Tejo was better fortified than any army post in the territory. The ranch headquarters were located in a box canyon with a high, five-foot-thick adobe wall closing the mouth, and only an Indian with an urge to commit suicide would have tried to climb down the steep walls of the canyon. They could try a siege, but with only a few men to feed, the amount of food Jesse had seen Miranda and Leola Rivera preserving and the spring to provide water, the Silver Tejo could outlast a siege far longer than the Indians could.

The hounds woofed lazily at him in greeting as he headed for the farthest corral. He, Rivera and one of the miners had spent a late evening building a wire-enclosed pen for them, partially shaded by a huge cottonwood. Jesse paused to tickle the closest one behind the ears, and the dog wriggled his rear end in delight.

The sole occupant of the last corral was a Hereford bull. His shiny red coat was unmarked except for the brand on his left flank, a heart enclosing an *S* and a *T*. Silky-looking white fur curled over the bull's broad forehead and massive chest. He was the finest bull Jesse had ever seen, and he could well understand why Miranda Hart wasn't risking his loss on the open range.

Rivera had told him that a number of cows had been brought to him to be serviced, but none lately. That the bull was annoyed about his lack of female companionship was obvious. Lonely and frustrated, he was pawing the ground and rolling eyes as red as his hide. When he caught sight of Jesse, he charged. In spite of himself, Jesse flinched, even though he knew the solid rails of the corral would contain the bull. The animal turned away at the last second and galloped twice around the edge of the corral, tossing his short horns, furrowing the dirt with his hoof and snorting loudly. Finally he skidded to a halt in a cloud of dust and glared at Jesse balefully.

Laughing, Jesse called out softly, "You getting a little randy, son? You need a woman? How about a fresh little heifer to—"

He broke off as he caught a flash of yellow through the rails on the other side of the corral. Miranda Hart was coming back from the orchard, carrying a basket loaded with ripe apples. As Jesse swiftly circled the corral toward her, he added one more to the mental list of people he would hire when he went to Deming. Despite what Rivera said, there had to be a woman desperate enough for money to brave the danger of working on the Silver Tejo.

Wordlessly he took the basket from her arms as he fell into step beside her. It wasn't that large or heavy; the woman had some sense, at least, even if she did seem determined to work herself into the ground. Again Jesse experienced a familiar yet inexplicable anger with her because she was taking so little care of herself and her unborn child.

When he'd taken the basket, she had flashed him a tired smile of gratitude and relief. An unconscious smile, he thought with a trace of bitterness. Although she was fastidiously polite to him on every occasion, he was certain Miranda Hart would never knowingly permit herself to smile at an outlaw.

He slanted a look down at her. Curling tendrils of chestnut hair that had escaped from the long braid down her back stuck to her damp forehead and heat-flushed cheeks, and there was a wilted droop to her usually straight back and shoulders. Shifting the basket to his other arm, he let his free hand rest at the small of her back. His touch was so light that she didn't appear to feel it as he guided her around an uneven patch of ground.

As they rounded the barn, a small boy came running toward them. Miranda bent to catch him in her arms, and the boy spoke in a breathless rush. "Susie's eggs have hatched, Mama! Come look!"

Jesse stood by, unnoticed. Probably five going on six, the boy was too old to be her son by Thomas Hart. Miranda Hart was a widow twice over. He hadn't seen the little boy before, but that wasn't surprising. Usually he rode out at sunup and returned long after sundown, so he wouldn't have seen the boy outside, and he took his meals in the kitchen, not in the dining room with the Silver Tejo's mistress and her son. The boy must take after his late father, Jesse decided, because with red hair and bright blue eyes, he looked nothing like his mother. His face seemed to be one giant freckle, and there was a gap in his grin where a front tooth should have been. A brown calico shirt and short brown pants covered his sturdy little body. The toes of his shoes were scuffed, and the knees of his black stockings were holey, signs that he spent a lot of time on his hands and knees in the dirt, like most little boys. It was a shame that his father would never know him, Jesse thought sadly. He was a fine-looking boy that any man would be proud to call "son."

Impatient, the little boy wiggled out of Miranda's arms and pulled at her hands to hurry her up. "Come on, Mama! Susie might hide her chicks, and then you won't get to see. There's a black one. I touched it. It was so soft—"

The boy didn't see the black boots until he stumbled over them. He froze, staring at the pair of long legs in black denim inches from his small nose. It was an even longer way to look up to the tall man's face.

The change that came over him astonished Jesse. One second the boy was full of life, happily chattering to his mother, his face glowing with excitement and wonder. The next second his little body was rigid, his face devoid of all life and expression, his eyes downcast. His words came out now in a helpless stammer. "I-I-I'm s-sorry, s-s-sir. I-I-I—"

Mercifully the boy gave up to stare miserably at his shoes. Jesse saw that the joy and laughter had vanished from Miranda's face, too. He knew his eye and bruises were a fearful sight for a young child. The sight of a big strange man with his mother might well have frightened him, too, yet he didn't think that was what had so disturbed the boy. There was some secret heartache here for both mother and son that Jesse would have given much to learn and, he realized with surprise, much to ease.

Miranda's hand on the boy's shoulder was as gentle as her voice. "This is Mr. McClintock, Tommy, the man I told you about. Remember? He's come to help us with the ranch." Her eyes rose to Jesse's with a wordless plea.

Jesse squatted. He was still too tall, but he was much closer to the boy's eye level. "Pleased to meet you, Tommy," he said quietly. He extended his hand, waiting for the boy to look up. Tommy's eyes flickered up to his, and his little hand darted out. Carefully Jesse closed his large hand around the small one and shook it. His eyes wide and solemn, the little boy nodded, then pulled his hand free, but slowly, almost as if he were reluctant to break the contact.

Jesse grinned at him suddenly. Immediately Tommy hid his face in his mother's skirts, but not before Jesse caught the glimmer of a grin answering his own. Jesse looked up, and Miranda Hart's smile thanked him silently. This time he knew her smile was deliberate. It shone like a light within her, momentarily banishing the shadows of weariness and sorrow, and made her beauty more heart catching than ever. He stared after her, and it was a long time after she and her son had disappeared into the barn before he finally picked up the basket and took it to the house.

Chapter Four

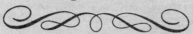

The man known to his people as One Who Yawns raised the flap of his U.S. Army field tent to greet the new day. He faced the east and began chanting his morning song to the rising sun. The first rays of sunlight washed over him, illuminating his face. Paradoxically, his life of physical hardship seemed to have slowed the aging process. Only the deep grooves around his stern mouth and the lines around his black eyes that came from continually scanning the horizon for enemies spoke of his fifty-four years. High cheekbones and a blunt blade of a nose stood out in high relief against the rest of his broad flat face. His barrel chest and thick shoulders were clothed in a faded red, calico shirt. The bare legs under his breechclout were skinny and a little bowed, but roped with strong muscles. As his head tilted to follow the sun's climb, thick black hair, untouched by gray, fell down his back to his waist. A cloth headband matching his shirt kept the long hair and sweat out of his eyes.

His song finished, he walked toward the small fire burning before his tent. His sixth wife handed him the rabbit she had split and roasted over the fire. He tore the meat from the bones with his strong teeth and fingers, washing it down with corn beer. As was the custom of his people, he ignored the woman.

Her long blouse was worn over a full, ankle-length skirt. Tucked under the belt cinching her blouse was a large knife. Her black hair was arranged around two willow hoops over her ears in the traditional style of their band—the Bedonkohes, the "enemy people." Others called them Chiricahua Apaches, but those were the whites' names, names that were meaningless to him.

Younger than him by more than three decades, his wife was not particularly pretty, and she was fractious, bickering continually with the other women. It was beneath his dignity to notice it, but the squabbling disturbed him all the same. He would have left her behind when he had broken away from the San Carlos Agency reservation the year before, but she was an expert *tizwin* maker. She knew exactly how much corn to ferment and the exact moment to stop the process. And her belly was big, proof that although he was a grandfather, he was still potent.

The man tossed away the last bone and relaxed back on his haunches to roll a cigarette. The makings came from a fold in the top of his knee-high moccasin. His fifth wife had made the moccasins. She had made them well. Too often in the past year and a half, he had had to abandon his horse and climb a cliff to escape a United States Army patrol or a ragtag company of *federales*, Mexican soldiers, but, like him, the moccasins had many more climbs left in them.

He puffed contentedly on his cigarette. He remembered all his wives with affection, but it would have been impractical to have had only one. He had traveled far in the years since the elders had tested his strength and courage in the rites that had proved his manhood. He had led war parties countless times to strike Mexican pack trains and ambush military patrols. He had even gone as far as what the Americans called California. The extended raids and visits had sometimes lasted months, and eventually he had had to find another woman to make his moccasins and his *tizwin* and warm his blankets on cold nights.

His latest wife set about making a fresh batch of *tizwin*. He could remember a time when some of their people still grew their own corn instead of stealing it from others. Tending his grandfather's melon patch when he was a boy, he had listened to the old man's tales of the days when all their people had been farmers, living in permanent villages instead of the tents and the temporary brush-and-stick *wickiups* they now built. They had grown fine corn and squash and beans, and traded with the pueblos along the Rio Grande. They had made expeditions to the great plains to hunt buffalo. They had even made their own pottery.

The Spanish had already come, but they were relatively few in number. The Comanches were more of a problem, but his people had been fierce warriors even then. Then the Mexicans had come from the south and the Americans from the east, squeezing them in between. The U.S. Army came with the settlers and built forts, and his people had been banished from land that had been theirs to use from the beginning of time.

The greatest of their chiefs, Victorio, had led them to what the whites called Mexico. His people paid little attention to the whites' squabbles over borders. His people had no borders. They did not need them, because they claimed no ownership of the land. All they wanted was the right to move freely over it. Their trading parties became war parties, raiding the Mexican and Anglo settlements to obtain the horses they needed to travel beyond the whites' reach. But the whites' reach was long and greedy, taking more and more, and the sedentary farmers became permanent nomads, living off the land. They became strong and harder to kill than the coyote. They ate berries, roots, seeds, cactus and crawling things to stay alive. They could go practically naked in freezing weather and thrive. And, his grandfather had told him proudly, they had become the most feared warriors in the Southwest.

He had listened as a young boy to his grandfather's stories and believed. He even believed the story of the pottery making, although, sadly, none of their women had the skill now. His mother had had a delicate bowl her mother's mother had given her. It had been white, painted with small black birds, her most cherished possession. It had been broken almost thirty years ago when an impatient soldier had shoved an old woman who couldn't walk fast enough to suit him.

He still believed the stories, but he no longer felt the excitement and pride he had felt as a boy. He felt only an endless weariness and an overwhelming sense of futility. As Victorio and Juh and Loco had before him, he was fighting a war he could not win. Now the American army pursued them even into Mexico. He never would understand why the Americans objected so righteously to the killing of a few foreigners they themselves had been killing only a generation before. All he could hope for was to delay the end until the whites were tired, too. Then his people would have a measure of bargaining power.

He tossed the suddenly bitter cigarette into the fire and rose, heading toward the outer perimeter of the camp. He resented the Americans, but he despised the Mexicans. They had killed his first wife and his first three children and his mother twenty-five years before. Until then, he had killed only when he had thought it was necessary, but even if his honor had not demanded it, he would have avenged the Mexicans' treachery. He had led a massacre of revenge and fought so fiercely that the other warriors were astounded. Until the death of his family, he knew he had not been held in particular esteem by them. He had lived as his name, One Who Yawns, implied, never leading and only following when there was a promise of excitement and adventure without too much effort.

The other warriors were so impressed by his newfound ferocity that they immediately made him the war chief. He did not have

Victorio's tactical brilliance, but he had hatred and an almost suicidal desire for revenge to compensate. Over the next two decades, he avenged his family's death many times over, and the
Mexicans learned what kind of justice the Enemy People meted out
to their enemies.

Eventually he became headman. There was no formal election,
no council of leaders to decide the matter; in the way of his people, the band simply began looking to him for leadership. Since he
had no hereditary right to the position of chief, he could not have
that title, but his enemies gave him the title of chief, anyway, and
a new name, because Spanish-speaking tongues could not wrap
themselves around his real name.

He heard his wife's strident voice as she argued about the best
way to make *tizwin*. He sighed wistfully. He wished there were time
to brew some *mescal*, but they would be moving on soon. The
federales would pick up their trail, if they hadn't already, and the
Enemy People would be on the run again. Still, he would have liked
a cup or two. *Mescal* was a friendly drink, easy on the head and the
belly, not like that red liquor the Indian agent had sold illegally at
San Carlos. Like the promises on the Americans' pieces of paper,
the liquor was a lie. It promised pleasure, but all it delivered was
an aching head and a sick belly.

Six years before he had put his mark on one of those papers,
because, in truth, he was tired. He had proved he was a great warrior and leader; he had earned much honor, and the idea of living
out his days in peace with his grandsons working his melon patch
had been very appealing. He had formally surrendered to the
American general Crook, and learned instantly the worth of those
paper promises.

His horses and other possessions had been seized immediately.
His honor was stolen from him almost as fast. Iron shackles were
riveted around his ankles, and he spent days in a corral like an animal, chained. He endured the humiliation, counseling his people
to be patient. The Americans would keep their promises once they
were convinced that the Enemy People truly meant to live in peace.

The Indian agent at the San Carlos reservation had interpreted
the promised ration of fresh beef as horns and hoofs and tripe. He
had endured that, too, and the cup of wormy flour allotted to each
adult every week. The agent did not consider it necessary to issue
rations to children. To supplement the starvation rations, they had
planted corn and melons. Just before harvest, soldiers destroyed
the fields, making them totally dependent on the agent for their
survival.

For five years he had tried to live in peace, watching insects swarm over the babies in summer, nearly devouring those who hadn't already died in the one hundred twenty degree heat, watching them freeze in winter when the promised blankets never arrived. He had endured until he could endure no more. One night the Enemy People simply slipped away. By the time the soldiers were mobilized to bring them back, they were in Sonora, safe in the sanctuary of the Sierra Madre.

He knew as surely as he knew his own death would come someday that they would have to return to the hated San Carlos—the sheer numbers of the American soldiers would defeat them eventually—but this time the Enemy People would have the cattle and wealth they needed to live with dignity and honor. He permitted himself a small smile. To the north, in the Floridas, there were plenty of cattle and silver, theirs for the taking. The time was not yet right, but soon . . . soon. . . .

He paused to watch his small granddaughter's attempts with a tiny bow and arrow he had made for her. Girls received the same lessons in weaponry and horsemanship as the boys. Women were expected to defend the band, to be able to ride and shoot, although adults never used bows and arrows anymore. They had no need to. They had the latest in repeating rifles, more ammunition than they could carry, tents and even the far-seeing glasses, all supplied by the United States Army every time the Enemy People ambushed a patrol. Still, he wanted the young to learn the old skills so they would not be lost, like the pottery making.

He clapped his hands with approval as his granddaughter finally hit a stuffed deer hide target. The little girl scampered over to him, demanding that he come help her look for her lost arrows. Agreeably he took her small hand in his, and Geronimo, the most hated and feared man in the United States and Mexico, went off to play with his granddaughter.

The back door of the main house swung shut behind Jesse as the rising sun gilded the east rim of the canyon sheltering the ranch house. Leola Rivera gave him a glance from the stove, where she was baking tortillas on the cast-iron top. "Good morning, *señor*. Your breakfast is almost ready." She spoke heavily accented English in a voice that was almost as deep as her husband's. Turning back to the stove, she stretched a thick pat of dough into a thin white circle over her fists as Jesse pulled out a chair at the scrubbed pine table. He watched her pinch a cooked tortilla off the stove top and slap down the new one in its place.

A few minutes later she set a plate down in front of him, and Jesse smiled his thanks. Señora Rivera took no chances that a man might leave her table hungry. The plate was heaped with frijoles, fried potatoes, a thick slice of ham, three eggs and two of the tortillas dripping with butter and wild mesquite honey. A thick salsa of green chile flavored the eggs and beans. Jesse was glad he had acquired the taste and the cast-iron stomach for chile, because Leola Rivera seasoned with the scorching peppers the way other people used salt.

Fifteen minutes later he pushed his empty plate aside and pulled his watch from his vest pocket, flipping open the cover. He snapped the watch shut and replaced it in its pocket, then relaxed back in his chair, stretching out his long legs under the table. There was no need to hurry. The ride to town would take no more than three hours, and he wasn't due at the livery stable for another five.

Idly he watched the middle-aged woman bustling around the kitchen as he sipped his coffee. Leola Rivera's face and figure were broad and plain. Her coarse black hair was liberally salted with gray and pulled back tightly into a bun that was more practical than attractive. Even in her youth, her own mother would not have called her pretty, but the *señora*'s large brown eyes had a lively sparkle. Those eyes had watched him closely the past week.

"If you are finished, *señor*, I will check your ribs now."

Standing, Jesse unbuttoned his buff shirt and pulled it off in what had become a morning ritual between the two of them. He held his arms out at his sides while Leola began unwrapping the linen strips around his chest. She had been doctoring his ribs all week. He didn't know if it was the poultices, the god-awful tasting tea she made him drink or the massages from her strong stubby fingers, but the heavy bruising had already faded to nearly nothing, and he could breathe without feeling as if a knife were ripping through his lungs.

Leola Rivera discarded the linen bandage and began testing the condition of the cracked bones with knowing fingertips. The swelling was nearly gone, indicating that the internal bruises were disappearing as fast as the external ones and that his ribs were mending. The poultices of wild tobacco and arnica, and the sneezeweed tea, had worked as she'd intended, although she suspected that the *gringo señor*'s own strong spirit and body were as much responsible for his healing as her skill.

Too bad all her patients weren't as cooperative, she thought wryly as she traced the damaged ribs around to his backbone to be sure neither was dislocated. Leola Rivera was a *curandera*, descended from a line of healers that stretched back almost farther than time. Their legacy had begun centuries ago in Europe and been passed down generation to generation, woman to woman, each preserving the knowledge and adding to it. One of her grandmothers had accompanied the *padres* and conquistadors to the new world. She and the daughters who followed her had incorporated the healing arts of the Aztecs and other Indians into their own, adding to their formidable knowledge of herbs and human nature.

Leola had acquired her skills from her father's eldest sister, a respected herbalist and midwife. As a child, she had tagged along with her aunt, absorbing the art of healing through observation and imitation. It had almost been as if a voice were calling her, commanding her to learn. Her *tía* had taught her the names of plants and herbs and the ailments they could cure. She'd learned what to pick where and when, and which parts of the plant to use for maximum benefit. At the same time, she had studied anatomy, learned the functions of the body's organs and the physiology and emotional peculiarities of childbearing and childbirth, and observed human psychology and the effects of fear and unhappiness on disease. All this she had learned without benefit of a formal education or even the ability to read. Her classrooms had been the hillsides around her home in Mexico and the bedsides of her *tía*'s patients, where she'd discovered how to feel a stomach lesion or where to snip an umbilical cord. Her apprenticeship had lasted fifteen years until she became a respected *yerbera* and *partera* herself. Then Señor Hart had come, recruiting men from the silver mines at San Luis Potosí for his mine in the United States far to the north. Manolo had decided that they would go, and, like a dutiful wife, she had followed him, but she had followed the voice, too. It had never weakened over the years; instead, it had been strengthened by her sure faith in God and His power working through her.

Jesse flinched a little as her fingers probed his ribs.

The *señora* laughed, a surprisingly girlish giggle. "You are ticklish, no, *señor*?"

He groaned, laughing as her fingers dug in again in a new place. "I am very ticklish, yes."

"Also very tall," Leola muttered, straining her bulky body up onto her toes to wrap a fresh roll of bandage around a man a foot and a half taller than she was. Obligingly, Jesse bent his knees.

She wound the linen around and around his chest, maintaining tension on the cloth. "You don't need another poultice or any more tea, and I think it is the last time you will need the bandages." Her tone was as brisk as her hands. With no change in inflection, she asked Jesse the question no one else had bothered to. "Did you steal that money and shoot that man?"

Jesse looked down into the sharp eyes waiting to judge his answer. "No, *señora*, I did not," he averred quietly.

Leola searched his face, then patted his ribs with a sudden smile. His answer only confirmed what she was already certain of. She had sensed no evil in the spirit of this tall *gringo*. She could not explain how she knew, any more than she could explain why the Lord had chosen her, but even Manolo would admit that she was very seldom wrong. "You can put on your shirt, *señor*." She gathered up the used bandage and left the kitchen, gently nudging aside the bemused woman standing in the doorway.

Watching Miranda, Jesse shrugged back into his shirt and buttoned it slowly. Had she heard Leola's question and his answer? Had she believed him?

As if she'd been startled out of a daydream, Miranda jerked her eyes away from his chest, groping for the enameled coffeepot warming on the back of the stove. "More coffee, Mr. McClintock?"

"Thank you, ma'am." Her clear lavender eyes gave no clue as to what she believed. He finished tucking in his shirt while she poured their coffee, then sat down across from him. As Jesse sat back down, it struck him that, were it not for the formality of their speech, the two of them might be husband and wife, enjoying the casual intimacy that allowed a man to put his shirt on in the kitchen.

"Is there anything you want from town, ma'am?"

Her gaze shifted slowly to him, as if her thoughts had been far away. "No," she said with an oddly guilty look. "Nothing, thank you." Her eyes dropped to study her coffee cup.

Actually, there was something she wanted, Miranda mused, but it wasn't worth a three hour trip to town just for a dish of ice cream . . . was it? With her thoughts busy elsewhere, her eyes had sneaked back to the smooth tanned skin exposed by the open neck of his shirt. Immediately she disciplined them back to her cup. She must ask Leola about these peculiar urges she'd been having lately. Surely they were simply a part of being pregnant, but some of them really were rather shocking.

Jesse stared across the table. The tip of her tongue was worrying that crooked tooth, a sure sign that she was fretting over something. She obviously did want something from town, but was too shy to ask him. Probably it was some feminine unmentionable she needed. He laughed slyly to himself. She would probably be shocked to learn that there were no feminine unmentionables he wasn't familiar with.

Maybe she had just been embarrassed by his half-naked state. Frowning, Jesse eyed her belly swelling above the tabletop. She was most definitely not a blushing virgin, yet there was a peculiar air of innocence about her that made her pregnancy seem almost an impossibility. He set down his empty cup, plucked his hat off the table and stood. "Goodbye, ma'am."

Her voice stopped him halfway to the door. "We haven't discussed your wages, Mr. McClintock."

The unexpected words startled an honest answer out of him that his pride would never have permitted otherwise. "I hadn't thought I would be getting wages. I'd figured I would just give up smoking," he admitted wryly. His tobacco sack was about empty, but he had decided he'd be damned if he would ask her for any money.

"You may be in my custody, Mr. McClintock, but you aren't in slavery," Miranda told him with a wry half smile. She pushed back her chair and approached him. "I understand you told Manolo to say that we'd pay anyone who came to ride for us sixty dollars a month and found." "Found," she had learned, meant room and board. "You realize, of course, that we'll be lucky to find anyone willing to work, even for that," she added, her shoulders slumping a bit. Consciously she straightened them as she looked up at him. "If the riders' wages are sixty dollars a month, then one hundred twenty dollars for the foreman seems fair."

Jesse grinned reluctantly. "More than fair, ma'am."

Pulling a small purse from the pocket of her plain gray dress, Miranda took out six twenty-dollar gold pieces and dropped the money into his palm. "Your first month's wages, Mr. McClintock."

"Thank you, ma'am." Jesse's fingers grazed hers as they closed over the coins, and he felt a curiously powerful heat in the scant touch. His smile was already turning sour in anticipation of her hand jerking back as if she'd inadvertently touched something filthy. Instead her hand stayed in midair, a hairsbreath from his, and he saw puzzlement in her beautiful eyes as she stared up at him, as if she'd felt the heat, too. After a few slow heartbeats, her hand dropped.

"You're welcome, Mr. McClintock," she murmured, and turned away, effectively dismissing him.

Jesse paused on the back porch to roll a cigarette. His watchdog for the day was mounted and waiting for him. Jesse laughed dryly to himself as he acknowledged the man's brief salute. With Rivera gone, one of the miners had been delegated to guard him, and he looked as if he would much rather have a pickax in his hands than the reins of a horse.

Jesse glanced upward as he opened the tobacco pouch. The sun was balanced on the rim of the canyon, tinting the cloudless sky pink and orange. Warm golden light was beginning to seep into the deep shadows in the canyon, but the air was still cool, a soft breeze carrying the sweet scent of the flowers blooming beside the patio. From up the canyon Jesse heard the morning song of a meadowlark, and he felt a stir of excitement, an anticipation of what the new day might bring.

Through the open door behind him, he heard Leola Rivera come back into the kitchen. She asked in Spanish if Miranda was going into town, but Jesse couldn't quite hear the reply. Leola agreed with whatever she'd said, adding that Deming probably didn't compare to . . . Jesse strained to hear where Hart had found his second wife. He missed the older woman's words, but Miranda's were very clear.

"No, it doesn't." Her laugh was husky. "Deming is a far cry from Eddie Street in San Francisco and the White Swan."

The thin cigarette paper fluttered to the ground, but Jesse didn't notice it or the spilled tobacco clinging to the front of his clean shirt. When he and Josh had sold the mine, they had decided to squander a little money on a trip to San Francisco. Newly married, Josh and Ellen were more interested in each other than in sight-seeing, and one evening Jesse had gone out alone to give them some privacy. He remembered Eddie Street very well. He remembered the White Swan even better. It was a whorehouse.

Chapter Five

It ate at Jesse like lye on bare skin. The chaste and proper widow had been a whore, spreading her legs for any man with money enough to buy her. Her price would have been high. He remembered standing on the boardwalk that night outside the White Swan, debating whether to go inside. He'd had no desire for a prostitute—he'd lost his taste for bought "love" in his youth—but he had been curious. For years he had heard about San Francisco's bawdy houses.

He'd finally raised the brass knocker beside a discreet red gaslight, and, after a silent once-over by a huge negro dressed up in a long-tailed black coat and stiff white shirt, he'd been admitted. The doorman had ushered him into a large room on the ground floor that had looked like the parlor of a very rich man. The women in it had looked like the kind to be found in such a parlor, enjoying afternoon tea, speaking in ladylike murmurs—except for their clothes.

Each one had worn a shimmering robe of cobweb silk that made them seem more naked than if they'd worn nothing at all. Another negro had taken his hat and politely asked his drinking preference, and seconds later a glass of the smoothest Kentucky bourbon he had ever tasted was placed in his hand. There had been no mention of payment.

He'd sat down to enjoy his whiskey on an ivory velvet couch just large enough for two people. None of the women had approached him, although he had been aware that he was the recipient of several modestly curious glances and a few bold ones. The other two men in the room, well dressed and considerably older than he, finished their drinks, then, their business with each other apparently concluded, they separated. Immediately each was joined by a woman, and they disappeared through a side door.

As he was swallowing the last of the bourbon, the negro had inquired if he wanted another. Jesse had shaken his head and stood. His curiosity had been satisfied. The man had returned with his hat and quietly pronounced a sum for the whiskey, and it had taken all of Jesse's self-control to keep from asking if he was joking.

Back out on the street, he remembered, he'd taken a deep breath of the salt-tanged fog to clear out the musky expensive perfume clogging his lungs. Everything he had heard about the sporting houses in San Francisco had been true. The women were beautiful—every one, he was certain, an expert in the tricks and delights of her trade—but even in that house Miranda Hart would have been queen. With her patrician grace and manners and her unusual beauty, a man could have fulfilled the fantasy that he was having a princess. Jesse wondered what the price had been to spend the night with a princess. And he couldn't stop himself from wondering, if she had been in the parlor of the White Swan that night, would he have paid it?

The woman sitting beside him on the buggy seat shifted. "How many men do you plan to hire, Mr. McClintock?"

"Ten." Jesse spit the word out, trying to get rid of the foul taste of self-disgust. It was the third time Miranda had attempted to start up a conversation; she had already tried the weather and the scenery. Jesse whipped up the black Thoroughbred pulling the buggy. Out of the corner of his eye, he saw Miranda's knuckles whiten on the edge of the seat as they jolted over the washboard ruts in the road.

Good, he thought nastily. That should keep her mouth shut. Maybe then he could forget the true character of the woman sitting beside him. As if matters hadn't been bad enough, she had come running out just as he was leaving to say that she wanted to go to town, after all, and he'd had to hitch up her damned buggy. He had toyed with the idea of letting his guard drive it, but the man had been barely able to keep the little cow pony he was riding under control. The spirited Thoroughbred would have had the buggy overturned in the first mile, and his conscience wouldn't allow him to let her or the child she was carrying come to deliberate harm. Cursing steadily under his breath, he had tied Lucky to the back of the buggy and taken the reins himself. He hated to make the poor horse eat dust all the way to town, and he'd be damned if he would drive her back. Some other fool could do it.

With another disgusted sigh, he slowed the Thoroughbred to a more reasonable, less bone-rattling pace. He might be able to shut Miranda Hart up, but he couldn't forget she was beside him. Her scent, not heavy musk but light and sweet, kept drifting past his nose, and although he was very careful not to touch her, the buggy's jouncing had thrown them together several times. His right arm was still burning from the soft pressure of her breast the last time.

She'd pulled away immediately, and Jesse hadn't been able to restrain a harsh snort of laughter at her false modesty. He'd bet she sure as hell hadn't pulled away like that from the customers of the White Swan. His hands tightened on the reins. He could just see her cuddling up to some rich old man, letting him take off her robe, letting him put his cold old man's hands on her warm young . . .

Miranda stole a quick glance at the ominously silent man beside her. For some reason he was in a foul temper. His arched eyebrows were flattened in a dark slash over his eyes, and the ends of his mustache were pulled straight down beside the hard tight line of his mouth, giving him a mean, almost evil look. She'd hardly expected a cozy chat, but she had thought they could at least be civil to each other.

She sighed quietly. She had so wanted to enjoy this day. When Leola had announced unexpectedly that she was going to visit overnight in the village where the miners' families lived and that Tommy wanted to go with her, Miranda had changed her mind and decided to go to town. She examined her hands folded in her lap. But not for ice cream, even if that was the absurd excuse she gave herself to justify the trip. The real reason was even more foolish. She had simply wanted to be with Jesse McClintock.

She unbuttoned the top button of her purple-and-white striped "town" dress and took off her bonnet. Pulling a handkerchief from her sleeve, she patted at the perspiration trickling down her throat. The heat under the black buggy top was stifling; even the breeze generated by their motion felt as if it came straight from a hot oven. Without thinking, she undid another button, trying to loosen the fit of her dress over her breasts. It must be the heat that made them feel so full and achy, made her nipples so tight and sensitive. Even the soft fabric of her chemise rubbing against them was an almost unbearable friction. Absently she plucked at the gaping neckline of her dress, trying to ease the chafing.

A vicious curse suddenly blistered the silence. More bewildered than shocked, Miranda turned to stare at the man beside her. A muscle jumped in his rigid jaw, and his mouth was drawn down even farther, as if he were trying to pull in the ends of his mustache and chew on them. Although nothing appeared to be wrong, he looked meaner than ever, still staring straight ahead, ignoring her as he had throughout this interminable ride. More to vent her exasperation than out of any hope of cooling off, Miranda fanned herself with the handkerchief and turned back to the monotonous scenery passing by. Well, she supposed, she could always count cacti to pass the time.

Unseeing, Jesse glared at the endless landscape of creosote, yucca and sand. He wished he had taken up the habit of chewing tobacco, because he could use something right now to bite down on, hard. When she was fidgeting with her damn dress, he'd had a momentary glimpse of heat-blushed flesh swelling lushly above a delicate bit of white lace. He was helpless to prevent it when his eyes strayed again, greedily following the slow slide of a bead of perspiration from the hollow of her throat. Unconsciously he licked his lower lip as the drop disappeared into the shadowy cleft visible above the last open button. He knew she wasn't cinched into any hard bony corset. Shifting uncomfortably on the seat, he gripped the reins so hard his hands ached, matching another ache. Under that pretty dress she would be soft, her skin like satin...

Miranda sat bolt upright on the narrow seat. He'd been planning to escape! That was why he was in such a snit! She'd inadvertently foiled his plan by wanting to go to town with him, and now, instead of escaping, he was having to play her coachman. She seethed with righteous fury. Over the past week he had seemed to take such a genuine interest in the Silver Tejo that she'd begun to believe he had resigned himself to the situation, but he was showing his true colors at last.

He might have had to postpone his plans, but he obviously hadn't given them up. That was why he had brought his horse along. No doubt he intended to slip away tonight and be long gone by the time they discovered him missing in the morning. Miranda smiled grimly to herself. Well, Mr. McClintock could just forget all about his fine plans. No matter how ugly he acted, he was going to keep the bargain he had made with her to save his miserable hide.

Manolo Rivera watched the approach of the buggy from the cool shade of the Harvey House Hotel's porch. The black Thoroughbred halted by the front steps, and Manolo gave up the shade and his comfortable chair to hold the horse's head while McClintock climbed out and tied the reins through a ring on top of the hitching post. Something had happened between the *patrona* and the big *gringo* on the way to town. Both of them looked as if they had been chewing on poison for the last five miles.

Jesse threaded the leather reins through the rusted iron ring, surreptitiously watching Miranda Hart prepare to take the high step down from the buggy to the street. She would have damned well sat there forever if she'd been hoping he would play the gallant and help her down. Whores—even retired ones—didn't deserve the same courtesies as decent women, he told himself righteously as he jerked the knot tighter.

Mindful of her body's new awkwardness, Miranda stepped down carefully, her skirt gathered in one hand, the other holding on to the buggy hood. Her heel snagged the hem of her dress, throwing her off-balance, and she dropped her skirt, grabbing for the buggy to steady herself. Her flailing hand clutched at the air, and Miranda knew with a helpless certainty that she was going to fall.

Both men turned at her cry. Manolo was closer, but before he could take a step, he was roughly knocked aside. McClintock leaped past him and was there to catch her in his arms almost before the *señora* had even started to fall.

Immediately Jesse eased the bruising pressure of his arms around her and set Miranda down carefully on the hard packed dirt. He still held her, his hands moving unconsciously up and down her sides to reassure her—and himself—that she was all right. They faced each other, scant inches apart, both of them breathing hard from the exertion and fright. "Ask for help next time," he growled with a fierce scowl.

The look she gave him told him what the conditions in Hell would be like before she asked him for anything, yet she had to fight a powerful reluctance before she managed to jerk free of the big, oddly gentle hands holding her. Without speaking, she stepped away from him. In the heartbeat that she'd been pressed against him after he'd saved her, every line of his hard, most definitely male body had been branded on hers, seared into her memory. Taking exquisite care not to touch him again, she leaned past him to snatch her small valise from behind the seat of the buggy, but in her condition, it was a frustratingly impossible reach.

With a muttered curse, Jesse grabbed the bag and thrust it at Rivera, who had come to stand beside them. Jesse heard a barely audible "Thank you," which sounded as if it had been forced out of her at gunpoint. He watched as she turned with a haughty swirl of her skirts and marched up the hotel steps, Rivera following dutifully with her valise. His mustache curled in derision when he saw two men coming out of the hotel tip their hats to her and stand aside courteously to let her pass. Jesse wondered if their derbys would have come off quite so quickly if they'd known that the respectable widow Hart had once been the queen of a San Francisco cathouse.

Manolo heaved his burly body into the buggy a few minutes later and gave directions to the livery stable. The dangerous outlaw who

he knew the *patrona* was convinced was planning his escape sat
relaxed on the seat, holding the reins negligently in one hand while
he took a drag now and then from his cigarette. He didn't look to
be planning anything more than finding out which saloon had the
coldest beer.

His wife scoffed at the idea that Jesse McClintock was guilty of
the crimes he'd been convicted of in Silver City, and he himself,
Manolo admitted, was beginning to wonder what game the old
judge was playing at. He sincerely hoped that Leola was right and
that McClintock wasn't planning anything rash, because he was
beginning to like him. He would be genuinely sorry to have to shoot
him.

Jesse turned the buggy and Lucky over to a boy at the livery
stable, then drew out his watch to check the time. It was a few
minutes past noon, but he had no illusions that he'd find any top
hands waiting for him inside. Every cattle ranch in the territory was
in the middle of fall roundup, and the good men would already
have jobs. All he could realistically hope for were saddle bums.
Pocketing the watch, he glanced at the short stocky man beside
him. "Well, Rivera, let's go see if we had any takers."

Ruebush's had the smell of livery stables everywhere, equal parts
horse, hay and fresh manure. There was a drowsy quiet inside as
the horses lazed in the midday heat. As his eyes adjusted to the
dim, dust-filtered light, Jesse heard the scratch of a match and saw
a brief flare of flame off to one side.

"Well, Jesse Mack, it doesn't appear that the Apaches have put
any holes in your sorry hide yet."

Manolo's gun was halfway out of his holster before he even
thought about it. Something in the low drawl had instinctively
provoked his reaction, an unvoiced threat, a menace, although
McClintock didn't seem to have heard it. Making no move for his
gun, he stood relaxed and easy, framed against the sunlight burning through the stable door, a perfect target.

"Tyree," Jesse said with a genuine smile of pleasure. "What the
hell are you doing here? I thought you had a job in Tucson." He
watched the man sauntering out of the shadows, the smell of his
thin cigar adding to the rich scents in the stable.

"I was passing through Lordsburg, heading that way, when I
heard about the big robbery in Silver City. When I heard the description of the desperado and his horse, I figured it had to be
you." Tyree's thin mouth lifted in a thinner smile as he took a draw
on his cigar. "I went back to Silver City to have a little talk with the
judge about convicting the wrong man."

Manolo eased his gun back into his holster. He was very curious about this friend of Jesse McClintock. A man's choice of friends said a lot about him. He already knew Tyree was not a cowboy. His white shirt, black string tie, black suit and clean shiny boots were proof of that, but if he'd needed any more, he had only to look at the well-oiled gun belted low on Tyree's hips, the holster tied down. He was black haired and tall, almost as tall as McClintock, but leaner. The dominant features of his face were a heavy black mustache and a hawk nose. Tyree had glanced his way when he'd reholstered his gun, and Manolo had been surprised to see that his eyes weren't dark, as he'd expected, but a rare pure green. There had been no expression in them. They had been as blank and cold as deep winter ice.

Before Jesse could reply, three men walked in the back door of the stable. He saw Tyree's left hand move, his fingertips casually resting on the butt of his gun. The men all had the same worn and weathered look, their eyes bleached and faded from years spent squinting against the sun. The man in the middle stepped forward. He dismissed Manolo Rivera with a neutral look. Tyree rated a wary glance. Then the man's faded brown eyes settled on Jesse.

"You be the one lookin' for hands?"

Jesse nodded. "I am."

"Sixty dollars a month and found?"

Another nod confirmed it.

The man rubbed his stubbled chin. "The Silver Tejo. That's in the Floridas, Apatch country?"

"Right."

The bulge in his cheek bobbed rhythmically as he digested that bit of bad news. "Hear it's owned by a widder woman. I don't know about takin' orders from no woman." Brown tobacco juice stained the yellow straw on the floor, subtly conveying his opinion that no man worth his salt took orders from a woman.

"She'll be paying your wages," Jesse said evenly, "but you'll take your orders from me."

The three cowhands exchanged a look, then accepted the job offer with sober nods.

The new hands were George Gearhart, Elmer Johnson and Shorty Brewster. Elmer and Shorty proved they could talk by introducing themselves, but left it to George to make conversation. He explained the reason they were looking for work. They'd drifted over from East Texas for a change of scenery and had found jobs on a small ranch. They'd been working there only a few weeks, when they'd come back after a Saturday night in town to find they were unexpectedly unemployed. While they'd been gone, Apaches had raided the ranch, murdering the owner and his wife and running off all the stock.

A few minutes later Jesse and Tyree pushed through the swinging doors of the nearest saloon. Jesse had felt Tyree's questioning eyes on him several times. Tyree wouldn't ask—he'd always figured a man's business was his own—but Jesse knew he was mystified by the situation.

The saloon had a fancy false front and a bare bones interior. The rough plank floor was strewed with sawdust to absorb spills and misses meant for the battered tin spittoons. A wooden bar, gouged and splintered, ran the length of the saloon, and a few mismatched tables and chairs were scattered over the floor. They ordered beers, then took their mugs to sit at a table in the back of the room. Manolo Rivera and the miner who had ridden in with Jesse and Miranda Hart bought beers and took a table between the other two men and the door. To make sure the Silver Tejo's foreman didn't run out on the job, Jesse thought, laughing dryly to himself. He took a long pull at his beer. It was strong and slightly bitter, but ice cold, thanks to the daily trains bringing in ice. "What did the judge tell you?" he asked when he set down the half-empty mug.

"Only where to find you," Tyree answered.

Jesse related the story of his capture and trial and the bizarre terms of his parole.

"So why haven't you skinned out for home and left the old gal to solve her own problems?" Tyree asked when Jesse finished. He glanced at the two men several tables away. "It doesn't look like there's much stopping you."

Tyree had naturally assumed that the widow Hart was as old as her brother-in-law, the judge, and for reasons he didn't choose to examine, Jesse didn't correct his false assumption. He shrugged. "I'd rather not have to shoot anybody. She'll decide I've given up the idea of escaping soon enough and drop the guards. Then I'll go."

Tyree accepted that. "How many men did you figure to hire?"

Jesse grinned crookedly. "Ten."

"How do you feel about Mexes? I seem to remember you speak the lingo pretty well."

"They don't know that," Jesse said with a brief glance toward Rivera and the miner. They hadn't heard Tyree's remark, he was certain. Tyree customarily spoke in a voice that didn't allow eavesdropping. He sighed heavily. "Right now, I'd hire anyone who knows the hind end of a cow from the front, even if he speaks Chinese."

"There's a Mex crew in town, brought a small herd of Brahmas up from Sonora. I met the boss in a poker game last night. He's only a kid, about twenty, the son of some *hidalgo*." Tyree relaxed back in his chair with a sardonic grin. "He's so damn pretty I feel like I ought to tip my hat every time I see him. I hear he's got all the girls in town panting after him, and there're a few fathers already cleaning their shotguns. But the kid must be all right. He brought that herd through Yaqui country without losing a head or a man."

"You think he'd be interested in just being a puncher?" Jesse's tone was plainly skeptical.

Tyree gave Jesse a sly wink. "I think his daddy told him not to hurry home. They have shotguns in Mexico, too."

An hour later Jesse had eight of the ten men he needed, when Francisco Jesús Antonio García de Moreno and his men decided that being ambushed by Apaches and chasing cattle through cacti sounded far more entertaining than playing pool and poker, drinking tequila and romancing the local *señoritas*. Even with Tyree's warning, Cisco Moreno had still been a surprise. Small and slight, with big black eyes, curly black hair and fine, almost delicate features, the young *hidalgo* did indeed look like a beautiful girl. It must be hard, Jesse thought with secret amusement, for a woman to know that Cisco Moreno was prettier than she could ever hope to be.

Jesse also hired a ninth man in the pool hall where he and Tyree had located Moreno. About forty, Frank Penny was a soft-spoken man with thinning brown hair and pale blue eyes. There was nothing out of the ordinary about him, yet Jesse felt a vague uneasiness about the man. Penny had the cat-eyed look of a gun hand who hired out to the highest bidder in local range wars, but that wasn't what was bothering Jesse most. It was Penny's hatband. A tawny ribbon of fur with a black stripe down the middle decorated the stained gray hat. Jesse recognized it as the strip of fur that covered a jaguar's backbone. Jaguars roamed the desert and foothills along the border, and he wondered if a beautiful animal had been killed just to make a hatband. However, Penny was an experienced hand, and Tyree had vouched for him, saying he had run across Penny a few years before in Tombstone.

Tyree racked up the billiard balls and gestured for Jesse to break the set. "Looks like you've got the ten men you wanted, Jesse Mack," he said.

The white cue ball hit the point of the triangle solidly, scattering the colored balls over the green baize. "Nine," Jesse corrected absently.

"Ten."

Jesse checked his shot and straightened slowly, looking at the man across the table. When he was a green cowhand, he'd practiced his fast draw, trying to earn the respect of the older hands, until he'd finally realized that nobody was much impressed by the fact that he could kill six fenceposts without reloading. Tyree must have had a different motivation. Even then he had been the fastest man with a gun Jesse had ever seen, and when they'd parted company, he'd known that Tyree wouldn't waste any more of his time punching cows. From the quality of his clothes and his cigars, it was obvious that his skill with a gun had earned him a good deal more than beans and blisters the past few years. "I thought you had business in Tucson."

Tyree's dark face lightened with one of his rare smiles. "Tucson's too hot this time of year."

Miranda crossed the railroad depot platform, heading for the Harvey Hotel. She had justified her trip to town by completing a few errands, including checking with the Wells Fargo agent to verify that the silver Manolo had brought into Deming yesterday was already on its way to the U.S. Mint in San Francisco. It was the first shipment they had made in months. The rich veins that had nourished the Silver Tejo for nearly twenty years were at last drying up, and within a year, Manolo predicted, the mine would no longer pay for itself, much less produce a profit. The Silver Tejo would be dependent on cattle, not silver, for its survival. And to ensure that—along with her own survival, and Tommy's—Miranda understood only too well that she was depending on a man she knew nothing about, and now trusted even less.

She paused at the open door of the hotel, drawn to look across the street as surely as if someone had shouted her name. The tickling sensation feathering down her spine told her who would be standing on the other side even before she turned her head. Her eyes were caught and held fast by Jesse McClintock's. He was too far away, of course, for her to see the expression in his eyes, but she felt the intensity of his gaze like a physical touch. For a long minute she was as oblivious to everything else around her as if she were trapped in a trance, watching the tall man standing on the board-walk across the street watch her. Then the steam whistle of an approaching train announced its arrival. Her eyes jerked free, and she walked through the door.

A small blond woman smiled at her as she took a corner table in the dining room, then she went on with her head-to-toe inspection of the young women lined up in front of her. Miranda dropped her bonnet and purse on the chair beside her and smiled to herself as she looked across the room. Celia Kershaw stood with her back ramrod straight, like a general inspecting her troops.

Celia examined the women under her command with an unsmiling face. This daily inspection reminded her of ones she herself had endured years ago. The purpose, though not the place, had been the same: to help assure that the customers were satisfied and would return again to spend their money.

The young women, dressed in white shirtwaists with black bow ties, black skirts and crisp white aprons, were as spotless as the linen tablecloths and polished wood floors. Celia nodded her approval and dismissed them to their stations just as the eastbound Santa Fe train chugged into the station. Hearing the hotel janitor out on the platform, beating a gong to attract customers, she took up her position by the door. Graciously she greeted diners, then, when the rush subsided, circulated around the room to make sure tables were quickly cleaned and reset with the heavy sterling flatware and fine china that were a Harvey House trademark. She quietly cautioned a new girl about keeping her station clean, including the glass cake bell that attracted crumbs and icing like a magnet, and when a customer jostled another waitress's elbow, sloshing gravy on her apron, Celia took her place while the girl went to change.

The train whistle blasted warning of the train's imminent departure, the last diners hurried out of the room and Celia released a grateful sigh. She had seen a waitress deliver a glass of icy lemonade to Miranda's table, and she had told the girl to make sure the glass was kept full. After a quick check to see that the girls were attending to readying the tables for the next meal, she pulled out a chair at Miranda's table and sat down. "You certainly look different than the last time I saw you." The fast friendship they had developed over the past year precluded any need for a more formal greeting.

Miranda laughed. "I certainly hope so."

Celia signaled one of the waitresses for a glass of lemonade for herself, then leaned across the table, her voice with its trace of a Cajun accent lowering automatically. "What in heaven's name were you doing in that getup? I could hardly believe it was you, you looked so awful."

Miranda's tone was very casual. "I had to go up to Silver City to hire a foreman."

Celia looked at her skeptically. "Why couldn't he come down here? You shouldn't be traveling that far in your condition. And why the disguise?"

Miranda answered the questions in reverse order with a bored shrug. "Oh, I decided it would be easier to travel as an old woman nobody would be interested in. And the man was rather busy at the time. He couldn't get away." It wasn't a lie exactly, Miranda assured herself. She was sure Jesse McClintock wouldn't be anxious to have the truth known, and neither was she. If the men he was hiring found out who he was, in essence, her prisoner, his authority would be undermined. Only Manolo and Leola knew the true circumstances that had brought him to the Silver Tejo, and she knew she could trust them to keep the secret. Even the guards he no doubt thought were there to prevent his escape didn't know. Their orders were to guard his back, not to keep him from getting away. After waiting so long to find a foreman, she couldn't afford to lose him. She knew she could trust Celia, too, but Miranda suddenly discovered she had a reluctance to talk about him, even think about him . . . perhaps because then she would also have to think about the disturbing emotions he seemed to arouse so easily in her.

Celia took a long drink of her lemonade. She wasn't fooled for a second. Miranda was up to something, and it most definitely involved that good-looking giant who had been with her last week. If she hadn't been up to something herself and pressed for time, she would have worked what was going on out of her friend. "Is your new foreman hiring men?" She already knew the answer. It was yesterday, when she had overheard Manolo Rivera telling a man to be at the livery today at noon if he wanted a job, that she had started planning, and the fact that Miranda had come gave her plan even more chance of success. She would have preferred someplace less dangerous than the Silver Tejo, but beggars couldn't be choosers. And she would beg, if necessary.

"Yes." Miranda's smile was relieved. "I think he's found a complete crew."

"A wrangler, too?" Celia asked, her attention seemingly on two girls snapping a clean cloth over the table between them.

Miranda paused with her glass halfway to her lips. "I'm not sure. Manolo didn't say." Leaving Jesse under the watchful eye of the other miner, Manolo had found her in the Wells Fargo office and reported on his success in hiring.

"I know a man who might be interested in the job."

"Who?" she asked curiously before emptying her glass. Celia Kershaw was a very attractive, very eligible woman, but more than once Miranda had seen her freeze an interested man with a frigid look from her lovely blue eyes. She wore her uniform of prim black dress and starched, virginally white pinafore like a nun's habit. A hairnet confined her hair as neatly as a wimple, the keys to the hotel hung about her waist like a crucifix and she watched over the Harvey girls as religiously as any mother superior did her convent. The only man she even seemed to know was Charlie Baxter. Miranda knew he had taken Celia for drives on her free Sunday afternoons and escorted her to the town's Fourth of July celebration and dance. Charlie had seemed to be getting rather serious, and she'd suspected that Celia was, too—until he had decided to live in a whiskey bottle.

Celia turned back to face her and said with elaborate casualness, "Charlie Baxter."

Miranda just managed to swallow the mouthful of lemonade without choking. "The drunk?" she said weakly. The hurt expression on Celia's face made her immediately chagrined at her unkind, although painfully accurate description.

"He has been drinking more than he should...lately," Celia conceded stiffly, "but he's not a drunk." She ignored Miranda's dubious look. "He's had some trouble. I know you heard about it, Miranda, how bandits attacked him two months ago. They took his wagons, his mules, killed John Pierce, his partner. He lost his freighting business, everything."

Miranda nodded reluctantly. "I did hear about it, Celia, but—"

"Charlie's a good man. He's just had some bad luck. All he needs is a chance, someone to believe in him. He's so good with mules and horses. He'd make an excellent wrangler," Celia argued persuasively, sensing that Miranda was weakening.

"No one has seen him sober for weeks, Celia. The Silver Tejo is a dangerous place. You know that. You've told me often enough," Miranda reminded her. "A man who can't keep away from liquor would be a danger not only to himself but to the other men who have to depend on him." Miranda smiled sympathetically and patted her friend's hand, clenched on the tabletop. "A job in town would be a better idea. I'll speak to—"

"He'll stay sober," Celia promised grimly.

Sitting back, Miranda considered her friend thoughtfully. Celia was on the edge of her chair, tensed and waiting for an answer. Whether she realized it or not, she was pleading for Charlie. She still believed in him, even if everyone else considered him a whiskey-soaked ruin. Miranda made an instant decision that she hoped she wouldn't have plenty of time to regret later, especially when she had a brief vision of a face with storm cloud eyes, a harsh line of a mouth and chiseled granite for a jaw. Well, she argued defiantly, as if the owner of that face were standing there in front her, if she could give a job to a convicted criminal, she could certainly give one to the town drunk. Especially when it was so important to Celia.

"Tell him to be at the livery stable tomorrow morning. We'll be leaving from there at dawn," she said finally, holding up her hand to forestall the other woman's gratitude. "But if anyone even suspects he's drinking again, Celia, he's off the ranch immediately. No second chances."

"One is all he needs," Celia said quietly. "Thank you." She breathed a deep sigh of relief and was about to order more lemonade for both of them, when a commotion at the door to the dining room drew her attention. With a sinking heart, she wondered if Charlie was going to get even that chance now.

Earlier in the day, she had promised one of the boys who habitually hung around the depot on Saturday mornings a quarter if he would find Charlie wherever he was sleeping off last night's binge and tell him that she wanted to see him. Apparently he had already gotten a start on tonight's spree before the boy had found him. Singing a bawdy song, he stumbled into the dining room, and with the exercise yelling at mule teams had given his voice, Celia was certain that even the guests on the second floor heard every word with absolute clarity.

Charlie's song was hysterically obscene, and in spite of herself, Miranda almost laughed, until she saw the heartsick dismay and genuine fear on Celia's face. The other woman was already on her feet, when Charlie ricocheted off the first dining table and tripped over a waitress station. China and glasses crashed to the floor, silverware went skittering over the polished planks in all directions and the cake bell holding a chocolate cake toppled. Miraculously the fragile glass didn't shatter but just rolled off unharmed. Coming to her feet, too, Miranda held her breath as Charlie teetered first one way and then the other, finally ending the suspense when he landed in a tangle of arms and legs atop the fallen cake, squashing it flat. She glanced uneasily at the woman beside her.

Celia gasped, sparing Miranda a distracted look. "I've got to get him out of here before someone sends for the sheriff. Last week he shot a man just for riding his horse in here." She saw not Charlie with a stupid drunken grin on his face and cake crumbs in his hair, but that poor dead cowboy lying in a pool of blood on the dining room floor.

"Come on, I'll help you." Miranda started around the table, but Celia's surprisingly strong hand held her back.

"No, Miranda, thank you, but this is my problem." She gave her friend one last look of grim resolution before starting across the floor. "Charlie will be there tomorrow morning."

Celia has more faith than sense, Miranda thought sadly, watching her issue rapid orders to the half-dozen Harvey girls still in the dining room. Charlie wouldn't be at the livery stable in the morning; he wouldn't be able to go that long without a drink, but at least no one else had witnessed this debacle. The girls scurried for mops and brooms while Celia commandeered the biggest of the waitresses to help her get Charlie upright and moving. He tried to help, too, but his legs kept folding up like overcooked noodles, making the women stagger, as well, so that they looked like three drunks instead of one, trying to carry one another off.

Miranda followed them at a discreet distance, but as soon as she walked out the door, she saw that there had been another witness after all, and any hope she'd had of keeping Charlie's problem a secret from his new boss—if by some miracle he did appear tomorrow morning—was promptly dashed. An expression of complete disgust on his face, Jesse McClintock stood a few feet away, watching the progress of the three people tottering toward the back stairs leading up to the staff quarters. He turned his head back to survey the mess Charlie had made, before his eyes finally flicked to her, coolly remote. Wordlessly he stooped and picked up the cake bell that had rolled to a stop at his feet; then, with a nod that just met the bare minimum of courtesy, he strode past her into the dining room.

Jesse was enjoying himself. He was enjoying the excellent steak on his dinner plate, he was enjoying the pleasant surroundings and he was enjoying Tyree's and Miranda Hart's reactions to each other. Tyree, who could bluff a man holding four aces into folding when he himself had only trash, hadn't been able to keep his jaw from sagging when he met the "elderly" widow Hart. And Jesse had especially enjoyed the way the widow's eyes had widened, then darted in alarm to Rivera, when he'd introduced Tyree and casually mentioned that he was one of her new riders.

Miranda rearranged the food on her plate again. It was well prepared and no doubt very tasty, but what little appetite she'd had had vanished as soon as Jesse McClintock had presented his friend

Tyree, then invited him to share the table with Manolo and her. The tall dark man had the same hard, dangerous look as the last men Thomas had hired. They had been professional gunmen, not cowhands, and—she didn't know why she hadn't noticed it before—Jesse McClintock had much the same look, too.

Jesse's pleasure evaporated rapidly as the meal progressed. It was no concern of his if she wanted to play with her food instead of eat it, he reminded himself. The fact that she was too damn skinny wasn't his problem. The Harvey girl who had brought their dinners returned to clear their plates and take orders for dessert. Silently Jesse signaled the girl to change the order from three slices of apple pie to four. Miranda's wedge of pie remained untouched, but the vanilla ice cream disappeared, he noted with grim satisfaction.

Miranda laid down her spoon and pushed away the pie. She hadn't ordered it, and when the waitress had set the plate down in front of her, she'd started to tell her so, but a hard look from across the table had kept her mouth shut. A piece of pie simply wasn't worth an argument. How a man could be so disagreeable without saying anything baffled her. The ice cream had tasted wonderful, though, and she laughed silently when she remembered that ice cream had been her excuse for coming to town that morning—a morning that suddenly seemed very far away.

"If you'll excuse me, gentlemen, I think I'll say good-night," she murmured, starting to push back her chair. Three other chairs immediately scraped on the wooden floor, and she saw Manolo moving behind her, but it was Jesse McClintock who pulled out her chair.

The three men reseated themselves, Jesse watching the two drummers, or salesmen, who were walking out of the dining room after Miranda Hart. He didn't like the bold way they were looking at her or the smirking laughter that had followed one's comment to the other. Worrying about an affront to her "honor" now? he chided himself scornfully, and deliberately turned back to the table.

Tyree was taking a thin cheroot from the inside pocket of his coat. "Well, I think I'll go play a little poker." He looked questioningly at Jesse.

"Sure, why not?" He glanced at the stocky Mexican sitting beside him. "Care to join us, Rivera?" He would, anyway, Jesse thought sourly, but the man deserved the courtesy of an invitation. It wasn't his fault that he had to play watchdog.

Manolo nodded, accepting the offer of a cigar from Tyree. Jesse declined one with an absent shake of his head. From his position he could see into the hotel lobby, and he followed the backs of the drummers' cheap suits up the stairs to the rooms above. He damn well wasn't going to go running after her, he assured himself, forcing his eyes away from the stairway. She wasn't his responsibility; she could take care of herself. He was no la-di-da gentleman, and she was sure as hell no lady.

Tyree lit his cigar and blew out the match. "Want to try the Bullhead first? There was a pretty good game going there last night."

Abruptly Jesse shoved himself back from the table and stood. "I'll catch up with you," he said absently, jamming his hat on his head as he headed for the stairs.

"Can't you get the door open?"

Miranda's fingers all turned to thumbs, and her room key clattered on the floor. "No—I—th-the key is stubborn." She'd heard someone coming down the hall, but the tingle of awareness that usually warned her when Jesse McClintock was near had failed her this time. Bending awkwardly, she groped for the key, but a lean tanned hand found it first.

Jesse fitted the key into the lock, cursing richly under his breath when it did indeed prove stubborn. Knowing he'd come on a fool's errand didn't improve his temper, either. Finally he felt the lock give, but he didn't turn the knob and step aside. Instead he leaned a shoulder against the frame, blocking the door. Giving her an insolently familiar smile, he used his bigger, brawnier body to deliberately crowd her smaller, slighter one, and she stepped back automatically into the corner where the hall dead-ended by her door, effectively trapped. It was a blatantly obvious move, but he saw no coy acknowledgment in her wide lavender eyes, certainly no invitation, no sexual awareness at all. Again he was struck by the air of innocence about her—until he remembered the ugly old hag he'd met in Silver city. She was skilled at creating illusions, an actress, and whores were the most skilled actresses of all, weren't they? They could make a man believe almost anything . . . even innocence.

She was tired, and loitering in a hotel hallway with a man at night wasn't the most proper behavior for a respectable widow, Miranda reminded herself, but she was loath to go into her room. She was intensely aware of the man—his size, the heat radiating from him, even the smell of him, clean, fresh, yet unmistakably masculine. Despite his inexplicable day-long churlishness and her annoyance with it, the presence of him so close to her, so big, so warm, so intensely male, was curiously reassuring and heart gladdening, like the strong bright sun finally breaking through a long siege of dismal gray clouds. "I hired a wrangler this afternoon," she said suddenly.

His dark eyebrows immediately snapped down. "I thought we agreed that I would do all the hiring."

With fastidious care, Miranda rearranged the light shawl she'd thrown on when the sun had gone down. "Actually, I don't believe we ever discussed it." Hoping to extend their two sentence conversation, she'd blurted out the first thing that had popped into her mind, and just as instantly regretted it. She met his darkening scowl with a bland smile. "Mr. Baxter is very good with horses. We're lucky he was available."

Her smile and words were guileless enough, but her tongue had flicked nervously over that crooked little tooth, a dead giveaway. Slowly he straightened away from the door. He dragged his eyes away from her mouth, then narrowed them on her suspiciously. If this Baxter was both good and available, why hadn't he been at the livery stable? Suddenly Jesse remembered the scene he'd happened on downstairs earlier and the feeling that she had played some part in it. "The drunk in the dining room," he said with flat certainty.

Miranda suppressed a sigh of sharp dismay. There was clearly no need for additional clarification; they both knew which drunk he meant. "He wasn't always like that," she said quietly. "Charlie Baxter and a partner had a very successful freighting business here in Deming. Then, a few months ago, bandits attacked them, stole their wagons and freight and killed Charlie's partner. He sold what little he had left and gave it to his partner's widow, and after that, he just didn't seem to care what happened to him anymore." Her voice almost faltered as she watched his mouth thin until it was no more than a cruel-looking slit beneath his mustache. "He really is expert with horses. All he needs is a chance," she finished softly, unconsciously echoing Celia's words.

Jesse snorted in disgust. "All that no-account drunk would be expert with is a whiskey bottle." Why the hell should it matter to him that she was practically begging for some rum sucker? he thought, furious with himself. Almost as furious as he was with the woman staring up at him with a quiet plea in her beautiful eyes.

Miranda could think of no rebuttal, and the continuing silence was unnerving. The face of the man in front of her was set and uncompromising, his eyes the dark color of a violent storm cloud, and she shivered suddenly, as if a cold draft had swept down the hall, chilling the air.

Jesse saw the slight tremor, and without thinking, he reached out to adjust her shawl where it had slipped down her arm. His fingers brushed her shoulder as he pulled it up, and he felt her shudder again. Her face was still tilted up to his, the graceful line of her throat exposed and vulnerable. Her eyes had darkened to a misty violet, and her lips were slightly parted, moist and so soft looking. She looked impossibly young and defenseless. His other hand came up of its own accord and joined the first one in arranging the soft wool, lingering to smooth it over her shoulders long after any wrinkles were gone. He felt the too sharp bones, and abruptly the resentment he had been nursing all day, cultivating into a fine righteous anger, drained out of him. The bitter internal dialogue he'd been carrying on with himself fell silent. Unconsciously his hands urged her closer, close enough that he could feel her soft, sweet breath, quickening and a little uneven, warming his throat and cheek. He no longer wanted to argue with her; he didn't want to think about what she had been, or the lie that she was. He looked down into the clear eyes that seemed open all the way down to her soul, and he wanted... His hands tightened convulsively. He wanted.

His long fingers had found the tight muscles in her shoulders, coaxing them into relaxation with gentle kneading. Her whole body was relaxing, yet every touch of those strong hands flickered through her body like lightning. How could that be? she wondered. Why wasn't her body tensing for the next jolt, instead of becoming more languid, almost liquid? She gave the puzzle only fleeting thought. The muted noises of the hotel around them receded even farther beyond the edge of her consciousness, and the long empty hallway, softly lit by gaslights, appeared to contract until it seemed the two of them were isolated in a small, dim room, completely alone. The warmth of their bodies flowed together as the air took on a musky sweetness. The animosity between them had faded away like an unsubstantial mist in the sunlight, and Miranda didn't want it to return, ever. For the first time since childhood she felt safe, cosseted and ... happy. The feelings had been absent so long that it took several moments to identify them, yet beneath them she sensed a stirring she couldn't exactly identify, a restlessness that wasn't satisfied with this comfortable languor, that wanted something much more, something vaguely disturbing. But she wouldn't think about that right now, she decided with even more vagueness as she gazed up into his eyes. They had changed. They were still a very dark blue-gray, almost black, but less violent now, softer. Just as the chiseled cut of his mouth, where her eyes were drawn next, was softer. His hands flexed on

her shoulders, drawing her even nearer, and she thought she saw
her name form soundlessly on his lips as his head bent and his
mouth came closer. Her arms lifted as, instinctively, she strained
up to meet his kiss.

A door slammed loudly down the hall, and heavy boots thumped
across the floorboards toward the stairs. Jesse and Miranda sprang
apart at the rudely intrusive noise like guilty children caught at
some forbidden naughtiness.

"You should be in your room. You have to be up early in the
morning."

His words were once again harsh and accusing, and Miranda felt
a powerful sense of loss like a physical blow, stunning her. It was
as if the few precious moments of quiet accord had never passed
between them, as if he had never touched her so...tenderly. His
hands were jammed in his pockets now, and he stood several feet
away, his body as hard and rigid as his expression. His words made
it clear that he wouldn't wait for any laggards in the morning.
Turning away from the cold glitter of suppressed fury in his eyes,
she opened her door. Pausing on the threshold, she gave him a brief
glance over her shoulder. "You won't have to wait for me, Mr.
McClintock," she said tonelessly, then shut the door.

Chapter Six

With an uncharacteristic lack of regard for her image, Celia ran as fast as she could down the hall. A dozen times she had been certain the large clock in the dining room must have stopped as she waited for the hands, dragging along at a worm's crawl, to reach eight o'clock. That was when the dining room closed for the evening and she was officially off duty, although she rarely even left until half past the hour, remaining to make sure that everything was in readiness for the following morning. Tonight she was out the door the instant the minute hand finally crept onto the twelve.

She closed the door to her room behind her. The man sprawled across her narrow bed didn't notice. Standing in the middle of the room, her hands on her hips, she stared at him as he suddenly rolled over onto his back and began snoring loudly. Charlie Baxter wasn't looking like any prize at the moment. His clothes were little more than filthy rags, his face was prickly with a scraggly growth of beard and his long brown hair was sticking out every which way. And he stank of stale beer, slopped whiskey and God knows what else. Celia didn't want to know.

She approached the bed and, with a grimace of disgust, began tugging off his boots. They were run over at the heels, the side seams burst, and his socks were more hole than wool. Holding the stiff socks as far away from her as possible, Celia carried them over to a small wicker wastebasket, trying not to breathe.

Prodding him hard with her small fist got no response, and with an impatient sigh, she began packing towels around his head and shoulders. She was much too small to drag him off the bed and manhandle him down the hall to the bathroom by herself, and she didn't want to ask one of the girls for help again. She didn't want to draw any more attention than necessary to the fact that she had broken the most sacrosanct Harvey commandment: Thou shalt not have a man in thy room. Despite being in a near panic of haste, she laughed dryly to herself. Such was her reputation that it would never occur to anyone that she might take a man to her room for lascivious purposes.

When she judged that there were enough towels to protect her bed, Celia retrieved the rose-painted water pitcher from her washstand. She had met Charlie Baxter the day she had arrived on the Santa Fe train from Kansas City, a year and a half ago. When she had stepped onto the depot platform, her heart had almost failed her. The "city" of Deming was a barren, brown wasteland, dotted with tents, wooden shack saloons and a two-story hotel with mustard yellow siding. If Mr. Fred Harvey himself hadn't asked her to come and manage the dining room in his newest hotel, she would have turned right around and gotten back on that train.

Charlie had been waiting on the platform for a shipment of mining equipment he was to freight up to the mines at Silver City, she remembered. He must have seen the shock and disappointment on her face, because he had come right over, tipped his hat politely and introduced himself. Then, before she had had a chance to protest his forwardness, he'd hoisted her trunk onto his broad shoulder and started for the hotel. Swallowing her protest, she'd followed her trunk. As soon as she'd caught up with him, he had begun talking about the big plans everyone had for that miserable pile of dust, and Celia had listened in spite of herself to talk of fine brick homes and hotels and a church and grass and trees and flowers. By the time her trunk was deposited in the lobby, she could almost see those houses and trees and flowers. Now, a year and a half later, she truly *could* see them.

Charlie became a regular for Sunday dinner, and she had soon realized what a genuinely nice, hard-working man he was. She had realized, too, that he wasn't coming by every Sunday for the food, and, in the face of his gentle persistence, she had broken her own commandment, one that had been inviolate for years, and allowed a man a place in her sterile life and heart. Then came the ambush. Charlie could have started over, but all the heart seemed to have gone out of him. She knew he needed someone—needed *her*—but he avoided all his old acquaintances, especially her, and she had stood by helplessly while he had sunk lower and lower into the private hell he wouldn't share with anyone.

Well, no more! Raising the full, rose-painted pitcher high, she paused for a moment to contemplate the snoring mess on her bed. She could be persistent, too, but not gentle, she thought with wry humor as she dumped the entire pitcher of water over Charlie's face. There was no reaction for a moment, and Celia started to panic, thinking she had drowned him. Suddenly the air in her room turned blue with mule train profanity, and flailing arms knocked the pitcher from her hand.

Stepping back out of range, Celia crossed her arms under her breasts and waited until he ran out of breath. "Please be quiet, Mr. Baxter. You'll disturb our guests."

Charlie Baxter gaped at her in total disbelief. "What the hell were you trying to do, woman?" he croaked hoarsely. "Drown me?"

"I thought that was what you were trying to do to yourself in a whiskey bottle," she retorted tartly.

Charlie tried to glare at her, but his eyebrows hurt too much to move. He moaned and shut his eyes against the dim light coming through the curtains and trying to blind him. "Go away. Let a man die in peace," he groaned piteously.

Celia stepped forward and began tugging at his arm. "Don't you dare go back to sleep, Charlie Baxter. I've gotten you a job. You have to be at the livery stable at sunup, and first you have to have a bath and a shave and a haircut."

Charlie risked the pain for a satisfactory glare. "What the hell are you talking about, Celia Kershaw?" he whispered furiously. His head hurt too much to yell. "I don't want any damn job. What I want is a drink."

"Well, you're not getting one." Celia had him in a sitting position and went to work levering him to his feet. "And I don't suppose you do want a job. Your job lately seems to be making people feel sorry for poor pathetic Charlie Baxter." She was panting with the effort of getting him to stand up. "Well, I hate to tell you, but people are tired of feeling sorry for poor old Charlie Baxter, the town drunk. They're beginning to say it's about time you sobered up and started acting like a man," she informed him heartlessly.

Celia got her shoulder under Charlie's left arm and heaved upward. He made it to his feet, and they swayed together precariously. Finally he stabilized, and Celia began guiding him toward the door, careful to keep her face averted from his. His breath alone was enough to knock over an elephant.

Charlie was helpless in the face of such determination. It was taking all his energy just to put one foot in front of the other to get down the hall. Celia unlocked the door to the bathroom, where she had prepared a bath earlier, and shoved him unceremoniously inside. Charlie stared at the full tin tub for a moment before understanding glimmered, then he automatically began stripping off his clothes. Celia demanded through the door that he hand them out to her, and he did so without argument. Then he climbed into the clawfoot tub and sank blissfully into the steaming water.

Slowly the steam penetrated his befogged brain, clearing it. He spied a cake of soap and decided he might as well make use of it as long as he was there. As he scrubbed away the layers of grime, he pondered why a sweet gentle little woman would suddenly turn into such a big bully. Nasty-mean bully, too, he decided. The woman was completely without pity, denying him even the tiniest little drink, just enough to stop the big bass drum beating inside his skull.

Too soon there was another peremptory knock on the door. He ignored it, but he had neglected to lock the door, and to his consternation, he saw it begin to inch open. He was frantically scrabbling for the washrag, lost somewhere under the water, when a small white hand appeared through the crack to drop jeans, a blue striped work shirt, socks and drawers on the floor. They were all new.

"Hurry up!" the bully's ruthless voice commanded him through the door. "You were due at the barber's ten minutes ago."

When Charlie came out of the bathroom a few minutes later, Celia pushed him toward the stairs. "When you've finished at the barber's, come straight back here." She gave him a hard look. "Don't even think about stopping for a drink. I'll have some dinner for you and tell you about the job."

Charlie gave her a weak smile and started down the stairs in a reasonably straight line. Half an hour later he was back in Celia's room. Freshly barbered and stone sober, he sat with a plate of chicken and dumplings on the small table in front of him, trying not to puke. The one dumpling he had forced down to please the woman hovering over him lay like a lead sinker at the bottom of his slowly churning stomach. What he needed was a drink.

And he would probably have had one, he thought, if his guilty conscience hadn't directed his feet to the barber shop instead of the first saloon he passed. Celia had gone to so much trouble for him already, even talking Henry Slavin, the barber, into keeping his shop open late, that he couldn't find it in his heart to disappoint her. The question was . . . why was she troubling herself with him at all? They had been keeping company together, but they had barely progressed past calling each other "Miss Kershaw" and "Mr. Baxter," although he'd been ready to skip over that respectable nonsense and on to more important matters the second he'd seen her step off the train a year and a half ago. Hell, he hadn't even found out if that prim little mouth tasted as sweet as he imagined, or if the small rigidly straight body under that proper black dress was as soft and delightfully curved as he suspected. Bandits had put an end to his plans for Celia Kershaw. He had nothing to offer her now, except a killing load of guilt as he tried to understand why John, who had a wife and two small children, had died, and he, who had had nothing but hopes and dreams, had lived.

"Well!" Celia clasped her hands together and smiled brightly as she sat across from him. "You look so much better. Those new clothes and the barber have worked wonders." Celia groaned dismally inside. The clothes did fit fairly well, his hair was neatly trimmed and he was clean shaven. His broken boots weren't too noticeable—she would have gotten him new ones, but she hadn't had any idea of his size—but his skin had a definite greenish cast. There were beads of clammy sweat on his forehead, and the whites of his brown eyes were a solid red. His hands trembled so badly he had hardly been able to hold the fork. Normally he was a nice-looking man with a quiet air of honesty and dependability. Now, despite the clean clothes and bath, the loud smell of whiskey still seemed to be on him, and she feared even a full night's sleep wouldn't blow it away.

Charlie gave her a dry look; he had seen what he looked like in the barber's mirror. He shoved the uneaten dinner aside. It was out of direct sight, but unfortunately he could still smell it. "Suppose you tell me about this job you've gotten for me?"

"You're going to be the new wrangler on the Silver Tejo," Celia said with far more enthusiasm than she felt. "You're to be at Ruebush's livery stable tomorrow morning at sunup. That's when they're leaving. There's a new foreman, too, a Mr. McClintock, but you don't have to talk to him about the job. Mrs. Hart has already said it's yours."

Charlie nodded fatalistically. He remembered hearing what had happened to the Silver Tejo's old wrangler. Ah, well, he hadn't been having too much success at committing suicide with a whiskey bottle; maybe he'd have better luck with the Apaches.

Celia picked up the dinner plate and placed it back on the tray. "I'll take this back down to the kitchen, then I'll be right back." She fingered her key in her pocket as she rose from her chair and started for the door. Charlie wasn't going to like it, but she was going to lock him in when she left. She couldn't take any chances that he'd sneak off while she was gone.

Charlie watched her, then took his first good look at the room around him. Besides the standard hotel bed, washstand, chair and wardrobe, Celia had added two armchairs with a small table between them, but the room was still barren, impersonal. There were no photographs, none of the trinkets women were usually so fond of, nothing to show for thirty years of living. She had never spoken of her past, either. It was as if Celia Kershaw had sprung full-blown, in a starched black dress, from a train one day. He remembered seeing her that first time, looking so lost and alone, shining like gold in the dust. "Why are you so bent on saving me from myself, Celia?" he asked her softly.

She stopped at the door with her back to him, then turned slowly to face him, and he saw her smile, off center and a little sad. "I'm not sure exactly. Maybe you're my good deed for the year. Or maybe—" her smile faded and for a moment her blue eyes were clouded and far away "—you remind me of someone I used to know."

"I'll pay you back, Celia," he promised quietly, standing up and going toward her. "Every penny...for the clothes, the barber." For believing in me when I don't even believe in myself, he added silently.

"Yes, you will, Charlie," she agreed matter-of-factly with a small smile for herself as he stopped in front of her. "With interest. I've made an investment in you, and I always expect a good return on my investments." She started to turn back to the door, when she felt the tray being taken from her hands. She looked up at Charlie questioningly.

"I'll take this back down for you." He saw the protest forming on her lips and the sudden alarm in her eyes. "Don't worry, the only thing I'll have to drink is water." He made a comical grimace of distaste that coaxed a little smile from her. "Hankins, the owner of the Tom Collins, has been letting me sleep in the back in exchange for swamping out the saloon every morning and giving me a bottle of rotgut every night. So far he hasn't gotten his money's worth. I owe him, too. I'll clean up the place tonight and sleep there." And maybe the work would take his mind off how much he wanted a drink. He saw the anxious doubt in her blue eyes. Shifting the tray to one hand, he gently brushed back the few stray wisps of golden hair that had dared to escape from the severe knot at her neck. His thumb lingered a moment to trace the clean line of her down-soft cheek. "I'll be at Ruebush's in the morning, Celia," he swore with quiet intensity.

As he pulled the door closed behind him, he heard her soft reply. "I know, Charlie."

Jesse had found Tyree and Rivera waiting for him at the bottom of the stairs. They ambled along the raised boardwalk, enjoying the clean evening air before they turned into the Bullhead, a noisy, smoky saloon. "The widow Hart is little younger than I expected," Tyree murmured, sending Jesse a sidelong look as they pushed through the swinging doors together. "Better looking, too."

Jesse laughed, but found he didn't want to discuss any of the widow's other "surprises."

After a few beers and several desultory hands of poker, they parted company. Jesse stood on the boardwalk for a moment, watching Tyree melt into the darkness, then started back to the hotel with his patient shadow. Charlie Baxter passed them, heading toward the saloon they had just left, and he looked after him, then silently shook his head to himself.

Charlie was tossing a bucket of dirty water into the alley behind the saloon an hour later, when he almost splashed a man passing by. The man didn't seem to notice the near miss. Because he had other things on his mind, Charlie grinned to himself. Down the alley were the cribs of the cheapest of Deming's prostitutes.

The town was asleep when the door to one of the cribs opened once again. A man paused in the narrow doorway, silhouetted against the dim light in the room behind him. A filthy carpet covered the rough plank floor of the shack. The bed took up most of the space, with a rickety chair for the customer's clothes and a table just large enough for a lamp cramped into a corner. The thin mattress was bare except for the stains on the blue-and-white ticking.

A limp green kimono hung on a crooked nail, and a string of Chinese lanterns dangled tiredly over the bed. The red paper of the lanterns was faded and crumpled, their festive cheer lost long ago. A very young Chinese Daughter of Joy lay huddled on the mattress, weeping silently, as if she knew the hopelessness of attracting any sympathy or help.

The weak lamplight was strong enough to pick out the oozing red weals raised on the pale skin of her back and buttocks and breasts. The man finished buckling his thick leather belt with its heavy brass buckle and put a hat with a band of black-striped gold fur on his head. Without a backward glance for the girl on the bed, he shut the door.

In no hurry, he took a cigar from his vest pocket, bit off the end and lit it, sucking the hot, acrid smoke deep into his lungs. It wasn't as fine as those cigars Tyree smoked, he knew. He'd be smoking one of those if that bitch in Prescott, over in Arizona, had come up to snuff, he thought dispassionately. Watching Tyree and McClintock from across the saloon earlier, lighting theirs, had set him to thinking again how she'd betrayed him, but he'd gotten rid of his hate. He felt better now, pretty damn good, in fact, so good that he could almost laugh about the time he'd wasted on that skinny horse-faced slut.

Nearing thirty, Martha Yount was the only child and heir of an elderly widower, and still unmarried because no man had been able to see past her buck teeth, slightly crossed eyes and the hairy mole on her crooked nose to the big cattle ranch she would someday inherit. The old man was hell to work for, but it wasn't long before Frank had had the bony, flat-chested daughter hot and panting in a dark corner of the barn, and he'd been seeing all those fat, sleek cattle wearing his brand. Then Yount had come to him one day and handed him his pay. His daughter was marrying the owner of a neighboring ranch. The ranches would be consolidated into one, and, of course, two foremen wouldn't be needed.

Of course. Just like that, after months of taking the old man's abuse and trying not to gag every time he'd looked at the daughter, he was sent on his way, with nothing. It seemed like that was the way his whole life had gone. Every time it looked as if he was about to make a big strike, someone would take it away from him and he'd be left with nothing but dirt. He'd gotten his revenge, though, he remembered with a chuckle. As he'd ridden out, he'd added a sack of lye to the main water hole, and he'd had a new vision, of those sleek cattle all bloated, up, dead.

Dropping the stub of his cigar, he ground it out under his heel. All women were lying whores, even the ugly ones. He'd learned that before he was grown. For a long time he hadn't understood the sniggers and catcalls of the older boys, or why the men who came by to visit Maizie—she'd beaten him with a belt the first and only time he'd called her "Mother"—always flipped him a penny and told him to go buy some candy. Finally one of the boys had explained it to him in terms he could understand. He hadn't believed it, so the next time a man tossed him a penny, instead of running off to the store, he sneaked around the back of the shack and watched through a crack between the warped boards. The sweet taste of candy sickened him after that . . . but he kept the pennies.

When he was ten, he'd come back one morning to find the shack empty, Lazy Maizie gone. Soon he was, too, stowing away on a wagon in one of the trading trains leaving Saint Louis for Santa Fe. The trader whose wagon he'd chosen had been a hard man, but fair. He'd stayed with him, traveling all over the Southwest, until the man died of blood poisoning from a broken leg six years later. He inherited the wagon and horses by default. He took the man's first name, too, Frank, because Maizie had never bothered to give him one—she'd just called him "Sonny." After the money from the sale of the wagon and trading goods was gone, he'd joined up with a trail drive leaving Texas.

That was when he'd needed a last name, but he hadn't taken the trader's. He'd taken Penny—so he wouldn't forget. He gave the dust and shreds of tobacco under his heel a final stomp, then began walking down the dark, deserted alleyway. All women were lying whores.

The rising sun was just touching the tip of the church spire at the end of the street when Jesse arrived at the livery stable. Cisco Moreno and his crew were already mounted and waiting in front, while George, Bill and Shorty sat on their cow ponies off to one side, silently sizing up the Mexican boys. Penny and Tyree rode up from the other end of town. Tyree, Jesse noted, had exchanged his suit for the standard uniform of a cowhand: denim pants tucked into the tops of high-heeled boots that were ideal for riding but hell to walk in for any distance, and a dark scarf tied around his neck over a muslin shirt without a collar. Collars flapped annoyingly in the wind, and a scarf offered better protection for the back of a man's neck, anyway. It could also double as a mask during a dust storm, or as a bandage or a sling.

Penny dismounted and approached with a smile Jesse thought was just a touch too friendly. He noticed Penny's spurs immediately. Generally a man chose spurs with large rowels that had just a few points, then blunted them. Few men intentionally wanted to cause an animal pain. Frank Penny's spurs had small rowels ridged with sharp points, but in all fairness to the man, Jesse told himself, the spurs looked new; maybe he hadn't had time to blunt the points yet.

Manolo Rivera drove up with a wagonload of supplies, Miranda Hart on the seat beside him and the miner guards sitting on the hundred pound sacks of oats in the bed behind. Today the Silver Tejo's mistress wore a white dress. She looked as fresh and cool as the morning and—his mouth tightened as he thought the word— virginal. Even knowing what she had been, he couldn't seem to rid himself of the illusion of her innocence, no matter how hard he tried. And he *had* tried, very hard. He couldn't understand it any more than he could understand what had happened to him in the hotel hallway last night.

Cisco Moreno immediately whipped off his sombrero, favoring her with a dazzling smile, and Jesse's mouth screwed a turn tighter.

The other men touched their hats respectfully, clearly dazzled by her. Everyone he'd met in town seemed to have great respect for her. Naturally Hart would never have told anyone where he had found her, Jesse thought sardonically. He had found himself treated with respect, too. Apparently Miranda Hart hadn't told anyone where and how she had found *him*, either.

He turned at the sound of someone else approaching on foot, more so he wouldn't have to acknowledge her tentative smile of greeting than out of any real curiosity to see who it was. With an effort he concealed his surprise as Miranda Hart's low, clear voice made the introductions.

"Mr. Baxter, this is Mr. McClintock, foreman of the Silver Tejo. Mr. McClintock, Mr. Baxter, the new wrangler."

Charlie started to offer his hand, but McClintock's stayed tucked in his pocket, so Charlie let his drop. Silently he endured the long, hard look of the tall foreman. He didn't have any confidence in Celia's assurance that he had the wrangler's job. Whatever Mrs. Hart might have promised, if this McClintock didn't want him, he wouldn't work an hour on the Silver Tejo.

McClintock finally spoke. "No horse, Baxter?"

"No," Charlie answered quietly. "No saddle, either." He knew what the big, hard man in front of him was thinking as surely as if he'd said it. No matter how low he went, a man never sold his saddle.

Jesse fought a helpless urge to laugh. A wrangler with no horse, not even a saddle. Hell, he had the shakes so bad right now he probably couldn't have stayed on a horse even if he had one. The only surprising thing about him was that he had stayed sober long enough to get cleaned up and report for his new job.

Miranda exchanged a worried look with Celia Kershaw, who was standing in the shadows on the railroad platform across the street. Charlie looked terrible, but at least he was sober. Holding her breath, she waited to see if Jesse McClintock would accept or refuse Charlie. If he refused, Charlie would be humiliated, Celia crushed and she would be faced with another confrontation with him. She wasn't sure she was strong enough this morning, not so soon after the scene in the hotel hallway, which still had her unsettled and confused.

Jesse caught the look passing between Miranda Hart and a small blond woman across the street. The same woman who had been carrying the drunken Baxter out of the dining room yesterday, he realized, and suddenly Jesse knew where the money for the man's new clothes had come from. He felt sorry for the woman. She'd wasted her money. Still, the man did have a peculiar dignity that kept Jesse from refusing him outright. And he wasn't going to give Miranda Hart the satisfaction of an argument over the man. The problem of Baxter would solve itself anyway; he'd be off the Silver Tejo before sundown tomorrow. He wouldn't be able to stay away from a bottle any longer than that. "All right, Baxter." As he nodded toward the wagon Rivera was driving, he saw the triumphant grin Miranda Hart flashed the little blonde. "You can ride in—"

He was interrupted by the jangle of bits and bridles as two boys led Lucky and the miners' horses out of the stable. Frowning, he stared at the unfamiliar horse with the Appaloosa and the miners' paints. It was a fine Tennessee Walking horse, nearly as large as Lucky, with a beautiful, unscarred midnight black hide. He was starting to speak to the stable boy about his mistake, when Charlie Baxter stumbled forward.

"Blackjack," Charlie whispered, running his hands down the stallion's withers as if he couldn't believe the horse was real. The horse whuffled a greeting and butted his head gently against Charlie's shoulder.

It had broken his heart to sell Blackjack. Ruebush had given him a fair price, and he had been able to give his partner's widow the price of a train ticket to get her and her children back to her people in Ohio with enough left over as a stake for a new life. He had avoided the livery stable ever since, but he hadn't been able to avoid seeing Ruebush occasionally riding Jack around town.

Charlie looked uncomprehendingly toward the stable boy and saw Calvin Ruebush, the livery owner, standing behind him.

"I sold your saddle, Charlie," the small, spare man apologized. "This is the best I can do."

For the first time, Charlie noticed that the saddle on Jack's back was near to falling apart. "It's—" Charlie cleared his throat. "It's fine, Cal."

"I was kinda surprised when Miss Kershaw said you wanted the horse saddled and ready to go this morning." Ruebush looked at Charlie curiously. "I know I told you I'd sell him back to you, but I didn't really expect..." Calvin Ruebush realized he was about to embarrass Charlie in front of his new boss. "I took real good care of him for you, Charlie," he finished lamely.

Charlie nodded. The back of his nose was burning, and his eyes were stinging. Blinking rapidly, he bent down on the pretext of checking the condition of the black's hooves. It had been so long since anyone had shown him such unselfish kindness, not since he had left home at nineteen, several lifetimes ago, to fight the Yankees.

Several months later, during a lull in the fighting, he was given leave to go home for a few days. All he'd found were the graves of his parents and younger brother, killed while trying to defend a few miserable acres of hard-scrabble ground. He had not gone back to his company, but drifted west instead, traveling by night to avoid the patrols looking for deserters. He'd been captured in Missouri by William Quantrill. Quantrill had given him the choice of a bullet or a horse and a place in his guerrilla force, and he'd soon discovered that being one of Quantrill's Raiders suited him just fine. He'd had a rage inside him that was threatening to burn him up and massacring Yankees kept it under control.

Three years later the war was over, Quantrill was dead and the fire had burned itself out. His skill with horses had been noted, and he received several offers to join up with the various bands that were forming when the Raiders broke up. He turned down Jesse James and Cole Younger and the Dalton brothers, and headed west once again. Over the years he heard of his old comrades from time to time, putting to use the hit-and-run tactics they had learned so well under Quantrill.

As Charlie Baxter swung into the saddle, Miranda saw the stable boy returning with her buggy, and she stood up, ready to trade the hard wooden seat of the buckboard for the buggy's padded leather. Sensing movement on her side of the wagon, she glanced down to see Jesse McClintock looking up at her, his hand extended. Their eyes and fingers met as briefly as possible as she stepped down, yet there was a whispered echo of the lightning she'd felt the night before. Silently he handed her into the buggy, and she waited to see if he would get in beside her.

A Chinese boy in his mid-teens came running down the street toward them. He tossed a bundle of clothes in the back of the wagon and clambered in. Behind him hobbled a grizzled little man, carrying a carpetbag that looked at least as old as he was. Miranda hid her smile. If the man's bowed legs could have been straightened, he would have been half a foot taller. She felt someone watching her and turned to meet Jesse McClintock's dark blue eyes.

His glance shifted immediately to the man now standing beside the buggy on the other side, wheezing noisily as he tried to catch his breath. "Toppy Burnham. He'll be cooking for the hands," he informed her shortly. "Toppy, this is Mrs. Hart. I want you to drive her buggy back to the ranch." He had assigned Toppy the task, knowing the cook's years of experience driving a chuck wagon would assure her safety. A harsh smile twisted his mouth as he heard Miranda Hart's gracious greeting and watched the old man try to stammer out a reply, then stow his carpetbag and climb up laboriously to the seat. Overwhelmed by the chance to sit so close to such loveliness, the old coot was probably close to wetting his pants, Jesse thought dryly. He mounted Lucky and nudged the animal into a fast trot.

As Charlie rode down the dusty street, he glanced toward the railroad depot. The early morning sun shining on Celia's golden hair made it look like a halo around her head. She raised her hand in a small wave that might have been meant only to brush back a wisp of hair. Charlie raised his battered hat an inch or so in a move that could have been just to settle it more comfortably on his head. He wondered, not for the first time, what she would do if some-day he just up and grabbed her and kissed her until the seams of that stiff black dress popped.

A few miles outside town, Jesse halted the small caravan. There was a canyon nearby that he hadn't had time to check for cattle, and now was as good a time as any. He sent the wagon and buggy on down the road with the guards. He debated sending half the men, too, but the word in Deming was that Geronimo and his band were still down in Mexico, at least three days' ride away.

The sun was straight overhead by the time they finished explor-ing the long twisting canyon and all the small draws leading into it. As he led the way back out to the road, Jesse saw the smoke, a black stain on the turquoise blue purity of the sky. The column of smoke rose from a point several miles away. With a curse, he touched his spurs to Lucky. From the color and the amount, he knew it wasn't a forgotten campfire burning itself out.

Chapter Seven

Smoldering timbers still sent the black smoke signal that had brought Jesse running. The unnatural silence was broken by an occasional pop and sizzle from the dying fire. From behind him, he could hear the sounds of retching. He swallowed back the sour bile in his own throat. He thought he had become inured to gruesome sights, but the inhuman viciousness of this attack was beyond anything he had ever imagined, much less seen.

The young couple who had owned the homestead lay on the ground near the charred pile that had been their cabin. The pink poppies the wife had planted for a bit of beauty in this hard land had been crisped by the fire. Whatever stock the couple had owned had been taken. Every living thing left behind had been slaughtered. A collie lay inside an empty corral, a dozen blood-blackened holes in its side as if it had been used for target practice. Bunches of rust and white feathers were trampled into the dust, no longer recognizable as chickens.

The couple's bodies had been stripped. The man's was hideously mutilated. The woman's body lay a few feet away, and from the obscene sprawl of her legs and the blood, Jesse knew she had been raped, repeatedly. He untied the yellow slicker behind his saddle and dismounted. Draping the slicker over her, he covered the woman as best he could. She had white blond hair and must have been very pretty—once. Tyree appeared silently at his side to spread his slicker, too.

George Gearhart recovered enough to find his voice. "Goddamn murderin' Apaches. We oughtta cut off the—"

"It wasn't Apaches."

The words, quietly spoken, silenced the loud voice. Standing, Jesse turned to see the rest of the men staring at Charlie Baxter.

"The hell you say!" George challenged him. "Are you blind, man?" His wildly gestured arm pointed to the yellow lump on the ground. "No white man woulda done that!"

Charlie gave Gearhart a brief look before his gaze rested on the lifeless yellow mounds on the blood-soaked sand. "The Apaches might have done that," he conceded, "but they wouldn't have taken the stock."

"Them murderin' bastards steal cattle all the time," Bill told him belligerently.

"But not sheep."

The men looked shamefaced at the sudden realization that Charlie had noticed what none of the rest of them had. The corrals were too low for cattle or horses; small cloven hoofprints covered the sand in the corrals, and then there was the stink. As cattlemen, they should have recognized it immediately.

"Who was it, then?" Jesse asked quietly.

Charlie met Jesse's direct look. "Renegades. They're mostly breeds, a few whites. The leader's said to be a Mexican breed named Leyba. Killing is the same as pissing to them. They don't think much about doing either one."

"Why would they bother with sheep?"

Charlie shrugged. "They steal whatever they find, and sheep bring a pretty good price down in Mexico."

"What about the army?" Tyree asked.

Charlie gave him a dry look. "The army has about as much luck catching renegades as it does Geronimo."

Jesse caught the reins of his horse and pulled himself into the saddle. "There's nothing we can do for these folks except see that they get a decent burial. We'll bring a wagon back for the bodies and—"

As he was swinging Lucky around to leave the carnage, his eyes had automatically charted the route the renegades would most likely have followed back across the border. The bodies of the rancher and his wife had been cold, but not stiff, meaning only a few hours had passed since the raid. The raiders, he had suddenly realized, would have had to cross the road to the Silver Tejo—just about the time Miranda Hart would have been passing by in her buggy on her way home.

He dug his spurs deep into Lucky's belly. The startled horse reared, then leaped forward, already at full gallop. Jesse didn't see the mesquite and prickly pear before them. All he saw was the tormenting vision of Miranda, splayed in the dirt like the rancher's wife, her pretty white dress a torn and bloody rag.

Sensing the urgency of the man on his back, Lucky picked up his pace on the open road. The tracks of the buckboard and buggy were easy to follow in the loose sand. Straining to see ahead through the fading afternoon light, Jesse sought a black buggy, unaware that he was praying he wouldn't see it. He knew the renegades would take the wagon—after killing the men. Suddenly a new, unthinkable thought came to torture him. The renegades might take Miranda, too, so they could take their time enjoying their prize.

A red haze of rage and near panic almost blinded him to the change in the tracks he was following. Reining in so sharply that the big Appaloosa nearly somersaulted trying to stop himself, Jesse leaped off the horse's back. Lucky stood, head down, his gray sides slicked with sweat, sucking air like a huge bellows.

Jesse crouched low over the roadbed. The wheel tracks disappeared in a confusion of cloven hoofprints, reappearing about twenty yards down the road. The hoofprints covered the wheel tracks, meaning that the killers had crossed the road after she had gone by. Leyba and his gang could only have missed her by minutes. His blood suddenly ran ice-cold. If they had missed her.

Dreading what he might see, Jesse forced himself to take a closer look at the tracks farther down the road leading to the ranch. There were no extras. No one had followed her. Leyba must have had only enough men to handle the sheep, none to spare on other "errands," he decided as every muscle in his body went slack with relief.

As he was remounting, the rest of the men galloped up, led by Tyree and Charlie Baxter. None of them questioned his abrupt departure from the homestead. From the grim looks on their faces, even the Mexican *vaqueros* had understood that Miranda could easily have crossed the renegades' path.

They rode the last few miles at an easy canter, letting their tired horses rest. Jesse found that although the desperate fear inside him had died, his rage hadn't. Instead it lived, flourished, until by the time he rode past the two guards on the gate, he was consumed with a righteous wrath. But not at the renegades. He was furious with the woman.

She shouldn't have gone to town...she shouldn't be so careless with herself...she shouldn't be so beautiful...she shouldn't have worried him so...she shouldn't have been a whore.

Although it was dark and long after suppertime, the triangle in front of the mess hall at the end of the bunkhouse clanged loudly as the men rode into the compound. Toppy Burnham, the new cook, stood on the porch, wearing a white towel tied around his waist with twine, like an apron. He had a meal waiting, Jesse noted with absentminded approval. The weary men dismounted, making use of the wash bench on the porch before they trooped inside.

Jesse bypassed the bunkhouse. A light still burned in the main house. The warm night air was sweetly scented by the flowers blooming beside the patio, but Jesse was in no mood to appreciate it. His boots pounded a loud, angry beat in the peaceful darkness as he strode along the porch.

The front door was open to the cool breeze, and soft yellow light spilled through the partially opened parlor door beyond it. Jesse stiff-armed the door, the force slamming it back against the wall. The noise was like a cannon boom in the quiet house. He glared around the room until he found Miranda Hart. "Why the hell aren't you in bed?" he snarled.

A wave of self-reproach immediately swamped his anger. She was frozen in the act of rising from her chair, her face paper white, her eyes wide with fear. One hand clenched the edge of the rolltop desk in front of her, the other was pressed to her swollen belly.

That one small gesture told him something he had wondered about. Miranda Hart wanted her baby. Her hand hadn't automatically gone to her breast, the instinctive gesture of a frightened woman; it had gone to her unborn child, to protect it. "I'm sorry," he said, guilt gentling his voice as he approached her. "I didn't mean to frighten you."

Miranda sank slowly into the chair. She wanted to collapse with relief; instead she straightened her back and composed her hands in her lap. "Did you want something, Mr. McClintock?" Her mouth quirked fractionally. "Besides to remind me about my bedtime?"

Jesse smiled in spite of himself. Whatever else she was, Miranda Hart had the class of a true lady. There she sat, coolly asking him what he wanted, just as if he hadn't scared the stuffing out of her only a few seconds before. He could see she had been about to go to bed. She was wearing a pale pink wrapper, and her face looked freshly scrubbed. Her hair was loose, the chestnut curls falling halfway down her back. He had thought about her hair, wondering how long it was, how soft—his hand rubbed unconsciously down his thigh—how it would feel curled around his fingers, brushing over his—

"I forgot to tell you about the Chinese boy," he rasped. "His name is Kwon Goon. He'll do the laundry, the men's, and yours, too. And since we have a wrangler now, Paco and Ramón can leave the remuda. They can chop wood, take care of the garden and orchard, the horses in the barn, and anything else you want them to do." Paco and Ramón were the two "hands" Miranda Hart had had before he'd arrived. Paco, supposedly fourteen, was no more than twelve, and his grandfather was more likely his great-grandfather; Jesse was sure the old man would never see seventy again. This was the best Jesse could do. Manolo had been right after all; he hadn't been able to find one woman in Deming willing to work on the Silver Tejo.

Miranda looked slightly dazed. "I . . . thank you." She flicked her tongue over her crooked eyetooth as she tried to puzzle out the reason for his unexpected consideration. "Leola and I will appreciate the help. Thank you, too," she added quietly, "for hiring Toppy." She had been dreading the fact that she and Leola would have to add feeding the hands to their other chores.

"You're welcome," he said gruffly, and a long silence followed while they stared at each other.

Miranda broke the silence at last. "Well . . . if there's nothing else . . ." She heard the hopefulness in her voice and finished hastily. "Good night, Mr. McClintock."

"Good night, Mi—Mrs. Hart," he said softly. Turning, he left the house, quietly shutting the door behind him.

Jesse whistled a tuneless song to himself as he curried Lucky. During the past week he had gotten into the habit of spending an hour or so in the barn every night after supper. The high walls of the canyon brought sundown early, and the barn was filled with soft shadows and a quiet peacefulness.

He stopped whistling as the first distant notes of a piano reached him. She always played for a little while every night after supper. The music was elegant, beautiful—completely out of place in this rude setting, yet somehow completely right, too.

A horse nickered nearby, and Lucky returned the greeting. Jesse gave the stallion a final pat on the flank and started for the tack room to put the curry comb away, pausing at the stall holding Miranda's gray Arabian. The young mare was a rare and very expensive animal. Hart must have bought the horse as a present for her in Mexico, from one of the *hidalgos* who specialized in breeding them. He knew the mare hadn't been ridden since the trip to Silver City. Apparently Miranda did have sense enough to realize she should give up riding until after the birth of her baby, Jesse thought grudgingly, resolving to take the mare out the next day for some exercise.

He was giving the mare's ears a scratch, when an itching between his shoulder blades told him he was being watched, and he knew when he looked that he would see the same bright blue eyes that sneaked furtive glances at him across the supper table every night. He took that meal now with the Riveras and Miranda and her son. Conversation so far had been limited to his terse progress reports and polite requests to pass food.

Turning, he saw Tommy sitting on a hay bale a few feet away. He straddled another bale and smiled at the little boy. Tommy smiled back shyly. He was making progress; when Jesse had smiled at him the first night, Tommy had bolted out of the barn like a scared rabbit.

"¿Cómo estás, mi'jito?" How are you, my little son? The greeting was a common one from an adult to a young boy. Jesse had noticed that Tommy chattered easily enough with Manolo Rivera, but always in Spanish. Since the boy seemed to find that language less intimidating, Jesse started their nightly conversations off in Spanish. He switched to English after a few sentences, but Tommy didn't notice once the conversation got going. He shifted languages automatically, equally fluent in both, although his English lacked his mother's elegant accent.

"Bien." Tommy eyed Jesse's vest covertly.

Miranda Hart would soon know he spoke Spanish, if she didn't already, but Jesse didn't particularly care anymore. Pretending he didn't was damned inconvenient, especially when half his crew couldn't speak English. He pulled a licorice stick from a pocket in his vest. He'd gotten the candy in town and had been luring the boy closer with it all week. He twisted the stick in half, offering a piece to Tommy. The child took it eagerly, murmuring his *gracias*.

"Isn't it about your bedtime?" Jesse asked in Spanish with mock sternness.

"Sí." The little red-haired boy grinned conspiratorially and tried to cram all the licorice into his mouth.

Jesse grinned back. The first time he had tried to tease the boy, his eyes had filled with tears, which he had tried desperately to hide. But a few seemingly casual questions had allayed Jesse's suspicions that Thomas Hart had beaten him.

Hart had simply ignored him, a much more subtle form of abuse, but Jesse could understand it. He felt as much sympathy for Thomas Hart as he did for the innocent little boy. It must have been hard for Hart to have another man's bastard living under his roof, a constant reminder of what his wife had been. Perhaps he had honestly thought he could accept the child, or maybe he had been so hot for the mother that he would have agreed to anything to have her. After it was too late, Hart must have discovered that the only way he could tolerate the boy was to pretend he didn't exist.

Yet it was unfair that Tommy had been the one to suffer. It wasn't his fault that his mother had been a— Without realizing it, Jesse shied away from actually thinking the word. Unless Hart had adopted him, the boy probably didn't even have a last name. She probably didn't even know who the father was. Jesse wondered if Hart had brooded about it, picked at it like a half-healed sore, keeping it open and festering between him and his wife. Jesse could understand that, too.

"*¿Jesse, cuándo vas a enseñarme cómo montar a caballo? 'iqQuizás mañana?*" When Jesse didn't answer immediately, Tommy repeated his question in English. "Jesse, when are you going to teach me to ride? Tomorrow, maybe?"

Jesse smiled down at the hopeful little freckled face. "No, Tommy, not tomorrow," he said gently. "Remember what I said last night?" The evening before Tommy had proudly shown him the small saddle Jesse had noticed before in the tack room. He said he had gotten it for his fifth birthday, and Jesse suspected he'd been polishing the dust off it every day since, wishing for a pony to put it on before he outgrew it. Tommy had said his mother took him for rides on her horse, but Jesse knew that sitting on your mother's horse with her hanging on to you was hardly the same as having a horse of your own.

Tommy's face twisted into a grimace of resigned impatience. "I remember. We'll look for a pony the next time we go to town," he said, reciting Jesse's words from the evening before.

"If . . . ?" Jesse prompted.

"If Mama says it's all right. But she will, Jesse!" he went on in a rush. "I know she will. We could go to town tomorrow."

In his eagerness, Tommy had slipped off the hay bale and grabbed Jesse's hand, as if trying to drag Jesse to town right that minute. Jesse closed his hand around the small fingers gently. "Now you know we can't go for a couple of weeks," he reminded him.

"Aw, Jesse—"

"You be sure you help your ma and do what she says, or she might not let you go."

Tommy heaved a gusty sigh. "All right."

They both heard Miranda's voice calling Tommy from outside.

"You better go in now," Jesse advised him with a wink.

Tommy nodded with obvious reluctance, drawing his hand away slowly. "Good night, Jesse."

Jesse reached out and ruffled Tommy's red hair. "Good night, son. I'll see you tomorrow night."

Jesse rode back into the Silver Tejo compound early the next afternoon. The past week had been quiet, almost boringly so. Were it not for the unusually large number of wooden crosses in the grassy plot of ground beyond the orchard and the nightmarish memory of the fired homestead, he would have found it hard to believe there could be any danger in the hot sleepy canyons of the Silver Tejo.

He had followed the raiders' trail over the crest of the Floridas into Mexico, but had seen no trace of them. Lookouts had been posted at the pass to watch for their return, but had reported nothing more than jackrabbits and the occasional coyote crossing the border. Despite their not-too-subtle hints that maybe they were wasting their time, he'd decided to leave them in place, for the time being, at least. The homesteader's wife, but with auburn hair instead of white blond, still haunted his dreams at night.

A few minutes later he walked out of the barn, passing Frank Penny leading in his dun mare.

"Boss." Penny acknowledged him in a voice that somehow made Jesse think of the dirty whispers of two men watching through a peephole as an unsuspecting woman took her bath.

"Penny." The foreman of a ranch was always "boss." Only Tyree called him by name, but, then, to Jesse's knowledge, Tyree had never called any man "boss." He glanced down at the other man's feet. "There's a file in the tack room, Penny." Frank looked blank. "Your spurs. The rowels look pretty sharp."

The smaller man ducked his head, as if embarrassed by the oversight. "Sure, boss," he mumbled.

Jesse stared after him, watching him lead his mare, plodding apathetically behind him, into the barn. Penny was just as good a hand as the rest; he worked hard, and he didn't bellyache. He couldn't fault the man, but he still didn't trust him.

The sound of childish laughter distracted him. Following the happy sound around the barn, he saw Miranda and Tommy running across the narrow patch of level ground between the back and the cottonwoods that grew along the spring. Knowing they were too intent on what they were trying to do to notice him, he leaned a shoulder against the cool adobe wall of the barn to watch.

He took the makings of a cigarette from his vest, grinning to himself. Miranda and Tommy had made themselves a kite. It was a crude effort, too little kite and too much tail, and neither of them knew squat about how to fly it, but they were giving it their best effort. They ran with the breeze, the kite trailing after them with the tail dragging on the ground. Miranda held up the skirts of her blue calico dress with one hand, the kite string in the other. Tommy ran along beside her, holding the ball of twine and yelling encouragement.

They ran out of running room and collapsed, panting, against the rough trunk of one of the massive trees. Jesse could hear Tommy's high-pitched giggle and Miranda's husky, breathless laughter. Their cheerful silliness was infectious, and he found himself laughing along with them. They caught their breath and gave it another try, running against the breeze this time.

The breeze caught the kite, lifting it rapidly over the tops of the cottonwoods. Tommy shrieked in delight and begged for the kite string. Miranda traded it for the ball of twine, taking the precaution of looping the rough string around the boy's small wrist. She stood beside him, her face flushed and tilted toward the sky. The breeze teased wisps of hair from the knot at the back of her neck, floating them around her cheeks and throat. Wrapping her arm around her son's shoulders, she hugged him to her side, and they laughed together, obviously pleased with themselves.

With a start, Jesse realized it was the first time he had ever heard her laugh. It was a carefree, exuberant and utterly natural sound, not the nervous, self-conscious titter of so many women, who seemed to think a good hearty laugh was an unpardonable breach of etiquette. Unaware of the soft smile on his face, he continued to watch them play, unnoticed.

The kite swooped, its tail flirting with the treetops, courting disaster. Jesse threw away his cigarette and bent to unbuckle his spurs. Spurs made tree climbing impossible. The kite's flight was going to be short-lived, and he wanted to be prepared, in case Miranda took it into her head to go after it.

A sudden gust sent the kite crashing into the tallest cottonwood. Miranda and Tommy looked at each other in dismay. "Oh, Tommy," she said ruefully. "I think the tree just ate our kite!"

Tommy stared at her for a moment, unable to comprehend why she was calmly rewinding the twine as if she planned to let the tree keep their kite. He caught at her hand and tried to run toward the cottonwoods. "C'mon, Mama! We can get it back."

Miranda held him back. "No, we can't, Tommy," she said with gentle firmness. "You're not big enough to climb the tree, and I can't."

"Sure you can, Mama," Tommy told her confidently. "You climbed the apricot tree to get the big ones on top, remember?"

"That was months ago. I can't climb trees now, not until after your little brother or sister is born."

"How long will that be?" he demanded in a tone rich with exasperation.

"Three more months. Remember I told you it would be around Christmas?"

"Three months!" The little boy groaned. He looked as if, had he been given any choice in the matter, there would never be any bothersome little brother or sister. His mother wasn't nearly as much fun anymore. She wouldn't go riding or carry him piggyback to bed, and now she couldn't even climb trees, all because of "the baby."

Miranda looked at Tommy's disgusted face with a wry smile. "I know it's a long time to wait," she sympathized. "I get tired of waiting sometimes, too."

An odd look crossed her face for a moment. Jesse, without the jingle of his spurs to announce him, had almost reached Miranda and Tommy without either of them being aware of his presence. The change in her expression had been so brief that Jesse wasn't sure what he had seen. Longing, perhaps? Fear? Her expression changed again, this time to one of unmistakable joy.

"Tommy, the baby is kicking. Would you like to feel it?" she guided his hand, laying it flat on her belly.

Tommy felt the faint flutterings through the calico, and his blue eyes went wide with wonder. "I feel it!" His eyes darkened abruptly with anxiety. "Does it hurt, Mama?"

"Sometimes." She smiled softly. "But it's a good kind of hurt."

Pulling his hand free, Tommy looked at her with obvious disbelief. He had never felt a "good" hurt, and this latest information only confirmed his suspicion that babies were far more trouble than they were worth.

At the edge of her vision Miranda saw the large man's hand reaching toward her rounded stomach. She was startled, yet she also felt oddly detached, almost as if she were caught in a dream, waiting for the hand to touch her. She felt her breath catch in her chest as if it were waiting, too. The hand came closer, long, tanned fingers spreading slowly. Just as the blunt fingertips were about to caress the soft calico, the dream ended, and with a gasp, she jerked back out of the hand's reach.

His hand burning as if it were on fire, Jesse jammed it in his pocket. He couldn't believe what he had almost done! Caught up in the intimacy between Miranda and her son, he'd almost done the unthinkable and touched her himself to feel the tiny life inside her.

Her wide eyes mirrored the shock he felt. The greatest shock was that he still wanted to touch her.

Blissfully unaware of the turbulent currents flowing over his head, Tommy grabbed Jesse's hand. "Jesse," he implored, "please get my kite out of the tree. Mama can't climb and—"

"Momentito, mi'jito." Tommy had addressed him in Spanish, and he had automatically answered in the same language.

Miranda's eyes widened even farther, and she stepped back another pace. Jesse McClintock was still full of surprises, it seemed. He spoke Spanish—quite well, in fact—a piece of information he had kept from them. And somehow—and this was an even bigger surprise—he had charmed Tommy.

Jesse watched the expressions flit across her face. From the sudden narrowing of her eyes and the frown, he knew the exact moment when she realized that he must know about the silver mine. The brief closing of her eyes and look of chagrin were signs of the frantic mental scrambling she was doing, trying to remember any potentially embarrassing remarks she might have made in his presence.

"You speak Spanish well, Señor McClintock," she said dryly in Spanish.

"Not as well as you, *señora*," Jesse answered politely in the same language.

A very unladylike snort escaped her. His words were polite enough, but Miranda suspected he was laughing at her. She could forgive him, though. Tommy was looking at Jesse McClintock with all the adoration and trust of a lovelorn puppy. For too long he had been desperate for the attention of a man and despairing, she knew, of ever having it.

Jesse tipped his hat, and again she heard silent laughter. He let Tommy drag him over to the tree holding their kite captive. She saw how Tommy's little fingers tried to reach around the tall man's big hand, and how Jesse automatically closed it to accommodate the small hand in his.

After handing his spurs and hat to Tommy, he swung himself easily up into the tree. For such a big man, he was marvelously agile. Tommy promptly put the wide-brimmed black hat on his own head, and his eyes and nose disappeared. Plunking down on the grass, he began buckling the spurs over his small shoes, and Miranda suddenly knew who was inspiring Tommy's unsubtle hints that it was time he had a pony to go with the little saddle in the tack room.

Thomas had given Tommy the saddle; he'd had it made especially as a surprise birthday gift. The gift had delighted Tommy and given Miranda the cautious hope that her husband was finally coming to accept the child. He had been a good man, though it had never been a love match between them. If she hadn't needed a home, security and money so badly, she never would have agreed to his proposal. She watched the small red-haired boy stand up and with his first step walk out of the spurs he'd worked so hard to put on. Thomas had had his needs, too.

Tommy forgot the spurs as his hero dropped down out of the tree with the kite. Jesse tore off half the rag tail, let out a long length of string and began loping toward her. Tommy's short legs were a blur as he strove to keep up with the long stride of the man beside him. It should look absurd to see a grown man wearing chaps and boots trailing a kite behind him, with a small boy with holey black stockings running for all he was worth beside him, yet Tommy and Jesse McClintock looked wonderfully right together, Miranda thought with an unconsciously wistful smile.

The kite was airborne in seconds. Jesse transferred the string to Tommy, and they both began backing toward her as Tommy, following instructions, let out the string gradually. He turned to flash a glee-filled grin over his shoulder. "You had too much tail, Mama, but Jesse fixed it," he told her kindly.

Miranda thanked the man beside Tommy for correcting her shortcomings as a kite maker with the briefest, coolest smile good manners would permit. His answering grin was broad and, she was certain, more than a touch arrogant. She cast about for something to put him back in his place while she watched Tommy slowly walking away, letting out still more string, until the kite was a white diamond dancing in the clear blue sky. When she noticed the position of the sun, Miranda felt a deliciously malicious thrill of satisfaction. She'd found her revenge.

"You're back rather early today, aren't you, Mr. McClintock?" she observed casually.

There was a wicked gleam lurking in those oh-so-innocent lavender eyes, like that in the slitted eyes of a supposedly napping tabby cat waiting for an unsuspecting mouse to happen by. He gave a very Mexican shrug of unconcern and answered her in drawling Spanish. "It is a hot day, and we have been working very hard. A little siesta cannot hurt."

The gleam got brighter. Just as Jesse judged she was ready to pounce on him for his shiftlessness, he spoke again. The drawl was gone; his words, though still in soft Spanish, were cool and crisp. "The last of the canyons are too far to ride out to and back in a day. We will be camping out for the next two weeks or so. The men needed time to get their clothes and bedrolls together, and Toppy had to stock the chuck wagon. We will be leaving at daybreak."

Miranda swallowed a growl of frustration. "Umm. Yes. Well, that sounds very...efficient, Mr. McClintock. Just—" her hand flapped uselessly at him "—carry on."

Jesse bowed slightly and tipped his hat with an exaggerated gesture. *"Muchas gracias, señora,"* he drawled. Despite the fact that she was speaking English, he had perversely answered her every time in Spanish, just to rub it in a bit more, he supposed. That, and he liked the way her soft mouth tightened prissily a little bit more at each word.

Nodding abruptly, she turned away. Jesse whistled between his teeth as he watched her stalk off, her back stiff and her tail twitching, just like a cat who'd pounced and missed.

Manolo Rivera lowered his head to hide the smile on his broad face. He had been passing by, when he had heard the *señora* and the big Anglo speaking in Spanish. Almost from the first, he had suspected that McClintock knew the language. Now, moving away from the tree where he had been eavesdropping, he headed for the bunkhouse. He had to make sure Cisco Moreno and his boys had enough ammunition before they left; then he was going to tell his wife this latest move in the game between Jesse McClintock and the *patrona*.

The young man stood up from the chair where he'd been lounging when he saw the older man approach. Manolo appreciated the gesture of respect. The *hidalgo*'s son was spoiled and took life too lightly, but he liked him. Had the good God seen fit to bless him and Leola with a son, he might be Cisco's age just about now. Not nearly so handsome, of course. Two plain crows like themselves could never have produced a peacock like Cisco.

After Manolo took one of the chairs on the bunkhouse porch, Cisco sat down again. He tilted his chair back against the wall, his dark eyes half-closed as he stared at the patio gate through which the auburn-haired woman had disappeared moments before. "La señora Hart is a very beautiful woman," he murmured in lazy Spanish. He, too, had observed the little scene behind the barn. He could not hear the words, but the language of the bodies of the big blond *gringo* and the *patrona* had been very expressive, especially hers when she had left him. *"¿Es verdad su esposo está muerto?"*

"Sí, es verdad. Her husband is dead. She is much older than you, and pregnant, of course," Manolo said repressively. He did not like the slyly speculative glint in this brash young cock's eyes.

"Una viuda." Cisco sighed sympathetically. "A lonely widow with a cold bed, and—" he slid Manolo a sidelong look "—not so old. And pregnancy is only a temporary condition." He gave Manolo a sample of the smile so many women had found irresistible. "I have always had a special fondness for auburn hair."

Manolo did not smile. He glanced toward the little boy and the big man flying the kite. "McClintock speaks excellent Spanish," he said in a seeming non sequitur.

Cisco's knowing grin widened slowly, showing perfect white teeth below his curly black mustache. "Ah, I see. Her bed is not so cold after—" He never would have believed the old man could move so fast. He didn't even see the hand coming that smashed his lips against his teeth.

"You will speak of the *señora* with respect," Manolo instructed him tonelessly, his fist bunched in Cisco's shirt, half choking him as the young man's toes scrabbled for the floor. "And if you are wise, you will not speak of her at all within McClintock's hearing."

Cisco nodded jerkily, furiously blinking back tears of pain and embarrassment as he swallowed the blood from his split lips. Abruptly Manolo released him, and he fell back into his chair in a clumsy sprawl.

Miranda set down her watering can and pressed a hand to the ache in the small of her back. Absently watching water drip through the pots of petunias hanging along the edge of the porch, she rubbed the dull ache over her right eyebrow with her other hand. It was a toss-up which ache was worse, the one in her back, the one in her forehead, or the one at the base of her skull, but she had only two hands. She sighed tiredly, her yellow dress cutting into her nonexistent waist. A look in her mirror this morning had only confirmed what she had already known. Every day she looked more and more like Bessie, their fat milch cow.

A loud laugh from the corrals drew her attention in that direction. The chuck wagon was hitched up, the horses jingling their harnesses, impatient to be off; the sun was up, and the men were just standing around drinking coffee, she noted with annoyance. Everything annoyed her this morning, most of all those heathen ruffians Jesse McClintock had hired as hands. To a man, they looked like a gang of singularly unsuccessful bandits. Miranda pulled irritably at the pins holding her braid in a knot at the base of her skull. The heavy braid swung free, easing that particular ache, as she stared hard through the patio gate, trying to see what it was exactly that made them look so raffish.

It was those damn mustaches! Every single man had one, even Charlie Baxter. Miranda shook her head sadly. They had corrupted him already. A week ago he had been nicely clean shaven; now he was sporting a brown growth on his upper lip that made him look as disreputable as the rest of the lot. Poor Celia.

One mustache was exceptionally obnoxious. Thick and dark and especially wicked looking, it outlined the wide curve of a firm upper lip, the ends turning down to frame the rest of the mouth. That mouth was laughing right now at something one of the men draped over the corral rails had said, the way it no doubt laughed at her behind her back.

Without thinking, she began jerking blossoms off the sweet peas vining over the gate, shredding them. Last night Tommy had asked her when he would be old enough to grow a mustache. Guess where *that* idea had come from!

She glared across the compound. There he was, wasting daylight, just lazily leaning one lean hip against the corral as he and Manolo had a chat. Her fingers tore off another flower and ripped it apart. Well, she might have to suffer insufferably smug kite flyers, but she did *not* have to suffer mustaches!

Miranda shoved the gate open, pausing for a moment to stare incomprehensibly at the denuded sweet pea vines, their petals littering the ground like confetti. With an impatient shake of her head, she slammed the iron gate behind her with a clang and began striding toward the corrals.

"Mr. McClintock!"

Jesse straightened away from the fence slowly and turned around to face the beautiful harridan accosting him. There was almost as much fire in her eyes as in her hair. "Good morning, ma'am," he said with an exaggerated politeness that underscored her rudeness.

"If I might have a word with you," she demanded imperiously.

"Of course."

They stepped a few yards away from the rest of the men. Miranda snapped her braid over her shoulder with a quick toss of her head. "When you come back, I do not want to see a single mustache."

Jesse gave her a mildly questioning look, keeping his smile to himself. She played "lady of the manor" very well.

"You all look like rapscallions," she felt constrained to point out.

One dark eyebrow rose. "Rapscallions?" he murmured.

Miranda nodded emphatically. "Yes! Rapscallions! I feel as if I am surrounded by a-a-a bunch of desperados!" Her sweeping gesture included all the men standing around the corral, trying very hard to appear as if they hadn't the slightest interest in this exchange between the boss and the widow Hart.

Jesse folded his arms across his chest, his hips swaggering as he adopted a blatantly male stance. "No."

There was an outraged gasp. "Yes, damn it! I want every one of those mustaches shaved—"

"*Señora.*"

"What is it, Manolo?" Miranda snapped over her shoulder.

"If I might speak with you a moment?"

After impaling the big man in front of her with a sharp look, wordlessly warning him to stay put, she wheeled on Manolo Rivera.

"*Señora*, for some men, shaving off their mustaches would be like cutting off their...manhood." His thumb unconsciously stroked his own luxuriant mustache.

Coloring at Manolo's frankness, she spoke without thinking, addressing the toe of her shoe making neat furrows in the dirt. "Well, he's got more than enough manhood! He would never miss his mustache."

Miranda could feel her neck and face glowing red hot as she realized what she had revealed. She seemed to have a totally unwanted fascination with Jesse McClintock's anatomy. Leola had reassured her that peculiar cravings and behavior were a normal part of pregnancy, so that had to be what made her so aware of his sexuality—and her own—but just how many more of these aberrations was she going to have to endure? she wondered a little desperately.

A quick peek upward caught the glint of humor in Manolo's eyes, and worse yet, she heard strangled laughter behind her. Furiously, her toe scrubbed out the neat furrows. Well, she couldn't help it! And he had to take part of the blame for wearing those tight pants. And today was even worse than usual. He was wearing chaps. The leather sheathing his long legs framed his pelvis perfectly, leaving little doubt about his sex.

Appalled, she felt the corners of her mouth twitch. To hide the smile, she rubbed her hand across her lips, as if considering Manolo's words. Jesse's height wasn't the only thing about him that was greater than average. Not that she knew from experience, of course, she assured herself hastily, but she had heard the girls talking...

Stiffening her back, she turned around with what she hoped was an implacable glare of command. One glance, and she knew the battle was lost. His face was blank, but there was a teasing, knowing twinkle lurking in those smoky blue eyes, and one corner of his mustache twitched.

"Perhaps it would be . . . unfair to ask the men to shave," she conceded with as much dignity as she could salvage.

Jesse was gracious in victory, allowing her a graceful retreat instead of an unconditional surrender. "Everyone could stand a trim." He smiled.

Suddenly her peevishness and assorted aches vanished, and she smiled back. "Have a safe trip, Mr. McClintock. We'll miss you," she added softly.

They had been out a week, when Jesse decided to take Charlie Baxter and check out a possible location to winter the ranch's remuda. The remuda was a herd of tough cow ponies, kept so the hands could alternate their personal mounts with horses belonging to the ranch. The country and the work were too hard on an animal for it to be ridden every day. Leaving the rest of the men branding calves, he and Charlie rode out shortly after noon. He'd gotten so used to his shadows that he hardly noticed the two guards trailing after him as usual.

Jesse glanced at the man riding beside him. Baxter said he'd found a long box canyon that would be ideal for holding the thirty horse remuda. There was plenty of grass, and a hot spring that would guarantee free-running water even during the winter. The narrow mouth of the canyon was blocked now by ocotillo, a cactus that grew in clumps of thick whips studded with long vicious spines, but hacking out an entrance and installing a sturdy gate would be no problem. Jesse was sure the site would be as suitable as Baxter had said. Every doubt he had had about the man had proved to be unfounded so far. He worked harder than two men, was an expert with horses as Miranda had claimed, and he hadn't, so far as Jesse could determine, drunk so much as a thimbleful of alcohol.

He looked ahead to the pocket canyon they had to ride through to reach their destination. The canyon was short and straight and appeared to flatten out at the other end. The floor and walls were sparsely covered with scrub oak and stunted piñon, nothing that would afford cover for an ambush. There had been no sign of Apaches or the renegades since they'd been out, yet the short hairs on the back of his neck prickled, as if a spider was crawling through them.

He reined in, and the three other men followed suit. Scanning the canyon inch by inch, he listened for any sound that was out of place. There was only the breeze sighing through the red and orange oak leaves and the piñon. There was nothing to see but rocks, sand and the runty trees. The only scent was a faint drift of skunk on the fitful breeze.

Lucky suddenly shied for no apparent reason. The horse might just be reacting to his own unease, Jesse thought as he brought the stallion quickly back under control, or maybe Lucky sensed something that he couldn't. Again his eyes searched the area, tree by tree, bush by bush, rock by rock. Nothing. Finally, nudging the Appaloosa with his heel, he led the way into the canyon.

They passed the midpoint without incident, and Jesse began to relax. Then, turning in the saddle to check behind them, he saw the sandy floor of the canyon inexplicably shift. Six Apaches rose out of the sand, yelling hideously and firing their repeating rifles even as they threw off the dirt-covered hides that had concealed them. One guard went down in the first volley. Returning their fire, he spurred Lucky for the other end of the canyon ahead. As he neared it, he cursed savagely, able to see now what he hadn't been able to see from the other end.

The canyon's straight walls were an optical illusion. One curved back, providing concealment for eight mounted warriors. At an almost leisurely pace, they rode single file across the end of the canyon, closing off that escape. Jesse spun Lucky in a tight circle, Charlie Baxter and the other miner right behind him, and made a dash back for the entrance of the canyon. Running down two of the Indians who had been hidden, he was scant yards from the canyon mouth, when a blinding yellow light exploded inside his skull. He felt unbelievable pain, then . . . nothing.

Chapter Eight

The last thing he remembered was pain mixed with blinding light. The first thing he was aware of was pain mixed with blinding darkness. The cause of the pain he understood immediately. From the line of fire that burned on the right side of his head—and the fact that he was alive to feel it—he knew the bullet had only grazed him. Still, his entire head ached as if something were trapped inside, kicking at his skull to get out.

His other senses told him that he was lying on his belly, on bare ground from the feel of the small rocks jabbing him and scraping his left cheek where it was pressed into the dirt. Cautiously he tested the rest of his body, tightening and relaxing muscles without moving. Everything seemed to be working, although his whole body felt as if he'd been run over by a stampede. Probably because he had been well pounded by the saddle he'd been slung over to get him wherever he was, he decided sardonically as a sharp twinge in his side reminded him his ribs were still healing from the last pounding they'd had. It was no surprise to find that his hands were bound, although his feet were free. From the sounds of movement and snatches of guttural conversation, he knew his captors weren't far away, but he had no idea how many there were. There had been about a dozen Apaches in the canyon, all men, but he heard women's voices now, too.

At last he considered the problem of his eyes. He smelled smoke, so a fire was burning nearby, yet there was only blackness against his eyelids. For one gut-seizing moment when he had first regained consciousness he had thought he was blind; then he'd discovered that the reason he couldn't see was simply that he couldn't open his eyes. Something was sealing them shut, and it had apparently been smeared across the lids, too, thickly enough to keep any light from penetrating. Perhaps it was some perverse joke the Apaches, but in any case, he fought the urge to rub the stuff away. He didn't want to call any attention to the fact that he was awake, not until he had had a chance to assess his situation and decide how he was going to escape. For the moment he ignored the small detail that he couldn't hope to do either if he couldn't see, concentrating instead on any sounds immediately around him. Was a guard close by? And what had happened to Baxter and the other miner?

A low urgent whisper from his left answered one question. "McClintock! Jesse! You awake yet?"

"Baxter?" His response was equally low.

"Yeah. How's your head?"

His dry laugh was almost soundless. "Hurts like hell. How about you—are you all right?"

"My leg isn't" came Baxter's laconic reply, and Jesse heard the pain tightening his words. "Ramirez didn't make it."

Ramirez was the other miner. He felt a bitter sadness at the loss of two more good men, but there was no time for it now. "What the hell's all over my eyes?"

"Blood. It must have oozed down from the wound on your head, then dried. You've been out for about six hours."

Six hours. That meant it was dark now. "Is anybody looking our way?"

There was a brief pause while he assumed Charlie was checking to see if they were being watched. "No."

Slowly, because a quick movement might attract notice, Jesse inched his bound hands up to his face. The movement forced feeling back into his arms, which were numb from being in the same position for hours with his weight on them. He was getting a taste of what it would be like to be staked out on an anthill, Jesse thought as he gritted his teeth against the fierce sting of returning sensation crawling up and down his arms. His hands stayed numb, although he could feel the cords binding them cutting deeply into his wrists.

The sticky blood had dried into a stubborn glue, and he had to rub hard before he could force his eyelids apart. Brushing away the loose crumbs of dried blood, he blinked, and gradually the blur in front of him came into focus. With the aid of the small fire they'd built to light the darkness, he could see that the Apaches had set up a temporary camp. He counted eleven men and five women. The presence of women didn't surprise him. He knew they often aided with their men and could be far more vicious. Wounded prisoners were turned over to them, not for their tender care, but for their amusement. In spite of himself, he felt his belly knot.

Tales of Apache torture got a lot of telling. He just hoped he and
Charlie didn't end up with a few to tell themselves—if they lived
to tell them.

Baxter was right—nobody seemed to be paying any attention to
them right now. The men were clustered around Lucky and Charlie Baxter's black stallion; the horses were apparently the main
topic of discussion. Each man wore a calico shirt, dirty muslin
breechclout, several cartridge belts and shin-high mocassins. Several of them also wore dark trousers under their breechclouts, U.S.
Cavalry issue from the looks of them, and all of them had their
faces painted with black and yellow ocher. It was hard to tell with
the paint, but they all appeared to be young; he was sure none of
them could be the old chief Geronimo. Several bottles were passing from mouth to mouth in the group. Whiskey bottles. Silently
Jesse encouraged their thirst. It would be hell of a lot easier to get
away if their captors were drunk.

His gaze shifted to the five women. He couldn't discount them,
though. Apache women could shoot and ride almost as well as the
men. Like the men, the women wore long calico blouses, cinching
them with a sash over a long skirt, and their faces were also painted
hideously with long stripes of black paint daubed across their
cheeks and foreheads and down their noses. They were pawing
through a pile of sacks and small barrels and other things he
couldn't quite make out in the flickering light. One woman held up
what looked like a slab of bacon with a gleeful shout. They must
have raided a store or a train of supply wagons, Jesse decided; the
sacks and barrels probably held flour, sugar and molasses. The
woman who had found the bacon next found a length of yellow
calico and began wrapping it around herself. Another woman
grabbed for it, and a screeching squabble ensued. The tug-of-war
ended abruptly when a third woman whipped a long knife out of
the sash around her waist and slashed the cloth in two. The two
squabblers shrugged, tucked the calico under their arms and went
back to their loot.

Turning his head a degree at a time, he looked around for
Charlie. His hands trussed, too, he was lying a few feet away,
propped up against the trunk of a skinny piñon. His right leg was
stretched out awkwardly in front of him. There was a black hole
high in the thigh, and his entire pant leg was soaked with blood.
Obviously Baxter wouldn't be able to escape on foot, but they
would stand little chance on foot, anyway, even in the dark. And
if he had to hold him on a horse, Jesse thought dryly, they wouldn't
stand a much better one. "Can you ride?" he asked in a low voice
that carried no farther than the man a yard away.

"Hanging on by my teeth if I have to," Charlie assured him, then added in an almost conversational tone, "the sooner the better. Looks like we're in for a roasting."

Jesse slowly turned his head in the direction Charlie was looking and saw that the women, finished with divvying up the spoils, were now out at the edge of the circle of firelight, gathering brush. The first one with a full armload approached, and Jesse closed his eyes to a bare slit that let him see nothing beyond the ground a foot in front of his nose. He heard the brush hit the ground a yard or so away; then two feet clad in skin moccasins came into view. The soles were cowhide, tanned with the hair still on. They projected beyond the toes, then had been turned back over and sewn down, for additional protection, he assumed.

One of the feet swung in his direction, and he forced himself to go limp, absorbing the hard kick like a lifeless sack of meal. He heard a grunt of disappointment; then the feet moved off and behind him. A few seconds later he heard the soft thud of a foot meeting human flesh, a long drawn-in hiss of agony and a high-pitched giggle of satisfaction.

The woman's footsteps, muffled on the sandy ground, faded, and cautiously Jesse looked back over his shoulder to Charlie. The other man's eyes were closed, and his face, even with the orange light of the fire, was ice white and clenched with pain. Fresh blood oozed out of the hole in his leg, and Jesse swallowed his rising gorge of sick, helpless fury. The squaw had kicked Charlie in his wounded leg so she could enjoy his suffering.

The brush pile grew higher by the minute. Jesse's skin crawled over his bones, drawing tighter, as if already trying to pull away from the flames. Charlie was right; if they were going, it had better be damn soon. One of the women came toward them from the direction of the campfire, her hands empty except for a burning stick. Jesse gathered himself. With no gun and his hands tied, his chances of saving himself and Charlie were about as good as those of a three-legged rabbit cornered by a pack of hungry coyotes, but he wasn't going to die without putting up one hell of a fight, he vowed grimly.

His left knee drawn up, his hands braced on the ground, he was ready to jump the woman, when the discussion over the horses suddenly erupted into loud shouting. The squaw tossed the branch away and hurried over to join the rest of the Indians, who were gathering into a loose circle. They'd moved closer to the fire, away from the horses, and in the flickering light, with their painted faces, they made a hellish sight.

The dispute seemed to be between the tallest of the bucks and a short, bandy-legged, barrel-chested one. From their gestures, Jesse guessed that the argument was over the ownership of Lucky and the black stallion. The smaller Apache's nose looked as if it had been smeared all over his face, and Jesse remembered the accounts of the latest Apache atrocities he'd overheard in Deming the month before when he, Miranda and Rivera had been passing through. The little one with the smashed nose must be Chatto, one of Geronimo's lieutenants. Apparently his own people weren't as terrified of him as the whites were, Jesse thought wryly, or liquor had given the buck challenging him a fool's courage.

The onlookers seemed to be offering their opinions, and voices got louder as the level in the circulating whiskey bottles got lower. The women, he noted with satisfaction, were drinking as freely as the men. One of the men abruptly staggered out of the circle, and a woman grabbed the half-empty bottle out of his hand as he reeled past her, heading toward the bushes near the rope corral holding the Apaches' horses. She tipped it up to her mouth for a long swig; then another woman snatched it away and a new squabble started over possession of the bottle.

He would have liked to wait until a few more of the Indians succumbed to the whiskey, to even the odds a little, but that was time he decided he and Charlie couldn't afford. As soon as the ownership of the two horses was settled, the Indians would turn their attention to the former owners. "I'm going after our horses," he called in a low voice to Charlie as he began to crawl into the darkness surrounding the camp.

Charlie's rushed whisper followed him into the deep shadows. "You'll stand a better chance on your own. I'll only slow you down. I can hold out until you send back h—"

"Just be ready," Jesse interrupted in a low rasp. Hugging the ground with his belly, he became another of the silent shadows. A light wind had come up, covering the soft scrape of his clothing over the sand. The breeze turned the cool moonless night chilly, but a clammy sweat stuck his shirt to his back as he waited for the shouts of discovery. Baxter was right; he would stand a better chance escaping alone, but he never even considered it. If he left Charlie behind, the man would have no chance at all.

He reached the bushes where the drunken Apache had disappeared a few minutes before. There was no sign of the Indian, and Jesse rose to his feet, staying low as he circled silently around behind the brush to the back of the corral. Without warning, the buck stumbled out of the bushes in front of him. For a frozen breath they stared at each other, the Indian with a comic expression drunken puzzlement on his face. Sobering rapidly, the warrior grabbed for one of the two pistols stuck in the heavy leather belt around his waist, when Jesse lunged to his feet. A wave of black pain and nausea almost knocked him back to his knees as he struggled to focus on the hazy figure behind the yellow dots dancing before his eyes. With a pure animal instinct for self-preservation, he defended himself with the only weapon he had: his bound, numb hands. He felt the shock in his shoulders as his clubbed fists found flesh and bone. Dimly he heard a dull thud, a quiet snap, and the warrior fell, his warning cry dying with him.

Jesse sagged to his hands and knees, head hanging down as he fought off unconsciousness. There were no cries of alarm, no shouts of discovery. The silent deadly confrontation had lasted only a few frantic heartbeats and, screened by the brush, attracted no notice. Gradually his heart slowed to a less frenetic beat, the dark fog in his brain cleared and the pain in his head settled into a monotonous throbbing. He crawled over to the body sprawled face-down in the dirt. From the unnatural angle of the head, he knew the man had died of a broken neck, dead before he had hit the ground. It had been the Apache's life or his, but Jesse took no pleasure or satisfaction in the man's death.

After rolling the body over, he eased the gun out of the lifeless fingers. His own gun, he noted as he reached for the second revolver and long knife stuck in the Apache's belt. Tied together, his hands worked clumsily, his numb fingers almost useless as he tried to remove the gun and knife. Carefully he laid the two pistols on the ground, then jammed the hilt of the knife tight between his knees. He slid the razor-honed blade down between his forearms and sawed at the rawhide cord around his wrists. Seconds later the tough leather strips fell to the dirt, and blood surged back into his hands, giving him another taste of the anthill. Ignoring the pain, he filled the cylinders of both revolvers, then tucked the extra one and the knife in his pants, keeping his own gun ready in his hand.

He stayed in a crouch until he reached the back of the rope corral, then cut through the rope strung between a couple of piñons. The ends fell free, but, as he had hoped, the horses didn't immediately realize their potential escape route. Careful not to spook them, he moved carefully through the herd. Lucky and Charlie's Blackjack were tethered to the rope on the opposite side, outside the corral. Quickly he untied Lucky's reins and the black's, then checked the location of each Indian. The whiskey had laid two of them out in the dirt, and several more were weaving aimlessly around the fire, while the rest kept up the argument.

Glancing across to Charlie, Jesse froze as he saw one of the women, a burning branch in her hand, staggering determinedly toward the brush pile. As soon as she reached it, if not before, she would notice that he was missing. Jesse vaulted onto Lucky's back, then raised the Colt in his hand. A seemingly random gunshot would cause confusion and might give him and Charlie a few more seconds than her shouts of warning would. He sighted the gun on her back, yet an ingrained inhibition against shooting a woman, even one who would be happy to kill him, made his finger hesitate on the trigger. The squaw stumbled on the uneven ground and sat down hard. For a few seconds she stared stupidly at the branch burning itself out in the dirt where she'd dropped it; then she fell over sideways with a drunken giggle and lay still. Jesse relaxed his finger on the trigger and, leaning across the Appaloosa's neck, cut the rope corral again. He guided Lucky back through the herd, leading the black stallion.

As soon as they cleared the opening on the far side, he yelled and fired several shots over the herd. The Indians' horses bolted out of the corral, with half of them stampeding through the camp, trampling one of the Indians lying unconscious on the ground and another who was too slow to get out of the way. As he kicked Lucky into a trot, the Apache horses were already disappearing into the night. Those Indians still on their feet scrambled in drunken confusion for whatever cover they could find and began firing blindly into the dark.

Jesse snapped off two more shots to keep their heads down. He saw one go down permanently before he leaped off Lucky's back next to the piñon where he had left Charlie. The wounded man had somehow managed to get on his feet, although, from the way he was slumped now, it was clear that the tree was all that was keeping him there. Jesse dropped Lucky's reins, certain that the big Appaloosa would hold steady, even through a Texas twister.

Uneasy with the loud gunfire and the smell of blood, the black stallion shied, trying to jerk free of the strong hand on its rein. Ruthlessly Jesse snapped the horse's head down, then snubbed the rein up tight just below the bit before the animal had time to pull away again. "Whoa, boy! Steady. Steady there." He spoke quietly as he braced his weight and power against the horse's. The stallion stamped and snorted, but finally responded to the implacable pull on its reins, sidestepping the few feet to its master.

Charlie lurched away from the tree to fall heavily against his horse's side. "Easy, Blackjack. It's me, fella." Grimly he hung on to the saddle, biting back a scream as Blackjack shied again and forced him to put his weight on his wounded leg to keep from fall ing. "It's just me, Jack, just me, boy," he whispered, patting awkwardly at the horse's neck. Hearing his master's voice, smelling him, the big stallion calmed. He stood still, legs trembling, nervous shudders rippling his sleek black hide. A shudder ran through Charlie, too, as he wondered just how in hell he was going to get himself into the saddle.

One glance at Charlie fumbling for the stirrup and Jesse knew the wrangler would never make it on his own. With a quick burst of strength, he literally threw Charlie into the saddle, hearing the not-quite-suppressed groan of agony as the other man's injured leg dragged across the stallion's rump. "Can you make it?" he asked as he handed up the rein.

"I can make it," Charlie ground out between gritted teeth, wrapping the leather strap tight around his hand.

An angry whine buzzed past Jesse's ear, reminding him that a random shot killed as easily as an aimed one. Giving Charlie a brusque nod, he ducked under the black horse's neck. The piñon and darkness hid them from view, but still the skin between his shoulder blades twitched. The Apaches were still shooting sporadically, but bullets weren't going to be random much longer. Even drunk, it was going to occur to them at any second that no one was returning their fire, and their next thought after that would be of their prisoners.

He took a few precious seconds to check that the foot of Charlie's wounded leg was secure in the stirrup, then turned toward Lucky.

"Behind you!"

Charlie's warning almost came too late. Jesse whirled in time to see a darker blur coming at him out of the darkness. Instinct made his hand draw his gun in the same motion, and he fired before he even thought about it. The hammer hit on an empty cylinder; they would all be empty, he realized with a sudden coldness in the pit of his stomach, because he'd fired all six shots earlier and hadn't reloaded. The coldness turned into icy detachment as he saw the silver glint of a knife. Trapped between the two horses and the tree, he had little room to maneuver, and the Apache would be on him before he could pull the other, loaded gun from his belt. Already he could smell the man, the strong, almost sweet scent of his death lust. As the Indian lowered his knife for the kill, Jesse chopped the gun down in a short vicious backhand, like a hammer. The butt caught the warrior over the ear, and Jesse felt the bone give.

The man was dead before the breath sighed out of his body, but momentum carried him forward. Face set in a snarling death mask, one of the Apache's arms wrapped Jesse in a macabre embrace, and he felt the cold sharp kiss of the blade as the knife slit his shirt. Jesse pulled free, and the lifeless body sprawled in the dirt at his feet. Feeling nothing but a weary emptiness, he explored the warm wetness trickling slowly down his belly. His fingers told him the Apache's knife had cut little more than a long shallow scratch in the skin, and he dismissed it, reloaded his empty gun, then handed the spare in his belt up to Charlie. The other man accepted it with a wordless nod, and Jesse turned to his horse.

They rode at a steady gallop, with Jesse in the lead. His innate sense of direction guided them out of the high narrow canyon where the Apaches had made camp, then took them east, toward the late-rising moon. After he judged they'd put several miles between them and the Indians, Jesse pulled up. He sat on Lucky, listening for any sound of pursuit. The earlier breeze had died with the moonrise, and sounds carried well in the still, crisp air. The Apaches would have rounded up their horses by now, but they'd apparently decided against a chase, because he heard nothing beyond the normal night rustlings . . . and the half-sobbing, rasping breath of the man beside him.

Dismounting, he moved to the side of the black stallion. In the thin light of the half-moon, the blood welling steadily from the ragged hole in Charlie's thigh looked black instead of red. Seemingly unaware of him, Charlie sagged in his saddle, eyes staring dully ahead, his hands white knuckled around the horn. Despite the chill in the night air, huge drops of perspiration ran down his death-white face. Jesse's respect for the man grew measurably. The hard ride must have been a torture as brutal as any the Apaches could have invented, yet he'd never made a sound. There was nothing he could do to ease Charlie's agony, Jesse thought in frustration, but he did have to do something to control the bleeding, or Baxter would bleed to death before he could get him to help.

After taking his scarf from around his neck, Jesse folded it into a pad, then placed it over the wound. It was soaked with blood almost immediately. Grabbing his shirt where the Apache's knife had slit it, he ripped off the lower half. Swiftly he wrapped the long strip of fabric tightly around Charlie's leg to hold the pad in place and maintain pressure on the wound. Charlie endured his rough ministrations in stoic silence, although Jesse felt the shivers of pain that ran through the man's leg every time he had to lift it. As he knotted the strip, he was gratified to see that the steady flow of blood had subsided to a seep. He glanced up to see that Charlie was watching him.

"Tie me on." Charlie's rasping voice was almost soundless with pain. He knew he'd reached the limits of his endurance. The only way he was going to stay on Blackjack was if McClintock tied him into the saddle.

With a nod of understanding, Jesse untied the lariat at the back of the saddle and proceeded to lash Charlie's boots to the stirrups. They could ride double, but they'd make better time riding separately, and to be honest, Jesse admitted as a wave of dizziness made his fingers fumble with the knots, he wasn't that sure he could keep them both in the saddle. Ignoring the throbbing in his head that seemed to increase with every heartbeat, he prized the rein free from Charlie's fingers, then tied his hands to the saddle horn. Now that he didn't have to worry about falling off, maybe Charlie would mercifully lose consciousness so he wouldn't have to endure any more suffering.

Keeping the rein of Charlie's horse, he put a boot in the stirrup of his own saddle. Bright, colored lights exploded in front of his eyes, and he shook his head to clear them away—a mistake, he discovered, as shards of pain stabbed the base of his skull. Fighting the pain and a sudden exhaustion, he hauled himself onto the back of his horse. Too bad there was no one to tie him in *his* saddle, he thought with grim humor as he kneed Lucky into a ground-eating, skull-jarring lope.

Miranda unwound the limp strip of grimy linen and dropped it on the kitchen table.

"Señora, no es necesario que usted se moleste conmigo. Por favor—"

"Yes, it is necessary, Ramón, and it is not a bother." She answered the old man seated before her in Spanish, pushing down with gentle firmness on his thin bony shoulders when he tried to get up again. She saw that the colorful walnut-sized knot straddling the hairline above his forehead was down from the hen's egg it had been three days ago and, satisfied, began winding a fresh strip of clean cloth around his forehead and spare white hair. "You know very well that Leola said your head is to be bandaged—" her tone was as briskly efficient as her hands "—and that you aren't to tax yourself." The bandage around Ramón's head was no more necessary than the one wrapping her left arm from the shoulder to the wrist, but Leola had prescribed them as a graphic reminder of her order to both her "patients" to take it easy.

Three days before some Apaches had appeared on the back rim of the box canyon protecting the ranch house, as they did from time to time. Miranda knew there was no way they could climb down—circling vultures always marked the failure of those suicidal enough to try—but her heart still raced with a helpless panic whenever she saw their silhouettes on the skyline. As usual they had vented their frustration with a chorus of bloodcurdling howls and a few shots that fell as harmlessly as raindrops. This last time, though, one of them had rolled a loose boulder over the rim that had started a small avalanche, and she and Ramón had been unlucky enough to be in the way at the bottom. A large rock had bounced off her arm with little more damage than a spectacular bruise, and since Leola was off in the miners' village attending a childbirth, Miranda could ignore her orders, but she was going to see to it that Ramón, who was not as young and strong as he thought he was, followed them to the letter.

"And you're to drink your tea, too," she reminded him. Finished with the bandaging, she handed him the cup steaming on the kitchen table.

Ramón took the tea with patently dubious gratitude. *"Gracias, señora."*

He drank down the tea, and Miranda smothered a smile as his scowl of distaste added a few more wrinkles to the mass lining his face. She felt not at all guilty that she was taking advantage of Leola's absence to avoid her own prescribed dose of the vile stuff. Made from the roots of *oshá*, a wild herb, Leola used it for everything from a skin wash for rashes to a cure for stomachache. She seemed to be of the opinion that while it might not cure whatever ailed you, it couldn't hurt, either. Since coming to the Silver Tejo, Miranda figured she'd drunk a barrel of it.

"Gracias, patrona," Ramón said again, this time with genuine sincerity as he handed back the cup.

"De nada, Ramón. I think I'll tie those last chiles you picked into strings today," she added casually as she gathered up the used bandage and the empty teacup.

Ramón rose from the kitchen chair with a speed and agility that belied his years. "Tying chiles is not proper work for a *patrona.*" There was reproof in his tone as the small spare man lifted a floppy straw hat almost as old as he was from the table, putting it on his head with a simple dignity. "I will do it."

Miranda kept her smile of satisfaction to herself until the back door had closed behind him. Ramón was far more concerned than she was with the propriety of the *patrona* of the Silver Tejo performing menial tasks, and making chile *ristras* had been the most menial—and least strenuous—task she could think of on short notice.

She followed him outside a few minutes later. For a long moment she just stood in the sunshine, absorbing the warmth and the serenity of the canyon. The sky overhead was blue and cloudless, and the air was so clear it nearly took her breath away. The sun shone pure and strong, turning the fall leaves on the cottonwoods into bright little hearts of newly minted gold as they fluttered in the light breeze. A killing frost had come a few nights back, followed by Indian summer, the grace period before the real cold of winter. The false summer was all the sweeter because she knew it could not last more than a few days. It was in moments like these, surrounded by this rough beauty, so precious because there was so little that was beautiful in this hard land, that she could almost forget the violence and death that haunted her home.

The only home she had ever had, imperfect though it might be, she thought with an inward sigh as she turned at the sound of childish laughter. Her somber thoughts lightened at the sight of Tommy chasing Susie's chicks. She and Tommy were safe here; the canyon was their haven, their fortress, both literally and figuratively, an island of security in the sea of danger that surrounded them.

Miranda laughed softly to herself as Tommy caught a small black chick and nuzzled it carefully against his cheek. She was glad to see him out in the sunshine, running about. He had been rather mopey the past few days—because a certain face was missing from the supper table at night, she suspected. She had missed it, too, she admitted reluctantly, just a little.

A faint whistle from the watchman down the canyon gave the signal that someone was coming, and minutes later the gates opened, admitting Leola and the two miners who had been pressed into guard duty to provide her with protection. Miranda reached the buggy as the older woman climbed down. "Did the birth go well?" she asked in Spanish.

Leola's smile was weary but fully satisfied. "Twins, as I had thought." She took Miranda's arm, not because she was tired, but because she knew the unspoken fears of the young woman beside her, and started them walking toward the main house. "The mother and babies are fine," she said with strong reassurance, then changed the subject. "There was dust in the west when I was coming back. Perhaps a dozen riders, coming this way fast."

Miranda tensed in automatic reflex. "Apaches?"

The Spanish woman shook her head. "No, and not bandits, either. They weren't trying to hide their presence. Soldiers, maybe. There was talk in the village of a raid the Apaches had made the day before. They attacked a wagon train taking supplies to Hachita, so the soldiers from Fort Cummings will be out looking for them." Her thick shoulders lifted in an unconcerned shrug. "If they are coming here, we will know who they are soon enough."

Miranda agreed absently. Before he had left, Jesse had told her that he and the hands would be working the outlying canyons...to the west. Unconsciously she rubbed her arms, trying to dispel the premonition that had suddenly turned the warm bright sunshine winter cold. She was being foolish. There were hundreds of square miles between here and Hachita, and there was no reason whatsoever to think that the Apaches had come across him, too.

As proof of Leola's prediction, there was another whistle from down the canyon, and the two women stopped to see who was coming now. The gates swung wide again, and a peculiarly strong happiness surged through her as she recognized the ranch chuck wagon with an escort of riders. Unconsciously she noted the grim, exhausted faces of the men while her eyes sought out one face in particular—and didn't find it. The wagon turned, and her surge of happiness collapsed, replaced by a hideous feeling of déjà vu as she saw the two riderless horses following it, tied to the tailgate. *No, not again,* she cried silently, remembering that terrible day seven months ago when the chuck wagon had returned, another horse with an empty saddle tied behind it. The fear and the pain this time were even worse, far, far worse.

Unaware that her cry of denial hadn't been silent, she shook off Leola's restraining hand and dashed back across the compound. The wagon stopped in the middle, and she shoved her way heedlessly through the crowd of horses and dismounting men around it. She rounded the corner of the wagon just as a tall, dark-headed man climbed down out of the back.

Jesse turned to see Miranda running toward him. In a move that was as unthinking as it was natural, he held out his arms, like a homecoming husband catching the wife who was happy to see him. He absorbed the soft impact of her body and instinctively gathered her closer.

"You're all right!" The words rushed out in a breathless, half sob of relief as, just as instinctively, she clutched at his shirt to pull him nearer still. Her voice, with a hitch of suppressed emotion, was muffled by his chest. "I saw your horse...tied to the back...and I—"

"Shh. Shh now," he whispered, unconsciously closing his eyes and rubbing his cheek against her soft, sweet-smelling hair. "I'm fine." Tightening the circle of his arm around her, he smoothed his other hand up and down her back while her warmth seeped into him, soothing his aching, battered body.

"What happened?" Manolo Rivera came pushing his way through the men and horses. He'd ridden over from the mine to see if his wife had returned yet from her midwifing duties in the village and had immediately known something was wrong when he'd seen the riders and wagon in the yard. Sensing Leola at his side, his hand automatically reached for hers. He glanced at her long enough to reassure himself that she was safe, then looked back to the tall *gringo*. "What happened?" he repeated the question with even less patience, his eyes narrowing at the sight of the *patrona* in McClintock's arms.

Eyes closed, Miranda was content for the moment to let words pass unheeded back and forth over her head. She loosened her grip on Jesse's shirt and, without thinking, burrowed her nose in his shoulder, only half hearing Jesse's terse description of the attack and his even briefer explanation of how he'd escaped and met the rest of the men out looking for them just before dawn. He smelled of sweat and dirt and horse, but he was alive—and wonderful.

Them. At last she faced the significance of the black horse tied beside Jesse's to the back of the wagon. Fighting another wave of sickening fear and guilt that she hadn't given a thought to anyone else being hurt, she tightened her hands in his shirt again and moved back to look up at him. As if it begrudged her even that tiny distance, his arm around her loosened only fractionally. "Is Charlie Baxter...?" She swallowed, but still couldn't say the word.

Jesse looked down into lavender eyes clouded with the beginnings of horror staring up at him. On its own, his hand stroked slowly up and down her back again. "Charlie will be all right," he assured her quietly. "He took a bullet in the leg and he's lost some blood, but he'll recover."

Leola was climbing into the wagon even before he finished speaking, forcing Jesse to move himself and Miranda out of her way. With movement, both of them finally realized their position—virtually locked in each other's arms. Awkwardly they moved apart. Leola stuck her head back out of the wagon and issued an order in rapid-fire Spanish for a litter. In her role of *curadera*, her voice took on a deeper resonance and a tone of inarguable command. The two men who had escorted her scurried to obey, and she turned to Jesse.

"Señor. Ven acá."

Jesse obeyed her order to come closer and submitted to a brief but thorough examination.

"You were very lucky, *señor*," Leola murmured as she pulled aside blood-matted hair to fully expose the shallow wound in his scalp.

"I know," he muttered, wincing as her fingers probed the swelling around the wound.

Satisfied that the injury was superficial enough to do without her immediate attention, Leola checked the knife cut on his belly and reached the same conclusion about that, as well. Straightening, she looked down at the young woman standing a few feet away, staring at him, her shock plain on her white, frozen face. *"Señora."* Leola spoke loudly to gain her attention, her tone sharp with authority. Miranda's eyes shifted reluctantly to her. "You can take care of the *señor*. I will see to this one here in the wagon."

Miranda felt her head jerk in agreement. She'd seen the blood on his head and face immediately, of course, seen his torn, blood-soaked shirt with yet more blood underneath on his exposed stomach, but she had been so glad just to see him alive that none of it had registered until now. "Certainly." She heard her own steady, amazingly calm voice and almost giggled. She didn't feel calm at all. A rush of delayed panic and another, stronger, rush of relief, swamped her until all she wanted was to give in to the hysteria she'd been fighting ever since she'd seen Jesse McClintock's horse with its empty saddle. Instead she lifted her chin and stiffened the tremble in her upper lip. "Please come with me, Mr. McClintock."

The men gathered around the back of the wagon automatically cleared a path for her as she turned toward the main house. Jesse watched her walk away, but didn't immediately follow. His eyes cut to the horses with their blanket-wrapped burdens, standing quietly in the midst of the others. He was certain Miranda hadn't noticed them. She'd pulled herself together just now with obvious effort, and he could only begin to guess what that effort had cost her. Without being told, he knew that she'd been reliving memories best forgotten, and he didn't want her to have any more to forget.

The other men followed his glance, then looked back to him, clearly waiting for orders. "I don't think Mrs. Hart needs to know about them," he said, his hard look taking in every man. He repeated the order in Spanish for the benefit of Cisco Moreno and his boys. His eyes met Rivera's, and he saw complete understanding and agreement. The Mexican majordomo was totally Miranda Hart's man, and though he knew Rivera still didn't trust him, in this they were allies. Relieved of the strain of her many chores by Ramón, his grandson Paco and young Kwon, she was looking less peaked and had even gained a little weight. Knowing about the deaths of the two miners who had been riding with Charlie and him couldn't bring them back, but it could undo the progress she'd made. He'd never mentioned the rancher and his wife they had come upon, either. Nor, he was sure, had Rivera, because both of them wanted to shield her as much as possible from the grimmer realities of life in this godforsaken country.

"The village has a little *camposanto*," Manolo said, glancing toward the small grassy graveyard behind them that already had too many white crosses. "I will send for the priest in Deming tomorrow."

"*Bueno.*" Jesse nodded his approval and started for the main house.

By the time he came through the back door into the kitchen, Miranda was ready for him. She gestured him toward the chair that was already pulled out and turned sideways to the table. After he seated himself, she moved to stand beside him, and he felt the touch of her fingers, cool and light, on his temple.

Miranda couldn't seem to get her fingers to work. She had seen wounds far worse than this, she reminded herself, right here in the kitchen, too, which Leola sometimes used for a clinic. Other men had sat in this very chair, their lives streaming out of them, while Leola worked to halt the flow of blood, mending the tears in their flesh as if they were a ripped shirt that could be salvaged with a few stitches and made serviceable again. Miranda had mended more than a few of them herself, often with blood up to her elbows, but after the months of caring for her dying father and seeing to all his needs—and the one brief trip outside to lose her breakfast the first time Leola had demonstrated the proper stitching technique—she had the stomach for it. She felt no disgust or queasiness when she treated a wounded man; rather, she was grateful for Leola's training and glad that she could help, and even felt a sense of pride in her small skill.

She urged her fingers forward again, and again they resisted. But this wasn't just another shirt, another body to stitch. This was *Jesse*, and as hard as she'd fought against acknowledging it, from the first moment she'd seen him in Willis's parlor, she hadn't been able to think of him as nothing more than another hired hand. Some of those hired hands had died because of Thomas's almost fanatic determination that the Silver Tejo would survive, no matter what the odds against it. She had accepted his determination—in truth, she'd had little choice—and tried not to think of the cost. After his death, she had carried out his commission to preserve the ranch as his legacy to his son, consoling herself with the illusion that the cost couldn't go higher. The army assured everyone that soon it would have the Apaches back on their reservation in Arizona and the bandit raiders dealt with. Then the miners could lay down their rifles and take up their picks and shovels again, and horses couldn't come back with empty saddles....

"You shouldn't have to do this. My head can wait until Leola can take care of it."

He was already rising from the chair before she absorbed his quiet words. Hastily she dropped her hands to his shoulders to press him back down onto the seat. Not narrow shoulders with sharp bones sticking into her palms like old Ramón's, she observed distractedly, but shoulders so broad and powerful that her urgent fingers hardly dented the solid muscle. "No! Sit down. Please. I—I was just thinking how best to proceed," she said quickly to cover her hesitation.

She sensed him looking at her but didn't meet his gaze. Finally he sat back down, and Miranda forced her fingers into his hair. It was stiff with dried blood, the rich dark color dulled and grayed with dirt. Carefully, trying to cause him as little discomfort as possible, she pulled apart the blood-and-dirt-matted strands to fully expose the wound and breathed a silent prayer of thanks when she saw the shallow groove in his scalp above his ear. Suddenly she had the almost overwhelming need to feel those strong arms around her again, to curl up on his lap and lay her head on his shoulder and weep.

Instead she took a steadying breath, then, as gently as she could, probed the swelling around the wound. His hair had protected him from worse injury, she thought as her eyes traced the path the bullet had clipped through the thick curls. Under the dirt and blood, his scalp was an ugly reddish-purple from blood that had congested under the skin. The vivid bruising silently attested to the powerful impact the bullet had made on his skull and the wicked pain he must have endured.

Was still enduring, she realized as a grimace twisted his mouth when she tilted his head to the light. Swallowing past a sudden constriction in her throat, she reached for a clean towel from the stack on the table beside her. Quickly she laid it over his shoulders, then wound another around his neck, much like a barber preparing a customer for a shave. Her knuckles brushed his chin as she tucked in the end of the towel, and his unshaven beard prickled her fingers. Small tingles penetrated her skin like the tiny lightning jolts she'd experienced in the hotel hallway the last time they were alone together. The sensation wasn't unpleasant.

Abruptly Miranda pulled her hands away, and plunging them into an enameled pan that was full of what looked like weak tea, she scrubbed them together roughly. Deliberately she focused her thoughts elsewhere. "I didn't see Procopio Ramirez and Jesús

García, the two miners who went with you," she remembered suddenly. "Didn't they come back with you?"

Jesse heard her real question under the spoken one. "They went on to the miners' village." It was a lie of omission for which he would be forgiven, Jesse thought. And it wasn't entirely untrue; by now, Ramirez and García should be making their last trip home.

Miranda wondered at the sadness that tinged his words. Her hands stilled. "Is Charlie really going to be all right?" she asked in a thin voice.

Jesse looked up and held her anxious gaze. "He's going to be all right," he echoed deliberately. "The bullet missed the bone, and it didn't look like it did too much damage to the muscle. He should be back on his feet in a week or two."

Miranda searched his clear dark blue-gray eyes and found only the truth. I should get word to Celia, she thought fleetingly as she turned back to the pan and wrung out a cloth that had been soaking there. She applied it to the wound in his head, and he flinched. So did she. "I'm sorry," she apologized in a tight whisper. "I didn't mean to hurt—"

"It doesn't hurt. I just wasn't expecting it," he said softly. As her hands had been, the wet cloth was cool against the hot throbbing in his head. "It feels good," he murmured.

She made a wordless sound that might have meant anything from disbelief to disagreement, but he wasn't lying this time. It did feel good. Enjoying the coolness of the cloth and the exquisite gentleness of her hands washing away the dirt and dried blood, he closed his eyes and felt the relentless ache in his skull ease. She washed his hair with repeated applications of the cloth, so carefully that hardly a drop escaped down his neck, making the towels she'd wrapped around him unnecessary. For several minutes the only noises in the quiet kitchen were the small swishing sounds of the washrag being rinsed out in the pan.

The sounds stopped, and her hands left his head. Jesse opened his eyes in time to see her spilling the filthy dark water into the soapstone sink. He watched her rinse the pan under the hand pump mounted over the sink, then refill it from what looked like a whiskey jug with the same liquid as before. "That looks like that same miserable stuff Leola kept giving me to drink when she was doctoring my ribs," he said suspiciously.

"It is," she confessed with a small sheepish laugh as she came back to him, carrying the pan. "It's her all-purpose elixir, supposedly good for anything and everything that's wrong with you. But it really is a good disinfectant," she added hastily, seeing his dubious frown. "It will keep you from getting an infection." She took another clean cloth and dipped it into the pan. "I just need to give your hair a final rinse."

"Just as long as I don't have to drink any of it," he muttered, closing his eyes again as she began her ministrations.

His expression was mutinous, his lower lip pushed out in a near pout, just like Tommy's whenever he was confronted with a dose of Leola's cure-all. Despite his size and the fact that he was very obviously a mature male, Jesse McClintock looked exactly like a little boy who didn't want to take his medicine. "I won't make you drink any," she promised him gravely. But Leola probably will, she added silently, stifling an unexpected giggle. Although she couldn't explain why, considering the grim circumstances that had caused him to be sitting there, needing her care, she felt extraordinarily relaxed, almost . . . happy.

"What's it called?" He wasn't interested in the answer; he just wanted to keep her talking so he could hear her soft, elegant voice.

"*Oshá*. It's a wild herb that grows around here. Leola digs sacks full of the roots every spring to make that awful tea." Finished with the rinsing, she unwound the towel from around his neck, taking care this time not to touch the soft bristles on his jaw. She scrubbed the thick towel gently over his wet hair to blot up the excess moisture. After a few moments she laid it aside and picked up an unlabeled tin, sliding open the top. Carefully she parted the damp hair away from his wound, then dipped up a quantity of the pale green salve from the tin.

"This will speed up the healing," she murmured as she dabbed the balm gingerly along the wound.

"That's what you gave me for my wrists, isn't it?" Eyes still closed, he had identified the salve by the soothing icy coolness on his head, not by sight—or smell. He couldn't smell anything but her, that sweet, utterly feminine scent that haunted his sleep at night and tempted him into daydreams he knew better than to dream . . . yet seemed helpless to resist.

She confirmed his guess in a soft undertone as she wiped off her finger. "Mmm-hmm. Leola makes *it*, too." Unconsciously she moved closer as she brushed back his hair to check her handiwork one last time. "I could put on a bandage," she murmured, more to herself than him, "but I don't think it's necessary, and you'll heal faster without it." As if they were detached from her body and she wasn't responsible for them, Miranda stared at her fingers leisurely combing through his hair. The warm air in the kitchen had finished the job she'd begun with the towel, and it was nearly dry now. She raised one hand slowly to watch his hair sift through her fingers and catch the light. He had beautiful hair, clean, shiny and dark, like the color of strong rich coffee. The curls twined around her fingers as if they were alive and trying to trap her. She was a willing captive. His hair was as she had once imagined it, thick and soft and so silky, almost like fur. Giving herself over to the luxurious sensation, she dragged her hands through it again, savoring the voluptuous rasp on the sensitive flesh between her fingers.

Jesse felt the tight muscles in his neck loosen and turn fluid. His neck arched, his head lolled, blindly following the direction of her gently stroking hands, rubbing against them, and he smiled to himself. Now he knew how a cat felt when it was being petted. He was so relaxed that he could easily have fallen asleep in this hard uncomfortable chair—except that he was too aware of her. His unconscious sigh drew her scent deep into his lungs. She was so close. Even with his eyes shut, he knew he had only to move his head a scant inch and he could rest his cheek on her breast and let the bone-deep exhaustion of forty hours without sleep overtake him. Or he could turn his mouth just a fraction and his lips would be at her nipple. He didn't need to have his eyes open to see the small pucker it made in the dark fabric covering her breast; the image was seared into his memory. He only had to undo the prim row of small black buttons and he knew he would find her breasts, full, ripe, underneath her high-necked, long-sleeved chaste dress. He would only have to part his lips and he could suckle, could nourish himself on her sweetness. The fantasy was so powerful that he could almost visualize her nipple, beaded and rosy and wet from his mouth, feel his hand plumping tender satiny flesh, taste her on his tongue. Yet the picture in his mind had little to do with sex, he realized with a vague surprise. It was more a symbol of peace, supreme contentment, a haven, and so sharp and real that the violence and tension of the past night and day seemed to be nothing more than a bad dream.

A loud scraping sound brought Miranda's head around slowly, as if she were just waking up from a deep sleep. She felt Jesse's head turn just as slowly under her hands at the same time. Across the kitchen, Tommy had dragged out one of the deep drawers and was using it as a step to the counter above. He climbed up, then reached down a gaily painted canister from the cupboard over his head. Clutching the tin against his sturdy body, he jumped down and came toward them. When Miranda realized that her hands were still moving through Jesse's hair, she dropped them immediately. She stepped away, and the delicate moment between them ended.

Tommy struggled with the top of the canister until he finally succeeded in twisting it off. He reached inside and pulled out a red-

and-white striped peppermint stick. His freckled little face and his bright blue eyes solemn, he extended the candy toward Jesse, saying with innocent assurance, "Here, Jesse, this will make the hurt go away. Mama always gives me one when I have a hurt to make it feel better."

"Thank you, Tommy," he said very gently. "I'll save it for later, all right?" As he tucked the candy stick into a vest pocket, Jesse caught a glimpse of himself in the polished chrome door on the stove front. Dried blood streaked his forehead and filled his eye sockets. The rest of his face looked almost as bad, and he'd forgotten that his shirt was half torn off and what was left was filthy with dirt and gore. He looked like some gruesome monster out of a nightmare, yet Tommy didn't seem frightened, or even startled, by his appearance. Because he was all too used to finding bloody men in the kitchen, Jesse thought grimly as he watched the small boy go back across the kitchen to put the candy tin away.

Miranda wrung out the cloth in the pan of *oshá* once more. She glanced at the man on the chair, her eyes not quite meeting his. "If you'll stand up, Mr. McClintock, I'll take care of the cut on your...stomach." He stood up as she directed, and her lowered gaze met exactly what she was supposed to take care of. Smooth, honey-toned skin stretched taut, defining the hard muscles underneath. A thin line of fine dark hair bisected his abdomen, gathered in a silky-looking swirl around his navel, then narrowed again to disappear below the waistband of his pants. The soft, well-worn denim fit and defined what was beneath it like a second skin.

She was almost grateful for the distraction of the wound on his belly. The knife cut was a thin, almost bloodless line a few inches long, even with his navel. From the single trickle of dried blood she knew it was blessedly shallow, little more than a harmless scratch, actually, but the realization that it could just as easily have been deep and fatal made her stomach churn sickeningly. Gently she touched the cloth to the rusty thread of dried blood on his stomach.

He grabbed the cloth out of her hand. "I'll do it," he said in a scratchy growl. Jesse washed the scratch on his belly roughly. She'd avoided looking at him when he'd taken the washrag away from her, but from the slow color rising up her throat and blushing her pale cheeks, he knew she had felt the same lightning shock he had when her fingertips grazed the bare skin of his belly. After giving the cloth a quick rinse and squeeze, he used it to scrub the blood and dirt from his face. He tossed the cloth back in the pan, and she moved to remove it from the table.

Tommy came back to the table and climbed up on the chair where Jesse had been sitting. Jesse felt the boy's small arm trying to span his broad back in a heartbreakingly sweet gesture of commiseration. He was glancing down at the little boy to give him a smile and quick hug, when Miranda reached for the pan of disinfectant. The loose cuff of her dress fell back, revealing a linen bandage that started at her wrist and wound upward until it disappeared under her sleeve at the elbow.

"What happened to you?" His voice was deceptively soft, belying the implacable grip he had on her wrist and the sudden, fierce light burning in his dark blue eyes.

"I just have a bruise. It's—nothing." Miranda tugged experimentally in an attempt to free her hand, but his hold, although not in the least hurtful, was fast.

Tommy's clear childish voice broke the small tense silence. "You should see it, Jesse. It's all different colors, like a rainbow, only not pretty. Some 'paches threw rocks down from the top of the canyon, and one of them hit Mama's arm." Tommy chattered on, blissfully oblivious to the thickening tension between the two most important adults in his life. "Ramón got hit on the head, too, but he doesn't have a big bruise like Mama's." Tommy's tone held faint disappointment.

Jesse's imagination had no trouble supplying the details that the child's explanation had left out. The rocks the Apaches had thrown had started a landslide, and he understood immediately what Tommy in his innocence did not: his mother could just as easily have been killed instead of getting an interesting bruise. Suddenly he was filled with a helpless fury. It was wrong for Tommy to think it was normal for mothers to patch up wounded men in the kitchen, wrong for a little child to have this knowledge and casual acceptance of violence, wrong for Miranda and her son to live in such a stupidly dangerous situation. His grip on the fragile bones in her wrist tightened almost to the breaking point. "Why do you stay here?"

With the strength that always surprised him, Miranda wrenched her hand free with a quick sudden movement. She met the bewildered and barely suppressed, impatient anger in his question with an infuriatingly expressionless calm. "Because it is our home, Mr. McClintock."

Chapter Nine

Geronimo took a leisurely stroll down to the spring near the band's camp to check on the horses. Nearly two dozen had been taken in yesterday's raid, along with several prisoners to ransom back his people the *federales* were holding hostage. The five captive women cowered at his approach, whining in fear like dogs. He did not look at them. Some of the men took Mexican women as concubines, occasionally even as wives, but he had never touched one and never would. He did not pollute his seed in dogs.

Even now he could remember the scene twenty years before when he and the other men had returned from a celebration they had been invited to in Janos, a village in northern Chihuahua. They had gone to trade, and the villagers had welcomed them. Afterward there had been dancing and food, and the *mescal* had flowed like water. The warriors had enjoyed the villagers' hospitality, little suspecting that while they danced and ate and drank, Mexican soldiers were attacking their women and children. He had returned to the camp to find his mother, his wife and his three children among the dead. One hundred others had been taken captive, to be sold as slaves.

He had placed the decorations that Alope, his wife, had made and the playthings he had made for his children in their *wickiup* and burned it. His mother's defiled home and property had been destroyed in the same way. They had been too few to avenge the villagers' treachery then, but four months later he had led one hundred seventy-five warriors back into Mexico, and they had struck Janos like a lightning bolt. Soldiers had come to stop them, and they, too, had been annihilated. For the past twenty years he had continued to exact payment for his slain family. He had heard that the Mexicans viewed him as a demon sent to punish them for their sins, and that made him smile with grim pleasure. They had much to atone for; their debt wasn't settled yet.

He stopped on the small hill overlooking the spring to survey the area, noting with satisfaction the horses, secured within a rope corral, contentedly cropping the thick grass that grew around the spring. His people never camped at the edge of a water source. Water in this dry land belonged to all creatures, and to selfishly keep the water to themselves, forcing others to thirst, would be unthinkable. The animals, birds and insects had once been human, too. It was only right that those who camped here now share water with those who had gone before.

After ducking under the rope strung between two cottonwoods, he ran a hand down the sleek flank of a fine black-and-white paint and nodded his approval to the two young men assigned to take care of the horses. The band's survival depended on the health and swiftness of their horses.

Walking back through camp, he stopped to exchange a few words with each of the forty men who had accompanied him on the raid the day before. Four crows flew low overhead, calling raucously, and he shivered under the warm afternoon sun. Four had a special magic for him. He had been the fourth son in a family of four boys and four girls. Four of his children had been murdered by the Mexicans, three when Alope was killed, and another later. Sometimes the magic was good, sometimes bad. He glanced away from the man speaking to him and saw a short, ugly man approaching. Today the magic was bad.

He returned the man's traditional embrace with little enthusiasm. A mule's displeasure had disfigured his face when he was a child, the kick permanently flattening his nose and giving him his name, Chatto—Flat Nose. Chatto liked himself and killing just a little too much. Several weeks before, he had killed an important American judge and his wife for no particular reason and kidnapped their five-year-old son. What had happened to the boy, Chatto never said. The murders and kidnapping had enraged the Americans and brought the soldiers down on them once again. He listened with feigned interest to Chatto's tale of his latest extravagance; he had already heard the truth from another. Chatto had not accompanied them on the raid to get horses and the hostages they needed to ransom back their people. Instead he had taken a dozen men—men who would have been useful on the raid—and ridden north across the border, undoubtedly further annoying the Americans so that still more soldiers would hound the Enemy People. He had returned with no hostages or horses, only a few

leaking barrels of flour and molasses—and without five of the men
who had gone with him.

Chatto's words to him were properly respectful, but the subtle
insolence in his tone spoke loudly of youth impatient with age. At
twenty-three, Chatto was young enough to be his son, and Geronimo knew the young man considered him a useless old man who
long ago ought to have done the honorable thing and stepped aside
for a much younger, stronger leader—himself, of course. Chatto
did not dare to challenge him openly yet, but the day was coming.
He had never thought to be the leader of the Enemy People, nor
even wanted to be, but once he had become the headman, he found
he liked the respect and power the position commanded. He knew
now he would never be satisfied with anything less, and he had no
intention of losing to this cocky young fool.

Chatto left to swagger and brag around the camp. The older men
turned their backs to him, but the younger ones didn't. His flam-
boyance made him very popular with the other young men of the
band because they were not wise enough yet to see that Chatto's
selfish seeking of glory was endangering the entire group. Geronimo turned away from the sight of the other man's posturing with
a snort of disgust. What the ugly runt and his admirers did not
seem to realize was that his wanton acts were only hastening the
inevitable day when they must surrender to the American general
Crook once and for all time.

When he reached his own campfire, his wife automatically
handed him a cup of the *tizwin* she had just brewed. He took a
deep swallow and considered the other disturbing news that he had
learned from Nah-tanh, one of the men who had gone with Chatto
on his raid, the one who had told him the truth of it. He had hoped
the woman would abandon the cattle and the silver mine when her
man was killed, but apparently she had found a new man. A dark-
haired giant, Nah-tanh had said, and fearless. He had killed four
of the five who had not returned himself, two of them apparently
with his bare hands. And Nah-tanh had said that the giant had a
remarkably beautiful horse, Geronimo thought a little wistfully.
One of the big ones with the spots he had heard about but never
seen. A tribe far to the north, the Pierced Noses, he thought they
were called, bred them. In Mon-Tana, he remembered suddenly.
The giant must be from there. Too bad he had not stayed in this
Mon-Tana, he thought sourly as he drained his cup.

Charlie didn't know which was worse, the itching or the boredom. It didn't matter, he finally decided. Another hour of either

one and he was going to be so crazy he wouldn't care anyway. The itching and the boredom both had the same cause—the bullet hole in his leg, which was, Mrs. Hart assured him, healing nicely. If the way it itched was any indication, it was healing *damn* nicely.

He looked over at the newspaper and stack of books on the small table at his bedside. Someone had brought a copy of the *Deming Headlight* back from town yesterday, but he'd read it twice already. The books came from Mrs. Hart's own library and were a rare luxury, but he was "read" out. What he wanted was to get out of bed.

Turning his head, he stared longingly at the crutch against the wall eight feet away. It might as well be eight miles, he thought gloomily. He'd finally talked Mrs. Rivera into giving him the crutch yesterday, so he didn't have to use that damned chamberpot anymore, but she wouldn't leave it within his reach. Where she thought he'd run off to, he didn't know, sighing in disgust as his head rolled back on the pillow. As much as he might want to get out of bed, the truth was that just going as far as the privy left him feeling as weak as a newborn pup.

He glanced around the whitewashed adobe walls, bare except for the crucifix over his bed and one small window, and sighed again. Apparently Mrs. Rivera was a great believer in the curative powers of fresh air and sunshine. The other days, she had had his bed carried out to the porch, and he'd been able to spend some time outside, but the good weather had turned, keeping him inside today. For a little while he entertained himself by watching gray clouds, every one of them the same, move slowly past the window.

Finally even that excitement paled, and he was back to staring at the walls again. He knew he was in the Riveras' house, not the main one where Mrs. Hart lived. It was a small house, one of several that were clustered between the main house and the corrals. Some of the married miners had lived in the houses at one time, he'd learned, their wives helping out in the main house, but they were empty now. The room he was in had the feel of a sickroom, and he knew he wasn't the first by far who had passed the time staring at these four walls while recovering from some malady. And most had recovered, he suspected. In a territory with few doctors, and most of them quacks, he knew that the Mexican population and not a few of the Anglos depended on healers like Mrs. Rivera for medical care. Besides the magic elixirs of fresh air and sunshine, she seemed to have more potions and remedies than a barker at a medicine show, but he was extremely grateful for her skill. She had dug the bullet out of his leg and cleaned the wound—

mercifully after giving him a healthy slug of laudanum—and was treating it with a poultice that looked to be mostly weeds, but whatever they were, they were doing the trick. She'd left the poultice off today, and he'd spent some time examining the hole in his leg. It sure as hell didn't look pretty, but there were no red streaks— a sure sign of blood poisoning—no oozing pus, no sign of infection at all. The edges looked healthy and already seemed to be healing over. Thank God for Mrs. Rivera, although he could have done without that evil-tasting tea she forced on him twice a day. They could have taken him to "Dr." Davidson whose advertisement he'd read in the Deming newspaper. A graduate of the "Missouri State Museum of Anatomy," he claimed, and promised cures for "nervous, mental and physical debility, especially those arising from early excesses and indiscretions of youth." If he'd fallen into the hands of a quack like that, he wouldn't be grousing about his leg itching; he'd be worrying about how he was going to find work as a one-legged wrangler—if he was able to worry at all.

The faint sounds of a wagon and women's voices reached him through the partially open window. It was probably Mrs. Rivera leaving, he decided. In the five days that he'd been there, she'd been called out to the miners' village twice, once to treat a child's broken arm and another time for an elderly woman with pneumonia. Both times Mrs. Hart had taken over his care, faithfully checking on his comfort every hour during the day and several times at night. Yesterday she'd even sat with him most of the afternoon. He'd helped her shell a mess of dry pinto beans while trying subtly to pump her for information about Celia Kershaw, until he realized that she didn't know any more about her than he did. He'd spent the rest of their time together discovering that the widow Hart was nothing like he'd imagined. She was reputedly one of the richest women in the territory and a lady through and through, but she was no snob. She'd talked with him as an equal, completely relaxed, discussing the books she'd loaned him, gossiping about the people they knew in common and revealing a dry, quick sense of humor that had him laughing more often than not.

Their afternoon of conversation and bean shelling had ended abruptly when Jesse McClintock had returned from scouring the surrounding country for any sign of the Apaches who had attacked them. Upon finding him with the widow Hart, McClintock had given him a look that had silenced him in mid-laugh and confirmed his speculations about the foreman of the Silver Tejo and its owner. The warm friendly manner she'd had with him became cool, almost icy civility with McClintock, and she had immediately departed for the main house, taking her beans with her.

Miranda Hart and Jesse McClintock were unconsciously providing him with the only amusement he had right now. Unable to do much of anything else, he'd devoted a great deal of time to observing them the past few days and speculating on their relationship. It was clear they were fighting—hard—against a powerful attraction for each other. To all appearances they went out of their way to avoid each other, yet their paths seemed to cross more often than could be considered mere chance alone. When they were forced to speak to each other, they took formality and politeness to excess—except for this morning.

Mrs. Hart had caught Jesse just after coming by to see how he himself was doing this morning, and a low-pitched, intense argument had followed, neither of them noticing his open window. Charlie had heard every word, including several rather unladylike ones after the argument had ended abruptly with the fading stomp of boot heels on hard-packed dirt. The gist of it had been that McClintock was taking the rest of the men out to finish the roundup that the Apaches had interrupted, and Mrs. Hart didn't want him to. He was still recuperating, she had reminded him—forcefully; the Apaches might still be around, and a few cows more or less weren't worth anyone else's being hurt, anyway. He had responded that Leola Rivera said his head was fine and none of their scouting trips had turned up any Apache sign. She countered with a direct order forbidding him to go, and McClintock had reminded her of their agreement that he was to have a free hand in running her ranch; then he'd stomped off.

Charlie frowned absently to himself as he tried to find a comfortable spot for his tailbone. That was the one thing he couldn't figure. What was McClintock doing on the Silver Tejo? He was the kind of man who would have his own ranch, not be running someone else's. Like Tyree—although Tyree was another story altogether—McClintock gave orders; he didn't take them.

Despite the fact that Charlie had done nothing more strenuous than eavesdrop all morning, his eyelids suddenly felt like lead. A day or two before he'd left Deming, he'd overheard a couple of traveling drummers talking in the bar. He tried to remember their conversation, but he suspected the rotgut he'd been drinking had fuzzed up his memory some. He gave up trying to keep his eyelids up. One had been telling the other some story about a road agent being sentenced to a ranch down on the border instead of a rope or the prison up in Santa Fe. The robber had claimed he was innocent, a cattleman from Montana....

* * *

Celia Kershaw paused in the doorway of the small room to stare at the man asleep on the bed. Charlie looked wonderful. His pasty barroom pallor, which had come from spending all his time indoors, either drunk or trying to get that way, was gone. In spite of his injury, his face still had a healthy tan, and the sharp hollows under his cheekbones had filled out, proof that he wasn't taking his nourishment from a whiskey bottle anymore. A dark blanket was pulled up to his waist, and he wore a clean, soft-looking plaid flannel shirt. His brown eyes blinked open suddenly, and she saw that they were clear and sparkling.

"Celia?"

There was uncertainty in his husky voice, as if he didn't quite believe what he was seeing. "Yes, Charlie. It's me," she said, feeling suddenly, unaccountably, shy as she approached the bed. Even his new mustache looked nice—not so big and bushy that it hid his sweet smile.

"What—" Charlie cleared the sleep out of his throat. "What are you doing here?" He'd been dreaming of her, and he wasn't sure yet that he wasn't still dreaming.

"I came to see you," she said simply. It hadn't been quite that simple. As soon as Miranda's man had given her the message, she'd shocked the Harvey Hotel manager by telling him at the height of the breakfast rush that she was leaving. The message had reassured her that Charlie's injury was not life threatening, but still she'd had an urgent, undeniable need to see him so she could truly believe it.

"How did you get here?" He stretched out his hand and was gratified at how willingly she put hers in his grasp.

His big rough hand felt wonderfully strong and warm around her small, soft one. Celia discovered that she craved physical as well as visual reassurance that he was all right. She shrugged diffidently. "I rented a buggy at Ruebush's." Leaving the hotel manager sputtering, she'd dashed across the street and convinced a reluctant Calvin Ruebush to rent her a horse and buggy, lying through her teeth about her experience handling both. She'd never driven a buggy before in her life, but fortunately the horse had known what to do.

"You came by yourself?"

Charlie's fingers tightened painfully around hers. "I was right behind the man Miranda sent in to tell me you had been hurt." Two miles behind, and out of sight, but the truth would probably have gotten her hand crushed. Besides, an appalled Miranda had already given her a severe scolding concerning her carelessness and a guarantee that she wouldn't be leaving without an escort. Charlie relaxed his grip, and she wiggled her fingers surreptitiously to restore circulation.

Charlie's eyes moved over her slowly, greedy for the sight of her. Sight wasn't enough. Curling his fingers around hers, he tugged her closer until her knees bumped the side of his bed. "You're wearing your uniform," he said absently. The starched nunlike black dress was wilted and gray with road dust, and her blond hair, always pulled tight into a neat bun on the back of her head, was a mess of flyaway wisps and dangling strands. He'd never realized that her hair was curly.

Finally the significance of her clothing struck him. "Today isn't Sunday, your day off. You should be working, shouldn't you?"

She became very busy examining the empty walls of the room. "They can get along without me," she said a little fiercely.

The realization that she had been so worried about him that she had risked her job to rush to his side gave him an inordinate amount of pleasure, but before he could think of a way to tell her, the pride he'd thought he'd drowned in a whiskey bottle suddenly resurfaced. "What's the matter, Celia? Were you worried about your investment?" His tone was insinuatingly nasty. "Don't be. You'll get your money back."

Her stricken look made him feel lower than a snake's belly.

"I wasn't worried about the money, Charlie. I was worried about you," she said quietly. "I—I'll say goodbye now. I need to get back before the supper rush." She tried to pull her hand free so she could leave before she embarrassed both of them with the tears she could feel backing up behind her eyes.

"Don't go, Celia. Please." He exerted a gentle, steady, downward pull on her hand, drawing her down onto the bed beside him. With his other hand, he tipped up her chin to make her see the truth of what he was telling her, and he almost cried himself when she raised her blue eyes to his and he saw them full of tears. "I'm sorry, Celia," he said gently. "I'm being a bastard because I'm piling up an awful lot of debts I don't know if I'll ever be able to repay. You, Mrs. Hart and now Jesse McClintock." His hand dropped away from her chin, and suddenly tired, he let his head fall back on the pillow. "He risked his life to save mine, you know," he told her soberly, closing his eyes.

He heard her soft whisper. "I know, and I'm very grateful to him." Celia was vaguely surprised to find herself sitting beside him on the narrow bed, his hand clasped between both of hers in her lap, his blanket-covered thigh tight and warm against her hip.

One corner of his mustache kicked up ruefully. "Yeah, so am I."

For several minutes neither of them said anything, and Charlie lay there, oddly content, enjoying the aimless motion of her soft fingertips on the back of his hand. Finally he heard a quiet sniffle, then her watery laugh.

"I bet part of the reason you're grouchy is that you're bored and your leg itches, right?"

Opening his eyes, he saw her smiling at him. "Right," he admitted with a sheepish grin. "How'd you know?"

"Miranda says you're not a quiet complainer." Her expression sobered as she touched the blanket covering his thigh hesitantly. "Does your leg hurt very much, Charlie?"

"It hurts something terrible," he assured her gravely. The dull ache in his thigh was gone; all he could feel now was the warmth of her hip pressed against him. "Maybe you could kiss it and make it well?" he suggested hopefully.

"I think not," she censured him prissily, vainly trying to turn her smile into a disapproving frown.

Gradually the teasing sparkle in his eyes was replaced by the light of sober intent. "Come here, Celia," he said softly.

"Ah . . . well! I should be going now," she chattered brightly. A small part of her laughed uproariously at her sudden attack of maidenly modesty.

"In a minute. Come here."

She tried to rise, but his hand turned swiftly in hers, catching her and holding her in place. "No . . . I have to . . . no."

"Come here."

His intense gaze exerted an even more irresistible pull than his hand. She shook her head a little desperately.

"Come here, Celia."

He repeated his soft command one last time, just before he pulled her down onto his chest and his mouth captured hers. Celia heard a soft sigh of surrender but didn't realize it was hers. His mouth was unexpectedly talented. Coaxing, not demanding; tender, not rough. His tongue teased her lips open, touched the tip of hers, and she moaned.

"The first time we did this," he whispered against her moist lips, "I'd planned to be standing up so I could feel every soft inch of you against me." She kissed with an endearing awkwardness, not as if the activity were unfamiliar, but rather as if it had been so long since she'd last done it that she'd almost forgotten how. She moaned again as he took her mouth once more, taking them both deeper this time, and her memory rapidly improved.

Celia tore her mouth away from his. Weakly she let her head rest on his shoulder, too limp to do anything more than try to gasp air into her starved lungs. Gradually she became aware that she was lying full length on top of him. She knew she ought to move, but her bones had melted, and she couldn't. He shifted slightly under her, and she had to bury her face against the soft flannel to stifle a wild giggle. He had said he had wanted to be standing up for their first kiss so he could feel every soft inch of her. Well, lying down couldn't have been so bad, either, she thought, suppressing another giggle. She could feel every *hard* inch of *him*.

Charlie shifted again with a groan, and a sudden guilty realization gave Celia the strength to move. She swayed unsteadily by the bed as she stared down at him in dismay. "Charlie, I'm so sorry! I didn't realize . . . lying on you that way . . . Is your leg hurting very much?" she asked anxiously.

Charlie reached his hand to her waist to steady her. "Sweetheart, you could hit me with a sledgehammer right now, and I wouldn't feel it." He knew he had a stupid grin on his face. Hers had a rosy flush, her soft blond hair was more mussed than ever from his hands and her big blue eyes looked as stunned as he felt. He laughed as she mouthed a silent "oh" when she realized that his groan had come from another kind of pain. As if they couldn't help themselves, her eyes strayed down to the pronounced bulge in the blanket, and her face got pinker. Her eyes snapped back up to his, and he saw a sultry glint that made him want to groan again.

Celia took the hand on her waist in both of hers. "I really do have to get back before supper." The foolishness of a five-hour drive for a ten-minute visit didn't occur to her. "Goodbye, Charlie." She pressed a kiss on his hard, callused palm, then laid his hand gently on his chest.

"Goodbye, Celia. Thank you for coming," he said with a formality that sounded ridiculous even to his still ringing ears.

She smiled at him fondly. "Don't be silly," she said, and with a little wave, she disappeared through the door.

Experimentally he ran his tongue over his lips and savored the lingering sweetness he found there—Celia's taste. Sighing contentedly, he closed his eyes. Once he had promised himself that someday he was going to kiss Celia Kershaw until the seams of that black nun's dress popped. He didn't know about hers, but his sure as hell had.

Miranda counted the stitches on her knitting needle the way she had done everything else the past week—with an ear cocked for the sound of men riding into the compound. Jesse McClintock had not given her any definite idea when they might be returning, only that it shouldn't take more than a week to complete the roundup. Manolo had suggested that several of the miners go along as guards, but he had refused, and she hadn't forced the issue. Although he didn't know it, she had found out what had happened to Jesús and Procopio, the two men who had been with him and Charlie when the Apaches had ambushed them. Although it had been Apache bullets that had killed them, she couldn't help feeling that their deaths were her fault.

She held up the long strip of deep green wool she had knitted. She was getting better, she decided objectively. The stitches were tight and even, and she couldn't see where she had dropped any. Satisfied, she began to bind off the last row of knitting. Christmas was six weeks away. She would continue Thomas's tradition of giving all the hands a Christmas bonus, but she had wanted to make a few more personal gifts, like the long winter scarf she was finishing now. She had already made another in the same color, and had one more project to complete before December 25.

Folding the scarf, she laid it over the arm of the wing chair she habitually sat in, then picked up her knitting basket and pushed herself up—something that was getting harder and harder to do, she thought with a rueful laugh. She crossed to a sewing rocker on the other side of the parlor and took one of several skeins of soft, deep blue yarn from the basket. She had bought the wool last summer, intending to make a shawl for herself, but last week she'd thought of a better use for it. After looping the skein around the spindles on the back, she sat on a hassock in front of the chair and began to wind the yarn into a ball. Her hands busy, her mind returned to a mystery she had been trying to solve during the past week. Why hadn't Jesse told her the truth about Jesús and Procopio? It was almost as if he were trying to protect her, but for what purpose? After their exchange in the kitchen, his opinion of her decision to stay on the Silver Tejo was quite clear. If anything, she would have thought he would have wanted her to know, as further proof of the dangers of staying here.

Engrossed in the puzzle, she missed the sounds she had been listening so hard for. It wasn't until she heard Leola's cheerful greeting and the deep masculine response that she realized the interminable week of waiting was over at last. Leaping up from the hassock, she kicked over her knitting basket, and balls of yarn unrolled in every direction over the parlor floor. She tried to grab the runaway balls, but all she succeeded in doing was getting her feet tangled up. Muttering in disgust at her own clumsiness, she dropped back down onto the hassock to unravel the mess of strings that seemed to wind themselves tighter the harder she pulled.

"That must have been some spider."

Miranda's head snapped up at the lazy drawl coming from the direction of the door. He was leaning against the frame, one dark eyebrow raised in sardonic question.

"My knitting basket got tipped over," she said with as much dignity as she could muster, then lost all of it when her bound feet tripped her up as she tried to rise and she plopped down again on the hassock.

Jesse struggled to keep a straight face at her comical expression of surprise. She shot him a look of pure annoyance before surveying the tangle of yarn crisscrossing the carpet, seemingly wrapped around every table and chair leg. A corner of her mouth twitched as she murmured, "It does rather look like some huge crazed spider tried to spin her web in here, doesn't it?" She slanted him another look; he grinned at her, and with a helpless shrug, she laughed.

"Well!" She directed a gust of breath upward in a vain attempt to blow a loose curl out of her eyes. "I guess I'd better clean this up." She started to get up again.

"Wait!"

Before she could stand, he was across the parlor and his big hands were on her shoulders, pushing her back down with firm gentleness, and she was on the hassock once more. Miranda looked up at him, more curious than annoyed. She hadn't even seen him move, she realized absently.

"Don't try to stand up. You might fall," he said gruffly.

Her curiosity turned to startled surprise when he crouched in front of her and raised her skirt. Bemused, she watched him matter-of-factly pleat the full skirt of her dress over her knees to expose her ankles, then reach for the shears that had fallen out of the knitting basket. She was wearing felt slippers instead of her usual high-button shoes, and he inserted the sharp point of one blade under the strands of yarn wrapped around her ankles, taking obvious care not to prick her or snag her black cotton stockings. He brought the blades together, and she was free of the multicolored web that had caught her.

She expected him to stand up right away. Instead, relaxing with one knee on the floor, he stayed where he was, and she felt his long fingers wrap around both her ankles. In wordless question she looked up to see that his eyebrows were drawn together in a frown.

"Your ankles are swollen," he murmured.

"Th-the baby." She cleared her throat. Now those long fingers were idly caressing her, sliding up and down her calves. "That's why I'm not wearing shoes."

He nodded his understanding, although his frown didn't lessen appreciably. With a final caress, his hands left her ankles, and he was on his feet, one of his hands extended to help her to hers.

After a moment's hesitation Miranda put her hand in his and let him pull her to her feet. She kept hold of him, because she wasn't at all sure she wasn't going to collapse right back down on the hassock again. The bones in her ankles seemed to have turned to the consistency of mush.

Finally her bones regained their normal solidity, and she gave him back his hand, then turned to the task of picking up the yarn balls scattered over the floor. "Did you have any trouble?" she asked, huffing slightly as, on her hands and knees, she stretched an arm under a chair for the dark blue ball of yarn she had been winding. Another hand reached it first, and Miranda felt herself being lifted, then deposited firmly in the high-back wing chair she usually sat in. The ball of yarn dropped into her lap.

"I'll pick up. You wind," he said in a tone that didn't leave room for argument.

Miranda wound.

He handed her four more balls of yarn and finally answered her question. "No trouble at all, not even a sign of it. If there's an Apache within fifty miles of here, I'd be surprised." They hadn't found any sign of the renegades, either, but Jesse didn't feel the same certainty about their absence from the area. Too many nights of waking up in a cold sweat from the same dream of finding Miranda like the homesteader's wife had given him a permanent knot in his gut.

Patiently he unwound a ball of gray yarn from around a table leg, then handed it over with the other three he'd picked up. "That's the last of it." She murmured her thanks. Mindful of his dusty clothes, he didn't sit down in the chair beside her as he wanted to but waited until she looked up at him. "There was a cavalry patrol about an hour behind us. I'm pretty sure they were heading this way." He glanced toward the window and the lowering sky visible through it. "They'd probably appreciate an invitation to spend the night with a dry roof over their heads. There's plenty of room in the bunkhouse."

Miranda nodded her agreement. "They usually stop when they're out on patrol. The officers always take dinner with us. You'll be here, too, won't you?"

She said it as if she didn't anticipate a negative response, and he didn't give her one.

Miranda rose from her chair and started for the kitchen. "I better warn Leola that we're expecting company for dinner, then." At the door she paused to look at him. "I'm glad you're back, Mr. McClintock," she said with a smile.

The officer leading the patrol was a young lieutenant serving his first tour of duty in the New Mexico territory, but he was already a veteran of two other Indian campaigns. Lieutenant Riddle's eyes, Jesse noted, had the wary narrowness of a man who had learned the hard way to keep a constant check on the horizon. Out of deference to Tommy, the conversation around the dinner table was kept innocuously general. But once dinner was over and Tommy in bed, the adults adjourned to the parlor, and the conversation got very specific.

"Does the army expect to capture Geronimo, Lieutenant?" Jesse asked as he poured brandy for himself, Manolo and the lieutenant.

Lieutenant Riddle grimaced as he reached for the glass of liquor. The grimace was partly due to the bluntness of the question and partly a reaction to the lingering effects of the red-hot green chile served at dinner. He swallowed the fine old brandy and wondered if he dared ask for a glass of milk. "Realistically, Mr. McClintock? No." McClintock had been introduced as the ranch foreman, yet he had a natural authority that made him seem less like a hired hand than the owner. Another swallow of brandy didn't calm the inferno in Riddle's stomach.

Setting down the snifter, he saw that McClintock, Mrs. Hart and Rivera were waiting for an explanation. "General Crook is convinced Geronimo will never be defeated by any army. What will defeat him is being constantly on the run, never having a chance to rest and refit. When he gets tired of the war trail, he will surrender and go back to the reservation."

Jesse glanced at Miranda to make sure she was paying attention. "Is there a chance of that happening anytime soon?"

"General Crook thinks there is," Lieutenant Riddle answered. "He received a message Geronimo sent through an intermediary two weeks ago, saying he was ready to live in peace, if the terms were right."

"He has said that twice before and surrendered twice before," Manolo pointed out dryly.

"That's true," the lieutenant agreed, "but he has been playing a deadly game by surrendering, then leaving the reservation again. He has to know he can't play it forever. If he surrenders this time and bolts again, he'll likely be executed the next time, or at the very least exiled to Florida."

"Why do you think he keeps leaving the reservation, Lieutenant?"

He smiled at his hostess. He counted himself fortunate indeed to have drawn this assignment, the chile notwithstanding. He hadn't seen a woman as beautiful and genteel as Miranda Hart since he'd left Philadelphia. "The conditions on the San Carlos reservation could have been better, ma'am," he said honestly. "General Crook is working, however, to improve them and the way rations are distributed. But there was also another problem. Geronimo's favorite pastime for years has been making life miserable for the Mexican peasants. Raiding is the Apaches' only organized sport, and Geronimo their most expert player, but he's getting old. The game can't be much fun anymore. He'll be giving it up soon," he said confidently.

"I sincerely hope so, Lieutenant," she said soberly. If Geronimo was suing for peace, then it might be only a matter of weeks before he was back on the Apache reservation in Arizona. She clung to that hope like a drowning woman clutching the rope that was going to save her.

Leola caught her eye and stood. Leola was reminding her that it was her bedtime, Miranda thought with an inward sigh as she stood, too. The three men rose courteously. "Good night, Lieutenant, Manolo, Mr. McClintock."

"I'll say good-night and goodbye, ma'am, in case I don't see you in the morning," Lieutenant Riddle said. "We'll be leaving at daybreak. My men and I thank you for your hospitality."

Miranda offered her hand to the lieutenant; he took it, but then, to her secret amusement, he bowed low over it instead of shaking it. "I hope you and your men have an easy journey back to Fort Cummings, Lieutenant."

Manolo excused himself shortly after the women left the room. "Do you know anything about a gang of renegades operating from across the border, Lieutenant?" Jesse asked quietly as he refilled the younger man's brandy glass.

Lieutenant Riddle tore his wistful gaze away from the doorway through which Miranda Hart had vanished and looked at the hard face of the man now seated across from him. "Leyba's gang? Oh, the army knows about them, Mr. McClintock," he said wryly. "There just isn't much we can do about them unless we can catch them on this side of the border. Unfortunately our treaty with Mexico only allows us to cross the border after Apaches, not murdering—" The young lieutenant used a word that wouldn't have been acceptable in Philadelphia.

"What about the Mexican army?" Jesse knew the question was naive even as he asked it.

Lieutenant Riddle's short laugh was more resigned than disgusted. "When the Mexican soldiers aren't busy fighting one another during their monthly revolution, they've got their hands full with the Apaches. Once Geronimo is back on the reservation, though, we'll be able to patrol the border more heavily and catch Leyba ourselves." He swallowed more brandy, wishing that he'd asked for that milk, after all. Setting down the glass, he frowned absently. "It's funny you mentioned Leyba. We just got a report that he and his gang robbed a bank in Mexico and got away with a thousand brand-new gold pesos, fresh from the mint."

Chapter Ten

Jesse stepped around the corner of the barn and out of the cold wind whistling up the canyon. The day was clear but blustery, as the weather had been since the storm that had come with the army patrol a week ago. Here on the lee side of the barn, the sun shone with more heat, and Tommy had found a small pocket of warmth to play in. He crouched beside the little boy kneeling in the dirt. "What are you playing, Tommy?"

"Ranch."

Jesse grinned at his one-word answer. "Ranch," he guessed, was the male equivalent of the "house" he remembered his sisters playing when they were little girls. Instead of dollies and tea parties, Tommy had cattle and roundups. None of his playthings were store bought, but were made of bits of trash and other unwanted items that he'd gathered and, with imagination, turned into toys better than any money could buy. His cattle were hard little winter apples, ones that had been too small to bother picking, so they'd been left on the tree. With their wizened skins and dark red color, it wasn't too hard for a little boy to see them as a herd of Herefords. He'd constructed corrals out of twigs and had his "herd" sorted according to size. Without being told, Jesse knew the small ones were the yearling calves, ready for branding, the middle-sized ones were the cows, and in one corral, all alone, was the bull—the biggest apple. In a tiny fire nearby, his branding irons were heating—several rusty bent nails he'd found lying around.

Tommy cut out a calf and reached for a branding iron. Cautiously he pinched the pointed end of the nail to make sure it wasn't too hot, then picked it up and applied the heated head. The apple skin smoked with a satisfying sizzle; then he turned the calf loose into the middle corral to find its mother. "What's your brand, Jesse?" he asked.

"My brother and I use *MC*," he answered as he watched Tommy brand another apple. He had told Tommy about Josh and their ranch in Montana. He'd wondered several times if Tommy had told his mother. Picking up a stick, he sketched a capital *M* with a *C* dangling off the right leg in the soft dirt. "Like this. See? We figured it would be hard for rustlers to burn over it with a running iron."

Tommy studied it, then nodded his sober agreement. "I wanted to make a different brand, but I couldn't bend the nails," he said with a sigh, and burned a circle on another calf.

Jesse picked up a loose nail lying in the dirt and straightened it with a quick twist of his fingers. Then he gave the pointed end a couple of bends and handed it to Tommy. "How about this?"

Tommy examined the nail with the point bent into the shape of a capital *T*, then gave Jesse a delighted grin. "Gosh, Jesse, thanks!" He immediately took all the other irons out of the fire, carefully placed the new one in the middle and added a small chunk of bark to build up the flames. Sitting back on his heels to wait for it to heat, he saw Jesse pick up the object beside the corral holding his bull. "That's the chuck wagon," he informed him.

"That's what I figured it was," Jesse said seriously, hiding a smile. The chuck wagon was an old cracker tin with holes punched low on opposite sides from each other. Wire ran through the holes for axles, and four empty wooden sewing spools had been threaded onto the tin for wheels. The ends of the wire had been bent into hubs to hold the wheels on, and when Jesse ran it on the ground for a few inches, it rolled right along. The toy was simple but cleverly made, and Jesse suspected it was Miranda's hands that had fashioned it.

Tommy's next words confirmed it. "Mama made it for me," he said proudly, then frowned. "But we never could figure out how to make good horses. We tried tying straw into horse shapes, but they kept falling apart. I tried the horses from my soldier set, but they were too small."

Jesse looked at the empty traces made out of twine and tied through two more holes punched in the end of the tin. Idly he estimated the size the toy horses would have to be to be in proportion to the wagon. His glance wandered to the stack of soft cottonwood that had been cut into stove lengths and stacked against the wall of the barn.

Tommy opened the back of the chuck wagon by taking the lid off the tin. "Dinnertime," he announced, and pulled out two apples and a fistful of cookies. He divided the cookies into two equal piles, then stared thoughtfully at the one left over. He peeked at

Jesse and saw that he was watching, so he broke the cookie in two instead of slipping it into his pile.

Gravely Jesse accepted an apple and his share of the scrupulously divided cookies.

Tommy munched happily in silence for a few seconds, then asked a question that had been uppermost in his mind for a week. "Jesse, can we go to town soon and look for my pony?"

Jesse looked down at the hopeful little face and felt a sharp pang of guilt. A month ago he had promised that they would go to town and look for a pony within a couple of weeks. The deadline had come and gone, but instinctively Tommy had seemed to understand that the roundup took precedence over everything else and said nothing. But the roundup was finished now, and Jesse suspected Tommy's patience had about run out. "How about tomorrow?" he decided.

Tommy's eyes lit with incredulous joy. He flung his arms around the man who had just granted his fondest wish and gave him a smacking kiss. "You mean it, Jesse? Really? Tomorrow?"

Jesse's arms closed automatically around the little boy to hold him still. "Tomorrow," he confirmed, then qualified it. "If your mother says yes. And Tommy," he cautioned, "just because we're going to town doesn't mean that we'll find a pony. There may not be any we want, or even any for sale."

"Mama will say yes," the boy said with absolute conviction, and didn't even bother to comment on the ridiculous idea that there might be no pony. When they got to town, there would *be* a pony.

Jesse smiled at Tommy's snaggle-tooth grin of supreme confidence. "I'm sure she will," he agreed. Unconsciously his hold tightened on the warm, sturdy little boy in his arms. The boy was intelligent, fine looking, strong and healthy, good-natured—in short, everything a man could hope for in a son. Whatever his parentage, how could Hart not have wanted him?

Remembering suddenly that men didn't do sissy stuff like hugging and kissing, especially a man with a horse of his own, Tommy squirmed out of the arms that held him. To cover his embarrassment, he slapped a brand on a couple of cows with his new iron and began thinking of good pony names.

Absently Jesse noted the holes in the knees of Tommy's black stockings as he crawled around in the dirt, playing with his horseless chuck wagon. Short pants and stockings were stupid clothes for a little boy, he decided. He'd had to wear them, too, when he was small, and he could still remember the seemingly permanent scabs on his knees and scrubbing off what little skin was left trying to get out the ground-in dirt. While they were looking for a pony tomorrow, they'd look for some long pants, too.

He heard a sound behind him and turned around to see Tyree coming out of the barn.

Tyree lit a cheroot as Jesse joined him. He squinted through the smoke from his cigar at the little boy playing in the dirt. "Short pants are the wrong thing for a little boy," he said.

Jesse bit off the end of the cigar Tyree gave him and lit it. "That's what I was just thinking."

Tyree glanced at the man next to him as he took a long draw on his cigar. "A man could do worse than a boy like that and a woman like his mother."

Jesse grunted noncommittally and changed the subject. "I think I'll go into town tomorrow, give the men a couple of days off, too."

Tyree nodded and looked down at the cheroot he held in his hand. "Good. I'm about out of cigars."

They smoked in silence for a minute or two; then Jesse asked casually, "Is that job still waiting for you in Tucson?" He knew the sixty dollars a month Tyree was earning here, although top wages for a cowhand, were only pocket money compared to what he usually earned.

Tyree puffed unconcernedly. "Probably not."

Jesse studied the glowing tip of his cigar. He knew why Tyree had taken a job that was far beneath his skills, why he hadn't moved on to one that wasn't. Tyree felt he owed it to him, because if he hadn't left Silver City when he did two months ago, Jesse wouldn't be here now. What had happened to him was pure, simple bad luck, Jesse knew. It had in no way been Tyree's fault, but he understood why Tyree considered himself responsible, because if the situation were reversed, he would feel exactly the same way. He would do exactly what Tyree had done and feel obligated to stay. "I don't imagine it would take you long to find another one, though."

Tyree stared at the fine Hereford bull in the corral across the way. No, it wouldn't, he agreed silently. In fact, he wouldn't even have to look. The job would find him. He turned slowly to face the only man he had ever trusted enough to call friend. "You firing me, Jesse Mack?" he inquired mildly.

Jesse met Tyree's cool green stare. "No. But there's no reason for you to think you have to stay," he said evenly.

Tyree took a long look around him. "A man needs a place to spend the winter," he said with a shrug. "This looks like as good a place as any."

* * *

It was a sign of the degree to which she was bored, Miranda thought, when she envied someone the chance to do laundry. From the window in her bedroom, where she'd been involved in the vital task of rearranging her dresser drawers, she watched young Kwon drape another sheet over the clothesline. Doing the laundry was a job she had at best detested, but right now stirring up a caldron of boiling clothes or skinning her knuckles on a scrub board sounded like heaven. Doing anything sounded like heaven compared to doing nothing, which was what she had been doing for the past week. The highlight of the past seven days had been dusting her piano.

She turned away from the window before the temptation overcame her to run out to Kwon and offer to pay him to let *her* hang up the clothes. Even a week ago, there had been little enough for her to do. There was nothing left in the garden or orchard to preserve, Kwon did the laundry now, Paco and Ramón were taking care of most of the livestock, and Leola had taken over nearly all the cooking and cleaning, but at least she had been able to gather eggs, feed the hens and chicks and milk Bessie if she wanted to. There was no need for her to do even that much, but, never having had a pet as a child, she enjoyed the contact with the animals, especially sweet-natured old Bessie.

Then one morning last week Ramón had gently taken the egg basket out of her hand in the barn and informed her with great courtesy that gathering eggs was his job from now on. When she had asked him who had assigned him that task, he had informed her that Señor McClintock had. Later that morning she had been reaching for the sack of chicken feed, when Paco had practically run her down to get to it first. Upon inquiry, she had learned that it was Señor Jesse who had decreed that her hand should not touch chicken mash. When Mr. Penny had come in with a full milk pail that afternoon, she hadn't bothered to ask who had told him to milk Bessie. She already knew.

She had thought that she would at least be able to putter about in the kitchen, but now Leola shooed her out every time she so much as put her toe across the threshold. She couldn't even make her own tea! She appreciated everyone's concern for her "delicate condition," but if they didn't let her do something, she was going to go completely daft! Miranda took her frustration out on a dresser drawer. The resultant slam was satisfying but hardly a solution to her problem.

Wrapping a shawl around her shoulders, she went out onto the back porch. Pulling her shawl tighter against the blustery breeze, she walked the length of the porch to the side of the house. Out of the wind, she sat down on a sunny bench. Now that her daily temper tantrum was out of the way, she could consider her problem rationally. And there was a problem, she admitted, sobering. She wasn't carrying the baby well, and Leola had told her bluntly that if she wasn't very careful, she could go into labor prematurely. Her pregnancy was far enough along that the baby might survive, but Leola wouldn't guarantee it. As if to punctuate her thought, Miranda felt a solid kick to her ribs. With a wry laugh, she rubbed her hand soothingly over her swollen abdomen. And so, as much as she longed for her pregnancy to be over, to hold her baby in her arms, she would put her feet up at every opportunity, take a nap in the afternoon, drink the noxious concoctions Leola pressed on her hourly and do nothing more strenuous than lift a teacup. Leaning back against the wall, she closed her eyes and turned her face up to the sun. She would even, she thought with a smile, suffer bossy kite flyers.

She was almost asleep, when the sound of laughter teased her back to wakefulness. The high-pitched giggle belonged to Tommy, and even while she was still more asleep than awake, she'd known the owner of the deep masculine chuckle. Sitting forward, she spotted the two of them over near the corrals and laughed herself. Tommy was beside Jesse, trying manfully to match him stride for stride. It was hopeless, of course. For one thing, his legs were about two feet too short, and for another, he hadn't mastered the walk. Miranda sighed unconsciously as she stood up to keep them in sight. Quite probably he never would. She suspected that lazy, long-legged, loose-hipped saunter was unique.

As usual, Tommy was talking nineteen to the dozen. All week the tall man had rarely been without his three-foot shadow, yet Jesse never showed any sign that he was tired of Tommy trailing around after him with his seemingly inexhaustible supply of questions. He was kind and patient with the little boy, giving him the male attention he so desperately needed. Tommy was a normal, happy little boy now, finally free of the fearful memories that had kept him trapped in unhappiness for so long. For that alone, Miranda knew she owed Jesse McClintock a debt she could never repay.

The minor-key notes that softly filled the shadows in the parlor hours later reflected her still pensive mood. Her fingers wandered over the ivory keys of the grand piano, finding their own music, as her thoughts wandered over the changes in her life and Tommy's since she'd met a tall stranger wearing handcuffs in Willis's parlor. The changes had been good ones, happy ones—yet she had never been less sure of her own emotions, felt less in control of them, than she did now. . . .

Jesse didn't know how long he had been standing in the shadows. A few minutes could have passed, or an hour. He had come to discuss the question of a pony for Tommy, when the music and the picture of her at the piano had arrested him at the door.

The only light in the room came from the single candle burning in the silver candelabra on top of the piano. The small pool of light illuminated both her face and her slim, elegant hands moving surely over the keys. In the soft candle glow, her skin took on a pearly luminescense that added an otherworldly quality to her beauty.

Whatever she was playing was quiet and dreamy, almost melancholy, like her expression, yet beneath the peacefulness he detected turmoil. There was no sheet music in sight. Was she playing from memory? Or her mood?

Miranda suddenly sensed that she wasn't alone. As she glanced toward the door, her hands paused on the keys. A shadow detached itself from the rest and came slowly toward her, but she felt no fear. She had known who it was when she'd felt the tiny tingle of awareness.

Wordlessly, Jesse gestured for her to continue. For a few moments after her fingers found their place in the melody, she continued to look at him; then she turned her attention to the piano. A few minutes later the last note faded into silence, and her hands rested in her lap.

Jesse waited until his voice wouldn't seem to be such an intrusion. "You play beautifully," he said quietly. "Is it your own composition?"

"Chopin's," Miranda said with a faint smile, "and thank you." Rising, she picked up the candelabra and carried it across the parlor. With the candle, she lit the lamp on the table between the two love seats and indicated that he should sit down.

The bright lamp banished the shadows to the corners of the room, yet a mood of intimacy seemed to linger that kept their voices low. "I expect you want to talk to me about a pony," Miranda said with a smile as he sat down across from her.

He gave her a rueful grin. "I didn't think Tommy would be able to keep it a secret." Jesse had purposely not brought the subject up at dinner because, in case she refused, he wanted to change her mind out of Tommy's hearing.

Miranda laughed softly. "He's so excited, he could hardly go to sleep. I finally had to threaten that if he didn't, he couldn't go with you tomorrow." Her smile faded into a worried frown. "Do you think you'll be able to find one?"

"I think so. I noticed Ruebush had a couple for sale the last time I was in town."

Miranda took a small purse out of the pocket of her dress and counted out several ten-dollar gold pieces, then laid the money on the table between them. "Will that be enough, do you think?" When he didn't immediately answer, she added, "I can give you more. The money's not a problem."

Jesse stared stupidly at the gold coins. Until she had put them on the table, he hadn't consciously thought about who would pay for the pony. Now he realized that unconsciously he had been planning to. He wanted to be the one who gave Tommy his first horse. "Uh, no." Dragging his eyes away from the money, he looked at her. "No, that's more than enough to buy a pony." He forced himself to pick up the coins and tuck them in a pocket in his vest.

"Well, if you're sure."

"I'm sure," he growled.

Miranda eyed him, at a loss to explain his sudden change in mood. Somehow she had offended him, but for the life of her, she couldn't figure out how. All she had done was give him the money to pay for Tommy's pony.

"Tommy needs long pants," he said suddenly. "I'll pay for them myself."

He said it as if he were daring her to disagree. "I—all right. That's very nice of you. I guess short pants for someone who spends half his time on his knees in the dirt aren't very sensible," she said with a weak attempt at humor. The fierce expression on his face didn't change. "But, then, I don't know very much about small boys," she mumbled, glancing away from him as she rubbed at the sudden dull ache over her right eyebrow.

Jesse didn't miss the gesture or the small grimace of pain. "That's all right. Neither do I," he said softly.

Miranda sensed that his mood had suddenly changed again. She smiled hesitantly. "At least you *were* one."

"Yeah." Jesse looked away before he became lost in her eyes. In the lamplight they looked darker, almost violet. He stood up in a sudden, almost violent rush. "Well, I'll see you in the morning," he said abruptly.

Peculiar moods and all, Miranda realized that she had enjoyed this time with him, and that she wasn't ready for it to end quite yet. "Are you giving the men time off to go to town, too?"

Jesse debated the wisdom of sitting back down and did it anyway. "Tomorrow and the next day. It'll probably be the last time for a long while. The weather's bound to turn sooner or later."

Miranda nodded. It was already the middle of November, and they had yet to see their first snowfall. "Are you keeping all the men on?" Surely she could think of something more interesting to talk about than the employment situation.

"They're all staying. We're going to have to winter the remuda here in the canyon, so we'll have to build extra corrals." After the Apache attack, he had decided against wintering the remuda in the isolated canyon Charlie had found. "There's firewood to gather, and the barn needs some repairs." He shrugged. "There's more than enough work for all of them." Christ! Surely he could find something better to talk about than how he was going to keep ten men busy all winter.

"None of that is work that can be done from a horse."

He caught the teasing laughter in her eyes. "No, it isn't," he agreed with a reluctant laugh. "But it beats riding the grub line." It was an old joke that a cowboy would do anything—as long as it could be done from the back of a horse. But when two out of three hands were laid off every winter and forced to ride from ranch to ranch, hoping to cadge a free meal and a warm place to sleep, most men were willing to swallow their pride and put a little wear on their boots if it meant a steady job.

"It—" A yawn caught her by surprise.

Jesse was on his feet immediately and reaching out a hand to help her to hers. "You should have been in bed an hour ago." His tone was gruffly gentle.

"I know." After smothering another yawn, she gave him a sleepy grin. Neither of them seemed to notice that she was on her feet so he didn't need to hold her hand any longer.

He drew her around the table until she was standing in front of him. "Is there anything you want from town?" he asked absently. She was practically asleep on her feet. Her eyes were almost too heavy for her to keep open, and her soft mouth wore a sweetly sleepy smile.

"No, nothing," she murmured absently. She didn't know where the thought came from, but suddenly it seemed perfectly natural that he should kiss her good-night. She closed her eyes and waited patiently, but she couldn't be sure if the light brush she felt over her temple was his mouth, or just her imagination, any more than she could be certain she hadn't imagined the whispered words she heard next.

"Good night, Miranda. Sleep well."

When she opened her eyes, he was gone.

Frank Penny felt an almost uncontrollable urge to rip the flimsy door off its hinges. He was certain he had seen the rag curtain over the small dirty window move. Finally he decided that if the Chinese whore didn't want his money, there were plenty of others who did, and he started back up the alley that stank of emptied slop jars and hopelessness.

"Lookin' for a little fun, cowboy?"

The whore was leaning in the doorway of a narrow shack across the alley. She had posed herself so that the dim light from the room behind her shone through her cheap cotton chemise. It limned sagging breasts, flabby hips and the roll of fat around her waist.

Penny skirted the greasy-looking puddle in front of her door. "How much?" he asked abruptly.

"Four bits." She named her price with just a hint of question in her rotgut-roughened voice, as if she would be willing to settle for less.

Penny shut the door behind him.

The whore held out her grimy hand. "In advance."

Wordlessly Penny flipped her fifty cents, and the whore turned to secrete it in a stained leather pouch hanging beside the bed. The pouch was the only decoration on the tar-paper walls. The only furniture was a rusted iron bedstead and an upended packing crate supporting a chimneyless kerosene lamp.

Turning back, the whore pulled the chemise over her head. "Now for the fun, cowboy," she said in a listless voice.

She had passed from hand to hand as often as the dirty coins that bought her. Her spongy drooping body was the same color as the underbelly of a fish. Her face was splotchy and swollen, her teeth were rotting and she smelled of stale sweat and puke, but in his mind Penny gave her silky auburn hair, lavender eyes, a beautiful smile and the sweet scent of flowers. "Yes," he said, undoing the big buckle and drawing his belt from around his waist. "Now for the fun."

An hour later, he was back in the alley. It had been better with the Chinese whore, he decided objectively as he walked toward the lighter mouth of the dark alley. He was thinking about finding a poker game, when what felt like an iron fist struck him in the back and his face slammed into the splintery siding on a building five feet away. Before he could orient himself, the iron fist struck again on the side of his head, and he was facedown on the ground, choking in mud and foul water as he gasped for breath. Hands

hauled him up, and he had a glimpse of a human fist coming at him
before lightning exploded in his head and he was on the ground
again. Something hot and wet was running down his chin, and he
dimly understood that his nose had split. He fumbled for his gun
before he remembered that it was back in his hotel room. The
wearing of sidearms is forbidden in town.

He was dragged up again, and that was when he realized that
there were two of them. A huge shadow danced in front of him
while his arms were jerked behind him until it felt as though they
were ripping out of their sockets. He sensed that the man holding
his arms was stockier than he was, but no taller. Clamping his teeth
down on the tearing agony in his shoulders, he let himself hang
limp as a rag doll. The shadow came closer, its arms raised.
Watching through slitted eyes, Penny waited until the shadow was
less than three feet away; then he lashed out with his feet.

One boot struck soft, unprotected flesh, and the shadow
dropped with a strangled cry. Surprise caused the man behind him
to momentarily loosen his grip. Penny was expecting it and took
immediate advantage. He bent double, then drove his body up and
back. His head snapped back, smashing the chin of the man behind him, and his arms were suddenly free.

Fumbling at his waist as he turned, Penny pulled a belly gun free
of his pants. The kind favored by whores and gamblers, the derringer held a single .22 caliber bullet. He emptied it at point-blank
range into the face of the man rising up from the mud. The man
made a small squeak, fell onto his knees in a macabre pantomime
of prayer, then toppled forward, burying his ruined face in the
mud.

Penny staggered around to find his other attacker writhing on the
ground, his hands between his legs, and mewling softly. The man's
eyes were open, and they widened when he saw Penny. They bulged
when they saw the descending heel of a boot. The mewling
stopped. Twice more Penny drove his heel into the man's throat.
One arm jerked away from his body as his eyes began to glaze over.
His fingers scrabbled briefly in the dirt, then went still.

Penny turned the man's face toward what light there was. The
man was Chinese. Crossing back across the alley, he bent to examine the other dead man. Most of the back of his head was blown
away, but dangling beneath the pink ooze was a long, thin braid.
Both men were Chinese.

Automatically he reloaded the belly gun and tucked it back into
its hiding place. Then he walked unhurriedly toward the street. The
fight hadn't attracted any attention, he was sure. The derringer
didn't make much noise, and nobody had come down the alley or

out of any of the cribs. Pausing at the alley entrance, he checked the street as a precaution anyway. There were people around, but he didn't hear any shouts or see anyone running toward the alley. It dead-ended at the back of a saloon, so he knew he didn't have to worry about trouble from that direction, either. The bodies would be found sooner or later, but there was nothing to connect them to him.

Stepping up onto the boardwalk, he strolled casually to the nearest watering trough. With his scarf he washed off the dried blood on his face and neck, then touched his nose gingerly. It felt twice its normal size and hurt like hell. He knew his face was scratched, and both his eyes were probably already turning black, but he'd been hurt worse.

The saloon door a few feet away swung open, spilling noise, bright light and two happy drunks out onto the boardwalk. Quickly he examined his clothes before the door swung shut and cut off the light. His vest, pants and shirt sleeves were covered with stinking mud. Using his scarf again, he scrubbed off as much as he could, until the cold breeze cutting through his clammy clothes convinced him he was clean enough.

The saloon door swung open again, and he looked inside. With a glance he saw that it was a bucket shop, the cheapest kind of saloon, serving watered-down rotgut and flat beer. Ordinarily he wouldn't set foot in a place like that—it reminded him of the places his mother had hung around—but tonight it suited his needs. He wasn't likely to run into anyone from the Silver Tejo, and nobody else would notice that he was dirty or had been in a fight.

Penny elbowed a place at the end of the crowded bar and shouted for a whiskey. After a short wait a bartender wearing a dirty apron around his fat belly slapped a shot glass down in front of him, poured it half-full and grabbed up his dime. Penny downed the shot and called for another. While he waited for the bartender to waddle his way, he tried to figure out why the two Chinese had attacked him. Briefly he considered the possibility that the attack might have been directed at him specifically, revenge for the Chinese whore, then dismissed it. Even if she had been in her crib and seen him, who would bother to avenge a whore? They got no more than they deserved. The two men had just been looking for a drunk to roll, he finally decided, then laughed to himself. It was just their bad luck that they hadn't found one.

Reaction to his narrow escape began to set in, and he felt himself shaking. His body and head ached, and still the damn bartender hadn't come. He yelled again, and the man finally came, cursing. He poured another drink, slopping it so that the glass was even less than half-full this time, and took another dime. Penny gestured for him to leave the bottle, but he was already turning away to shout obscenities down the bar at another impatient customer.

"Can I buy you a drink, *amigo*?"

The voice sounded like the rasp of scales over sand. Frank Penny turned his head slowly to look at the man beside him. His first thought was that he was the meanest looking son of a bitch he'd ever seen. His second was that the man's reptilian appearance matched his voice. Smooth eyelids slid down over small bright black eyes when he blinked, which Penny suspected wasn't often. A narrow tongue darted out to wet very thin lips, and he was vaguely surprised when it was pointed, not forked. His nose was long, also very thin, and sharp. His face was more of the same, with the addition of the worst smallpox scars Penny had ever seen. His hair was black, not thick, and cut so that it lay close to his skull. "*¿Cómo no?*" he said, automatically answering the question in Spanish, the language the stranger had asked it in, a language Penny spoke almost as well as English. He didn't like the faint tremor he heard in his own voice, so he repeated his answer, stronger this time, in English. "Sure, why not?"

"Why don't we sit down?"

The stranger led him to one of a few small tables at the back of the saloon. Then he produced a bottle, not of the rotgut the saloon sold that tasted like horse piss, but a bottle of golden, aged tequila. After the first few swallows had slid like honey down Frank's throat, the stranger's soft voice no longer sounded like a hiss, and he forgot to wonder why the man had picked him out of the crowd at the bar. Covertly he studied him. He was no taller than him, and thinner, almost slight, and dressed like a rider, although his hat was the flat-crowned Spanish style. He spoke Spanish like a native, too, but from his lack of the usual mustache and other facial hair, Frank guessed that the man was most likely a half-breed. Mexican and half Yaqui probably, he decided as he took another drink.

Leyba counted it his greatest talent that he could sum up a man's strengths and weaknesses at a glance. He tipped another drink into the *gringo*'s glass. Especially his weaknesses.

The *gringo* had interested him as soon as he had come through the door. Studying him from across the room, Leyba had seen a man who was afraid of almost everything, but not a coward. He had been in a fight, and the odds had been against him, but he had won. He knew that because, although the *gringo*'s face was battered, his knuckles were not burst or even bruised, indicating that one man had held him while at least one other had hit him. If it had been only one man, even a coward would have had the natural instinct to throw up his hands to protect his face and would have sustained some injury to them. He discounted the possibility that the *gringo* had been knocked unconscious, then beaten, because the beating would not logically have stopped with only a broken nose. His lips would be split, also the skin over his cheekbones, and most likely his jaw would be broken. None of that had happened, and from the air of self-satisfaction about the man, he had prevented it from happening himself.

He filled the *gringo*'s glass again, while his own drink remained untouched. "The woman over at the bar, in the red dress," he murmured. "She is pretty, no?"

Frank's glance slid over the small woman with milk-white skin, delicate features, soft black hair and big dark eyes. "She's a whore," he muttered.

"Ah, my friend, are not all women?" Leyba laughed and saluted the *gringo* with his glass. Another weakness. The *gringo* muttered his agreement and gulped down his tequila. Leyba set down his own glass, still full, and reached for the bottle again. His eyes strayed to the woman in red. He would remember her for later.

He looked at the *gringo*'s hat on the table. "I have been admiring your hatband, *amigo*. Jaguar, is it not? There are many of them down along the border. You are from around here, then?" he asked casually.

"The Silver Tejo," Frank mumbled, and emptied his glass again. He appreciated the fact that the stranger was not stingy with his liquor. His opinion of the man rose as the level in the bottle lowered.

Leyba's hand convulsed on the bottle. The Silver Tejo! He could not believe his luck. He had long coveted the riches of the Silver Tejo, but the ranch was too well defended for him to take more than a few stray cattle. What he had finally decided he needed was a man on the inside of those high adobe walls, and he knew, with absolute certainty, that he had just found him. Without thinking, he picked up his glass and drained it. Still, he would have to be very careful, play this man like a hungry fish, tease him with the worm, then finally let him take it, and the fish would hook himself. "I have heard of it," he said thoughtfully. "You are the foreman?" Leyba already knew that he was not, but he was curious to see if the *gringo* would lie.

"No, I am the *segundo*. A man named McClintock is the foreman." Second-in-command on a ranch as big and rich as the Silver Tejo was as important a job as that of foreman on a smaller ranch. Frank wondered if he should tell the stranger that.

Leyba nodded. The *gringo*'s answer showed intelligence. He didn't doubt that the man would lie, but it wouldn't be a stupid lie that could easily be found out. He liked his men to have intelligence. And ambition—although a moderate amount of both was best. He didn't want someone questioning his decisions, and he didn't want to find a bullet in his back someday. "I think I heard someone mention this McClintock. He was captured by the Apaches, no? Tied up and wounded, and still he managed to escape." He repeated the gist of a story he had overheard earlier. "And he killed some, no? How many did they say... two? Or was it three? A man with *huevos*." He slanted a look at the other man. It was possible he had some loyalty to or liking for this McClintock.

"Four," Frank admitted grudgingly. He had *huevos*—balls—too. "He shot two of them, though. He got a gun."

"Then he must have killed two with his bare hands. *Huevos con huevos*," Leyba murmured, pushing a little harder.

"Other men have *huevos*," Penny muttered. He didn't like the turn the conversation had taken suddenly, and the stranger hadn't refilled his glass for several minutes.

"The Silver Tejo. I hear it is owned by a woman, a widow. She is old and ugly, no?" Leyba asked idly, stalling for a little time to think in what direction to push next. He filled the *gringo*'s glass; then, out of unconscious habit, he took a coin out of his pants pocket and began tapping it on the table.

"She is old and ugly, no. She is young and very beautiful," Frank said, pleased with himself at his little joke. The stranger laughed appreciatively as Frank picked up his glass. He set it down again, empty, and noticed the coin in the stranger's fingers. It was a gold ten-peso piece. The sight of a peso didn't surprise him—this close to the border, Mexican money was accepted as readily as American—but the peso looked brand-new, shiny, with none of the nicks and scratches a coin acquired in circulation, and it reminded him of something, something he felt it was very important that he remember.

His glass was full again, but he ignored it, thinking hard. Was it that he had seen another coin like that recently? No... it was a something about a bank robbery... something one of the soldiers had said when they'd stayed at the ranch last week....

When he remembered all of it, he felt as he had in the alley when the iron fist had struck him. Slowly he reached for the glass in front of him and drained it in one swallow. The soldier had said the band had been robbed by the gang of renegades led by a man named Leyba, a Mexican 'breed. It was Leyba's gang that Baxter thought had fired the sheep rancher's homestead, too, he remembered absently. Could it be that this was the man himself? No doubt there was a price on his head, a reward for his capture. Unconsciously his hand went to the small bulge the belly gun made under his belt. Dead or alive. The reward would probably be a big one, maybe enough to buy a little place, start a herd.... The vision in his head, though, wasn't of a small ranch house and a few cattle. Instead he saw all the times he had had success in his grasp, only to have it snatched away, all the times he'd been cheated out of what he deserved. The ugly horse face of Martha Yount gradually dissolved into one with beautiful lavender eyes and a sweet gentle smile.

His hand moved away from his waist. "There's a mine on the ranch, too," he said carelessly. "Silver. The widow ships a load of it every few months to the mint in San Francisco."

"There are guards, no doubt, and no regular schedule for the shipments." Leyba's casual tone matched his.

He nodded. "Still, it wouldn't be hard to take the silver when it's on its way to Deming. Usually there are only two guards and the driver of the wagon."

"If one knew when the silver was being shipped," Leyba pointed out.

"If one knew," he agreed.

Absently Leyba toyed with the coin. Perhaps he wasn't the only one fishing. Intrigued, he studied the man across the table. The man met his gaze, and he saw excitement, greed...and fear. Could it be that he knew who he was? It didn't seem possible. It was a matter of pride that he always made sure there was no one who could identify him. He dangled the worm to see if the fish would bite. "How would one find out when the silver was being shipped?"

"Someone who worked on the Silver Tejo, someone who could find out when the silver was to be shipped, would tell him."

He felt a strong tug on the line. "Such a man might also be able to find out if the rumor is true that the widow's husband hid much silver before he died. It is supposed to be buried in a tunnel under the house."

Frank could feel the sweat running down his back as the black eyes focused steadily on him. He forced himself not to look away. "Such a man could."

"Even if it is there, it would be no easy thing to get it. The gates guarding it are always closed, and they are high and strong."

Frank licked his dry lips. "The gates would be open."

Leyba prepared to set the hook. "Still, there would be the guards," he said.

"The guards would not be a problem," Frank said deliberately.

Leyba kept his smile of satisfaction to himself. A man with a conscience was of no use to him. The fish was securely hooked. He tossed the gold piece up in the air. "What would such a man want for doing all this?"

Frank reached out and grabbed the gold coin on its descent. "Why don't we find a quieter place to talk, and I'll tell you Señor Leyba?"

The black snake eyes went utterly blank and cold, and Frank Penny wondered if he had made a fatal mistake. Then the thin slit of a mouth opened, and words hissed out softly. "*Sí, amigo.* As you say. Let us talk."

Chapter Eleven

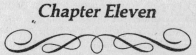

Hello, cat." Miranda spoke softly as she looked up at a granite boulder that had rolled down from the canyon rim at some long forgotten time in the past and stuck before reaching the bottom. On top of the huge rock sat a bobcat, looking down at her. "Would you like something to eat? Hmm? Look what I brought you tonight." She set down a tin plate of meat scraps and backed away. She had seen the bobcat from her window for the first time a week ago in exactly the same spot and watched for him every night since, and each night he had returned, appearing as silently and suddenly as a ghost.

She retreated into the deep shadows at the back of the house and waited. The cat was sitting in a shaft of moonlight, and Miranda could see him as clearly as if he were sitting in a patch of bright sunshine. He was the largest she'd ever seen, a male in his prime. His thick gray fur looked almost silver in the moonlight, speckled with faint black spots. Black bars divided the darker gray fur of his front legs, the gray fading to cream on his broad chest, throat and chin. Thin black lines on his face radiated into a broad cheek ruff, contrasting with his long, elegant white whiskers. His ears stood up, the tips ending in small black tufts.

His yellow eyes gleamed as he turned his head toward her, keeping her in view, she knew, even in the shadows, and for a long time they stared at each other. Then the cat stood up, and she saw his black-tipped bobbed tail as he stretched out his long front legs and arched his back in a lazy stretch. His big front paws kneaded the rock; then he crouched down, his belly hugging the stone. Miranda held her breath. The first night she'd seen him, she'd thrown on some clothes, then dashed into the kitchen for some meat scraps, hoping to entice him closer. She'd had a plate ready every night since, but he always refused to come to it while she was watching, although every morning she had found it empty. Her breath sighed out slowly as suddenly he leaped down and approached. Keeping a wary eye on her, he ate daintily until the plate was clean; then, with a final glance in her direction as if to say thank-you, he turned and disappeared into the night.

Slowly she walked back along the porch circling the house, her felt slippers making no sound on the boards. A tiny foot or fist jabbed her sharply under the breastbone, and Miranda laughed softly. "We can't seem to agree on a bedtime, can we?" she whispered, patting her abdomen gently. The past few nights, the baby had decided it was playtime, not bedtime, which was why she had been up to see the bobcat. She paused at the front door before going in, unconsciously rubbing at the ache that seemed to have settled permanently in the small of her back. The night was dark and cold and quiet, so quiet that she heard the creak of the barn door opening. A tall figure wearing a long coat was briefly outlined against the square of soft yellow light before the door creaked shut. On a whim, she stepped off the porch and headed for the barn.

"What were you doing out, Penny?" Jesse knew his tone was abrupt, but he made no attempt to soften it.

Glancing at the tall man standing just outside the stall, Frank Penny pulled the saddle off his dun mare. "I was just checking on the remuda," he said neutrally. "Saw some cougar sign over there this morning. I thought it might come back tonight, and I didn't want the horses to get spooked and scatter."

Jesse nodded shortly. This morning he'd assigned Penny, Cisco Moreno and his boys the job of moving the remuda to a small box canyon two ridges over until the corrals were finished. There were at least one or two of the big cats in the area, and it was logical that there would be sign in the canyon. "Aren't Shorty and Bill on guard duty over there?" he asked sharply.

"They're there," Frank said quickly as he gave his horse a quick rubdown before McClintock saw how sweated up she was. "I just wanted to take a look up top." He'd had to ride hard to make the meet with Leyba, then harder yet to get back before his absence caused comment.

"Did you see anything?"

Frank stepped out of the box. "I didn't see anything tonight, but it probably wouldn't be a bad idea to keep checking." It would give him an excuse to be out again.

"How about Bill and Shorty? They see anything?"

Frank gave an easy shrug. "I didn't ride down to find out." It was the truth, he thought smugly, in case McClintock asked the other two men if they'd seen him. "I figured I'd have heard shooting if they had."

Without responding, Jesse moved down to the last stall. It was a birthing stall, wider and roomier than the others, and its occupant at the moment was a heavily pregnant bay mare.

"I'll stay with her, boss."

Jesse glanced from the mare to Penny, standing a few feet away. "That's all right, Penny. I'll stay. It's her first foal, and I want to be here in case she has any trouble." That was why he had come down to the barn. He'd sensed it was nearly the mare's time by her pacing when he'd checked on the horses after supper.

Frank nodded, turning away. "I'll turn in, then. See you in the morning, boss."

Jesse heard the barn door closing a few seconds later and fought the urge to spit on the floor. Penny left an ugly taste in his mouth. He was almost certain that the man hadn't been out because he was concerned about cougars, but there was no way to prove it. If he was lying, he'd covered himself neatly with that story about not riding down to talk to Bill and Shorty. If he could, he would simply tell the man to draw his time, but in fairness, he couldn't. Penny was a competent hand and caused no trouble, yet he couldn't shake the feeling that the man was trouble, bad trouble.

The mare turned her head and nickered a greeting, and Jesse took off his coat, laying it over one side of the stall. The barn was cool, but the stall was warmed by the mare's heat. She was a fine Thoroughbred, part of the breeding stock Hart had imported from Kentucky. From her restlessness, he was sure she was in the early stages of labor, and if it went like most first foalings, they were both in for a long night. He stepped into the stall and ran a hand along her swollen belly. The skin was stretched as tight as the head of a drum, and beneath his hand, he felt a sudden strong contraction. The horse squealed, as if in surprise. He rubbed his hand soothingly over her, and she settled.

Jesse leaned back against the stall to wait, and his thoughts drifted back to Frank Penny. Penny kept to himself and said nothing about his past, but that wasn't unusual. Often a man worked for a season on a ranch, then left, and nobody had even known his full name. His broken nose had been obvious, and he'd admitted to getting it in a fight in Deming, but he'd been closed mouthed about why or who with. He got along with the other hands well enough, and as much as Jesse hated to admit it, he had been the logical choice as ramrod. There had to be somebody to make decisions when he wasn't around, and since half his crew was from Mexico, it had to be somebody who spoke Spanish as well as English. The only other man who spoke both languages besides himself was Penny. Even Tyree didn't—not that Tyree would have wanted the job, Jesse thought with a wry laugh.

The mare squealed again, and Jesse put a hand to her halter, then led her out of the stall and into the wide aisle that ran down the center of the barn. As he walked her slowly, they passed the old milch cow in her stall. The black-and-white Holstein turned her head to give them a sleepy glance, and Jesse patted the cow's wide rump as they passed by.

"Too bad Bessie can't give you a few pointers, girl," he said to the mare, laughing softly. His laughter died abruptly. That was something else about Penny that made him uneasy about the man. On his own, he had taken on the job of milking Bessie so that Miranda didn't have to. It was a thoughtful gesture, but he wondered if it had just been an excuse for Penny to see her, get close to her. He laughed dryly at himself. Of course it was. Any one of the men would have stumbled all over himself to get close to her, to look on loveliness instead of a cow's behind, to catch a whiff of sweet feminine scent instead of manure. He'd made it a point to be in the kitchen a couple of times when Penny delivered the milk, and there had never been anything suspicious or even remotely objectionable in the man's behavior toward her. He handed over the milk, Miranda thanked him, Penny tipped his hat respectfully and went on his way. Yet once or twice, when Miranda was outside, Penny had watched her with a look that made the short hairs on the back of Jesse's neck stand up. It was the look of a fox—hungry, greedy and sly—spying a juicy young hen. But you can't fire a man for looking, he reminded himself, and maybe the reason you don't like him doing the milking is because you wish you'd thought of it first.

The mare snorted and suddenly stopped short. Legs stiff, she stood with her head down until the contraction passed. Jesse patted the glossy hide covering her long neck. "This isn't much fun for you, is it, girl?" he said in sympathy. The mare raised her head and rolled her eyes as if in agreement. Tugging on the halter, he started her up the aisle again. When they reached the birthing stall, the horse plodded in on her own and lay down with a heavy sigh.

Jesse made himself comfortable on the clean straw close by and leaned his head back against the side of the stall. Absently he looked around him. Lit only by the lantern hanging on a nail across the way, the big barn was full of shadows. He heard the small rustlings and quiet snores of the sleeping animals and a small squeak that ended abruptly as one of the barn cats caught a midnight snack. The air was rich with the smells of warm, living animals.

Suddenly he closed his eyes and laughed helplessly. This sure as hell wasn't how he had figured to spend his time in New Mexico. After contracting for the cattle he'd come to buy, he had planned to visit some of his old haunts, play a little poker, get drunk a few times, maybe find a warm woman for the cold nights. He hadn't planned to spend his time midwifing a horse.

His laughter fading, he opened his eyes and stared blankly at the other side of the stall. Two months had passed, and he noticed that he hadn't "escaped" as he'd promised himself he would at the first opportunity. He'd made excuses to himself for not leaving, but finally he'd faced the fact that he had no intention of leaving anytime soon. Miranda Hart had taken a chance on him, and he owed her. He felt an odd sense of responsibility for her, and for her son. He couldn't leave until he was sure they were safe.

Jesse shook his head with a sardonic chuckle. At least that was the excuse he was giving himself now. It had disturbed him more than he cared to admit when he had handed over his father's watch to the old judge that it was going to his brother and not his own son. He had been grateful at the time that he had no son who would have to grow up fatherless, no wife to struggle with having to raise a family alone. Yet paradoxically he had been profoundly saddened to realize that all he had to show for thirty-three years of living was . . . no one. He would have left no one behind to mourn him. Oh, Josh would have cared, his mother and sisters, even Ellen a little, but they had others, others they cared about more. There would have been no one who was exclusively his to cry for him. He was alone. He had led a selfish life, living only for himself. He'd whored and caroused, traveled around and worked as he pleased. It had taken a near hanging to show him how empty his life had been. Now he could do something for someone else, something utterly unselfish, wanting nothing for himself.

The rusty hinges of the barn door creaked, and he stood up to see who was coming in. Or was this, he thought as he recognized the person closing the door, the most selfish act of his life to date? Was he staying because he wanted everything?

"Good evening, Mr. McClintock." It seemed odd to call him "Mr. McClintock" when he was always "Jesse" in her thoughts, Miranda mused, but convention and the situation demanded formality between them.

"Good evening." He hadn't been able to call her "Mrs. Hart" for weeks, though he wasn't sure why. Maybe it was because he thought of her as "Miranda" or more and more often—as

"Randy." He hadn't consciously decided on the nickname, but it seemed to fit her somehow. And, although he knew it was dangerously stupid to think so, the private name seemed to make her exclusively... his. The nature of some of those thoughts—especially when she was Randy—made the formality of "Mrs. Hart" absurd. He thought about her too damn much, he sighed inwardly. "What are you doing up so late?" He'd intended the words to be brusque, unwelcoming, but they came out only gently chiding, instead.

"I couldn't sleep," she said absently, staring past him to the mare lying in the straw. "Is Red Lady ready to foal?"

"It'll likely be a few hours yet, but tonight's the night." Under her coat she was wearing the dark wool dress he'd seen her in at supper, but he suspected she'd been in bed, then redressed, because her hair was down, a mass of pillow-mussed curls framing her face and falling past her shoulders. In the lantern light they shone with a dull fire. "You shouldn't come down here alone late at night," he said quietly.

She turned to give him a smile. "I knew you were here. I saw you come in a few minutes ago, right before Mr. Penny left."

He saw the shadow cross her face before she turned back to the mare. "Did he say something rude to you? Make an advance?" he asked in a sharp tone.

She gave him a startled glance. "Oh, no! He's always very polite and respectful. It's just that he...gives me a funny feeling when he looks at me." There was a trace of nervousness in her quick laugh. Miranda thought of the sharp mean line of a mustache above a thin mouth and small ferretlike eyes. "He's never done anything improper," she added hastily when she noticed the hard line of Jesse's mouth. "I'm sure he's a very nice man, and I'm just being silly." She dismissed the subject of Frank Penny for one more pleasant. "Tommy will be so pleased with a new foal."

"Did he go to bed all right tonight?" he asked after a minute. Apparently Miranda also sensed that something wasn't right about Penny, and he resolved to keep a closer watch on the man.

She laughed. "At last, after we had the same argument we did last night about his sleeping with his new pony. I've finally convinced him, I think, that there isn't room for both of them in the same stall and talked him into bed."

He stared after her as she moved into the stall and knelt beside the mare, patting her as she spoke softly. He believed she could get a reluctant little boy into bed, especially when she'd had so much practice in getting older, bigger boys into bed, too. Of course, none of them would have been reluctant, he thought, but the usual bitterness that came whenever he thought of her in the White Swan didn't come tonight. He'd come to terms with her past, he realized, and finally understood how unimportant it was. Sometimes good women found themselves in hard circumstances, forced to make even harder choices in order to survive. He didn't blame her for that, or for taking Hart's offer of a better life for herself and her son. Many women would simply have abandoned a child who would only have been an inconvenient accident, anyway. Whatever she had been before, she was a hard-working, decent woman now, and a kind and loving mother. She deserved his respect and admiration; she'd earned it, the hard way.

She gasped suddenly, and her hand went to her stomach. His hand went immediately to her shoulder. "What's the matter?"

She laughed ruefully as she patted her stomach. "The baby has hiccups, I think."

The mare's sharp hooves lashed out as she struggled to get her feet, and Jesse jerked Miranda back out of danger. "You shouldn't be here," he growled as he went to the mare's head to steady her.

"I'd really like to stay," he heard her say softly behind him. "Perhaps I can help."

"It's a messy business," he warned as he turned the mare and led her back out to the center aisle, where he began to walk her again.

"So Leola tells me," Miranda said under her breath. She walked on the opposite side of the mare, her hand on the horse's shoulder. "You and I are in the same fix, Red Lady," she told the horse wryly.

"When is your baby due?" Her slenderness accentuated the mound under her coat and made it seem as if the birth were imminent, if not already past due. He knew the question was too intimate for a man to ask a woman unless he was a very close relative. Motherhood was considered a woman's most honorable occupation, but pregnancy was treated as something almost shameful. A round belly was tangible proof that a woman had known a man carnally, allowed him to satisfy his lust and low urges with her, a reminder that the pure and noble state of motherhood was achieved only with some sweaty tussling between the sheets. That she might have enjoyed the tussle was unthinkable in the prudery of the times. A woman as a sexual being, Jesse knew, was too disturbing for most people to consider.

If she thought the question improper, she gave no sign of it. "Around Christmas, but every time I catch a glimpse of myself in a mirror, I think I should have had her three months ago. I look bigger than Bessie." She laughed ruefully.

" 'Her'?" he asked with a grin.

Miranda shrugged. "Leola thinks it's a girl. She's generally right."

She paused, and the mare halted automatically beside her. They were stopped before a stall where a small black-and-white pony was asleep on its feet. Miranda smiled unconsciously at the sight of the small saddle thrown over a saw horse just inside the stall. Tommy had named his pony Sam, and he inveigled Jesse into another riding lesson every chance he got. She smiled up at Jesse as he came to stand beside her. "Tommy is so happy with his pony. Thank you for finding him, and for the long pants and boots. It was very nice of you to buy them for him. I think he loves them almost as much as he does Sam."

"A boy can't learn to ride very well without them," he said shortly. It was stupid, he knew, but it still rankled that he hadn't bought the pony for the boy himself. He started to lead the mare on, but Miranda's slim hand on his arm stopped him.

"I know Tommy is pestering you at every opportunity to take him riding. I don't want him to become a nuisance, so if you don't want—"

"He's not a nuisance," Jesse said evenly. "I'm happy to teach him."

"Well—thank you, then. I appreciate it very much."

He nodded abruptly, and they continued walking the mare in silence.

"I guess everyone made it back from town all right?" Miranda asked after they'd made the turn at the door and started back up the aisle.

"They did," Jesse confirmed, then chuckled, "but I think a couple of them still have sore heads."

Miranda savored the sound of his deep laughter. "I expect Cisco romanced as many girls as he could find."

"I don't imagine he had to look too hard," Jesse said, laughing dryly. Cisco Moreno's romantic prowess was already becoming a legend in Deming.

Miranda laughed with him, then said with studied diffidence, "I wonder if Charlie Baxter saw Celia Kershaw." Charlie was fully recuperated now and had made the trip to town with the others.

Jesse slanted a look across Red Lady's back and met Miranda's innocent look with a bland expression of his own. "He might have. I saw him heading over toward the Harvey Hotel after he left the livery stable." Baxter and the little blonde seemed to have some peculiar kind of courtship going on that only the two of them understood. He saw Miranda's small satisfied smile and hid one of his own.

The mare stopped suddenly, grunted and strained. Jesse saw the strong contraction convulsing her belly. "This may not take as long as I thought, girl," he muttered. Red Lady tried to lie down in the aisle, but he urged her back to the birthing stall, instead, and as soon as the horse entered, she collapsed on her left side.

Resting an elbow on the side of the stall, he watched her. Miranda leaned beside him, unconsciously bracing herself against the hard planks to relieve the ache in her back. "You seem to know as much about horses as you do cattle, Mr. McClintock. Manolo told me you doctored his buckskin's sore leg and fixed it right up."

"I learned from an old hand when I was just a green kid." He laughed reminiscently. "Stumpy Bates was his name, and he was so stove up he could hardly walk, but what that man didn't know about horses wasn't worth knowing. We had this horse in the remuda that was crazy about mesquite beans. Every chance he got, he'd find a bush and start eating. The beans won't hurt an animal—in fact, cattle can live on them in drought, and the Indians eat them—but too many will give a horse colic and kill him. So Stumpy picked a mess of beans and put them in a pan with gun powder and kerosene, just a little, not even enough for the horse to taste it. He fed it to the horse, figuring it would give him a bellyache and teach him a lesson, and sure enough that horse had the granddaddy of all bellyaches that night. Stumpy thought he might have to repeat the dose, but the horse was a fast learner. He never went near another mesquite bush." He laughed again at the memory, glancing past her to the mare lying on the floor of the stall.

Miranda's answering smile turned hazy as she became absorbed in the intriguing way his mustache curved when he laughed. Vaguely, she remembered once ordering him to shave it off; now she wondered where such an idiotic idea could have come from. It was thick and dark and framed his straight white teeth and firm bottom lip so perfectly. What would that black bandit mustache feel like, whisking over her own tender flesh? she wondered absently. Would it feel soft and silky like his hair, or would it be rougher, stiffer and tickle a little? Miranda felt suddenly too warm and unbuttoned her coat without thinking about it. And what would that firm, hard-looking mouth feel like against hers? Would it be gentle and tender, coaxing her response—or would he use his lips and tongue and teeth to take what he wanted? The graphic detail of her thoughts shocked her, but not as much as the realization of how much she wanted to know.

"I think it's time."

At his soft murmur, she raised her eyes slowly, still half-lost in her daydream. "Yes," she whispered.

As Jesse spoke, he saw that she was staring at his mouth, a dreamy expression on her face. When she raised her eyes to his, he felt as if he'd caught a fist in the gut. Her eyes were soft and dark and unfocused, and for the first time he saw sensual awareness in them, awareness of him as a man, and desire. On its own, his head bent, he took a step toward her.

Her eyes focused suddenly, and he stepped back quickly as she shook her head hard, as if she were trying to clear it. Her lips parted, and the tip of her tongue touched that crooked tooth.

"I—I'm sorry. What did you say?"

He turned abruptly toward the mare. "I said I think it's time. Red Lady should have her foal anytime now."

Miranda looked on as he knelt beside the mare, talking to her in a low hypnotic murmur as he rubbed her belly. "Easy, girl. You've got a ways to go yet. Are you a little scared this first time? Hmm? I know, it's a little frightening, not knowing what to expect, but everything will be all right. I'll take care of you."

Although he meant the words for the mare, Miranda felt oddly reassured, too.

After several minutes, Red Lady began to pant rapidly, and Miranda could see muscles rippling and straining. "This must be hurting her," she said in a thin voice.

Jesse looked swiftly over her shoulder. Her face was white and tense as she glanced from the horse to him. "She's in a lot of pain, isn't she?" she asked, her voice even more strained than before.

There was genuine concern for the horse in her voice, but he heard the undertone of very real fear, too, and saw it in her shadowed eyes. Briefly his gaze shifted to the swelling beneath her breasts. Her own time was near, and naturally she must have a few fears, even if she'd been through it before. Perhaps Tommy's birth hadn't been an easy one, and this was bringing back frightening memories. "She feels some pain," he allowed, "but probably not as much as you think, and when it's over, she won't remember it. She'll just know she has a fine new baby to take care of."

Her expression said she wasn't convinced. "Why don't you go back to the house? I'll come up later and tell you whether it's a boy or girl," he promised with a faint grin.

Miranda felt her tight face relax a little. "No, I'll stay. Maybe I can help."

Jesse was going to argue, when the mare whinnied loudly. When he looked back at her, she was struggling to her feet, in obvious distress, which he knew wasn't normal. Quickly he examined her.

"What's wrong?"

He swung around, startled for a moment to see the wide-eyed woman standing behind him. Jesse cursed under his breath; he'd forgotten he had an audience. "The foal is turned wrong, and she can't give birth. Go back—"

"What are you going to do?" Distantly Miranda realized that she just naturally assumed he would know how to help the mare.

"I'm going to turn the foal." Rising, he gripped Miranda's shoulders and tried to turn her around and push her out of the stall. "Now I want you to g—"

She resisted. "Aren't you going to need help?"

"Yes! I'm going to get one of the hands," he confirmed impatiently. "Now g—"

"Why do that when I'm already here?" she pointed out reasonably.

Jesse stared down at her, taking in the stubborn set of her chin and the equally stubborn set of the shoulders under his hands. He chewed on a corner of his mustache in a rare moment of indecision. He didn't need strength; he just needed an extra pair of hands, but it was going to be very messy and could well upset her, especially in her condition.

Miranda made the decision for him. Reaching up, she pushed his hands away, then stepped quickly around him. "I'll stay with her while you go get whatever you need."

"All right," he agreed with reluctance, then added forcefully, "but if she starts to kick or thrash around, get out of the stall—immediately!"

"I will," she promised.

He was back with a bucket of water and a bar of soap in what seemed like only seconds. Miranda looked on as he stripped off his shirt and washed, then thoroughly resoaped his left hand and arm. The smooth golden skin covering his broad back and shoulders dimpled from the cold, but he seemed oblivious to it. Plucking up a length of twine that had been soaking in the bucket, he quickly tied a slip knot at one end, then went to work.

Miranda supposed a true lady would have been repulsed and appalled, maybe even managed a swoon or two, by watching something so messily intimate, something that might even be considered obscene, but she was too fascinated to worry about it. His hand would make two of hers, yet was so gentle that the mare appeared to feel no discomfort. After a few seconds he handed Miranda the end of the twine with his free hand. "Hold that and pull when I tell you," he instructed.

"What are we going to do with the string?" she asked softly.

"We're going to straighten the foal's legs. I push and you pull. Now pull—don't jerk! That's a girl, like that...steady... steady...there we go."

A tiny foot appeared. Jesse unslipped the knot, they repeated the procedure, and a second foot joined the first.

"Now stand aside." Miranda moved against the stall door and watched as he took hold of the tiny feet and began to pull gently, but the mare took over with a mighty heave, and seconds later, a wet, wiggling foal was lying on the straw. Jesse looked up at her with a grin of satisfaction. "It's a colt, and he's perfect." Miranda grinned back at him, then laughed as the mother nudged him aside to get a first look at her new baby.

He cleaned up with the soap and water, and Miranda silently handed him his shirt, almost sorry to see him put it back on and cover up such a magnificent chest. For a few minutes they stood together, watching the mare nuzzle and lick her colt. After several unsuccessful attempts, the colt finally made it to his feet, wobbling precariously on his rickety legs.

Jesse spoke quietly, "You know, I've seen this a hundred times or more, and yet I still feel a kind of reverence and awe every time I see a new life coming into the world." Shut up, he commanded himself silently, before you make any bigger an ass of yourself.

But Miranda's soft tone matched his. "It's as if you're watching an ages-old drama that you've seen countless times before. You know the ending by heart, yet it's still as fresh and new and exciting as the first time you saw it."

They smiled at each other in perfect understanding; then Jesse reached past her for his coat. After a final look at the mare and her new son, now busily enjoying his first meal, he took the lantern off the nail and guided Miranda down the aisle. Outside, she waited for him while he secured the door. The moon was down, but the black sky was clear, and the millions of twinkling stars provided a cold, bright light. Jesse extinguished the lantern and left it hanging by the door.

She gave him a quick smile as he came to stand beside her. Tilting back her head, she sighed, her warm breath a puff of mist in the chill air. "It's so beautiful tonight. If you lived to be a thousand, you couldn't count all the stars."

The night was still and quiet, the canyon wrapped in deep sleep, and Jesse had the fanciful notion that they were the only two people awake in the world. "There's the Big Dipper," he murmured and felt Miranda's glance on him.

"Do you know the stars?"

"Some of them. I had an astronomy book once, and when I rode herd at night, I'd try to pick out the constellations. I've forgotten most of them, though."

Miranda sighed regretfully. "I only know where the Big Dipper is. Where's the Little Dipper?"

"Find the two stars on the side of the Big Dipper opposite the handle." He waited until she nodded, indicating that she had found them. "Now line them up and follow the line up to a bright star."

"I see it," Miranda murmured as she found the brightest star in the sky.

"That's the North Star, and it's the last star in the handle of the Little Dipper. See it now?"

Miranda tried, but couldn't see anything that looked like a dipper. "No."

Jesse moved to stand close behind her and raised his arm beside her head. "Sight along my arm."

Miranda followed the line of his arm to the end of his pointing finger, then shook her head in frustration. "I still can't see it."

Sliding his hands into her hair, he fitted his palms to her skull and tilted her head gently. "See it now?"

"I see it," she whispered. He was so close that she could smell him, warm and quintessentially male, and feel the strong beating of his heart against her back.

"The curving constellation just to the right is Draco, the dragon." He moved her head again, sliding his hands deeper into her hair to feel it curling around his wrists. "And back to the left is Cepheus, the one that looks like a house with a pointed roof." Her hair tickled his nose, and he barely resisted the urge to bury his face in its sweet-scented softness. He rubbed a curl surreptitiously between his fingertips, relishing the feel of it, but it was too easy to imagine feeling that silk floss on other parts of his body, and regretfully, he released the curl.

"I see them." The muscles of her neck were so lax that only his hands were keeping it up, she thought, and shivered.

"You're cold," he muttered with concern.

"No, I—" His coat settled over her shoulders, and she was instantly enveloped in warmth. His strong arms followed, crossing over her shoulders from behind and drawing her back against his long hard body. "Now you're going to be cold," she murmured, but made no effort to move.

"I'm fine," he said softly against her hair, and smiled to himself. He was so hot he doubted he'd be cold in the middle of a blizzard.

Miranda rubbed her cheek absently on the rough canvas collar of his coat, the coat he had selflessly sacrificed to her so she wouldn't be cold. It reminded her of the other sacrifices he had made, and she felt the sudden sharp prick of guilt.

She turned inside the circle of his embrace, and his hands slipped down her arms to keep her close as he looked down at her with a question in his dark eyes.

"I knew you weren't guilty of any of the crimes you were convicted of the first time I saw you in Willis's parlor," she said quietly. "But I was so desperate for someone to help me save the ranch, I pretended you were and went along with his crazy plan. Tommy has told me about your brother and your ranch in Montana. I'm more grateful to you than you'll ever know for everything you've done for Tommy and me, but why haven't you left and gone back home?" she asked him in honest bewilderment. "You must know that I would do nothing to stop you." She felt another, sharper, almost killing stab of guilt at how much she was praying he would make yet another sacrifice and stay just a little longer.

Jesse looked down at her pale, sober face. Because I just realized I love you, Miranda, he told her silently, and there's not one thing I can do about it . . . except stay until I'm sure you and your son will keep your ranch. Then I'll go home, alone. "Like Tyree says, a man has to spend the winter somewhere. This is as good a place as any," he said with a faint smile.

She searched his face for a long moment; then she turned away with a silent shake of her head. He saw the glitter of tears before she averted her face. He dropped his hands from her arms before the temptation to pull her tight against him and kiss away her tears and test the softness of her mouth became too great. She slipped his coat off her shoulders and gave it back to him without speaking or looking at him. Jesse took it, but he didn't put it on as he stood alone in the cold darkness, watching her walk away from him.

Miranda emptied her teacup and came to a decision. "Leola," she said, setting the cup on the saucer, "I want you to go into Deming and find someone to help out here. Between your work as a *curandera* and all there is to do here, you don't have time to sit down, much less sleep."

With a weary smile the older woman looked up from the tortilla she was patting between her hands. "It is true that I am a little tired. Perhaps tomorrow—"

"Today," Miranda interrupted in a firm tone. "Everyone here and in the village is well at the moment, and—" she glanced out the window at the few clouds scattered across the blue sky—"the weather is clear. You'd better take advantage of the chance to go while you have it." She stood, a process that was getting harder than ever to accomplish lately, she thought ruefully, and crossed the kitchen. After relieving Leola of the half-finished tortilla, she encouraged her toward the door. "Go put on your hat and coat while I find someone to hitch up your wagon and two men to escort you."

Leola dug in her heels. "But *señora*, who will take care of you and Tommy?"

"Tommy and I can fend for ourselves for a few days. Even if you find someone right away, don't try to come back today. Stay overnight, at least." Miranda opened the door politely, then practically shoved the older woman through it. "Perhaps you could find a Chinese girl willing to come," she called after her. "Kwon has certainly proved a treasure."

A few minutes later she acknowledged Leola's last baleful look with a cheerful wave as the woman drove through the gates, escorted by two of the young men who'd come with Cisco Moreno. Keeping her eyes steadfastly away from the tall man watching from the nearest corral, Miranda smiled down at the small boy at her side. "Well, Tommy, let's go make cookies, shall we?"

Jesse sat up in bed suddenly, unsure what had woken him. All he heard was the screech of the wind outside. The few puffy white clouds that had been in the sky that morning had become heavy and dark, reaching from horizon to horizon by midafternoon. The light breeze had shifted to the north and blown itself into a gale by dusk, and by morning he expected the season's first snow.

Above the scream of the wind, he thought he heard a thudding on his door. Grumbling under his breath, he threw back the blanket, reached for his pants and, a few seconds later, yawning, opened the door.

It was blown out of his hand and slammed back against the wall. The snow had come a few hours earlier than he had anticipated, and in the form of a blizzard. The sudden frigid sting of the wind brought instant tears to his eyes, temporarily blinding him, and before he could blink them away, something wet and very cold fell heavily against his bare chest. Automatically one of his arms wrapped around it, registering a vaguely human shape even as he was jerking whoever it was inside and reaching for the door with his free hand to shut out the snow and cold.

The door shut, he set the cold, wet bundle of clothes away from him. The figure was so snow covered that he couldn't tell who it was. Dark wet hair was exposed as gloved hands unwound a snow-caked scarf, followed by a pair of twilight eyes, huge and frightened.

He was already reaching for her when she gasped, "Jesse, I-I think the baby's coming!"

Chapter Twelve

Jesse immediately understood the implications of what she had just said. Leola Rivera was in Deming, and there were no other women on the ranch, so she was turning to him for help. A spasm of pain crossed her pale face. He assumed it was a labor pain, until he looked down and saw his fingers vised around her arms. He eased his grip, but didn't release her. "When did the pains start?"

"Right after dinner." The panic she had felt when the sudden gush of water had told her that the pains she had been feeling all evening weren't the false alarm she had thought they were faded. It had started to diminish, she realized, the instant he had opened his door. "They're coming closer together now, about ten minutes apart."

He nodded, dropping one of his hands to lead her to his bed. "We have plenty of time, then, right? Sit down, and I'll finish getting dressed."

"I suppose we have plenty of time," she murmured, giving him an uncertain look he didn't see.

Jesse dressed swiftly, then shrugged into his coat. She was getting cumberously to her feet as he came back to the bed. He stripped the blanket off the bed and quickly wrapped it around her, noting that her dress was soaked past her knees. "I wish you had some dry clothes, but this will have to do," he muttered as he adjusted the wool until he was satisfied that her head and face were completely protected. "Can you breathe all right?" Taking her muffled response for assent, he bent and put one arm beneath her knees.

Miranda felt herself being lifted and knew he had opened the door when an icy blast of air hit her, cutting through the thick wool as if it were thin cotton. She shivered involuntarily and tucked her head down against his shoulder. With her arms trapped under the blanket, she was helpless to hold on to him and just had to trust that he wouldn't lose his grip on her. She needn't have worried, she thought a second later, when his arms shifted and suddenly she was being held so tightly she could hardly breathe. She felt him step off the porch, and then, impossibly, he began to run.

The trip to the house took only seconds, but they were the longest seconds of his life. Too late he realized that the driving snow had cut the visibility to nothing, and he could only guess whether he was headed in the right direction, relying on instinct and prayer to guide him. All the stories he had ever heard about people freezing to death within yards of safety and warmth came back to him now with grimly graphic clarity. The frigid gale snatched his breath away and tried to knock him off his feet. His lungs burning and his legs feeling as if they were made out of lead, he was sure he had missed the house, when something solid almost accomplished what the wind hadn't. Falling backward, trying desperately to keep his balance and not drop his precious burden, Jesse blinked his eyes clear just long enough to see that he'd run into the patio wall. Gambling that the blank space he saw to the left was the open gate, he stumbled through it. Instantly the wind was cut in half, and he knew he'd hit the jackpot. Protected by the high walls surrounding it, the patio was a haven of calm compared to the open compound. He staggered up onto the porch, and his momentum carried them through the front door.

Jesse kicked the door shut behind him and carefully set Miranda down. After the bone-cutting cold and the roaring wind and darkness outside, the sudden warmth and quiet seemed almost unnatural. The entry hall was brightly lit, and he began to unwrap the frozen blanket to see how she had fared. He was halfway through, when he felt Miranda's body clench and heard her gasp, muffled by the blanket still covering her face. "Another contraction?" he asked. Feeling her nod in response, he held her until the spasm passed, then finished the job of getting her out of the blanket.

Her face free at last, Miranda stared up at him. Snow had caught in his hair, eyebrows and mustache, turning them white. The snow was melting now and running down his face and neck, but he seemed not to notice. "You should have worn your hat," she said inanely.

He didn't waste time answering. Rapidly he stripped her of her heavy coat, muffler and gloves, then turned her and gave her a gentle push, starting her toward a hallway that he guessed led to the bedrooms. "Get out of the rest of your clothes and into bed. I'll be there in a minute."

He drew in a long breath, then let it out in an even longer sigh that was ragged around the edges. Absently he ran his hand through his hair, scattering a small shower of water droplets, then wiped the hand slowly down his face. Now what the hell was he supposed to do! Finally he roused himself, removed his coat and wet boots and started down the hall after her in his bare feet. Thank God one of them had been through this before and knew what she was doing.

Every door along the hallway was closed but two, and those rooms were dark. He knocked quietly on the first closed door, got no answer and opened it anyway. The light filtering down the hall from the entry was enough to see that the room was indeed a bedroom, but it had the mustiness of disuse. He bypassed the next door in favor of the open one across the hall. It was a bathroom, and a quick glance through the next open door confirmed his guess that it belonged to Tommy, and that the little boy was still soundly asleep. He assumed the rooms beyond were extra bedrooms. Going back to the second door, he knocked again and heard a low voice telling him to come in.

The bedroom he stepped into was as feminine as the first one had been masculine. So she and Hart had not shared a bedroom, he thought, but he had no time to analyze why that fact pleased him. There was a door connecting the room with the one next to it. Miranda was standing in front of it, drying her hair with a towel. Her clothes were a sodden pile on the floor, and now she wore a voluminous white flannel nightgown that covered her from her neck to her ankles. "I thought I told you to get into bed," he said, taking the towel from her.

She gave him a vague smile as she lowered the towel. "I just wanted to get my hair dry first."

He took the towel out of her hands, and she stood docilely in front of him, head down, while he scrubbed it over her wet hair. After a few passes, he tossed the towel toward the pile of wet clothes. "It's dry enough. Now get into bed."

The covers on the wide bed were already pulled down. She sat down on the edge and turned carefully to brace her back against the pillows stacked against the high headboard, and he swung her legs up onto the mattress. He was tucking the quilt and top sheet around her, when she suddenly gripped his hand, and he looked up to see that she was in the throes of another contraction. After a minute or so it passed, and she relaxed back against the pillows with a tired sigh.

"They seem to be coming a little closer together now," he said as he drew up a chair to sit beside her. "How long did your labor last the first time?

Miranda stared at him blankly. "The first time?"

Worry made his tone sharp with impatience. "Yes! You know, when you had Tommy."

She stared at him in confusion, then realized that no one had ever told him. "This *is* my first time. Tommy is my stepson. His mother was Thomas's first wife. She died giving birth to him." She glanced away from him, but Jesse saw the flash of fear in her eyes. "Even Leola couldn't save her," she whispered.

Jesse breathed a soft obscenity as he stared down at her. She knew even less about this than he did. Guilt suddenly jabbed him as he remembered her white face and the fear in her eyes last night as she'd watched the laboring mare, and his casual dismissal of it. No wonder she had looked so scared. And now she was stuck with a midwife whose only experience was in pulling calves and foals.

He was trying to think of something—anything—to say, when he heard the slam of the front door, followed by a muted shout.

"*Señora!* Where are you? Are you—" Manolo Rivera broke off at the sight of the big man coming from the direction of his mistress's bedroom. With a stunned glance, he took in bare feet and an untucked, half-buttoned shirt. "McClintock! What the hell are you—"

Jesse interrupted him without preamble. "The *señora* is about to have her baby, and we're the only help she's got."

"*¡Madre de Dios!*" Manolo crossed himself. "She's having the baby now? Tonight?"

One glance at Rivera's green face and Jesse knew he couldn't count on any help from him. In fact, he was going to have to keep him completely away from Miranda if he didn't want the man keeling over in the middle of everything. "Get the stoves and fireplaces stoked up—the house is cold," he ordered brusquely. "Then bring me all the clean sheets and blankets you can find, and after that, boil some water." Just what the hell he was going to do with boiling water, Jesse didn't know, but it sounded like a good idea, and it would keep Rivera busy and hopefully on his feet in case he really needed him.

The other man's color improved dramatically as soon as he understood he wouldn't be asked to help with the birth. "I will," he said with fervent gratitude. "I am sorry, but these things..." Manolo's hands fluttered uselessly, like broken bird wings. "I know nothing about them," he added apologetically, his voice still shaky with the masculine panic he'd felt at the thought that he might be called upon to deal with this, the ultimate feminine mystery.

Jesse brushed aside his apology with an abrupt gesture. "That's all right. Just get some heat in here, then take care of the linens and the water. I'll take care of Miranda."

Following his own orders, he built up the dying fire in the small corner fireplace after he returned to her room. He was feeling more than a touch of panic himself, he thought as he added the lumps of coal, but surely Leola Rivera had briefed her on what to expect.

Her answer to his question on that subject didn't untie any of the knots in his stomach; they only got tighter. "She's told me almost nothing." Miranda made a gesture of helpless frustration. "I think she was afraid it might upset me, and I didn't insist, because I never dreamed she wouldn't be here when my time came."

"Well, don't worry." She didn't need to; he was worrying enough for both of them. Ignoring the chair, he sat on the bed, took her hand and gave her what he hoped was a reassuring smile. "It can't be much different than it is for cows and horses." She managed a smile in return, and even, amazingly, a tiny laugh at his lousy joke.

He clasped her hand between his and almost despaired when he felt how small and fragile it was compared to his. "Miranda, I promise you that I'll take the very best care of you I can," he swore to her softly.

Her other hand came up to touch the side of his face. "I know you will, Jesse." Her hand caressed his cheek, then dropped back to her side.

She looked at him with such trust and confidence that he had sudden difficulty swallowing. There was a sound behind him, and he turned, almost grateful for the interruption. Tyree's long lean body filled the doorway, and Jesse saw his curious glance toward the woman in the bed. "I'll be right back," he whispered, brushing a kiss across her hand before he gave it back to her.

Tyree followed him down the hall until they were out of earshot of the bedroom. "I was watching the storm through the bunkhouse window, when I saw you come running out of your room carrying something," he said. "When you didn't come back, I figured I better make sure you hadn't gotten yourself lost. I ran into Rivera bringing a sack of coal up from the barn, and he said you were here."

Tyree didn't ask directly, but it was obvious from the tone of his voice that he was wondering what the hell was going on. "That was Miranda I was carrying. She'd come to tell me that she was in labor."

Immediately Tyree backed up a step, throwing up his hands as if he were trying to ward off some unspeakable horror. "Don't look at me, Jessie Mack! I don't know one damn thing about birthing babies. That's your specialty."

"Only the four-legged ones," Jesse reminded him dryly. "But I think between the two of us, Miranda and I can handle it. I'd appreciate it, though, if you'd stay, in case Tommy wakes up. I don't want him walking into his mother's room at the wrong time, and Rivera's looking none too reliable at the moment."

Tyree lowered his hands, and Jesse almost laughed at the look of profound relief on his dark face. "That I can do," he agreed.

Two hours later, Miranda decided ruefully that her labor really wasn't going much differently than the mare's had the night before. For both of them, it had turned out to be a long and frankly tedious process. Jesse had been with her every second, for which she was extremely grateful. He had closed the door behind him after returning from talking with Tyree, and they'd been left alone, for which she was also grateful, except for one brief interruption. When Jesse had answered the knock on the door, Manolo's arm had appeared with clean linens and then, inexplicably, a huge steaming kettle of water. Jesse had set it on the hearth near the fire, then seemingly forgotten about it.

There wasn't nearly as much pain as she had feared, for which she was also extremely grateful. Instead the contractions, which were coming closer and closer together now, were more like pressure slowly building in her abdomen. At the moment, eyes closed, she was recuperating from the last one. It had been the strongest one yet, coming before she'd had time to catch her breath from the one preceding it.

"You're doing fine, Miranda. Just a little longer, honey. Relax now. Everything's going to be all right. Before you know it, it'll all be over, and you'll be holding your baby in your arms."

His voice soothed over her as gently as the hand rubbing her abdomen through the soft cotton of her chemise. It was like last night, when he had been talking to the mare, she thought vaguely. Even though his words hadn't been meant for her, they had been curiously reassuring. Now they calmed her fears and renewed her flagging strength.

She hadn't realized she had spoken her thoughts aloud until his stroking hand stilled suddenly and she felt him looking at her. She opened her eyes in time to catch the expression on his face. It was oddly bittersweet, as if her inadvertent revelation had somehow made him both joyously happy and incredibly sad at the same time.

She was still staring at him, trying to puzzle out why, when the next contraction came, and every muscle in her body clenched.

When it passed, she was exhausted and completely drenched with sweat. She opened her eyes to see Jesse's face inches from hers. This is taking its toll on him, too, she thought tiredly. His blue-gray eyes were bloodshot, his dark eyebrows pinched together, and deep lines bracketed his mouth.

"Are you still with me?" he asked softly as he wiped the sweat from her hot face and neck with a damp cloth.

"I'm here, but maybe you better start looking for some twine," she joked weakly.

He didn't laugh. Instead his entire body went taut, and new lines appeared in his face. "Do you think something is wrong?"

"No. It's just that I'm so tired," she said with a weary grin.

He rinsed the cloth in the bowl from her washstand, then wrung it out and folded it, placing it on her forehead. Miranda almost moaned aloud at the wonderful coolness of it. He'd stripped the quilt and top sheet off the bed an hour ago, and then, while he'd turned his back, she'd dispensed with most of her modesty and her heavy flannel nightgown in favor of a thin chemise, but she still felt as if it were a hot summer day and she'd been running miles under the roasting sun.

Another contraction seized her, and she felt the irresistible urge to push. She gritted her teeth and groaned, not because it hurt, but from the sheer physical effort.

"Is the pain very bad?" His voice was a rough rasp as he tenderly stroked the damp curls off her forehead. "Manolo says there's a bottle of laudanum in the kitchen. I can get it in a second, and—"

"No, it isn't that bad," she panted. "It's just that this is—" she gave a breathless little laugh "—*hard work*."

The next contraction *would* have to make a liar out of her, she thought dimly, as she endured a sudden pain so great she thought her body must surely be splitting apart.

When it had passed, leaving her too weak even to pant, she heard him say in a strained voice, "I think this is it, Miranda. Sure you won't change your mind about the laudanum?"

His hands were under her shift now, and she could feel them moving, gentle and sure, over the tightly stretched skin. She shook her head once in response to his question, not wanting to use any energy even to talk, because she knew she was going to need every drop for the next contraction. Instinctively she knew she should be higher in the bed.

Jesse saw her struggling to sit up and guessed immediately what she wanted. He lifted her, then braced her with pillows under her shoulders and upper back. He felt her muscles tighten again and glanced down to see that her knees were raised. He moved swiftly to the end of the bed and, without ceremony, hiked her sweat-soaked chemise out of the way. This was no time for false modesty, he decided, prepared to tell her so if she voiced any protest. He glanced up to her face and realized that she hadn't even noticed. Her eyes were squeezed shut, and there was an expression of intense concentration on her face.

Another wave of pain caught her, but this time she rode on top of it, and it wasn't so bad. When it released her, she wanted nothing more than to just go to sleep, but she heard Jesse's deep voice, alternately demanding and cajoling.

"Come on, Randy. Damn it, don't give up on me now, sweetheart. Push."

Drawing strength from his strong, steady voice, Miranda obeyed.

"That's it . . . that's it . . . I see the baby's head. One more time, honey. *Push*."

She heard her own long, low groan, then a startlingly loud shriek of annoyance, then Jesse's voice, now sounding oddly hoarse and choked.

"Oh, Randy, it's a girl. A perfect beautiful little baby girl...and she has your hair."

She felt one more, small contraction and a slight tugging. When she finally found the energy to open her eyes, he was kneeling beside the bed with a tiny red bundle in his arms. Impossibly small arms and legs thrashed, while an astonishingly powerful set of lungs expressed outrage at the whole situation. She raised her eyes to his and saw that they were curiously bright. His broad smile lit his whole face, taking away the lines of weariness and tension, she thought absently, unaware that her own smile mirrored his. She held out her arms, and he started to place the baby in them. She shook her head, and suddenly he seemed to understand what she wanted. Holding the baby carefully to one side, he leaned down and met her mouth with his. They shared a kiss that celebrated their success and the wonderful miracle of life.

Without her permission, her eyes closed. She felt him draw back, then place her baby on her breast, and she closed her arms gently around the tiny body. The baby quieted instantly. She felt the quilt settle over both of them, and then she was asleep.

Jesse stared down at the woman and baby sleeping peacefully in the wide bed. It was hours past midnight, almost dawn, and he was exhausted, but he was unwilling to leave just yet and find a bed for himself. Miranda had immediately fallen into a sleep so deep she never stirred even while he changed the bed, bathed her and dressed her in a clean shift. He'd finally found a use for all that water Manolo had boiled, he thought, laughing softly to himself. And he'd also used some to sterilize his knife before he'd cut the umbilical cord, he remembered absently.

He had bathed the baby, too, and wrapped her in one of the soft knitted blankets he'd found stacked in the small cradle next to Miranda's bed. He'd taken her out to show her to Manolo and Tyree, feeling possessively proud and peculiarly pleased with himself, as if he were showing off his own child, then placed her back in her mother's arms. He knew the other two men were waiting for him so they could all toast the birth of the baby with a bottle of fine Kentucky bourbon Manolo had been saving for a special occasion, but still he made no move to leave.

Easing down on the bed, he gently brushed the tangle of auburn hair off Miranda's cheek. Tonight truly had been a special occasion, perhaps the most precious of his life, he thought as he watched her sleep. Except for the faint violet shadows under her eyes, sleep had erased the signs of exhaustion from her beautiful face. Her baby, her color already fading to a rosy pink, slept beside her. Her tiny mouth worked as she slept within the security of her mother's arm. The faces of both mother and child wore the same sweet expression, and he wished it were possible to have a photograph of Miranda and her tiny daughter asleep together; then he immediately knew he would not have shared this precious moment with anyone, not even to have a permanent record of it. He didn't need one. Until he breathed his last breath, he would carry this picture of them in his heart, take it out in quiet or lonely times to gaze on it and remember this wondrous night.

Miranda shifted gingerly onto her left side, but several sharp twinges reminded her that she was a brand-new mother. Laying her cheek on her hand, she stared out the window toward the boulder where every night for the past eight the bobcat had waited for her to bring him his treat. Last night she'd left it before the blizzard started, and now the empty plate would be buried under the ten inches of snow Manolo had said had fallen. The blizzard had blown itself out while she was sleeping, but she was still sure the cat wouldn't come. He was no doubt lying up in some snug, dry spot, dreaming of summer.

On the other side of the frost-painted window the new snow sparkled in the moonlight. The sky had cleared, and she didn't have to be outside to know that the temperature couldn't be much above zero. Manolo had also said the road from Deming wouldn't be passable until it warmed enough to melt the drifts. That meant Leola would not be returning anytime soon, but she wasn't worried. She and her baby were fine.

She stretched out her arm to the cradle next to the bed and carefully peeled back the pink blanket. Miranda laughed softly at herself. She couldn't seem to keep from sneaking peeks every few minutes at the tiny little girl in the cradle. As Jesse had said, she was perfect and beautiful.

Miranda rolled over onto her back with a groan that had nothing to do with her assorted aches. She didn't know how she was going to face him. Covering her face with her hands, she groaned again. She was slowly dying of embarrassment. The coup de grace had come when she had woken up and been mortified to discover he had washed her and dressed her in a clean nightgown, handled her body as if she were a baby, too, while she'd been asleep!

Sliding her hands down from her face, she caught sight of the open door connecting her bedroom with the one next to it. The door had never been left open before, and when she'd asked Manolo about it, he'd said that Señor McClintock had opened it so he would hear her if she needed anything. In answer to her bewildered look, he had explained that the *señor* was sleeping in that bedroom, and there was another embarrassment to deal with. Manolo's tone had implied that it should have been perfectly obvious, and she also hadn't missed the implication that Jesse McClintock was now "the *señor*." Whatever doubts Manolo had had about him—and she knew he'd had plenty—had all magically vanished last night. She wouldn't be at all surprised to hear Manolo call him "*patrón*."

There was a knock on her partially closed door. "Come in," she called out softly before thinking. The door swung open, and her worst fears were realized.

"Toppy sent up some stew from the bunkhouse for you."

After setting the tray he was carrying on top of a small table, he reached for one of the extra pillows scattered at the foot of the bed. Because she was being very careful not to look directly at him, it was a few seconds before Miranda realized he was waiting for her to sit up so he could stuff it behind her back. Cautiously she pushed herself up; he positioned the pillow, and she sat back. He placed the tray over her knees, and Miranda stared down at the food, suddenly realizing she was ravenous. The stew looked and smelled delicious. There were two huge split sourdough biscuits that looked so light she suspected only the weight of the butter and honey melting over them was holding them down. And last, but definitely not least, there was a hefty portion of dried peach cobbler. "Thank you, Mr. McClintock," she murmured, reaching for the neatly folded linen napkin.

The tray was whisked off her lap so quickly she might have thought she'd only imagined it if not for the lingering warmth on her lap and the wonderful aromas. Against her will she raised her eyes to the tall man standing over her, her supper in his hands.

"Don't you agree that 'Mr. McClintock' sounds just a little ridiculous after what we shared last night, Miranda?" he asked her in a deceptively mild tone. "I'll wager I saw parts of you your husband never did."

Her face turned pink, and her eyes widened with shock at his bluntness, and Jesse braced himself for the eruption. Suddenly her eyes crinkled shut, and he was startled by a burst of laughter.

"Oh, Jesse, I'm sorry," she gasped. "I sounded like a proper prig, didn't I? The truth is I'm more than a trifle mortified, and—" her eyes dropped back to her lap "—I really don't know what to say to you except..." Her eyes lifted to his and held steady. "Thank you," she said soberly.

"I was glad I could help," he said with a soft smile, and set the tray back in place.

A few minutes later Miranda looked down at the empty tray in front of her and muttered in disbelief, "I can't believe I ate all that."

"There's obviously nothing wrong with your appetite."

His smoky blue eyes teased her as he removed the tray and handed back her teacup, refilled. Along with her supper, he'd brought a pot of tea and two cups. As he settled in a chair a few feet away with his cup, she asked, "Where's Tommy? Except for a few minutes this afternoon, I haven't seen him all day."

"He spent most of the day down at the bunkhouse, learning how to play poker and cuss."

Miranda's laugh became a groan as she settled back against the pillows.

"How do you feel?" Jesse asked her, frowning.

"Truthfully?"

He nodded.

"As if I just spent three days on the back of a very fat horse," she told him with a wry grin.

The tiny bundle in the cradle beside the bed reminded them of her presence with a sudden cry. Jesse bent and picked her up, then traded the baby for her mother's teacup. Setting it on the night-stand, he sat down on the edge of the bed. He touched a finger to the baby's cheek, marveling at the incredible softness of the skin under his rough fingertip. A tiny fist grabbed his finger and tried with surprising strength to drag it into the little rosebud mouth.

"I introduced Tommy to his new sister, but I don't think he was very impressed," Miranda said dryly.

Jesse laughed. "Have you picked out a name for her yet?"

Miranda waited until he looked up before she answered. "Her name is Jessica," she said with soft smile.

"Are you my sweet baby Jessa? Are you? Hmm?" Miranda nuzzled her nose gently against a tiny squashed one and was re-warded with a loud hiccup. Laughing, she hugged the freshly bathed and dressed baby close. She really was a sweet baby, if one ignored the early and definite signs of a healthy temper, Miranda thought wryly as she settled into a rocking chair and unbuttoned the front of her dress. And if "Jessa," the nickname that had im-mediately seemed to evolve from Jessica, sounded suspiciously like "Jesse," she would ignore that, too.

A little while later she laid the sleepy, sated baby in her cradle and tiptoed to the door. She glanced toward the other door in the room with an unconsciously wistful sigh. It was closed again. He had stayed for several nights, until he was certain that neither she nor Jessa might need him, then he had returned to the bunk-house.

She started toward the kitchen but detoured to the front door, when she heard footsteps on the porch. The weather had been bit-ter for four days; then, with the fickle unpredictability Miranda had come to expect of the desert, a south wind had blown in an almost balmy warmth that had melted the snow in a day. Knowing she would wait no more than a day for the road to dry out, Miranda had been expecting Leola all afternoon.

The older woman was just reaching for the handle when Miran-da opened the door. "Leola!" She enveloped the smaller woman in an exuberant hug. "I'm so happy you're back. Wait until you see my surprise!"

"I am happy to be back, and I have a surprise, too, *señora*." Leola returned Miranda's embrace with a warm one of her own, then suddenly froze. Gripping Miranda's arms, she pushed her away so that she could get a good look at her. "You had the baby! *Por Dios*, I knew I should not have gone! When did you have it? Are you all right? And the baby? How is the baby?"

"The baby's fine, I'm fine, everyone is fine," Miranda assured her. Linking her arm through Leola's, she started walking toward her bedroom. "Except perhaps Manolo," she qualified with a laugh. "I'm not sure he's recovered yet. The delivery took a lot out of him."

Leola turned to her, aghast. "Manolo delivered the baby?"

"No, Jesse McClintock did," Miranda said blandly, secretly enjoying the stunned expression on the older woman's face. By then they were at the door of her bedroom, and she led Leola to the cradle beside the bed. Pulling back the pink blanket, she showed off her surprise.

Leola bent and peered at the tiny head with its cap of auburn curls. "Would you like to hold her?" Miranda asked in a whisper.

Leola shook her head and straightened. "When she wakes for a feeding," she whispered back absently, giving Miranda a look that said she still couldn't believe it.

Miranda took her arm again and led her to the kitchen. "Here, sit down, Leola. I'll make you some tea." She pulled out a chair at the table and gently pushed Leola down onto it.

While Miranda made the tea, Leola stared blankly around the kitchen as if she'd never seen it before. Miranda set a cup of tea in front of her, and the older woman gulped it down as if it were a shot of whiskey. "Now," she demanded, setting down the empty cup, "tell me everything."

Miranda gave her an edited version, and several minutes later Leola nodded, a disgruntled expression on her face. "It sounds as if he did you and the baby no harm," she admitted grudgingly, "although I cannot be certain, of course, until I examine you both."

"He did us no harm," Miranda affirmed softly.

"How do you feel now?"

Miranda gave a rueful laugh. "Well, a week ago I told Jesse I felt as if I'd been riding a very fat horse for three days. Now it's down to two days, and the horse was skinny."

Leola laughed, then gave her a sober look. "Are you having any problems?"

"No. Toppy has been sending meals over, and Jesse takes Tommy with him every morning, so I haven't been doing much but eating, sleeping and taking care of Jessa, who also—" she grinned "—doesn't do much but eating and sleeping." Miranda frowned suddenly. "I'm not sure I have enough milk, though. Jessa nurses well, but then she seems to be hungry again in just an hour or two. Can you give me something so I will have more?"

With a vague nod, Leola changed the subject. "Isn't that one of the dresses you wore before you became pregnant?"

Miranda looked down at the brown wool shirtwaist she was wearing with a pleased smile. "Yes. I was surprised it fit right away. I guess I didn't gain as much weight as I thought."

Leola could have told her that she hadn't gained nearly enough, especially not enough to support a nursing baby. She pushed back her chair and stood. "I do have something for your milk. I'll get it right away."

Miranda's voice stopped her as she was leaving the kitchen by the back door. "Wait! You didn't tell me your surprise."

Slapping her broad forehead with her hand, Leola whirled around and hurried to the front door, instead. "Ay, ay, ay! I forgot all about her."

Miranda followed more slowly. "Her?"

"I found us some help, a girl in Deming." Leola threw open the front door. "Her name is Emma Lee Stamm."

Miranda walked through the door and bit back her startled exclamation.

The girl was still standing where Leola had left her. She hadn't seen her, Miranda supposed, because she had been so intent on Leola that she had never looked beyond her. She looked now.

Emma Lee Stamm looked like a scarecrow some farmer had left out in the weather too long. Leola had called her a girl, but her age was impossible to determine. The skin of her face was reddened and rough from countless sunburns and peelings. The skin on her hands was cracked, and Miranda saw several healing sores. Her hair might once have been strawberry blond; now it looked like pinkish-orange straw that had been hacked off by a dull scythe. Emma Lee looked to be her own height or a bit shorter, but with her skeletally thin body and ill-fitting, too short dress she looked taller. Most ragpickers would have turned up their noses at that dress. It was obviously a cast-off, calico, although what color it had been originally was anybody's guess. Her shoes were broken and looked as if they would slop on her feet every time she took a step. The man's coat she wore was much too large for her, and dark wool rubbed shiny. Her eyes were the worst. A washed-out green, they were vacant and lifeless, as if her soul had already abandoned her poor husk of a body.

Leola gently drew the girl forward. Against her concave chest, she clutched what Miranda finally decided was an Indian cradle board. "Emma Lee, this is Señora Hart, the lady I told you about." Leola spoke slowly, each word distinct, as if she were speaking to someone with a limited command of English—or a half-wit.

The empty eyes shifted to her, but Miranda saw no awareness in them. Taking her cue from Leola, she spoke distinctly in a kindly tone. "Hello, Emma Lee. I'm happy to meet you. Welcome to the Silver Tejo." She reached out and took the catatonic girl's free hand, giving it a gentle squeeze. It was like squeezing the hand of a rag doll, except that a rag doll didn't have sharp bones poking through its fabric skin. When she released it, the girl's hand flopped back to her side and hung there limply.

"I'm going to take Emma Lee to my house now, *señora* but I will come right back." She touched the girl's shoulder, and Miranda saw that she cringed, as if in anticipation of a blow, although she made no attempt to ward it off. Leola stepped off the porch, and Emma Lee plodded after her in her too big shoes like a docile cow. Miranda stared after them until they disappeared around the corner of the patio. At no time had the girl spoken.

True to her word, Leola was back sitting at the kitchen table in less than ten minutes. "I know what you are going to ask, *señora*. Why did I bring back someone we are going to have to take care of, when I was supposed to find someone to help us?"

As Leola spoke aloud what were indeed her thoughts, Miranda heard how selfish they sounded.

"I truly do not know why," Leola admitted. "There is just something about the girl...." She shrugged helplessly.

The bewildered expression on Leola's face was almost comical, but Miranda didn't laugh. Something about the scarecrow girl touched her, too. "Who is she?"

"Soldiers found her with some Apaches, not part of Geronimo's band, though. Apparently one of the men had taken her as a wife. Since Deming was the closest town, the soldiers took her there, thinking someone might know her. All they could get out of her was her name."

"She won't speak, then?" Miranda asked. Leola shook her head with a sigh. "Did anyone in Deming know who she was?"

"Many people remembered that a family named Stamm had been attacked by Apaches two years ago on the road between Deming and Lordsburg. The bodies of the man and woman were found, but there was no trace of their fifteen-year-old daughter, and everyone assumed the Indians had taken her. Someone remembered that the daughter's name was Emma Lee."

"It's obviously her, then," Miranda murmured. "Did anyone in Deming know if she had any relatives?"

"Several people said the family had been going to visit the father's brother in Lordsburg when they were attacked, so Lieutenant Riddle, the one who stayed here last month, sent a telegram to him. He still lives there, but—" Leola's mouth turned sour "—when he found out that she had been living with the Apaches and had been the wife of one, he wouldn't take her. Her uncle seems to think she should have had the courtesy to kill herself, as any decent girl would have done, and saved the family embarrassment," she finished dryly.

Miranda's tone was equally dry. "If her father was anything like her uncle, she's probably better off an orphan." She looked at Leola thoughtfully. "How did you find out about her?"

"I saw the *teniente* in Deming, and when he found out why I was in town he told me about her. He said the army couldn't keep her, and that if nobody would take her in, they were going to have to send her to the insane asylum in El Paso. When I went to see her, the army doctor told me he thought that was where she belonged. She was too simpleminded to be of any use to anybody."

Miranda gave her a knowing look. "And you don't agree."

"She has been badly treated, and I think she has had a wound to the spirit that may take a long time to heal. Perhaps she will never be healed completely, but I do not think she is simpleminded. Nor does she belong with *locos*," she said with more than a trace of righteous indignation.

Miranda studied the woman across the table from her. If Leola said Emma Lee Stamm was not simpleminded or crazy, she was quite prepared to believe her. The *curandera* had an almost uncanny insight into people's hearts and minds. She knew, too, that the older woman's common sense, innate kindness and strong faith affected as many—if not more—cures than her herbs and potions did. "Well!" Miranda clapped her hands together briskly as she rose from the table. "First off, we had better do something about finding her some decent shoes and a new dress."

Chapter Thirteen

Miranda set the empty baby bottle on the table, shifted Jessa to her shoulder and gave her back a gentle pat. The tiny baby produced a booming belch, and two of the three women in the kitchen laughed. "We're going to have to work on your manners, Jessa," Miranda scolded with mock sternness, snuggling the baby back in her arms. Jessa gave a sleepy gurgle, and a few seconds later Miranda heard a soft little snore.

"She seems to be taking the milk well." Leola glanced up from the fresh beef she was cutting into chunks for stew. Emma Lee sat beside her, methodically dicing potatoes and carrots with a small knife.

"I guess it's best that the tea you gave me to increase my milk didn't work after all. She'd doing a lot better on Bessie's milk than she did on mine," Miranda agreed ruefully. After a week of the cow's rich milk, Jessa was fussing less and sleeping better. "She's gained at least a pound, I think."

Leola slanted a look at the too thin young woman across the table from her. The sage tea had worked exactly as it was supposed to. Miranda had assumed it was to increase her milk supply, and Leola hadn't enlightened her to the fact that the tea stopped, not increased, the flow of a mother's milk. Sometimes what patients wanted was not always what was best for them. "Perhaps you should be drinking Bessie's milk, too, then. You also need to gain weight."

Miranda wrinkled her nose in distaste. "Never. The only thing I hate worse than milk is that dreadful *oshá*. And yes, I drank my daily dose," she hastened to add, pointing to the empty cup on the counter beside the sink when she suspected that Leola was about to ask. Her glance cut quickly to Emma Lee. Emma Lee had seen her spill the tea in the sink when Leola's back was turned. The girl's eyes met hers, and for a moment Miranda was sure she detected a glint of humor in them, making the bleached-out green seem suddenly brighter. Then she blinked and Miranda was staring into the same faded emptiness as before.

No, Emma Lee wouldn't give her away, Miranda thought sadly. She would willingly drink a gallon of Leola's nasty tea just to hear one word from the girl. She followed Leola around as if she were an old pull toy of Tommy's the older woman was dragging behind her. She did whatever Leola told her to do, so obviously she could hear and understand, but she had yet to make one sound.

Physically, however, it was obvious that she was recuperating from her two-year ordeal. No longer did she resemble a scarecrow. The dresses Miranda had given her helped, as did the shoes—fortunately they wore the same size—but the real improvement in her appearance came from the weight she was gaining and Leola's healing salves and creams. Already her face was looking less burned and her hands were healing. Leola had even concocted something for her hair that had it looking less like straw and more like the real thing. Each day she looked less like an old woman and more like the seventeen-year-old that she was, and each day Miranda's heart ached for her a little more, that one so young should have suffered so much.

"*Señora*, before I forget, I brought some more *romero*." Leola wiped her hands, then dug around in the pocket of her skirt.

"*Gracias*, Leola." Miranda accepted a small tin of powdered rosemary and started to put it in her pocket.

"Perhaps you should use some now."

Miranda slid open the tin and put it on the table, instead. That Jesse had not treated Jessa's umbilical cord with a proper dressing had been the only real fault Leola could find with his midwifing skills. She was treating it now, and Miranda knew her overconscientiousness was not meant as a criticism, but as a way of making amends for not being there when she needed her. It was unnecessary, but she understood the *curandera*'s need to do it.

After placing the sleeping baby on her knees, she gently unwrapped the blanket and eased down the flannel diaper to expose the healing scar of her navel. She sprinkled on a pinch of the grayish-green powder; then, as she rewrapped Jessa, the baby's eyes opened sleepily and she began to cry. Miranda rocked her in her arms, softly crooning her back to sleep with a wordless little tune. At the sound of the back door opening, she looked up and smiled at Jesse coming in from outside.

Another sound, indistinct yet definitely human, drew her eyes and his to the girl sitting across the table from Miranda. Oblivious to the others in the kitchen, Emma Lee was staring at the baby in Miranda's arms. The expression on her face—the first emotion of any kind she had shown—was one of ravenous hunger, as if she were a starving wolf and the baby a hunk of meat. The girl still held the small paring knife in her hand, and Miranda knew a moment of unease. The first three days, Emma Lee had carried the cradle board with her, reminding her of Tommy and the stuffed toy bear he had dragged with him everywhere when she had first come to the ranch. The girl had left the cradle board in her room after that, but Leola said she suspected she slept with it at night, and it hardly took a genius to figure out the reason why. Emma Lee had committed another unpardonable "sin" while she'd been held by the Apaches, which no doubt would have further damned her in her uncle's eyes.

Sensing Leola's eyes on her, Miranda glanced toward her. With an almost imperceptible nod, Leola indicated that she should give her baby to Emma Lee. Without taking the time to figure out why, Miranda's eyes flew to Jesse. He glanced at the girl, studied her for a moment, then looked back and nodded. He stepped behind her and pulled out her chair, and Miranda stood. She went around the table and stopped beside the girl, who had followed Jessa's progress with her hungry stare. "Emma Lee," she said quietly, extending the sleeping baby toward her, "would you like to hold Jessa?"

The girl's head snapped up, and Miranda saw that her dead green eyes were alive with a mixture of hope and disbelief. Warily, as if she expected the baby to be snatched back any second, she reached out her arms. Miranda gently placed her daughter in Emma Lee's arms, then stepped back. Slowly, as if she still expected Miranda to take the baby away from her, Emma Lee drew the baby to her breast. As if sensing the change in who was holding her, Jessa fussed in her sleep. Emma Lee rocked her gently, and the baby, seemingly realizing that the arms that held her now were no less careful or loving, settled. For long seconds Emma Lee held the tiny warm body close, her head bent, her body rocking back and forth slightly.

Jesse came to stand beside Miranda and she reached automatically for his hand. His strong warm fingers laced through hers as they looked down on Emma Lee and Jessa. For long seconds the girl held the baby close, as if drawing comfort from her tiny warm body. At last she raised her head, and Miranda saw two huge tears rolling down her thin cheeks. She knew Jesse had seen them, too, by the convulsive tightening of his hand on hers. Miranda felt the hard pressure of tears behind her own eyes as Emma Lee smiled at her, a smile of gratitude and heart-wrenching sadness. She held the baby out so Miranda could take back her daughter, then she went back to cutting up the potatoes and carrots in front of her.

Miranda glanced up at Jesse, and they smiled at each other in unspoken understanding. His smile was soft and a little sad, a reflection, she knew, of her own.

Hours later he was smiling again, but there was no trace of sadness now, Miranda thought as she watched him with his namesake. He had volunteered to hold Jessa while she warmed the milk for her evening bottle, and when she had come back into the parlor, the tiny girl had been staring up at him intently, seemingly fascinated by his mustache. Her small fist flailed upward as if she were trying to touch the thick swatch of dark curly hair curving above his straight white teeth. Miranda could understand her daughter's fascination. She wanted to touch it, too.

She was starting toward him to take the baby, when he motioned for her to sit down, indicating that he would bring Jessa to her. While she settled in her armchair, his long body rose with the smooth easy flow of muscle that characterized all his movements. He was one of the biggest men she had ever seen, yet there was never anything clumsy about any of his movements. As he shifted Jessa into the crook of his arm, she noted how confidently he handled her, automatically supporting her head and keeping her squirming body secure in his large hand. He had been good with her from the first time he'd held her, right after her birth, Miranda remembered. Just as she remembered the endearments and the odd nickname he had used. Randy. She'd never heard the name used for a woman before, yet, strangely, she liked it. Because it was something private, and therefore special, just between the two of them? she wondered.

"Leola doesn't think she will have any problems because she was born early?" he asked.

She was almost startled when he placed the baby in her arms. "I don't think she still quite believes we managed it on our own, but she admits Jessa didn't suffer any ill effects from her early birth, except for being too skinny."

Jesse chuckled as the baby began to suck with noisy greed on the rubber nipple stretched over the top of the bottle. "And she's making up for that now."

"I know." Miranda laughed. "She's a terrible pig."

Jesse heard his deep chuckle harmonizing with Miranda's light sweet laughter as Jessa's little forehead wrinkled with a fierce frown of concentration while she worked to empty the bottle as quickly as possible. Taking the armchair within touching distance of hers, he relaxed. He wouldn't trade these evenings with her for all the riches the Silver Tejo mine had ever produced. He had begun lingering after dinner, staying longer and longer each night. His excuse at first had been that he wanted to be there in case Miranda needed help of any kind, but after a few days of recuperation, that pretext was an obvious one, even to him. He was here simply because he enjoyed these quiet, peaceful times with her, and he wasn't about to give them up.

Miranda set the empty bottle aside, shifting the baby higher in her arms as she stood. Jesse stood quickly. "Here, let me tuck her blanket back around her." He tucked all of an inch of loose blanket around the now sleeping baby, his fingers brushing Miranda's arm. He used every excuse, however flimsy, to touch her, and if a legitimate one didn't present itself, he invented one, he thought wryly. He wanted to touch her constantly. He wanted a hell of a lot more than that, he admitted with a silent sardonic laugh, but he wanted just to touch her, too, and not only in a sexual way. He wanted to touch his finger to her cheek, to see if her skin was as smooth and soft as it looked. He wanted to trace the elegant arch of her thin eyebrow, brush his finger over the tips of her long dark eyelashes, tickle the delicate pink shell of her ear. He wanted to nuzzle the fine dark hair on the nape of her neck to see if it was as downy as it looked. What he really wanted, he guessed, was to discover her, to play with her as if he were a small boy again and she were a fantastic toy he'd just been given.

Miranda left to put Jessa in her cradle, and while he waited for her to return, he added a log to the fire that was keeping the large room cozy, then pulled the two overstuffed chairs closer to it. He turned when he heard her returning and saw that she was carrying a tray. After setting it down, she filled the two cups she'd brought in and handed him one. Jesse accepted a cup, hiding a smile at seeing hot chocolate in it instead of the usual tea. He couldn't remember drinking cocoa since he was about ten years old.

Miranda sank into the comfort of the overstuffed chair, tucking her feet under her. After taking a sip from her cup, she murmured, "Sometimes, when I was a little girl, my mother would sneak down to the kitchen of whatever hotel or boarding house we were staying in and make me hot chocolate."

She turned to him, and he saw that her smile was soft and a little hazy. While she'd been gone, he'd turned down the lamp so that the room was now lit only by firelight. The flames gave her face a golden glow and picked out echoes of their own fire in her hair.

"Didn't you ever live in a house?" he asked quietly. The past week they'd shared stories of their childhoods, and he'd gotten a picture of hers as being spent almost constantly on the move with the traveling company of actors her parents had formed.

She shook her head with a laugh. "For years our 'house' was trunks of costumes and props. Even after the acting company settled permanently in San Francisco, my parents preferred living in a hotel. This—" she glanced around her "—is the first real home I ever had."

Was the lure of a home part of the reason she had married Hart? he wondered. Sharing the intimacy of Jessica's birth had removed the conversational barriers between them—most of them, he amended silently. She'd mentioned in passing that she'd met Hart in San Francisco, but she hadn't been any more specific than that.

"After my mother died when I was seventeen, my father and I moved to a small hotel. It had a wonderful view of the bay," she reminisced.

"Did you take your mother's place in the company then?" She was staring into the fire, her eyes dark pools of shadow reflecting yellow points of flame.

"No, both my mother and father had always been opposed to my acting, but I did take over the other responsibilities she'd had. She handled the company's financial matters because she'd always had a better head for figures than my father. I had been helping her for the past year, so it was only logical that I take over. I did that for six years, until my father became ill."

"What did you do then?"

She'd set her cup aside, seemingly forgetting it as she became lost in reminiscence. "I took care of my father," she said simply, but beneath her matter-of-fact tone he heard the quiet desperation she had felt at knowing she was going to lose the only family she had. "The other members of the company bought out my father's interest in the theater, and for a while we lived on that, but eventually I had to find a way of supporting us. There aren't many ways a woman can earn money, at least not what I needed for my father's care, but I was fortunate. One of the theater patrons was..." She paused suddenly, and her tongue flicked the crooked tooth as she stared at him. He looked back, waiting to see if she would mention the White Swan. "The madam of a brothel. She heard about my father's illness and offered me a job—as the piano player."

How he kept from showing a reaction, Jesse didn't know, except that he guessed he was too stunned. Absently he remembered seeing a grand piano in the parlor of the White Swan, a larger version of the piano across the room. At least now, though, he understood that peculiar air of innocence about her that had seemed so at odds with what he'd thought had been her past. He'd accepted it, but still he was too human not to feel relief at learning she had not been a whore. Even though the feeling made him ashamed—he knew he had no right to pass judgment on her—he couldn't deny that he was very happy to learn that she had not known countless men. Then he realized that much of the relief he felt was for her, not himself, thankfulness that she had not had to sell herself, not had to live the hard life he'd imagined for her.

"I don't tell everyone that," she admitted with a small laugh.

"I don't imagine so," he agreed dryly.

"Ah, well, anyway, the job wasn't enough to pay all the expenses of my father's illness, so she loaned me the additional money I needed. After my father died, I moved into the White Swan—that was the name of the place—to save money so I could settle the debt as quickly as possible."

"I imagine you could have settled it a lot faster if you'd—" He couldn't think of anything but a crude term or an even cruder obscenity.

She knew what he meant. "That's what Mrs. Hargreaves, the madam, kept telling me," Miranda agreed with sardonic humor. "I think that was the real reason she hired me. She thought she would eventually convince me to try something other than playing the piano in the parlor. She guaranteed me that within a year I could repay her and earn enough for a start in a new life."

Jesse could almost feel sorry for the woman, knowing her frustration at having such a money maker living under her roof and not being able to earn a penny off her.

"After she saw that she wasn't going to convince me to become one of her 'girls,' though, she decided she would find me a suitable husband, instead. However, since all the candidates for my hand were customers of the White Swan, few of their proposals involved marriage."

Jesse couldn't suppress a burst of delighted laughter at her droll tone. "How many prospects did she find for you?" He knew the madam had found at least one, but there had to have been others.

Miranda laughed wryly. "She had several, but there was one she was really enthusiastic about—a don Pedro Álvarez from Sonora," she said with mock grandeur. "He was in San Francisco visiting his cousin, and when he asked about me, Mrs. Hargreaves investigated him immediately. She found out that he was eight years older than I was, a widower with two little girls and the richest man in Sonora."

"But he was short, fat and ugly, right?"

"Oh, no." A faint, purely feminine smile played around her mouth. "He was well built, very handsome and—" she cocked her head, looking at him appraisingly "—almost as tall as you."

"But he had a bad reputation."

She shook her head. "He seemed very nice, and Mrs. Hargreaves said everyone spoke highly of him."

"Then why didn't you marry him?"

She gave him a puzzled look at his disgruntled tone. "Well," she said, sighing, "Mrs. Hargreaves thought I was very foolish, but he didn't know any English, and I didn't speak Spanish then, and I didn't see how we were going to be able to have any kind of a marriage if we had to speak to each other through an interpreter for months on end. Sooner or later one of us would have learned the other one's language, of course, but it just would have taken too long, so I said no."

With a practiced eye, he raked her body in the soft blue wool dress she was wearing. "Oh, you'd have been 'communicating' very well by the time the wedding night was over. You'd probably even haved learned a little Spanish, too."

Miranda took a hasty sip of her hot chocolate and almost choked. When she finally looked up, the expression in his eyes arrested the cup halfway to the saucer. The mocking humor was gone. Now his eyes were sober, intense—and wanting. They were filled with a reflection of the same desire she felt herself, the same desire she had been feeling since she'd first seen him that night months ago, wearing chains. Never having felt it before, she hadn't understood at first the strong attraction she felt for him, the powerful emotions stirring through her, the longing that was a persistent, physical ache deep inside her. These new feelings had frightened her and, with her pregnancy, had been too much to cope with, so she'd repressed them, ignored them as best she could. The look in his storm-cloud eyes said that whether she was ready or not, she was going to deal with them now, was going to acknowledge the desire that had been building steadily between them, because his patience was at an end.

He came to his feet, and without consciously willing it, she was suddenly on her feet, too. The cup and saucer that had been in her hands had somehow gotten to the table, she realized vaguely. They stood inches apart, and with slow deliberation, his eyes locked on hers, he closed the distance between them.

The kiss was a consummation, a sealing. There was nothing tentative about it, only a sense of naturalness, a rightness. His hands rose automatically to her shoulders, cupping them to bring her closer. One of her hands rose to his cheek, the other sliding around his neck, and her lips parted for him to enter.

For a moment he flicked the tip of his tongue against that crooked tooth; then he deepened the kiss, tasting, seeking. His arms slipped around her, his hands on her back, guiding her fully against him. He felt the hand on his jaw drop to his waist, then glide around to the small of his back. Her hand molded itself to the hollow there, exerting a subtle pressure, and his hips moved of their own accord against hers, pressing their bodies closer.

Jesse felt himself sway, and his eyes flew open. He was dizzy! Dizzy—just from kissing her. He'd never gotten dizzy before from kissing—not even when he was fourteen years old and he'd finally talked Ellen May Parsons into letting him kiss her. He didn't even get dizzy when he was deep inside a woman, his body pumping hot and sweet into hers. Closing his eyes, he gave himself up to the exciting novelty.

She started to withdraw, and he tightened his arms around her, one hand moving up swiftly to hold her mouth in place. "No," he whispered against her lips, which felt moist and slightly swollen from the pressure of his. "Again, Miranda. Kiss me again."

Her lips parted to draw a shaky breath, and he took shameless advantage, sliding his tongue between them again, deeper this time. He widened his stance, and one hand slid down, his fingers spreading, kneading, holding her high and hard against him.

Miranda moaned softly. Her body seemed to be melting like warm butter wherever it was touching his. His mustache was crisp and soft at the same time, an erotic abrasion against her upper lip; his mouth was alternately hard and demanding, soft and coaxing in turn.... She couldn't begin to name all the confusing sensations she was feeling; she just knew she didn't want even the smallest one of them to stop. Never had she imagined that you could feel such pleasure, such joy, from just kissing, from simply holding and being held. Hesitantly her tongue touched his. Cautiously it advanced to explore the sharp ridges of his teeth, the soft slickness of the inside of his upper lip, the firm muscles of his inner cheeks. Rapaciously it gathered all his tastes, the rich sweetness of the hot chocolate he'd drunk, a hint of tobacco and a darker, sharper tang that she knew instinctively was his own. His mouth shifted slightly, changing the angle of the kiss, and her hand slid up into his hair and tightened convulsively in the rough-silk curls.

"No...please, please..." Suddenly she was desperate that he might try to pull back, to deny her what she was so hungry for, to take away the fascinating mouth that was giving her so much pleasure before she was ready to give it up. And if it was like this just sharing kisses, what would it be like, she wondered dimly, if he took her down the hall just a few steps away, laid her on her wide comfortable bed...

"Shh. Shh, Miranda. Easy, sweetheart. I'm not going anywhere yet." There was a hint of humor and more than a hint of satisfaction in his husky crooning whisper as his tickly mustache brushed light soothing kisses over her cheeks, forehead and nose. The meaning of his words penetrated at the same time that she realized she had a handful of his hair, the curls wound tightly around her fingers to make sure he didn't go anywhere. With a little embarrassment and much greater reluctance she loosened her grip and let his hair slide slowly free before she dropped her hand to his wide shoulder.

With a final kiss, he eased his mouth away, and drawing a deep, uneven breath, Miranda hid her hot face against his shoulder. She could feel him hard and pulsing against her, and there was a corresponding moist heaviness between her thighs. She probably should feel embarrassment about that, too, she thought, but she didn't. She couldn't, not when, like the kiss, it felt so natural, so right. With another sigh, she started to push him away.

His mouth was immediately at her ear, his breath a warm tickle. "Stay, Miranda. Don't go yet." He spaced soft, openmouthed kisses down the vein throbbing in her neck. "Let me hold you a little longer."

She acquiesced, because in truth she couldn't do anything else. It might be insanity to stay, but it was *right*.

The need clamoring through him was quieting, slowly. Jesse rested his cheek on top of the silky head tucked beneath his chin and closed his eyes. If he'd needed any further proof that she'd done nothing more than play the piano at the White Swan, he had it now. Her response had been everything he could have wished for—and more—but it had been unschooled, as sweetly naive as it had been passionate. And it had surprised her as much as it had him. Her helpless response gave him an intense satisfaction. Hart might have had her first, but he hadn't awakened her passion.

She stirred against him, and he cursed silently. It had been an unconscious move, he knew, but it had rubbed the nipples of her breasts, still hard with her arousal, against his chest and reminded him that there was a part of him that was still hard, too, that wanted to rub against her. He almost groaned aloud at the mental image that thought conjured up, and he cursed himself again. As the one with greater experience, he recognized that it was his responsibility to lead the way and, perhaps more important right

now, to know when to call a halt. Caught off guard by her unin-
hibited response, he had already let things go too far, but, God help
him, there was one more thing he had to do before he let her go off
to her bed—alone. With the lightest of touches, he slid his hand up
her ribs to capture her left breast. He countered her startled jerk
with a gentle hand and stifled her gasp with his mouth. "I just want
to touch you, Randy. Please. Nothing more," he whispered between soft biting kisses.

The feel of those soft mounds with their hard centers pressing
through her clothes, his shirt, burning into his chest, had been
slowly driving him insane. He felt her relax as his hand weighed the
softness of her, felt the shudder that went through her as his palm
rotated slowly over the hard little nub, then felt her start to melt
again as his fingers shaped it through the soft fabric.

He gave her one last hard kiss, then quickly set her away from
him. He saw the quiver in her soft mouth, the turmoil of emotion
in her eyes. "Good night, Miranda," he said, his voice a low rasp.

Her eyes searched his for a long moment, though she wasn't sure
what she was looking for. His eyes met hers unflinchingly, burning with a clear steady light, and she nodded unconsciously in rec-
ognition, satisfied. "Good night, Jesse," she whispered, giving him
a soft, tremulous smile.

Jesse heard the quiet click of the latch on her door a few seconds later and echoed it with a sigh. He knew it wasn't locked, but,
her recuperation aside, he knew he wouldn't have opened it tonight. She wasn't ready to make love yet. Make love...that was the
term he had been trying to think of before, when they'd been talking about her only playing the piano in the White Swan. That was
what you did with a woman like Miranda—not any of those crude,
obscene words he'd thought of earlier. You made love, long, sweet,
unimaginable love. And they would—he'd already promised himself that—but not until the shadows of guilt had left her eyes.

Not guilt because she thought what she felt for him was wrong,
that what they would do was wrong, because he was certain she
didn't. Miranda was a strong woman. If she'd thought that, she
wouldn't have kissed him, no matter how much she loved him. And
she did love him. He was as certain of it as he was that she felt no
guilt because of it. Of all the emotions he'd seen in her eyes just
now, the strongest had been love, shining pure and bright, but
dimming that bright light were the dark, deep shadows of guilt.
Small shadows had been there almost from the first, before the
love, guilt over the unfairness of what had happened to him and
her part in it. The shadows had grown after his scrape with the
Apaches, then gotten even bigger and darker after he'd told her

about his dreams for his ranch in Montana. He shouldn't have told her yet, he realized now, but, relaxed and comfortable with her, the words and dreams had just slipped out, and now she felt even guiltier, knowing at last why he'd been accused of robbery and attempted murder and what the reality of his conviction and sentence had done to those dreams. She was blameless; if anything, she had saved him, but he knew by the shadows in her eyes that she didn't see it that way. In her mind she represented the destruction of those dreams. She felt she owed him for that, that she should do anything she could to make up his loss, and he was just selfish enough that when they made love for the first time, he wanted her only motivation to be love, not guilt, nothing but the desire to finally consummate that love. She owed him nothing, and he wanted nothing from her but her love.

Quietly he closed the front door behind him, then paused on the porch for a few moments before going back to his room in the bunkhouse with its narrow, cold bed. He had until spring to convince her, until spring when it was time to head north, back to Montana and home, until spring—when Miranda, Tommy and the baby would go with him to begin rebuilding the dream.

"Bang! I got you, you Apatch sonofabitch!"

Chuckling to himself, Jesse leaned against a stack of hay bales to watch Tommy stalk Susie and her chicks at the back of the barn, picking them off with his finger six-shooter and loud "bangs!" punctuated with realistic imitations of gunfire and enthusiastic profanity. Tommy dispatched another Indian with a single shot and a well-used, particularly obscene description of his sexual preferences, and Jesse winced through his suppressed laughter. He'd better remind Tommy again to watch his language around ladies. Miranda would probably use an entire cake of soap to wash that word out of his mouth.

"He certainly picked up some colorful additions to his vocabulary down in the bunkhouse, didn't he? Can he play poker as well as he can swear?"

Jesse turned around warily. The thick straw on the barn floor had muffled her approach, and he hadn't known she was there until he'd heard her dry murmur directly behind him. He took in her arms folded across her chest, the perturbed pinch of her tight lips, the elegantly arched eyebrow raised in sardonic inquiry—and the gleam of amusement in her eyes. "Not yet," he admitted honestly. "So far he's shown more talent for cussing."

Miranda agreed with an exasperated sniff, then found herself reluctantly laughing along with him as Tommy killed off another chicken with a remarkably creative hair curler in Spanish.

"Where did he hear *that* one?" she demanded under her breath.

"That's one of Cisco's favorites," Jesse said absently. At her narrow look, he added hastily, trying to keep a straight face, "Don't worry, I'll have a serious talk with him, and I'll speak to the men about watching their language around him, too."

Tommy disappeared after the chickens, out of earshot, and Miranda frowned after him. "Little boys are so bloodthirsty. When some of the miners' families still lived here in the canyon, those little boys used to play shoot-em-up, too, all the time."

Without thinking about it, Jesse took her arm to lead her toward the stall holding Red Lady and her colt. "I played it when I was small, and little boys a hundred years from now will probably still be playing it. I think it's natural, but—" he gave her a reassuring grin "—it doesn't mean he's going to grow up killing every chicken he sees on sight."

His hand was warm and firm on her arm. It was the first time he'd touched her in a week—since that night in the parlor when she'd discovered how devastating a simple kiss could be. Except that there had been nothing simple about that kiss or the ones that had followed it. Apparently it hadn't been that simple and easy for him, either. He still came to spend the evening with her in the parlor, and conversation was still just as relaxed as before, but both of them were being cautious with each other, careful about touching—or not touching. They were seemingly waiting, though she wasn't sure for what.

When they reached Red Lady's stall he let go of her arm, and the spot his hand had been heating immediately went stone cold. "The colt is growing so fast," she murmured, crossing her arms on the closed door of the stall to watch the mare suckle her foal.

He leaned beside her, almost, but not quite, touching. "I think Tommy's got his eye on him already, for when he outgrows Sam," Jesse said, laughing.

Laughing with him, Miranda caught a flash of movement behind them. Putting a finger to her lips, she directed his attention with her eyes to the short stack of hay bales a few feet away.

Jesse turned his head just in time to see the bright red top of Tommy's head as he ducked down behind the hay. Apparently having run out of chickens, Tommy was looking for new victims.

Both of them straightened away from the stall casually, waiting for Tommy to make his move. They didn't have to wait long. Two seconds later Tommy burst from behind the hay bales, shooting as fast as his finger and mouth could move. "Bang! Got you Mama!" He whirled and fired from the hip. "Bang, bang! You're dead, Jesse!"

Miranda clutched at her chest dramatically; then, with a long, piteous moan, she sank down in a slow death spiral. Jesse was so busy admiring her performance that he almost forgot to "die," too. Grabbing his belly, he groaned, staggered forward a few paces, then fell back on the clean straw, breathing his last with a convincing death rattle.

In a cautious crouch, Tommy approached the two bodies sprawled in the clean straw, his gun still ready in case they were only playing possum. Finally, satisfied, he straightened, blew on the tip of his finger and holstered it in his pocket. Jesse was good, but Mama was a better dier, he decided objectively.

Through slitted eyes Jesse watched the little boy suddenly slap his little butt and gallop off, already in the middle of his next adventure. Rolling over onto his belly, he propped himself up on his elbows to look down at Miranda; her eyes were closed, and she was still lying on her back in the straw. Several strands of hair had pulled loose from the knot on the back of her head and curled around her face and down her neck. Her shawl had fallen off, the tail of her long-sleeved white blouse had pulled out of the high waist of her dark blue skirt and the button holding the high, lace edged collar closed had popped, exposing her throat. Her cheeks were pink, and her lips were rosy from biting them to keep from laughing when she was supposed to be dead. She looked like a woman who'd just had a quick tumble in the straw and loved every second of it.

"Is he gone?" she whispered, her lips barely moving.

"Um-hmm." There was no need for him to, but Jesse heard himself answering in a near whisper, too. The barn was empty except for the two of them and the animals, and lying in the straw, it was warm, the air scented with the sweet, sunshine smell of dried grass. Strong winter sunlight shone through the windows on the south side, but by the time it reached the floor it was softer, gentler.

Her eyes opened, and he saw they were bright and sparkling with laughter. Suddenly she wrinkled her nose and made a terrible face. "Ugh! I have straw in my mouth, and it tastes terrible," she said, giggling. Her hand came up to get rid of the straw; then she smiled up at him, seemingly in no hurry to get up.

Jesse decided he wasn't in any hurry, either. Slipping two fingers into his vest pocket, he worked one of the pieces of hard candy he'd bought for Tommy the last time he was in town out of the small bag. "Close your eyes and open your mouth."

She gave him a wary look. "Why?"

"Come on, Miranda, just do it. I promise you'll like it," he wheedled.

After another hard look, she closed her eyes and opened her mouth a fraction of an inch.

"Wider." She opened one eye to give him a suspicious scowl, and he laughed. The eye shut, her mouth opened a little wider, and he popped in the candy.

He watched her taste it with a cautious tongue; then her mouth curved in a delighted smile. "Umm. Raspberry, my favorite." She sighed blissfully, her eyes still closed as she sucked on the candy.

"Let me taste."

Her eyes opened quickly; then the expression in them changed as they met his. The lids seemed to grow heavy, and the sparkle he saw now was the spark of excitement. They shut slowly as he lowered his head. His tongue demanded a taste of her sweet mouth, and her lips parted immediately.

"Mmm. My favorite, too," he murmured, then took another, longer, taste. Her arms came up to lock around his neck as she kissed him back, taking a taste of her own. He let his elbows collapse, settling his chest and hips over hers. Sliding his hands into her hair, he tilted her mouth up so he could perfect the seal of their lips. Their chests and bellies rubbed languidly together, and he eased one long leg between hers. Her knee rose slowly, her thigh rubbing along the outside of his, and he snugged his leg higher and tighter in the notch at the top of hers.

Miranda heard her own soft moan and his deeper answering groan as their hips rocked together gently, creating a warm friction. Miranda broke the seal of their mouths and kissed her way down his jaw and throat to the red bandanna circling his neck. Her tongue took a delicate lick beneath it. She tasted salt and man, a combination far more pleasurable and potent than the candy. She felt his hand working the top button on her blouse, and she twisted her shoulders slightly away from his to give him access. Swiftly he freed that button and the next two. His fingers slipped inside, and the almost scorching heat of his hand burned through the thin batiste that covered her breast. The nipple rose immediately, almost as if it remembered his hand and had been hoping for that knowing touch again.

Slowly, almost lazily, his long fingers moved until his hand finally covered the hard wanting peak and softer flesh beneath. Miranda let out a long breath and felt herself sinking deeper into the straw. The warm gust of his breath stirred her loose curls, and his mustache brushed her neck as his lips nuzzled softly; then his head settled on her shoulder, his body hard and heavy on hers. Their bodies were aroused, their position intimate, yet there was something curiously sexless about his hand on her breast, Miranda thought hazily. That large warm hand, his reassuring weight, his head lying so sweetly on her shoulder, made her feel cherished, safe, protected.

For long moments they simply lay together, silent, unmoving, just absorbing the wonderful warmth and feel of each other. Finally he raised his head, and she knew he was looking at her. Her eyes were closed, and when she opened them, she saw by his soft, almost sleepy smile that he had been feeling the same emotions she had.

He brushed the loose tendrils of hair back from her cheeks, then pressed a soft kiss on her mouth. "We'd better get up before someone wanders in here," he said with a wry smile.

His hand slowly withdrew from her breast, but this time the warmth remained, a heat that seemed to melt into her body to penetrate her heart. He did up the buttons of her blouse, then rolled to his feet and offered her his hand to help her up.

Miranda straightened her clothes, then tried to repair the damage to her hair.

"Here, let me," Jesse said softly, coming to stand in front of her. His long fingers plucked out a few bits of straw, and tucked and pushed pins in tighter; then he stepped back to survey the results. "I think you'll do," he said solemnly.

"Not with all this straw all over me, I won't," Miranda said, laughing. With limited success, she tried to brush it off the back of her navy wool skirt. Jesse finished the effort with a few brisk swipes of a currying brush that had been lying on top of a nearby hay bale. She smiled her thanks; then they both turned toward the small figure yelling for them at the front of the barn.

"Mama, Manolo is looking for you."

Outside, Manolo met them at the first corral, where Tyree and Frank Penny were repairing a broken rail.

"*Señora.*" Manolo tipped his hat, then nodded at the tall man beside her. "*Señor.*" He nodded silently to the two men working nearby, then glanced briefly over his shoulder to make sure the wagon parked by the main house was being tended to. "*Señora*, there is enough silver for another shipment to the mint in San Francisco. I think it should go tomorrow, while the weather is still good."

Miranda looked at him in surprise. "I didn't think we were going to have enough to ship until spring."

Manolo heard the hope in her voice and was sorry that he had to dash it. "We hit a pocket of very rich ore, enough for another shipment after it was smelted, but there won't be another one," he said with absolute certainty. "The vein has nearly run out. As I told the *señor* yesterday—" he nodded toward her companion "—I think this will be the last full shipment."

Miranda absorbed this news. It was not unexpected—she just hadn't expected it quite so soon. She also absorbed the fact that Manolo had told Jesse before he had told her and realized that she wasn't really surprised. Although his loyalty was unquestionable, she had known that Manolo was not completely comfortable working for a woman. Since the night of Jessa's birth, there had been a subtle shift in his attitude toward her. He was as respectful as ever, but she had several times caught his eyes shifting to Jesse, as if for confirmation, before he acknowledged one of her orders. "Very well, Manolo." She turned to Jesse. "Will you arrange for a couple of the hands to go along? I expect the miners would be more than happy to relinquish guard duty to them."

He nodded, then addressed Manolo. "Is that the silver in the wagon?" He nodded toward the wagon by the main house with the tarp-covered, chest-sized lump in the back.

"*Sí, señor.* I thought I would leave it in the house tonight for safekeeping, then load it in the morning so we can get an early start."

"Good. I'll tell the men to be ready at daybreak." For a moment he watched the miners struggling to lift the heavy chest out of the wagon. There was little need to move it to the house, but he knew Rivera was taking no chances. The mine superintendent had asked him the week before if he would like to see the mine, and he had of course said yes. The operation was an efficient one, but from the size of the pile of tailings, he knew the rumor he'd heard around Deming that a fortune in silver was buried under the Silver Tejo ranch house was just that—a rumor. The blooded horses, the prime Hereford bull, the house with its fine furnishings—that was where Hart had buried his "fortune." Over the years the mine had produced a comfortable income, but no more than that. He suspected Hart had left Miranda with very little other than a dying mine and a cattle ranch that would never pay for itself.

He turned back as the boss of the Mexican miners spoke again.

"*Señora* . . . there is something else."

His obvious dismay warned Miranda that Manolo had more bad news. "What is it, Manolo?"

"Several of the miners had asked me to tell you that they and their families will be leaving after Christmas, to go to the mines in Silver City."

"How many of them, Manolo?"

He cleared his throat. "About half of them, *señora*. But there will be enough to finish the last of the vein," he added quickly.

"But they would all like to go, wouldn't they, Manolo?" she asked perceptively.

"*Sí, señora,*" he said heavily. "The Santa Rita mine is going to open a new tunnel the middle of next month, and the owner sent a man down to the village, trying to recruit miners. All of the men could have jobs if they went."

"Ask them if they'll stay until the first of the year. I'll send a message to the owner of the Santa Rita mine to tell him that all of the Silver Tejo miners will be coming."

"*Gracias, patrona.* The miners will appreciate that, and I guarantee that they will stay until the new year." The burly miner tipped his hat again and started to turn away.

Miranda stopped him with a hand on his arm. "What will you and Leola do, Manolo?" she asked softly.

"Leola and I will stay as long as you need us, *patrona*," he said firmly.

Jesse waited until the burly miner had crossed the compound to the wagon before he said quietly, "He would like to go to Silver City, too."

Miranda gave him a bleak look. "I know. I'll talk with Leola about it. I'm sure the owner of the Santa Rita mine would be overjoyed to get someone of Manolo's experience." She stared across the yard at the thick adobe walls of her home. They looked just as solid, just as sturdy, as before, yet suddenly she didn't feel as safe.

At the sound of a childish voice, Miranda turned, and Jesse saw the determinedly cheerful smile she put on for the little red-haired boy running toward them. The mine would be closing sooner than she had expected and that could only aid Jesse's own plans, but still he felt sorrow for her. She was going to lose friends, people she loved, and the loss would be hard. He only wished he could make it easier for her.

Tommy skidded to a stop in front of them. "Mama, Jesse, come see what I made!"

"What is it, Tommy?" Miranda asked.

"I can't tell you. It's a surprise," he explained, dancing from one foot to the other. He grabbed Miranda's hand and almost jerked her off her feet in his impatience. "Come on!"

"Whoa!" Jesse clamped a gentle hand on Miranda's elbow to steady her and a slightly less gentle one on Tommy's shoulder. "Your mother and I will come with you in a minute, son, after I talk to Mr. Tyree and Mr. Penny."

"Yes, Jesse," Tommy said in a subdued voice.

Jesse covered the few feet to the corral in one stride. "Tyree," he called, "you want to take a load of silver into Deming tomorrow?"

Tyree looked up from the rail he was about to hammer into place. "Well, I don't know, Jessie Mack. I'm having so much *fun* here." He looked at the hammer in his hand with disgust. "But I suppose, as a favor to you, I'll force myself."

Jesse was grinning at him when Frank Penny spoke up. "I'll go, too, boss, if you need another man."

Jesse's smile vanished. "All right, Penny. Be ready to leave at sunup." He started away, then turned back. "Tell Charlie Baxter and Moreno I'd like them to go, too." A few extra men couldn't hurt, he reasoned. There had been no sign of trouble from either the Apaches or Leyba's gang for weeks, but that only made the short hairs on the back of his neck stand up straighter.

Penny watched the man and woman walking away, smiling down at the small boy, who was holding their hands and skipping between them.

"Ready, Penny?"

Hastily he picked up the rail to hold it in place for Tyree to hammer. "Ready," he said. Tyree hit the first nail, and Frank glanced back at the three people walking toward the barn, focusing on the woman. Oh, yes, he was ready. More than ready.

"I thought maybe you had forgotten our deal, *cuate*."

Cuate was a more familiar, friendlier term than *amigo*, but Frank Penny didn't feel reassured. "I didn't forget, Leyba, but I couldn't see any point in a long ride unless I had something to tell you," he said, risking a subtle complaint. The meeting place Leyba had chosen was a cave several miles from the mouth of the canyon that guarded the Silver Tejo. The entrance was between two slabs of rock, one sitting in front of the other with a narrow gap in between, which created the illusion that they were one solid piece of rock from a distance. Even up close, no one would suspect they hid the opening to a huge cave. How Leyba had found it, he didn't know, and he hadn't asked.

He did know that Leyba didn't waste his time at the cave, on the chance that he would show up. The 'breed was alerted by someone who was watching for him, but who the man was or where he kept watch, was something else Frank didn't know.

"So, *cuate*, what did you ride this long way to tell me?" Leyba drew out a knife and began to clean his nails.

Frank eyed the length and sharpness of the blade and swallowed before he spoke. "They're shipping a load of silver to Deming tomorrow. There'll be five men. I'll be one of them." He swallowed again. "It-it'll be the last load, too. They're shutting down the mine. The silver's run out."

Leyba looked up slowly. "So. There will be no more after tomorrow." Idly he tapped the knife on his palm; then he suddenly pointed it at the man crouching on the other side of the small fire. "Then you, *amigo*, had better find a way for us to get in and get all that silver buried under the widow's house, no?"

With an effort Penny kept himself from recoiling from the razor sharp point inches from his chest. "Let's worry about tomorrow first."

"I will worry about tomorrow, Señor Penny. You worry about the other. Soon, no?" He feinted with the knife, laughing when the other man flinched and almost fell over backward.

Penny slipped through the slit between the rocks a minute later, Leyba's laughter still ringing in his ears.

Chapter Fourteen

Jesse opened the front door of the ranch house and took a deep appreciative sniff. He'd seen the silver off on its way to Deming, set the rest of the men to doing their chores, and now he was going to steal a little time for his own pleasure. For the past few days the kitchen had been producing nose-teasing odors that had the whole house saturated by now. Some of them were the same smells of Christmas that he remembered from his childhood—spices, roasting nuts, baking cookies—but mixed in were smells unique to New Mexico—red chile, lime cooking with dried white corn, and the cedary scent of juniper. Green boughs hung over the door and picture frames, and a wreath of the tied branches heavy with tiny purple berries and shiny apples decorated the center of the dining table. The house looked and smelled ready for the holiday that was a few days away—except for one important item.

In the kitchen he found the three women hard at work, making yet more food. Leola was grinding lime-cooked corn for tamales, Miranda was buried to her elbows in a bowl of dough and Emma Lee was turning the handle of a meat grinder while feeding chunks of cooked meat, raisins and apples into the top. Even Tommy had been pressed into duty. Armed with a small hammer, he was cracking walnuts.

Miranda looked up from her bowl in time to see Jesse whisper something in Tommy's ear. Whatever he'd said, it got a favorable reaction, because Tommy grinned hugely, scrambled down off his chair and ran out of the kitchen. After winking at Leola's frown when he stole a handful of raisins, Jesse came over to her. He was close enough that even with the other scents in the kitchen, she could smell the cold clean smell of winter on his long white heavy canvas duster.

"What are you making?" he asked between raisins, peering into her bowl.

"The dough for *empanaditas*—mincemeat turnovers. Emma Lee is making the mincemeat."

At the sound of her name, Emma Lee glanced up with a shy smile, then as if she'd startled herself, quickly looked back down at the meat grinder. Jesse raised his eyebrows in silent comment, and Miranda nodded with a pleased smile. "I'm going to take Tommy out to find a Christmas tree," he said, now filching one of the chunks of citron soaking in brandy in a bowl in the middle of the table.

Miranda laughed at the terrible face he made when he popped the citron into his mouth. "Thank you. He keeps asking me when we're going to put up the tree."

"How big a tree do you want?" He got rid of the taste of the citron with a chunk of apple.

"One that will fit in the parlor," she said wryly. "The one Manolo cut last year was only ten feet too tall."

Tommy came dashing back into the kitchen, wearing his coat and mittens. "Mama, Jesse's going to cut a Christmas tree, and I'm going to help him," he said importantly.

She smiled at him fondly. "I know, poppet. Remember, keep your coat buttoned."

Fearing that Jesse was going to succumb to that bad habit grown-ups had of wasting time talking when there were much more important things to do, Tommy pulled on his hand. "Let's go, Jesse. I know where there's a really big tree."

Miranda rolled her eyes, and laughing, Jesse let the little boy drag him out of the kitchen.

Outside, Jesse retrieved the ax he'd left by the front door, then followed Tommy around the back of the house. The sun was shining out of a clear blue sky. There had been no more snow since the blizzard the night of Jessica's birth, but the air was cold. As he watched the little boy running ahead of him, the toe of his boot kicked something and sent it clattering over the loose rock at the base of the canyon wall. Bending, he picked up a battered tin plate.

"That's for Mama's bobcat," Tommy said, running back to him.

Jesse swallowed a disbelieving laugh. "A bobcat?"

"Uh-huh. Mama says he lives in a cave." Tommy gestured vaguely toward the upper wall of the canyon. "But he comes down every night and sits on that big rock and waits for her to come feed him."

Jesse looked up at the huge granite boulder partway up the side of the canyon, poised as if it were about to roll down on the house below. Moving directly below it, he saw the tracks in the few patches of bare dirt.

"Mama's let me stay up to see him a couple of times. He's real big and pretty." He glanced up worriedly at the big man. "We're not supposed to tell Leola, though, because she says bobcats steal chickens, and she might want somebody to shoot him."

"We won't tell her," Jesse assured him gravely as he came back and carefully set the tin plate down in its place, then took Tommy's hand and started walking up the canyon. From what Miranda had told him of a childhood spent in hotel rooms and boarding houses—hardly the places where a child could keep a pet—he understood why she made pets now out of chickens, an old cow—even a wild cat.

During the next hour they found several likely trees, but after serious discussion on the finer points of each, they kept looking. Finally Jesse spotted a tree at the base of the back wall of the canyon. It was a piñon, about six feet tall and perfectly formed. A scarlet Virginia creeper twined through the thick green branches to make a natural garland, and a few cones remained as additional decorations. After several wistful glances at a thirty-five-foot, long-needled pine close by, Tommy guessed that the piñon would be all right.

As soon as Jesse opened the back door into the kitchen, he knew something was wrong. The pans and bowls were still on the table, just as they had been an hour before, still full of food, but there was no sign of Miranda or the other women. It was as if they had just suddenly vanished. Swiftly he searched the house with Tommy as his white-faced silent shadow. In Miranda's bedroom, he saw the empty cradle—and Toppy sitting in the rocking chair, calmly feeding the baby her bottle.

As soon as he saw Jesse in the doorway, the cook gestured with a gnarled finger to his lips. Jesse saw that the bottle was empty, and that Jessica's eyes were nearly closed. Toppy set the bottle down on the floor, then stood up carefully on his bowed legs. He walked on the toes of his boots to the cradle, laid the almost sleeping baby on her stomach, then patted her back when she started to whimper. If he hadn't been in such a hurry to find out what the hell was going on, Jesse thought absently, he would have laughed at the sight of the grizzled old cook playing nursemaid.

Jessica quieted, and Toppy tiptoed to the door. Jesse took him by one skinny arm and hustled him down the hall, pulling him to a stop by the front door. "Where are the women?"

Toppy took one look at the grim expression on the face of the man towering over him and decided that now was perhaps not the best time to mention that he was about to break his arm. "They're over at Miz Rivera's, takin' care of Cisco. Miz Hart asked me to take care of the baby." The steel fingers crushing his arm relaxed fractionally.

"What happened?"

"Bandits tried to take the silver, Tyree said. They got four of them, but Cisco's horse took a bullet and fell on him. Busted up his leg pretty bad, so they brought him back here before they took off again." He wiggled his arm hopefully, and after an absent-minded glance down, McClintock released it.

"Took off where? After the bandits?"

Toppy shook his head, rubbing his sore arm discreetly. "Back to Deming to deliver the silver. They took the rest of the men to ride shotgun."

Jesse stared past him for a minute, thinking. It was what he would have done himself. With four of Leyba's gang killed or wounded, they would hardly be likely to try to take the silver again right away. Glancing down, he saw Tommy beside him, his small face still unnaturally pale and still. "Your mother is all right, Tommy," he reassured him, squatting down to Tommy's level. "She and Leola are taking care of Cisco, and I'm going to go see if they need any help. I want you to stay here with Toppy and help him with your sister. All right?"

Tommy nodded solemnly.

After a smile and a pat of approval for the little boy, Jesse rose swiftly to his feet, his face sober again. "I'll be back as soon as I can," he said to Toppy as he pulled open the front door.

Leola heard the door of her house open, but she didn't look up from what she was doing until she sensed the visitor watching from the doorway. Even then she spared only a quick glance upward. "I am glad you are here, *señor*. I am going to need a pair of strong hands."

And a strong stomach, Jesse added silently. Looking as pale as death, Cisco Moreno lay unmoving in the same bed Charlie had occupied scant weeks before. His lack of movement was no doubt explained by the half-empty bottle of laudanum on the night-stand. His lack of color was explained by the gruesome condition of his right leg.

His pant leg had been cut away to expose his leg from ankle to hip. Halfway between his knee and his hip, two jagged ends of bone poked through the front of his thigh. It was not a neat wound. The broken thigh bone had obviously ripped and torn its way through muscle and skin, and there had been a great deal of blood. The wound was still oozing, even now. Quickly Jesse glanced at Miranda and saw that while she was nearly as white as Cisco, her hands were steady as she held his leg still for Leola's ministrations. Emma Lee stood behind the older woman, passing her items from the small pharmacy on the nightstand as she asked for them. Jesse moved to stand beside Miranda, but the *curandera* redirected him to the end of the bed.

"We are almost ready for you, *señor*." To the silent girl behind her she murmured, "Hand me the blue bowl and a clean cloth, Emma Lee."

As Leola wrung out the cloth in the dark colored liquid in the bowl, she kept up a steady monologue that Jesse realized was for Emma Lee's benefit. Probably to keep her mind off the grisly mess of Cisco's leg, he thought.

"This wash is made from Oregon grape, Emma Lee," she murmured, using the English name instead of the Spanish. "It is used to cleanse the wound to prevent infection." She finished washing the area around the ragged puncture and as much of the wound itself that she could reach. Fortunately there seemed to be little dirt. "All right, *señor*, now I need your strong hands. Grasp his knee firmly, and when I tell you, pull straight toward you."

Jesse placed his hands as instructed, while Leola positioned her hands at the top of Cisco's thigh and Miranda held the uninjured leg steady.

"Now, *señor*!"

Jesse pulled steadily, and the ends of the white bones disappeared. The pain penetrated the fog of laudanum, and Cisco groaned and thrashed, trying to free himself from it. Immediately Emma Lee grabbed his flailing arms and crossed them over his chest, half lying on him to use her weight to hold him still. Jesse heard the ends of the broken bone grinding against each other; then Leola Rivera gave Cisco's thigh a quick twist and there was an audible click as the ends of the bone snapped together like the pieces of a puzzle.

Cisco sank back into unconsciousness, and Jesse and the three woman relaxed. Leola Rivera rested for a few seconds, then bent to examine the set of the bone.

"*¡Perfecto!*" she announced, and picked up the washrag and blue bowl of Oregon grape wash again. When she was satisfied that the wound was as clean as possible, she handed the bowl and cloth back to Emma Lee, then asked for a clean strip of linen and the two small tins on the nightstand. "This is wild tobacco, Emma Lee," she said, pointing to a light green pile of ground leaves and stems. "It will ease the pain. And this is Apache prayer plume." She indicated a similar pile, only brown in color. "It will draw out any infection that forms." She applied the poultice with brisk, economical movements, tying the ends tight, then gestured toward the wooden splints leaning against the side of the bed.

As Jesse looked on, Miranda handed one across, keeping the other for herself. Working together efficiently, they passed a fat roll of linen bandage back and forth, binding the splints to the leg to hold the ends of the bone in place while it knit back together. Miranda had done this before, he realized. She might not have the *curandera's* knowledge of herbs and medicines, but her hands were every bit as deft.

"I have heard," Leola commented as she tucked the end of the strip under the splint and knotted it tightly, "that some of the Anglo doctors now use white plaster to hold the bones while they heal, although I do not see how it could be used if there is an open wound. Closed off from the air and the necessary medicines, the wound would fester and eventually the arm or leg would have to be cut off."

"The Apaches grind up the bark of a cottonwood tree." The voice was dry and raspy, as if it hadn't been used for a long time, the words slow and hesitant, as if the speaker had to search for the right ones. "They boil it, then strain out the fibers. What is left they put around the broken arm or leg, and when it hardens, it forms a shell that holds the bone in place."

Three pairs of eyes snapped up in astonishment. The fourth pair, light green, was intently examining the face of the young man lying unconscious on the bed.

"Do the Apaches have any other... interesting cures like that, Emma Lee?" Miranda asked in a careful voice. All three pairs of eyes were now locked on the thin girl bending over the bed.

"They have a lot of them, some of yours—" she glanced up briefly to Leola, then back to Cisco "—like the wild tobacco. For pain they grind up a red seed and mix it with a little *mescal* and drink it. It seems to work."

"I have heard of it," Leola said thoughtfully, suppressing her excitement. Secretly she had long desired a chance to learn some of the Indians' cures and medicines. "Perhaps you can tell me some of the others later," she suggested in a casual tone.

"I will." Emma Lee spoke almost absently as she tucked the blanket at the foot of the bed around the injured man. She looked up at Jesse suddenly. "What color are his eyes?" she demanded with an odd fierceness.

"Very dark, almost black." Jesse automatically used the same subdued, careful tone as the others. It's almost as if we're afraid we'll somehow frighten her back into silence, he thought, watching her closely.

Emma Lee nodded almost dreamily. "That was the color of my baby's eyes. He was eight months old. The first wife of the Apache they gave me to couldn't have any children, and she was jealous of my son. So she killed him." Emma Lee looked at each of them in turn with an odd kind of detachment; then she burst into tears.

The two hours following Emma Lee's calm revelation were the most traumatic, emotionally wrenching she'd ever experienced, Miranda thought as she walked slowly back to the main house. Two years of horror, unspeakable brutality, grief and almost inhuman suffering had poured out of Emma Lee like the pus out of a festering wound. Yet when the girl had sobbed out the last of it and fallen asleep, exhausted, on Leola's bosom, Miranda had sensed that she was cleansed. Emma Lee, despite her terrible ordeal, had a chance at a normal life now.

It would take an exceptional man to accept what had happened to her, but—she glanced up at the man walking at her side, his arm tight around her—they did exist. Her own tears had fallen freely during Emma Lee's agonizing recounting of her life with the Apaches, and several times she had seen that Jesse's eyes were unashamedly wet.

"It's amazing that she survived," he said quietly.

"I know," she agreed softly, "but I think she's going to be all right. Leola's plan to have her take over Cisco's care will be good medicine for her, too. It will give her someone to worry about instead of herself, and show her that she has value."

Jesse leaned against one of the new corrals built to winter the remuda, shaping the small chunk of cottonwood in his hand with his pocket knife. The cuts of the sharp blade in the soft wood were precise and sure, but they were automatic. His mind was on the attempted robbery of the silver shipment the previous day. Because of their late start—the second time—the men accompanying the shipment had not returned until this morning. He had heard Penny's report, along with Rivera's and Charlie's, and all three were in agreement on the essential details. The attack had come as they were riding across a deep arroyo, one where the high walls turned on both sides close to the crossing, hiding whatever was around the curving corners. Eleven renegades had been around the corner yesterday, and it had been only dumb luck that none of the five men from the Silver Tejo had been killed. Tyree had heard a horse whinny a fraction of a minute before the attack, but those seconds had been enough for the men to whip their horses up and out of the arroyo and take cover behind the wagon. They had picked off four of the bandits as they'd come charging up out of the gully. The rest had turned tail, abandoning their fallen companions, who, unfortunately, had all been dead, meaning there was no one to question.

Cisco had suffered his broken leg giving chase, when his horse had stepped in a prairie dog burrow and snapped its leg. Cisco's foot had become tangled in the stirrup somehow, and the horse had fallen on his right leg, breaking it. At least they hadn't had to shoot Cisco, he thought with morbid humor.

It was obvious that the ambush had been planned. The question was: who had tipped Leyba off that the silver was being shipped? It could only have been someone from the ranch, and he was hoping the fourth man he hadn't heard from yet might have the answer.

"That one looks like a Morgan."

Jesse laughed dryly at Tyree's drawled comment. "I'm doing well to make it look like a horse, much less any particular kind." Snapping the knife closed, he slipped it and the cottonwood horse he'd been whittling into one of the deep pockets of his duster. He rolled a cigarette while Tyree leaned back against the corral and found a cigar. Cupping his hand around Tyree's match, he drew deeply on the cigarette, then slowly exhaled the lungful of hot smoke. "Do you have any thoughts on who tipped off Leyba?" he asked almost mildly.

Taking a puff of his cigar, Tyree nodded. "But I can't prove it," he said aloud.

"Who?"

"Penny. He went out late two nights ago. By the time I saddled up, I couldn't see where he'd gone, so I waited. He came back about three hours later. His horse was lathered up, as though he'd taken a hard fast ride. When I asked him about it the next morning before we left, he said he couldn't sleep and had decided to go cougar hunting, see if that big cat was still around the canyon where we had the remuda." Tyree took another leisurely puff. "I checked this morning. The freshest tracks in the canyon and up on the rim are at least a week old."

From the suddenly bitter taste of the cigarette, Jesse realized how much he'd wanted it to be Penny, and how disappointed he was that there was proof that it might not be. "Charlie and Rivera both say he shot a bandit who was drawing a bead on Cisco."

Tyree blew a perfect smoke ring. "If he is in with Leyba's gang, the smartest thing he could have done was to shoot one of them. You know that, Jessie Mack."

He ground out his cigarette. "Yeah, I know it. The hell of it is, I can't think of a way to make him tip his hand."

Tyree shrugged. "All you can do is watch him and wait." He had a sudden thought. "Do you suppose one of the six dead bandits was Leyba?"

Jesse gave a disgusted snort. "I couldn't be that lucky. Where's Penny now?"

"He and Shorty and a couple of Cisco's boys rode out just ahead of me to make sure the cattle still have plenty of feed."

Frank Penny slipped between the two slabs forming the entrance to the cave and forced himself to walk slowly across the sandy floor to the other side of the small circle of scorched sand where the fire usually was. Even though it was daylight, he wished there were a fire anyway. There was little natural light in the cave, and it was cold. He shivered once. He hoped Leyba showed, because he couldn't risk coming again. From his sharp questions, he knew McClintock was suspicious, and he was certain Tyree had tried to follow him the last time. Coming today in broad daylight had been chancy, but it hadn't been hard to give the other men with him the slip. He would claim later that he had gotten lost for a while in the maze of canyons.

"Leyba?" he called finally when he saw no one.

"Behind you, *amigo*."

Startled by the low voice that sounded more than ever like the hiss of a snake, Frank whirled around, his hand on his gun. Leyba must have been waiting outside, hidden, then come into the cave behind him. He saw that the 'breed's hands were empty, so he relaxed, letting his gun slide back into the holster.

"Why did you shoot one of my men, *cuate*?"

Too late he saw that Leyba's hands were not empty. He'd been too busy looking for a gun that he'd overlooked the thin knife Leyba was now tossing lightly in his palm. He could feel the sweat running down his spine and smell the stink of his own fear. Hooking his hand casually on the big buckle of his belt, he felt for the deringer tucked inside his pants. He didn't dare try to outdraw that knife, but if he could reach the derringer... "One of your men was so stupid he couldn't keep his horse quiet," he said boldly when his thumbnail caught under the hammer of the little gun. Slowly he eased it up. "A man with me heard it and warned the others. Then your men came charging out of the arroyo like fools, and I was forced to shoot one so the others wouldn't become suspicious."

Leyba stopped tossing the knife, and Frank waited, in an agony of indecision. He had the belly gun snugged between his thumb and his pants, ready to pull it out. Should he go ahead and shoot Leyba now? Or take the chance that Leyba would accept his explanation.

Suddenly Leyba put the knife away, sliding it into the sheath at the small of his back.

"You are right, *amigo*, my men were stupid. When will they try to move the silver again?"

"It's already in Deming," Frank said with as much spiteful satisfaction as he dared. He hated Leyba, he suddenly realized. Someday he would like to see the half-breed snake down on his belly where he belonged. "As soon as they took the one that was injured back to the ranch, they left again. That silver is probably in San Francisco by now." He eased the gun back down into his hiding place. "I didn't see you with the rest of the gang," he said in a more careful voice.

Leyba shrugged. "I did not think it was important enough to need my personal attention, but—" he gave Frank a slow, unblinking stare that sent another slimy runnel of sweat down his spine "—I will give my personal attention to the silver buried under the ranch house. When can we get it?"

"Remember my cut. I want the same as with the shipment, twenty-five percent—and the woman."

"She is yours, *amigo*, and the cut is fair," Leyba said equably.

"You'll need more men, too."

"I have them already. What you saw yesterday was only half."

"The last night of the month, everyone will be celebrating the new year. They will be drinking, and no one will be worrying very much about the gates. I'll open them after the celebrating is over when everyone is sleeping off the whiskey and tequila."

"It is an adequate plan, *amigo*. We will be waiting."

Leyba laughed softly to himself as Penny vanished through the cave entrance. The stupid *gringo* was worried about his cut. His cut would be a bullet in the back—after the gate was opened. He tested the sharp blade of the knife under his thumb. And *he* would have the woman.

Chapter Fifteen

So this is what you see from up here, cat," Miranda murmured. Huffing a little from the hard climb, she wrapped her skirt around her knees. The gray boulder where the bobcat sat nightly like a lord on his throne commanded a view of the box canyon from the high front gates to the back wall. She had seen the same view from the rim once, but the buildings had looked like cracker tins, the men like Tommy's lead soldiers. Here the perspective was much closer, everything life-size, like a stage setting she had stepped out of so she could watch from the wings until her next scene.

For a moment she tilted her face up to the sky overhead. It was clear today, but hazy, the winter sun cold and flat. It was not the ideal day to be sitting outside on a rock, she thought humorously, but she had been restless, feeling the need to be free of thick, confining walls, the need to *move*. Gradually her breath came easier, her body, overheated from the exertion of the climb, cooled to a pleasant glow and she was content simply to sit and enjoy a rare moment of solitude.

There were two days until Christmas, and there was nothing left for her to do. All the food that could possibly be made had been. The house was decorated, Tommy had already hung his stocking from one of the war lances on the chimney and Jesse had set the tree up in a bucket of sand in the parlor the evening before. Tommy had carefully painted the cones on the branches with a solution of Epsom salts that had dried into sparkling white crystals that looked like new snow. The three of them had popped popcorn in the fireplace, then strung it to make a long garland to go with the beautiful red one of Virginia creeper. The rest of the decorations—the Mexican painted tin angels and fanciful animals, the blown-glass fruits and polished tin candle holders—wouldn't go on until Christmas Eve.

For a time she watched the scene below. The horses in the remuda lazed in the new corrals, their shaggy winter coats giving them a wild, untamed look. Red Lady's colt frisked in another, while his mother looked pleased with herself. Men were working to haul feed to the remuda, Mr. Penny was coming toward the house with the milk pail and Tommy was playing at the side of the barn, but the tall figure she was always unconsciously on the alert for wasn't in sight.

She was too far away for sounds to reach her, but suddenly the heavy gates opened, and she knew the signal must have been whistled to allow someone entrance. A rider came through on a buckskin horse. It was Manolo, and she wondered how many more times she would see him ride through that gate. He had taken her letter to the owner of the Santa Rita mine, along with the last small shipment of silver, and she knew that the adobe houses in the miners' village would be standing empty and abandoned by this time next month. Manolo and Leola would be the next to leave, probably after the six weeks or so Leola had said it would take Cisco's leg to heal. She did not want to think about how much she was going to miss them, especially Leola, who had welcomed a frightened young stranger and made her feel less alone, less an outsider. She would have to bear their loss, because she could not ask them to stay when there was no longer anything there for them. Manolo needed a mine to manage, and Leola needed people who needed her skills.

Miranda's gaze dropped to the flat roof of the fortresslike house below her. What she needed was right here. The house was her haven, her security, hers and Tommy's, and now Jessa's, too. People could leave, *would* leave, but the house would remain. Cattle and horses, not silver, would support it now. She had the stock and the determination, and she would find trustworthy men to help her. The army would solve the problem of the Apaches and the renegades, and the gates to the house would finally stand open. Until then, nothing could harm it; her home was safe.

There! You see? she told herself with a laugh. There's nothing to worry about. But it wasn't the laugh of a woman with nothing to worry about. It wasn't strong and confident; it was weak, with an odd note of desperation, and she put her hands over her mouth to keep the sound inside.

A man had come out of the barn, immediately picking up a small shadow, and started across the compound with that familiar loose-hipped, long-legged stride. There was someone else whose loss would be hard to bear. The sound blocked by her fingers now had an added note of despair. The pain of Jesse's loss wouldn't be hard it would be unbearable, like the loss of a limb, a vital, necessary part of herself.

The house blocked her view, and she could no longer see him. *A vital, necessary part of herself.* Because she loved him. When had it happened? The night of Jessa's birth? Perhaps it had been the morning she'd told him to shave off his mustache. She smiled at the memory of her ridiculousness. It hadn't been any particular moment, she suspected, but rather a gradual process, beginning the night she had been confronted with a chained stranger and felt the first stirrings of an emotion she didn't understand. She understood it now, and it was time to stop giving it coy names like desire, attraction, or any of the dozen others she'd used to try to disguise its true identity. It was love, pure . . . but not so simple.

Suddenly feeling cold, she pulled the old sweater she was wearing closer. He would be leaving, too, in the spring. It was nothing he'd said, just a restlessness that she sensed in him, too vague to be identified by any particular word or action. He was anxious to go home to Montana, back to his ranch—though without the cattle he'd come to buy—and they both knew she could do nothing to stop him. But she was going to try. With everything she had and was, she was going to try. She was going to offer him a home here, a ranch already stocked with the cattle and fine horses he wanted. She would be offering herself, of course, as part of the enticement. He cared for her, she knew, and for Tommy and Jessa. With her head bowed to her knees, her hands, which had been pressed over her mouth, pressed together now in an attitude of supplication. Surely, surely, he wouldn't refuse an offer like that.

"What are you doing up there?"

Her head snapped up and she turned toward the quiet voice below her. She had been so engrossed in thoughts of him that she hadn't heard him approach over the loose rock and hard ground. He stood now at the foot of the slope looking up at her. After the rather formal clothes of the men she had known in San Francisco, the Western style of dress had seemed too casual, almost raffish, but now she thought how frivolous those high beaver hats, long-tailed coats, brocaded vests, fancy white ruffled shirts and silk cravats and shiny patent leather shoes were. They were as frivolous as the men who wore them. Jesse was wearing the white canvas duster that was the standard winter coat in the West. Split to the hips in back and hitting at mid-calf, it protected a man against the weather whether he was on foot or, more important, on a horse. Underneath the unbuttoned coat, his tight black pants were tucked into the tops of long, close-fitting, square-toed, high-heeled black boots. His vest was worn black leather, his shirt plain dark flannel topped with a red bandanna, and his black hat was wide brimmed and low crowned. He chose his clothes for practicality, not fashion, and there was nothing dandified about them, any more than there was about the man who wore them. His face was tanned instead of the pasty white of city men, his body lean and hard, not soft and beginning to run to fat. Nothing about him was frivolous or pretentious; he was big, strong, physical and, quite simply, the most wonderful-looking man she had ever laid eyes on.

"I was just seeing what the bobcat sees when he sits up here," she answered finally, standing up. Gathering her skirts, she scrambled down off the rock and began to pick her way back down the slope. Her feet got away from her, and she finished the descent in a breathless rush.

He caught her, the impact of her body hard against his, leaving her even more breathless. For a moment she felt his arms strong and secure around her and smelled his warm musky scent; then he set her away from him. With a small, soundless sigh she fell into step beside him.

He looked down at her head, just level with his shoulder. What had she been thinking all alone on that rock? For a split second after she'd raised her head, he'd thought he'd seen a lost, almost desperate look in her eyes.

He resisted the urge to run his hand over her hair, to straighten her sweater, to take the hand that was so tantalizingly close to his as they walked. He sensed the tension in her, the same tension he'd been living with for weeks. With her limited experience, she probably didn't know exactly what was causing it, but he did. Desire, lust—whatever name you gave it, it was a physical symptom that came from being unable to satisfy a hunger that had nothing to do with meat and potatoes. He hungered for a taste of her soft white skin, her sweet giving mouth, her warm pliant body. And even as he thought it, he knew a taste would never satisfy him. Only the whole feast would do, and even that, he was certain, would never be enough.

"Have you seen Cisco this morning?" he asked.

"Yes. He seems better. His fever is down, and there's still no sign of any infection. Emma Lee has hardly left his bedside."

"It's a good thing she can't understand Spanish," Jesse observed dryly.

Miranda laughed her agreement. Out of his head with fever, there had been no curbs on Cisco's scatalogical tongue. As they rounded the back corner of the house, she glanced across the yard, and her gaze fell on the butchered steer hanging from the block and tackle at the top of the barn, curing in the cold dry air for their holiday dinner. "Do you know what I wish we could have for Christmas dinner?" she said wistfully. "A goose. The last Christmas we were in England, I remember we had one. It was so good. If I close my eyes," she said, suiting the action to the words, "I can still taste it."

Her face was lit by a soft, unfocused smile as she savored the memory, and for a moment he had a glimpse of an auburn-haired little girl, her twilight eyes shining with the wonder of Christmas.

She opened her eyes with a sigh and gave a rueful laugh. "That's one problem with living on a cattle ranch, I suppose. There's plenty of beef, but never anything else."

"There's a flock of wild geese on the slough," he said. "Why don't you put on your riding clothes, and we'll go get one or two? The scouts haven't reported any sign of Apaches or Leyba's gang, and the fresh air and exercise would do you good. You haven't been out of the canyon for months."

He was rewarded with another glimpse of the happy little girl as she clapped her hands with a delighted smile. "Oh, do you really think we could? I can be ready in—" Her smile and delight started to fade. "But what about Jessa? Tommy could go, but—"

"Leola will take care of Tommy and Jessa. I'll go tell her while you get ready." As much as he enjoyed the little boy, he was going to be selfish, Jesse decided. He wasn't sharing Miranda with anybody this afternoon.

Her smile came back immediately. "All right." She took off in a flurry of skirts, then whirled when she was halfway to the front door. "I'll be ready in five minutes!" she promised.

The heavy gate swung shut behind them minutes later, and with the thud of the crossbar dropping into place, Miranda suddenly felt wonderfully free and light, as if she'd been given a reprieve at the last second from some long and tedious task. The temptation of a ride—and the time alone with Jesse—had been too much to resist. She was going to forget her worries and simply enjoy this wonderful, unexpected treat.

He glanced over at her with a frown. "Are you sure you're going to be warm enough?"

She gave him a dazzling smile as she nudged the Arabian mare into a light-footed lope. "Oh, yes. I have my woollies on."

Jesse urged Lucky into a canter after her. If she was wearing "woollies" the sheep must have been damn near bald, he thought, chuckling to himself. She had on a brown suede divided skirt that fitted every sweet curve of her slim hips without so much as the hint of a wrinkle and revived a familiar ache that riding a horse did nothing to relieve. With the skirt she wore English riding boots and a short black jacket over a white blouse, with a stock tied high around her neck. She'd plaited her hair into a long braid and left it to hang down her back, beneath a flat-crowned, Spanish-style hat. She looked like a proper English lady out for an afternoon's ride in the park.

Once out of the canyon, they left the road and traveled cross-country. A long, dark line low on the western horizon warned of an approaching storm, but Jesse ignored it. They would be back in the canyon long before the storm hit.

Miranda pulled up suddenly, then sat on her gray mare, gazing toward a pile of burned timbers about a quarter of a mile away. "That's where the sheep rancher and his wife lived, isn't it?" she said quietly without turning her head. "The one you all took such care I shouldn't know about."

Jesse cursed under his breath. "How did you find out?"

She looked at him then with a sad smile. "I overheard Manolo telling Leola about it. He said it was Leyba's gang."

He nodded curtly, silently repeating the obscenity and adding a few more, then turned Lucky and kicked him into a trot. The mare's hoofbeats sounded behind him after a few seconds, and he settled his horse into a smoother gait. They put a quick mile between them and the burned-out homestead, and Jesse saw that her somber mood had lightened when she turned with a smile to point out a short skein of geese, black necks stretched out in eager anticipation, flying in the same direction they were riding.

They topped a small rise, like a hump in the desert's back, and stopped again. The horses puffed clouds of steam into the chill air like small locomotives, while out of habit Jesse scanned the horizon and the low foothills a mile distant. Automatically he noted a small cabin tucked between two of them. Turning back in the saddle, he looked toward the slough. It was a shallow depression where an underground spring made a brief appearance, then disappeared back under the sand, creating an oasis of cottonwoods, willows and salt cedars in the midst of yucca and cholla.

A blue-gray mist hung over the area, seeping across the desert surrounding it, making it seem as if they were about to ride down into a calm sea. Miranda touched her heel to the mare, and the responsive horse started toward the line of tall cottonwoods that marked the course of the spring. They rode across several low hummocks that rose like islands out of the sea of mist, giving her the fanciful illusion of being on a boat, riding the ocean swells.

In a sparse stand of willows at the upper end of the slough, Jesse dismounted with that smooth flow of muscle she so admired and slipped his rifle out of its saddle scabbard. She, too, dismounted, withdrawing the rifle on her saddle out of habit. A year and a half ago she'd never even held a gun in her hand, she thought absently. Now it seemed unnatural to be without one. After tying up their horses, he led the way quietly through the thin trees toward the water.

Miranda stood on the edge of the marshy ground and looked across the dull water. It appeared black, very cold and slightly oily. The bare gray branches of the cottonwoods looked like gnarled fingers scratching at the pale sky. The sun was shining, and geese were honking cheerful greetings back and forth, but there was a something almost... sinister about the place, she thought, and shivered. A few seconds later she was laughing at her foolishness as Jesse angled through a denser thicket of chest-high cottonwood whips that ended abruptly at the edge of a quiet pool. A raft of geese floated in the middle, within range of the rifles, but out of range of dry feet, so he turned, taking them deeper into the marsh.

Moving silently on the soft ground, they worked their way through a break of salt cedars; then Jesse halted abruptly, cocking his head to listen. Miranda paused behind him and heard the beating of wings overhead. Jesse threw up his rifle, but by then the Canada goose was over the water, and he lowered the gun with a disgusted look. Grinning, Miranda shrugged, then pointed questioningly toward a faint game trail that wound through the trees.

As they followed it toward the center of the slough, Miranda realized it was getting darker. The sky overhead was no longer clear, shreds of cloud and mist were turning it a leaden gray. She was reaching for Jesse's sleeve, when a dozen geese suddenly exploded into the air behind the thin screen of willows in front of them. His arm reached back a split second later and his hand clamped on her shoulder, jerking her face down onto the damp, sour-smelling dirt. More than a little annoyed with him, she planted her palms on the ground and strained against his hand, but succeeded only in raising her head even with his knee where he was crouched beside her. "Jesse!" she began in a furious whisper. "Why did—"

"We've got company," he informed her in a terse undertone. Relaxing his hand on her shoulder, he gestured that she could come up to her knees, but no farther. He pointed silently across a small patch of open water, and through the mist, she could see several human forms flitting between the cottonwoods. Someone else had apparently come looking for a goose dinner. She was about to make a small joke to that effect, when the mist swirled and cleared for a moment and she saw that they were Apaches.

"What are we going to do?" she whispered. Amazingly, she felt little fear—because, she realized, she was with Jesse.

"I don't think they spotted us. We'll go back the way we came and get the hell out of here."

Like wraiths of fog themselves, they moved swiftly through the mist-shrouded trees. A branch snapped nearby, and Miranda found herself facedown in the dirt again. The hand locked on the back of her head kept her there for interminable minutes, until Jesse was satisfied that the danger had passed; then he grabbed her elbow, yanked her up and took off in a crouching run. Miranda stumbled after him, keeping her head down to avoid getting slapped by the branches whipping back behind him. They missed her face, but they snatched at her hair, bringing tears to her eyes several times as the long strands got tangled, then tore free.

Without warning he stopped, and she ran into him, half knocking the wind out of herself. He seemed oblivious to the impact, merely reaching a hand back to steady her. While she was still struggling for a decent breath, she heard his soft curse.

"They left someone with their horses."

Cautiously, Miranda rose up enough to peek over his shoulder. About twenty yards directly in front of them, a young Apache stood with six horses. "We're going to circle around to the left," he said directly into her ear. "Keep low and don't make a sound."

His warning was completely unnecessary, Miranda thought. She wouldn't be making a sound; she wouldn't even be breathing.

They almost made it. Just as they were reaching a dense stand of willows that would have assured their invisibility, the eerie silence of the marsh was shattered by a rifle shot, followed almost simultaneously by a loud whine an inch over Jesse's head.

Miranda felt herself flying impossibly through the air until a solid tree trunk brought her to the ground again. It was several seconds before her dazed brain cleared enough to understand that he had picked her up and literally thrown her into the thicket. Coming up onto her hands and knees, she saw him with his back to her, facing the direction they had just come from. For a moment all was silence again, and Miranda had the wild thought that perhaps the Apache had decided he'd seen an animal, instead, but the sudden shouts killed that hope almost as fast as it had sprung up. She didn't need to understand Apache to recognize the sound of human wolves hot on the scent of their prey.

Jesse levered off three quick shots as he backed swiftly toward her. "They're not sure how many of us there are, so they're being cautious for the time being, but they'll start circling around to trap us pretty quick," he said in a low voice as soon as he reached her. "Our horses are about twenty-five yards straight behind us. You go first. I'll be right behind you."

She knew he wouldn't be right behind her. He was going to stay, was going to sacrifice himself to make sure she got away safely. "No," she said quietly.

His face was harder than she had ever seen it, the skin drawn so tightly over his cheekbones that she was vaguely surprised it didn't split. He grabbed her and shoved her hard toward their horses. "Yes, Miranda! Now get the hell going."

A snow squall began sifting small flakes through the trees as she swung around to face him once again. "I won't leave you," she said in a steady voice.

"Damn it, Miranda!" His voice dropped from a near shout to a low cruel hiss. "Remember the sheepherder's wife? Maybe you didn't hear all the details of what they did to her. The Apaches won't be any different than Leyba's men. You'll be raped by every man. If you're lucky you'll lose consciousness after the fourth or fifth one, but they'll wait until you revive, and then they'll start all over again. They'll enjoy it more that way. You'll pray to die, and you will, but not before you spend an eternity in hell."

Her face was as white as the snow catching in her dark hair, but she didn't move, and Jesse knew a fear and desperation unlike any he had ever felt before. Suddenly her eyes widened, and she raised her rifle. He spun, and they both fired at the same time. A body slid slowly down between the trees. Jesse swung back around, almost crazy in his desperation to make her go. "They're circling around. Now will you g—"

As he swung around, his hand, halfballed into a fist, struck her cheek. Involuntary tears of pain filled her eyes, and her hand rose reflexively to her cheek. Then, with visible self-control, she lowered her hand, and he felt sick at the sight of the bright red imprint of his fist on her white cheek. "Miranda, please...please go." His agonized whisper broke in the middle.

"Not without you," she enunciated clearly in a low, fierce voice.

Jesse hesitated only a heartbeat; then, with a despairing curse, he grabbed her hand and began weaving a zigzag course through the trees. The air was suddenly full of blood-freezing cries and gunshots. Twice bullets came close enough for him to feel their hot breath as they sped past his head, and once he heard Miranda cry out softly. When he jerked around, already stopping, she shook her head, pointing to her ankle to indicate that she'd only turned it, and motioned for him to keep going.

The course he'd chosen meant they had to cover three times the distance to the horses than they would have if they could have simply run in a straight line. Every breath burned in her lungs, and her legs felt like tree stumps she was trying to drag behind her, but

Miranda kept moving. All her concentration was focused on the man ahead of her, gripping her hand so hard she was sure the bones were crushed. The snow squall intensified, hiding them from their enemies' eyes, but hiding their enemies, too. Miranda tried to listen to the sounds beneath the rising wind, but could hear nothing but her own rasping breath.

The howls and cries behind them had died away, and there were only a few sporadic shots, but Jesse halted in a crouch at the edge of the stand of willows where their horses were tied. He could see his horse and Miranda's through the eddying snow, but no other movement. "Ready?" he whispered, his eyes intent on the scene in front of him.

He heard her whisper raggedly in return, "I'm ready."

Tightening his hold on her hand, he rose and sprinted through the scattered trees. Jerking the reins of the Arabian mare free, he shoved them into Miranda's hand, then boosted her into the saddle with a rough shove on her bottom. Seconds later he was mounted and urging Lucky into a gallop through the trees. The mare needed no urging. Terrified by the gunfire and the storm, she raced ahead, clearing the trees a few lengths ahead of the Appaloosa stallion.

A small snow devil swirled suddenly in the mare's path, and the horse, already spooked, reared in panic. Jesse watched in horror as Miranda struggled for control, then began a slow inevitable slide to the ground. She fell, and the horse galloped off, disappearing into the storm. She was back on her feet almost immediately, and Jesse was spinning Lucky toward her, when the muffled report of a rifle alerted him to the danger behind them. Four Apaches were riding out of the swirling snow, looking more like ghosts than human beings. He fired the rifle still in his hand, then sheathed it and kicked Lucky into a full gallop toward Miranda. Understanding what he was going to attempt, she began running in the same direction, her arms held high. Tightening his thighs and knees around his horse, he leaned from the saddle, arms outstretched. He had one brief glimpse of her white face and wide frightened eyes; then his arms closed around her at the same time that she grabbed a fistful of his coat, and he snatched her up. Lucky absorbed the impact and extra weight in his steady stride.

Jesse righted himself in the saddle, lifting and turning her sideways to cradle her in front of him. For several minutes he gave Lucky his head, letting him put as much distance as possible between them and the Apaches. Finally he slowed the stallion to a walk and listened for sounds of pursuit. There were none, and he guessed the Indians had abandoned the chase in favor of seeking shelter from the storm. Which was what they had better do, he thought grimly. The storm could very easily accomplish what the Apaches hadn't.

The closest shelter was the little cabin in the foothills. Trying to get any bearings with the sleet obscuring everything past Lucky's nose was impossible, so he simply trusted his instincts and turned Lucky into the wind. He felt a hard shiver run through the body in his arms. Jesse tore open his coat, then pulled the edges around her as tightly as possible. She'd lost her hat, and he could feel her long hair whipping around them both. With his free hand, he tucked it down inside his coat, turned up the wide collar and snugged her closer.

The stock on her blouse had unwound, leaving her throat exposed, and Miranda felt the icy kiss of the sleet on her bare skin. Ducking her head, she tucked her cheek into the hollow of his shoulder. With his arms holding her securely, her eyelids began to grow heavy, and incredibly, she fell asleep.

Jesse wasn't sure if it was his instinct or Lucky's, but one of them found the little cabin. Its solid black bulk loomed suddenly out of the cold dense whiteness surrounding them, and Lucky stopped on his own, head down, by the door. Stifling an incredulous laugh that she could have fallen asleep in the middle of a snowstorm on the back of a horse, he said softly, "Miranda, wake up, honey, we're at a cabin." He felt her stir against him; then the top of her head rubbed his chin.

"Where are we?" she asked sleepily.

"At a cabin," he repeated. "About a mile or so from the slough. Can you stand up if I put you down, sweetheart?" He felt her nod, then lifted her and let her slide slowly down Lucky's shoulder. She stumbled then steadied herself and moved away.

As he swung down off Lucky's back, Miranda went to the door. "Anybody home?" he called to her.

"No." But in the tradition of offering shelter to any stranger who might need it, the owner had left his door unlatched. Miranda moved farther into the small cabin, leaving the door open. The pale light of the storm was enough to show her that the cabin consisted of only one room, and that a kerosene lamp sat on a table. She groped around the base of the lamp and was rewarded with a box of sulfur matches. She struck one, holding her breath against the acrid smoke, then raised the glass chimney and touched the match to the wick. A bright yellow light immediately chased the darkness back, and after adjusting the flame, she looked around her.

"It looks like a miner's cabin," Jesse said, stamping the snow from his boots as he shut the door, then set his saddle beside it.

"I think so," she agreed. The cabin was roughly finished and furnished. The floor was of uneven planks, with wide gaps between them. Several more planks made up the crude table and two benches. The rest of the furniture included a wooden barrel, where it looked like the miner tossed his dirty clothes, several packing crates for cupboards and a bed. There were both a fireplace and a small cook stove, with an enameled coffeepot and a cast-iron kettle on it. Several gold washing pans hung on the wall, while a collection of picks and shovels leaned by the door. There was a set of assaying scales on the table by the lamp, and Miranda could see a few bright glints of gold dust caught in the rough grain of the wood.

Jesse glanced around the cabin. There was every sign that the prospector lived alone—one chipped enameled cup, one battered tin plate, one bent fork and spoon in the open cupboard—but the bed was built for two. Either he'd once had someone to share it with, or he was an optimist, Jesse thought to himself with a laugh. It was solidly if crudely made, like the table and benches. One side was anchored to the wall, the other supported by two legs, and there was a mattress, but no other bedding.

At the sound of a clank, he turned to see that Miranda had started a fire going in the little stove, using the kindling that had been stacked beside it. Larger logs were piled haphazardly along the rude hearth in front of the fireplace. She closed the small door of the fire box, then backed up to it, rubbing her arms as she waited for the heat to penetrate her damp clothing. "Was there a place to put Lucky out of the storm?" she asked.

Jesse nodded as he stripped off his coat and hung it on a nail pounded into the wall by the door. "There's a lean-to out back."

Miranda fixed her gaze on the lamp. Suddenly she felt unaccountably nervous. "I wonder where the miner is?"

He shrugged. "He probably went into Deming to spend Christmas. You need to get out of those wet clothes, Miranda."

"I—uh—yes. I suppose so," she agreed, but made no move to do it. She watched his hat and vest join his coat. Then he straddled a bench and pulled off his boots one at a time, standing them beside the bench, and her nervousness doubled. He wiggled his toes inside his socks, and that funny, unconscious, natural little gesture relaxed her, banishing her nervousness to somewhere beyond the door. This was Jesse, she reminded herself, the man who had delivered her child, the man she loved. She had no secrets from him. Reaching up, she felt for the buttons of her jacket and began to undo them. After taking off her jacket, she hung it on another nail on the wall nearby. "Whoever he is, he certainly likes nails," she muttered under her breath.

"What did you say?"

The words were spoken almost in her ear, and, startled, she jerked around. He had come up behind her, his sock-clad feet making no sound on the wooden floor. His shirt was unbuttoned and hanging loose, exposing a narrow strip of smooth golden-brown skin.

She licked her dry lips before speaking. "I-I said he likes nails. Whoever he is. The miner, I mean," she chattered inanely. Her nervousness was creeping back in under the door, sifting in with the fine snow, bit by bit.

He nudged her down on the bench, squatted in front of her and patted his thigh. It was several seconds before Miranda realized that he wanted her to prop her foot there while he eased off her boot. When the second one came off she had the sudden urge to rub the arch of her foot over the hard muscle she felt under her heel. Instead she stood quickly, forcing him back onto his heels to get out of her way.

For several minutes she made a show of examining the contents of the miner's "pantry," an open-sided packing crate he had nailed high up on the wall. She heard the door of the little stove open and the thunk of several logs; then it shut again, followed by the grating slide of the damper to adjust the air flow. "Are you hungry?" she asked brightly.

"Yes." His answer was soft and close behind her.

"Well, it seems we have beans, flour, coffee, molasses—"

"That's not what I'm hungry for."

She turned around slowly to face him. "No?"

"No," he affirmed quietly.

"Then—"

"I'm hungry for you." He answered the unspoken question she already knew the answer to. "And I think you're just as hungry as I am."

Her throat suddenly too tight to speak, she nodded dumbly. That was what it was, not nerves, but hunger. Well, perhaps a few nerves, she admitted with a silent rueful laugh. Slowly he approached and reached down to take her hand, leading her to stand beside the bed. She saw that while she had been wasting time inventorying the pantry, he had spread the blankets from the bedroll he always carried tied behind his saddle.

Slowly, as if he didn't want to startle her again, he took the hand she held and placed it behind his neck. Her other hand just naturally seemed to follow, and he settled his own hands on her hips, drawing her closer inch by inch as his head dipped. She watched his eyes turn from smoky blue to dark blue to almost black before hers finally slid shut the second before his mouth touched hers.

His mouth was hard on hers for a heartbeat, then softer, not making a request or a demand, but simply acknowledging his right to take. Her lips parted easily, and his tongue swept inside, over-powering hers, then drawing back to let her take what was her right. Her tongue dipped and tasted and teased while her arms locked more tightly around his head, her hands spreading to comb through the curly hair above his ears, then close gently, luxuriating in the rough silk feel of it trapped between her fingers.

One hand slid down to her bottom, bringing her body into full contact with his, and she rubbed against him unconsciously, wanting the fit to be closer. He groaned deep in his chest and freed his mouth to brush light quick kisses over her face, her nose, her chin, her cheek. His lips detected the swelling, the slight abrasion on the smooth skin, and his head jerked back.

Her eyes opened slowly, a question in them.

"Miranda, I didn't mean to hit you." His voice was a rough, urgent rasp as his hands came up to frame her face. "It was an accident. I'd never hurt you. I love you."

"I know," she said softly. Reaching up, she took one of his hands to cradle it in hers. She studied it as if she had never seen it before. Like the rest of him, his hand was long and lean, graceful and strong. This hand had held both guns and her baby, she thought. It had both killed and delivered life. It had touched her, given her such pleasure, and she wanted to feel its touch again, without the restraint of clothing, with nothing to keep bare flesh from bare flesh. "I love you, too," she averred.

Jesse had to shut his eyes against the rush of emotion surging through him. When she had refused to leave him, he had been so frightened and so angry with her, yet he'd felt a perverse kind of satisfaction that she was willing to die with him rather than save herself at his expense. Eyes still closed, he brought their mouth and bodies together again. Miranda gave herself up to the kiss, only vaguely aware of his hand working the buttons of her blouse loose. He opened them all and pulled the blouse free of her skirt, but didn't remove it. Instead his hand dropped to another set of buttons, the ones on her skirt, and slowly, agonizingly slowly, he freed them, too; then he stepped back and she felt his hands brushing her bare shoulders, slipping off the blouse. His knee nudged between hers, and she shifted her legs apart to let her skirt slide down.

As it hit the floor with a soft whoosh, Miranda heard his soft question. "Are these your 'woollies'?"

His finger was hooked in the neck of the long-sleeved close-fitting shirt that covered her chest, and she nodded without opening her eyes, because suddenly it was just too much effort.

He'd been almost right about the bald sheep, Jesse thought with another chuckle. Her shirt and long drawers were made of the thinnest, softest wool he'd ever felt. He ran his finger inside the neck, tracing her collarbones, then pulled it free to trace a line between her breasts and lower, enjoying her small quiver. His finger reached the bottom hem over her belly, and he gripped it with both hands to raise it up over her head. Then, loosening the tie at her waist, he eased the drawers down her long legs, and she stepped out of them. Lastly he tugged off her long woolen socks.

She was wearing a camisole and short drawers under the woolen underwear. He pulled her back into his arms and ran his hands over her back, watching her face as he massaged and stroked. Her eyelids fluttered, but did not open, and her head dropped to his shoulder with a soft groan of pleasure as his fingers made their way down her straight spine to the small of her back. It was warm in the cabin, and there was no need to hurry. He was going to prolong their first time together for as long as he could stand it. Greedily, he wanted to act out every one of the fantasies he'd imagined all those nights when he'd sat chastely with her in the parlor, and keep every detail locked in his memory forever.

His long fingers spread over her bottom, and his openmouthed kisses teased down her chest, while his hands gently kneaded the firm flesh filling them. He reached up to loosen the satin ribbon threaded through her camisole, then opened the first two buttons, and Miranda waited, waited for his hot mouth to reach her breast. Instead, just as she felt moist warmth through the thin linen, he turned her around and pulled her back against him. His hands resumed their slow massage across her shoulders, down her sides, over her midriff, avoiding the flesh that most wanted to feel his touch. Even without it, her nipples had beaded and puckered so tightly that they ached. She sagged back against him, and felt him widen his stance to trap her thighs between his. She felt him hard against her hips and rubbed without thinking, drawing a moan from both of them.

Soon, she thought, soon he would touch her breasts. She tried to will his hands in that direction, but she couldn't seem to concentrate hard enough; she could only feel, a hot achy fullness that she knew instinctively would be relieved if only he would *touch* her. His fingertips slipped under the waist of her camisole and skimmed back and forth across the bare skin of her abdomen, a breath away from the curves above, and Miranda couldn't contain her groan of frustration and longing when they went no higher.

Soon. He would touch her breasts soon. Jesse let his hands glide over her belly and back up, circling around her full breasts under the cloth, but not touching. Not yet. She ached to be touched, and he ached to touch, but the waiting was such a luxurious torture. Silently she twisted against him, trying to move beneath his hands, to make them give the attention her body craved. Then the soft undercurve of her breast brushed his knuckles, and he'd had enough torture.

The camisole was whisked up her arms and over her head, and Miranda gasped as his hands closed over her bare breasts. The roughened skin of his fingertips was deliciously abrasive on her sensitive nipples. Squeezing, shaping, he eased the ache, but it only moved lower, concentrating in an emptiness at the top of her thighs. She clamped them together in an effort to fill the emptiness, but it wasn't enough.

"That won't help, Randy," his deep voice whispered in her ear, one arm anchored around her middle, while his other hand glided lower, over her belly, until it found the new ache. His long knowing fingers began to rub it away, relieving it…and making it worse.

Miranda heard herself moan. I'll be so ashamed when I remember this later, she thought, letting him touch me like this. But now she couldn't help it. She wanted him to touch her; her body demanded it.

"Open your legs, Randy."

Mindlessly she obeyed his husky command, shifting her thighs apart, and moaned yet again when his hand covered the place where she hurt the most.

"That's right, honey. Tell me how good it feels when I touch you here."

Her answer was her buckling knees. Only his arms, holding her against him in a gentle vise, kept her on her feet.

"And here."

Those clever fingers stroked and maddened, offering an even more insidious pleasure. They created an unbearable friction between the fine soft linen and her ultrasensitive flesh. She sensed that the fabric was damp, but she was past feeling any shame. She was only sensation and need now, and when the warmth of his hand was abruptly removed, she cried out at the uncomfortable rush of coolness when only heartbeats before there had been such heat.

"Shh, it's all right. I'll only be gone for a minute. I just want to get you out of these."

She felt his fingers at her waist, pulling at the drawstrings. She wanted to demand that he hurry, but her body was in riot. All she could do was lean back against him, trembling, in a fever of need she could only pray he would fulfill. His nimble fingers worked the knotted bow loose, and she dimly felt the linen skim down her thighs and calves. There was more coolness, but she didn't care, because all her attention was focused on his hand, which was back where she wanted it, warmer than before, the sensations more incredible than before.

"Ah, Randy, you're so soft."

His words were a scorching gust across her skin as his mouth seared the sensitive hollow between her shoulder and throat, racking her with a new set of unbearably pleasurable sensations. His hand dropped to her bare belly, splayed across it, supporting her for his ministrations. One finger probed, and she gave a high thin cry.

He knew no one had ever touched her like this. The startled little flinches he felt with each new touch proved it, and he almost lost control from that knowledge alone. It made her new for him, virgin, as if she had never been touched by any man. He knew he had no right even to want that—he was certainly no untouched virgin—but he was too human not to be pleased.

"You're so hot, sweetheart, so hot, so ready."

Miranda barely heard the low rasp in her ear. She sensed that she was on the verge of some tremendous discovery, some incredible experience, and she knew for a certainty that she wasn't meant to go alone.

With that quick strength that still surprised him, she twisted in his arms. Her hands, which had been hanging limply all this time, now grasped his head.

"No!" Her eyes were bright with determination and an odd confusion. "I want…" She shook his head in her frustration. She didn't know what she wanted. She only knew what she *didn't* want.

He watched her, wary, every muscle in his body tensed. Surely she wasn't going to refuse!

"I want you with me!" She finally cried, and knew that she still hadn't made herself clear. Not knowing what else to do, she pulled his head down roughly and covered his mouth with hers, telling him her demands, her frustrations, in one devastating kiss.

For a moment Jesse was too stunned by her power to return the kiss; then his mouth caught hers, matching demand for demand, frustration for frustration, while his fingers tore frantically at his own clothing. He jerked his mouth free long enough to whisper, his voice harsh with self-control, "I know what you want, Randy."

He laid her back on the bed. She raised her knees automatically, and he didn't waste any time fitting himself between them. She was ready, and he was past ready. With one slow stroke he buried himself deep inside her, gritting his teeth at the sensations he'd never felt before. This was way beyond dizzy, he thought with a kind of wonder. This was like dying, only dying of a pleasure so unbelievable that it couldn't get any better. He pressed his forehead against hers, forcing himself to hold still inside her. He'd heard her small gasp of shock at his entry, seen her hands clench in the blanket, and he knew her body needed time to accommodate itself to him.

Finally he sensed a subtle relaxation, and he began to move with a slow rhythm, letting her become reacquainted with a man's possession, only he wasn't sure anymore who was possessing whom. And he'd been wrong; it *could* get better.

"Randy, oh, sweetheart, you're so tight, and it's so good . . . so good."

Miranda felt her body readying itself for the discovery, the experience, and she began to be afraid. She tried to hold back, to retain the control she sensed she was too rapidly losing.

Jesse sensed her fear and smoothed his hands down her satiny thighs, lifting them. "Wrap your legs around me, Randy. Hold on to me, love. I'll take care of you."

Blindly Miranda did as he commanded. Her senses were so filled with him that she could do nothing else.

He felt the first small convulsions begin deep inside for her, then the answering ones in his own body. "Now your arms Randy . . . around me. Hold me." She obeyed again, but he felt her still resisting the release he knew would be scalding, soul deep endless.

He slipped his hand between their bodies and found the small point of incredible sensitivity he'd pleasured so exquisitely before "I want you with me, Randy." He unconsciously echoed her earlier words. "Don't stay behind . . . come with me, love."

Her body jerked and seized his in a paroxysm of delight that sen shudder after shudder deep through him until he realized he wa feeling his own release as well as hers. Dimly he heard a lon scream and a low agonized groan, and he knew he'd been right. I *was* scalding . . . soul deep . . . endless.

Chapter Sixteen

There was no better way to wake up, Miranda decided, than in the arms of the man you loved, warm, blissfully relaxed and snow-bound. She didn't have to look out the one window of the cabin to know that the world outside was wrapped in a cold white blanket. The light in the room had an odd bluish brightness that lacked the power of the sun. Raising her head from its comfortable niche in his wide shoulder just far enough to see over his even wider chest, she glimpsed icicles hanging like jagged teeth from the low eaves. The snow had stopped falling sometime during the night, but dawn appeared to be just a colorless smear in the heavy clouds.

The cabin was almost as cold as the icicles, she thought, snuggling back down under the blanket. It was tightly built, but the fire in the stove had burned out, so she wrapped herself around the warm body next to hers. Jesse was as warm as any stove, and you didn't have to worry about getting burned when you touched him. That thought brought a faint frown to her face. The night before had been . . . unimaginable, because her experience had been so limited that she couldn't have pictured such physical sensations, such soul-wrenching emotion. And she *had* gotten burned—in a fire that had consumed her totally, then recreated her again so that she felt new, reborn.

Yet there was a niggle of disappointment. One thing she had imagined as she stared across the parlor at him, night after night, had been touching him, exploring him, satisfying her—to be blunt—curiosity about him. He had taught her things about her own body last night that she'd never known and never would have guessed, and it made her cringe a little to remember them now, but—could his body feel the same incredible pleasures? More important, could she give him that pleasure? And, most important, did she have the courage to try?

She buried her nose against his shoulder and felt his arm tighten around her, then relax. She had woken several times during the night, and each time he had been touching her—his arm around her, his hand on her breast, her hip, once his long leg thrown over hers, as if he wanted to be sure of where she was at all times. Her nose suddenly itched, and she rubbed it against his shoulder. She could smell herself on him, she thought with a small shock. Surreptitiously she sniffed her forearm. His scent was on her, and on both of them she smelled the same earthy, musky scent of their lovemaking. Somehow there was something stunningly primitive and erotic about that.

Slipping up a little in the bed, she watched him sleep. He was lying on his back, and she studied him, able to look her fill for once without worrying about being caught staring. In profile his jaw and nose were even more bluntly masculine, his bottom lip a little fuller. The dark stubble on his cheeks and jaw added a roughness that she found oddly, compellingly appealing.

She was reaching out to touch it, when his head turned suddenly and he opened his eyes. He smiled, bringing a sudden warmth to the room as he tightened his arm to draw her closer. Miranda felt her body go very soft and yielding against his. He closed his eyes on a deep sigh, and for a moment she thought he'd gone back to sleep; then she saw his lips move.

"The first one awake lights the fire—old bunkhouse rule."

She made a point of looking around the small cabin. "This isn't a bunkhouse."

"We'll pretend," he muttered around a yawn. He could feel her growing warmer as she tried to work up the courage to get out of bed naked in front of him. She was so endearingly shy, he thought as he sat up suddenly and threw back his half of the blanket.

She had modesty enough for both of them, Miranda thought as she clutched the blanket to her chest, and he had none. Which she appreciated. Busily her eyes examined the strong length of his thighs and the hard round muscles of his calves as he hopped from one long bare foot to the other on the icy floor. She laughed heartlessly at his grumbled complaints, then laughed harder when he scowled at her over his shoulder. He crouched in front of the stove, and her laughter died to a soft sigh. His shoulders were broad, his torso tapered down to his narrow hips and tight buttocks. He got the fire going, then stood with a smooth ripple of muscle that elicited another sigh. Completely unself-conscious about his nudity, he moved around the small cabin, filling the coffeepot with water from a large crock, throwing in a handful of beans, then setting it on the stove. Several drops of water skit tered crazily on the hot cast iron, reminding Miranda of some of the sensations that had skittered crazily through her the night before.

He stoked the stove, then came back to the bed, and she got to appreciate him some more. She started at the top of his head and unabashedly let her gaze drift downward. His dark hair was wonderfully rumpled. His neck was a strong column of corded muscle; his chest was deep, his belly flat and hard. And the part of him that defined him as unmistakably masculine was as well proportioned and strong as the rest of him.

She raised her eyes back to his, and he said quietly, "Turnabout's fair play, Miranda."

Miranda felt her cheeks growing warm, but she held his gaze and dropped the blanket.

After another deliciously lazy hour in bed, where she discovered that she did have the courage to satisfy at least a little of her curiosity about his body, necessity forced them into their clothes and outside. Miranda stood on the flat rock that she imagined was the porch and absorbed the cold white beauty of a world that had disappeared in a foot of snow.

Jesse came tramping back around the corner of the cabin. "Guess who's in the lean-to with Lucky?"

"My mare?" she asked in disbelief.

He nodded. "She was probably right behind us last night."

"I wondered if maybe she would go back to the ranch, but I'm glad she didn't," Miranda confessed. "They're going to be worried enough about us without having one of our horses show up riderless."

"I think they'll figure we're holed up somewhere," he said, unconcerned. "In the meantime, look what else I found." With a flourish, he produced a large galvanized washtub.

"Come on, Randy. You're not going to let all this nice hot water go to waste, are you?" Trying to keep a straight face, Jesse enjoyed her indecision. On the one hand, he knew she wanted a bath; on the other, he knew she was still too shy to be comfortable splashing in front of him. If he were a gentleman, he'd put a blanket up for her, he thought. But, then, he'd never claimed to be anything so civilized.

"There can't be more than five inches of water in there. That's hardly a proper bath," Miranda pointed out, feeling gauche and unsure of herself.

"Then we'll use it like a hip bath." He held out his hand.

" 'We'?" She gave him a thoughtful look, then put her hand in his.

"Will you put your camisole and drawers on for me?" Wrapping a blanket around her like a huge towel, he drew her toward him.

Even after their bath together, she still felt a little shy. "Why?" she asked softly.

"Because," he whispered, nuzzling her nose with his, "I like taking them off you so much."

He caught the short tail of blue satin with a gentle bite and tugged it loose. His hand worked down the line of tiny pearl buttons, loosening them one by one while his mustache nuzzled the linen and lace aside to bare what he was seeking.

"You smell so good. I want to smell you, taste you, all over," he growled. He licked the taut points of her nipples; then his mustache brushed them dry with an exquisite tickle. The tiny blue rivers of her veins showed with startling clarity against her white skin. He traced each to its source with his tongue, until he finally gave in to the demands of the hands clasping his head and captured the rosy nipple in his hungry mouth. He suckled, drawing her deeper and deeper into his mouth, then treated her other breast to the same tender care.

Whisking gently down her midriff, his mustache and mouth stopped at another barrier of white linen and lace. The sheer fabric was a white mist over the dark triangle at the top of her thighs. Less patient now, he used his fingers to loosen the strings and push the material out of his way. His mustache stroked over her like a soft brush, painting lazy swirls on her belly, dipping into the hollow of her navel. The pointed tip of his tongue stippled her hip.

"I love this little mole." The tip of his tongue covered it, daubing on warmth. "It's shaped like a little heart." His fingers gathered the misty white fabric and pulled it with tantalizing slowness down her legs and off; then his mustache brushed long light strokes back up from her ankle, over the quivering flesh of her inner thigh. He painted a symmetrical pattern on her other leg, reaching higher.

Her hands held his head. "Jesse?"

He raised his head and saw that her eyes were wide and uncertain. "Let me, Randy." Reaching up, he took her wrists and held them out to the side as he lowered his head.

At the first touch of his tongue her breath caught in her throat and she resigned herself to dying. Her death was a glorious one moments later; then she was astonished to find she was still alive. She felt him smile as he pressed a gentle kiss above the dark tangle between her thighs; then he raised his head.

Her arms were open to him, and he filled them, lowering his body over hers. Her eyes were wide with wonder and delight as he slid into her welcoming warmth. She took him with no pretense, no coyness, only open, honest passion and love. Her body drained his, and he felt like a virgin, new and reborn.

Jesse lay sprawled over her, his head cushioned on her breast. He was too heavy for her, he knew, but he wasn't going to move. He was totally relaxed, totally at peace with himself. When had a woman looked at him with such delight? he wondered hazily. Not a few had stared with wonder when he'd taken his pants off, he thought, laughing wryly to himself, but not Miranda's kind of wonder, and never with such delight. To be the object of that kind of delight and wonder was a privilege few men ever enjoyed, and he wanted to bask in the afterglow like a cat curled up near a warm fire. He nestled his head deeper on her breast and felt her hand come up to stroke his hair. He wondered if she knew "nice" women weren't supposed to enjoy this. They were supposed to lie stiff and passive beneath their husbands, suffering their carnal attentions stoically. They were never supposed to find any wonder and delight. His mouth curved in an unconscious smile as he closed his eyes. Well, if she didn't know, he sure as hell wasn't going to be fool enough to tell her.

He was crushing her, but it was such a lovely way to die that she wasn't going to complain, Miranda thought dreamily as her fingers sifted through his hair with random movements.

Suddenly he rolled onto his back, then picked her up and draped her over him like a warm living blanket, before covering her with the real one. She lay utterly relaxed against him, and he sensed the perfect opportunity to satisfy his curiosity about a few things, but knowing he had no right to ask.

He ran his hands slowly up her back and across her shoulders. "Why did you marry Hart, Miranda?" he asked quietly.

A pleasant drowsiness was slackening her muscles, making her body completely malleable under those wonderfully talented hands, making resisting anything, especially something as easy as answering a question, too much of an effort. "He was a good man. He needed a wife, a mother for his son, and I needed to get away from the White Swan." She sighed and found the energy to raise her head to look at him. "I suppose it sounds rather cold-blooded put that way. It wasn't a love match, but I liked him, and, more important, I respected him. And I think he felt the same way about me. He always treated me very well."

You may not have loved him, Jesse told her silently, studying her sober honest expression, but I'd be willing to stake my life that he loved you. When a man went looking for a mother for his son, he didn't bring home the piano player in a whorehouse. "Why did you need to get away from the White Swan? Were you badly treated?"

"No, I was very well treated, in fact, by both Mrs. Hargreaves and the girls." She braced her folded arms on his chest, unconsciously squirming her hips into a more comfortable position that had him swallowing a groan. "I think they looked on me as their rather naive little sister, although—" she gave a rueful laugh "—I was older than at least half of them. But in many ways it was such a sad place. The girls were beautiful, the house was beautiful, but there was a kind of ugliness, too. I felt sorry for the girls, for the kind of life they had settled for. Some of them had children, but they couldn't live there, of course. They were living with families, being raised by foster mothers the children thought were their own. Their real mothers would see them once or twice a month, and their children called them 'auntie.' You couldn't have any kind of a real life in the White Swan, yet the girls pretended they did. I knew I would probably have had to stay there another year to settle my father's debts and earn enough money to begin a new life somewhere else. Thomas offered me a real home, a real life, and I took it, because I was..." She stopped, unwilling to reveal what had been her worst fear for herself.

"Because you were afraid you might become like them? Accept the kind of life the White Swan offered?" he guessed perceptively. Her swift downcast look told him that he'd guessed right. Gently he tipped her chin back up with a finger. "You never would have, Randy," he said firmly.

She gave him a quick little smile, and they were silent for a few moments.

His hand stroked over her bare hip, and she stretched against him like a contented cat. Then he spoke again. "Why was Hart so cold to Tommy? His own son?"

Her expression became sad, and she laid her head back on his chest. His arms crossed over her back to keep her warm and close. "He told me once that every time he looked at Tommy, he saw his first wife, lying dead after his birth. They had been married almost twenty years, had built the Silver Tejo together, but their one regret was that they'd never had a child. She'd never been able to carry a baby more than a few months. When it became clear that she was going to keep this one, he told me they were so happy, made so many plans. Then she died. He knew it wasn't right to blame Tommy, and he loved him in his way, but he just couldn't be a father to him. I felt so badly for both of them.''

Her lashes brushed his chest when she blinked, and he felt that they were damp. She sighed, and he stroked her back gently in silence. Finally he spoke. "I knew you worked in the White Swan before you told me, Miranda,'' he confessed quietly.

Her head came up slowly.

He answered the wordless question in her eyes. "I overheard you mention it to Leola one day, and I knew what it was.''

"And you thought I was one of the girls,'' she said quietly.

He nodded.

"How did you feel about that?''

"I hated it,'' he said honestly, "but then I realized that what you had been or done before didn't really matter. Who you are now is what matters. That's the woman I love.''

She searched his face for the truth and found it, then leaned down to give him a long kiss. "I love you, Jesse.''

He traded her kiss for kiss. "I love you, too, Miranda,'' he whispered, smiling against her mouth. "And I like it.''

Their idyll was about over. The sun was shining through the small window, and shadows of the icicles dropping from the roof fell past it occasionally. The snow was melting, and soon they would no longer have any excuse not to go back home, Miranda thought, feeling a little sad.

She glanced around the poor cabin with a soft smile. It was hardly a storybook castle complete with moat to keep the dragons at bay, but for the past two days it might have been. They had needed this time together, time safe from the dragons of everyday problems, time to devote exclusively to each other and to find out what was important between them. What was most important, she prayed in an endless litany, was that he would stay.

"Are you going to eat that last peach?'' he demanded.

Miranda looked at him sitting cross-legged on the bed, facing her. He was wearing his pants, and she was wearing his shirt, and they had been eating Christmas-morning breakfast in bed—finishing it off with a can of peaches their unknown host had provided. "Yes!'' she said defiantly, and stabbed at the last golden half in the can. They fought a brief duel for possession of the sweet fruit, but she had the fork, while he only had the bent spoon, so it was no contest. She claimed her prize and held it aloft in victory, then watched his grinning white teeth steal half of it. Quickly she stuffed the rest in her mouth before she lost it, too, and grinned back at him.

He took the can out of her hand and tipped it up, and she watched the strong muscles of his throat work as he drank the last bit of sweet syrup. He set the can and utensils on the floor; then his arm locked gently around her neck and he lay back, drawing her over him. The arm around her neck tightened, pulling her deeper into the kiss, and his mouth was a lure she couldn't resist. Her tongue searched deep, and his teeth raked it lightly, making her groan.

"You have the soul of a hussy, Randy," he murmured.

"Tart."

He licked at her lips, tasting the peach. "Uh-uh. Sweet, not tart."

She pulled away slightly. "No," she began seriously, "I meant 'tart' is what the English call a hus—"

He chuckled deep in his chest as he drew her back down to his mouth. "I knew what you meant, Randy. You're a sweet tart, then." It was his turn to groan as she parried the thrust of his hips with hers.

For a little while they teased each other with the feel of their bodies rubbing together, bellies, thighs, chests, until teasing was not enough. His shirt and pants disappeared, her warmth and softness fitted his hardness, and the never ending kiss deepened as he drove into her body. The pleasure for both of them grew hotter and deeper until it ended in a series of soft explosions that left them both shattered.

Jesse fought the muscle-melting lethargy afterward so that he could enjoy the simple pleasure of holding her while she slept, naked and boneless in his arms. He would be forever grateful to the unknown man who'd built this rough cabin, grateful for their two days here. Finally they had had a chance to relieve the tension between them, to give the love they had for each other physical expression.

She sought greater closeness in her sleep, snuggling against him, and he hugged her tighter. He had wanted to discover her, play with her like a new toy, and he'd told himself that it wasn't sexual, but he'd lied. He hadn't played, hadn't discovered, all that he wanted. But, then, he probably wouldn't live that long, he thought, laughing softly to himself. She was still too shy—though she was rapidly losing her shyness, he decided with a reminiscent smile. She had a frank and honest sensuality, and her response to him had been gratifyingly eager and total. He closed his eyes, supremely satisfied. She would be going north to Montana with him in the spring.

By midafternoon the snow had melted enough for them to travel the few miles back to the ranch. Miranda wished she had a gold piece to leave on the table as she took one last look around the small snug cabin. The money would probably have puzzled the miner who owned the place, and it would have been far too much for the few supplies they'd used, but she would gladly have paid a thousand times as much for these past few days.

Outside, their horses stood saddled and waiting. The sky was a cloudless blue over the snow-dusted desert. The spiky crowns of the yuccas were filled with snow, but the warm wind from the south said they would be empty in another day.

Miranda turned to Jesse, and in his blue-gray eyes she read the same odd sense of melancholy she was experiencing. Silent, he reached an arm out to her, and she went into his embrace. The kiss they shared was sober, as if both of them sensed that they were leaving far more than the little cabin behind.

The sun set just as they were entering the ranch canyon, and Miranda paused to enjoy the glorious spectacle. It looked as if the horizon were on fire. Scarlet flames licked at the edges of the lowest clouds, burning them white-hot. The upper clouds were billows of purple smoke in the orange sky, while their bottoms were vermillion with the reflection of the fire.

"Are there sunsets this beautiful in Montana?" she asked softly.

"Yes, just as beautiful." He looked around him at the endless dirt and sand, the sparse bits of green, the bare brown mountains. "But the mountains are green there, and the valleys have grass up to a horse's belly. There are deer and elk and trees so big you can't reach your arms around them."

She gave him an unconsciously wistful smile, and they started into the canyon. They rode in silence, the horses' hooves muffled in the snow. For the past hundred yards, small towers of stacked pitch pine burned brightly to guide their way through the darkness.

Miranda answered his questioning look. "They're *luminarios*. Traditionally they're burned on Christmas Eve, to light the way for Joseph and Mary, but I guess they saved them for us, to light our way home."

* * *

Their welcome was certainly warmer than the one poor Joseph and Mary got, Miranda thought wryly. More *luminarios* lit the compound, making it as bright as midday. Even the bunkhouse emptied as they rode through the gates, and she struggled to keep from laughing as Toppy planted a smacking kiss on her cheek, then turned bright red to the top of his grizzled eyebrows. Tommy was overjoyed to see them, but more because Leola had decreed that Christmas would not be celebrated until they had returned, she suspected, than because he had been especially worried about them.

"Where did you hole up during the storm, boss?"

Penny's question was natural, but Jesse was sure he heard a subtle insinuation in it. "A miner has a cabin about a mile from the slough," he said easily. He phrased his answer to deliberately convey the impression that they'd had a chaperon for the past three days. He wasn't going to let Miranda be the subject of sly looks and bunkhouse speculation.

She flashed him a grateful look. They had done nothing wrong, but she needed the respect of these men.

"Mama, will Father Christmas come now that you're back?"

Taking Jessa from Leola's arms, Miranda looked down at Tommy, who was tugging on her riding skirt. She had introduced him to the story of Father Christmas the year before, and for the past month he had been trying so hard to be good that it was almost painful to watch. The last thing she wanted tonight was a huge celebration—she wanted time to think about what had happened in the miner's cabin, to savor it—but one look at Tommy's hopeful little face and she knew she couldn't ask him to wait another interminable night and day, when he'd already waited so long to enjoy the results of all that good behavior. "Yes, I'm sure he will." She ruffled his bright red hair. "In fact, I'll bet he's filling your stocking this very minute." She made a silent request of Leola over his head, and the older woman slipped out of the crowd around them. She knew where the oranges and chocolates, along with the red bandanna and tiny spurs that were the only gifts he'd wanted, were hidden.

For a minute Tommy was too stunned to believe that what he'd been waiting for, for what seemed like forever, was finally going to happen. Then he whooped and started for the house.

"Whoa!"

A hand of gentle iron abruptly halted his mad dash, and he looked up at the tall man whose hand was on his shoulder.

"Father Christmas doesn't like anybody to see him. Sometimes little boys who try get rocks in their stockings," Jesse told him gravely.

Tommy considered the possibility that the red bandanna and spurs he was absolutely certain were going to be in his stocking might turn into rocks, and decided he didn't really care what Father Christmas looked like anyhow. Besides, he thought, drawing his shoulders back and hooking his thumbs in the waist of his pants—he should have remembered to ask Father Christmas for a belt, too, a big wide one like Jesse's—men didn't go running off to see what somebody had left in their socks.

"Why don't you come down to the barn with me and help me unsaddle the horses?" Jesse suggested.

Tommy agreed with one last wishful look toward the house.

Plans were made to meet again in an hour up at "the big house," where tonight they would all eat together. As the crowd was breaking up and Miranda was wondering how she was going to manage a bath and prepare enough food to feed twenty people, all in an hour, Emma Lee's still rusty-sounding voice stopped her. "Mrs. Hart, did you get the goose?"

Miranda's eyes met Jesse's for a moment. Neither of them had given a single thought to the original purpose of what had ended up being a three-day "ride." And what a ride, a ribald little imp reminded her. "No, Emma Lee," she said solemnly, struggling to keep a very satisfied smile off her face, "we didn't."

Miranda started to blow out the small white candle in the tin holder, then paused. She wasn't ready to dim the Christmas tree's beauty just yet. Instead she blew out the parlor lamp, leaving the candlelit tree as the only source of light. The bright yellow flames reflected off the polished tin backs of the holders, making the tree look as if it were lit by tiny stars. A giant gold-foil star crowned the top. The gaily painted tin angels and animals, glass ornaments and frosted cones caught the candle glow and transformed the sturdy piñon into a glittering fantasy.

Everyone had left an hour ago, but still she lingered, gazing at the tree, half believing she had been caught up in a fantasy herself, one that had begun three days ago. This Christmas was the most special she had ever had, and the memory of it would always be one of her most precious. Their dinner had been long on desserts and short on everything else, because there hadn't been time to prepare the roasts and Yorkshire puddings she had planned. Nobody had seemed to mind, though. Presents had been given out, along with the hands' bonuses. Emma Lee had stared at the delicate cameo brooch as if she couldn't believe someone had given her something so precious and beautiful. Miranda had finally had to pin it on her herself, so that Emma Lee would believe it was really hers. The pink shell and gold-filigreed brooch had been her mother's, but Miranda knew she would have approved of her daughter's decision to give it away. Of all people, Emma Lee needed a bit of beauty in her life. The girl had thanked her simply, with tears in her eyes, then left the celebration with a plate of food for Cisco, so he wouldn't have to be alone at this happy time.

Miranda had found a quiet moment to give Tyree the present she had for him. The taciturn man had seemed oddly touched by the long green scarf she'd knitted for him, and she'd been glad she'd followed through on what had seemed like a rather silly whim at the time. For a moment, as he had gravely promised her he would indeed wear it, she had seen a crack in the armor of aloofness he wore, and had a glimpse of a man underneath who did not realize how lonely he was. Charlie's scarf she would save; she hadn't been surprised when the men had told her that he was spending Christmas in Deming. No doubt camped in the Harvey Hotel dining room, she thought with a smile.

They'd all enjoyed Kwon's goggle-eyed pleasure in his first American Christmas, and everyone had had almost as much fun watching Tommy empty his holey black stocking as he had doing it. He had gone to bed with the red bandanna tied around his neck, and only the promise that he could try the spurs out first thing in the morning had kept them off his feet. He was asleep now, dreaming, of course, of riding his horse, with four hand-carved wooden ones under his pillow.

After the presents, everyone had gathered around the piano to sing carols. The men, slicked up in their best shirts and shined boots, had stood around self-consciously at first, but soon even Toppy, who had been tongue-tied since his impulsive kiss, was calling out a request. Tyree had a surprisingly rich bass, and he had astonished everyone—himself most of all, she suspected—by singing a verse of "Silent Night" in French. Their untrained voices had made music no professional choir could ever hope to match. She had looked up from the piano once at the hard faces of the men, soft now with happiness and contentment, and wished that the peace and goodwill filling the room would last for more than just a day. Her eyes had lingered on Jesse, with Tommy's sleepy head on his broad shoulder, singing slightly off key in his deep raspy voice. She was studying how the light highlighted the angle of his face, when he caught her staring at him and smiled. Th memory of what had passed between them burned hot in his smoky blue eyes, and she wondered if Father Christmas might not be real, after all. Never had she been given a gift more precious or unexpected than their few stolen days together.

Now she sighed and turned away from the tree to look for the candle snuffer for the top branches. She had never found the right moment to give him his present, another foolish whim, she suspected. Perhaps tomorrow, although it would seem even more foolish then, once Christmas was past.

She was reaching for the snuffer on top of the piano, when a sound from the parlor door made her turn her head in that direction.

"I have something for you, but I didn't want to give it to you in front of everyone," he said quietly.

How long had he been standing there, watching her? She didn't know, but she sensed it had been a long time. "I have something for you, too," she admitted with a sheepish grin, reaching for the package she'd stuffed behind the cushion of her chair. Smoothing out the wrinkled white tissue, she handed it to him. "Tommy was so pleased with the horses you carved for him. He wanted to put them together with his chuck wagon tonight, but he fell asleep."

"I'll help him with them in the morning." The pleasure on the little boy's face when he'd unwrapped the box and seen the horses had more than made a few nicked fingers worthwhile.

He undid the satin ribbon tied around the tissue. The ribbon reminded him of the green one he had been carrying around in his pocket for the past few months.

"I hope you like it. I knew that you hadn't brought a lot of clothes with you, and it gets so cold here sometimes. I thought maybe you could use something warm." She watched him unfold the dark blue-gray wool and hold it up to look at it. "I hope it fits," she added anxiously.

"I like it very much, and it will fit," he assured her. With genuine pleasure he examined the sweater, noting the neat, even stitches, the carefully sewn buttonholes and the horn buttons. That she had spent so much time and effort on something for him selfishly pleased him even more, and his pleasure only strengthened his resolve to ask the question tonight that his better judgment was still telling him to postpone. Like a kid waiting for Christmas, he was tired of waiting. He wanted his present *now*.

He put on the sweater and buttoned it across his chest to show her that it did indeed fit.

"Do you really like it?" she asked, keeping her eyes on her hand as she smoothed out a tiny wrinkle on his shoulder.

He answered her foolish question with a soft kiss. "I really like it. Thank you, Miranda." She started to move away, but he caught her hand to keep her. "I made this for you," he said, putting a small chamois bag in her hand.

With a smile of delight, she loosened the drawstring of the soft deerskin bag and shook out the contents. A silver bracelet fell into her palm. She held it up with a wondering smile. It was a wide band, plain except for the narrow scalloped design worked into the softly gleaming surface along each edge, which gave it a simple elegance. "You made this? It's beautiful."

"My brother and I used to play around with making jewelry when we had our gold mine. The silver is from your mine. I got it from Manolo."

He dismissed his effort with a careless tone, but his boyishly pleased grin showed her how much it meant to him that she had liked it. But "like" was much too weak a word, she thought. She put the bracelet on her wrist, and his hand moved to help. Turning her arm, she admired it from all angles. "How did you do the design? You must have had some special tools."

He laughed. "A hammer and a nail head." At her look of disbelief he laughed again, then added, "We never had any special tools. Josh made Ellen's wedding ring by putting a cork the same size as her finger in the cap off a bottle of Dr. Parker's horse worming medicine and pouring molten gold around it. He didn't tell her, of course."

"Of course," Miranda said, giggling. Her laughter died away at the suddenly sober expression on his face.

He took her hand between his and stood, head down, as if he were studying it. Then he raised his head and looked directly into her wide questioning eyes. "Miranda, I want you to marry me."

He didn't say any more, and for a moment Miranda was too stunned to speak. Then she found her voice as she threw her arms around him. "Oh, yes! Yes, Jesse, yes. I'll marry you." She punctuated each word with quick kisses all over his face. "I love you."

Jesse captured her mouth with a long, sweet, deep kiss, then released her long enough to lead her to one of the love seats. They sat down, knees together, and he took her hand again, the plans he'd made night after lonely night tumbling out. "If we can't find a buyer for your ranch before we go, I'm sure Judge Hart will handle the sale for you and forward the money." Privately, he doubted anyone would buy the Silver Tejo. "I figure we'll round up the stock the first of March, sell off the cows with calves and take the rest. It's a long drive, but we should make Montana by early sum mer." He surveyed the parlor. "We should be able to fit any furniture you want to take in a couple of wagons. It might be a while—" he gave her a rueful grin "—before I can afford to build a house big enough to hold it all, but we can store it in the barn."

"Go?"

The whispered word interrupted his last sentence. As he finished it, he realized that the warm hand in his hand turned ice-cold, her shining eyes had dulled and her rosy face, flushed with happiness and kisses seconds ago, was now white, pinched and unsmiling. He felt a cold dead spot in the pit of his belly as he said quietly, "Yes, Miranda. Go. To Montana. That's my home, and it will be yours and Tommy's and Jessa's, too, after we're married."

"But the Silver Tejo is our home." She said in the bewildered tone of a little girl who had been given a wondrous gift, only to have it suddenly snatched out of her hands.

"Sweetheart, it doesn't make any sense to keep two ranches when they're so far apart. We couldn't run them right. My ranch is the better of the two, so that's the one we'll keep." At the despairing look in her eyes, the coldness in his belly began to spread. "I know it won't be easy for you to leave the Silver Tejo," he said gently, trying to rub some warmth back into her hand. "You have memories here." Most of them bad, he added silently. "I understand that, but we'll make new ones, together, in Montana."

No, he didn't understand! She couldn't leave. "But you don't even have any cattle on your ranch in Montana. How could that one be the better one?" she asked a little wildly.

A dull flush rose up his neck. "Do you think I asked you to marry me so I could get my hands on your damned cattle, Miranda?" he asked with deceptive softness.

She was as shocked by that suggestion as she had been by his plans a minute before. "No! Of course not! I know you're not that kind of man."

"That's right, I'm not." He bobbed his head for emphasis. "But just in case you have any doubts, I plan to have Judge Hart draw up papers before we leave giving you and Tommy and Jessa sole possession of any cattle and horses we take, as well as proceeds from the sale of the Silver Tejo. You can do whatever the hell you want with them." He forced himself to stop and take a deep breath when he felt himself losing control. He wasn't angry because she doubted his motives in asking her to marry him. He'd known she hadn't even before the words left his mouth, but he was scared, and his fear was manifesting itself as anger directed at the person who was making him frightened—and at himself. He had just assumed that she would want what he wanted because he wanted it so badly. He had expected a discussion and maybe having to do a bit of persuading, but he had honestly never thought he would have any trouble getting her to agree to go.

The coldness in his belly was reaching toward his heart, chilling him so that he suddenly shivered. "Miranda," he said with a calm he didn't feel, "we don't have to take the cattle at all, if you don't want to. We can sell them here. I just thought that since I would eventually be buying some anyway, we might as well take yours. I was thinking that Josh and I could start up a timber operation, and buy the cattle from you a few head at a time." He stared down at the hand lying so still and cold in his for a minute, then raised his head, giving her a direct look. "I never intended that they should replace the ones I would have bought if I hadn't lost the money. To be honest, except for what it will mean for Josh and his family, I don't even care about the money being gone anymore. I have you, and in my mind, that's a more than even exchange. Even if I'd had all the money in the world, that would still be true."

His simple eloquence as he testified to his love brought tears to her eyes and despair to her heart. The money had been stolen from him, with the nicety of a trial to make it legal, of course; he hadn't carelessly lost it. Yet he still accepted responsibility for it because that was the kind of decent, honorable man he was. A woman would have to be insane to give up a man like that. *But she couldn't leave her home.*

"I promised Thomas that I would keep the ranch as Tommy's inheritance. Jessa's, too, now." A trace of desperation began to creep into her voice. "The ranch is the *land*, the *house*, not the cattle. The cattle can be yours, just as I am, so there's no reason for you to go back to Montana. Don't you see? The Silver Tejo already has the cattle you want, and horses, too."

The coldness was grabbing at his heart now, threatening to freeze it. "There's every reason, Miranda. Montana is my home. I damned near broke my back grubbing in the dirt to get it, all the time dreaming of the ranch I'd have someday. Now I want you to come with me, to help make the dream a reality."

"And this is *my* home!" she cried, snatching her hand away from him and standing. "I can't leave it!"

He rose slowly from the sofa to face her. "A home? The Silver Tejo?" He shook his head. "This isn't a home, Miranda." He gestured toward the heavy wooden shutters with gun ports cut in them that the fine velvet-and-lace curtains couldn't quite hide. "A *home* doesn't have shutters on the windows to keep the bullets out

It doesn't have armed guards and a high wall surrounding it. And if you live in a real home, it's safe to go out for an afternoon ride."

She had her back to him, trying to ignore him. He stepped around in front of her, grabbing her chin to force her to face him, to face the truth about her "home." "And what about Tommy? Do you think if he were living in a real home he'd think it was normal to find his mother patching up bleeding men in the kitchen? Is it his inheritance to learn his numbers by counting the crosses in the graveyard out behind the house? How many more is he going to count, Miranda? How many more people are you going to sacrifice to your *home*?" The tears running down her white cheeks glistened in the candlelight from the Christmas tree, and he saw her shoulders shake in a silent sob. He was being brutal, and he knew it. It was hurting him as much to say these things as it was hurting her to hear them, but he was fighting for his life, and, if she would only see it, for hers and her children's, too. "Will it be his inheritance to count your cross someday, too, Miranda?" he asked her softly. "Jessa's? His own?"

Her shoulders shook again; then she straightened them and, jerking her chin free, took a quick step back. Hands that had a fine tremor wiped the tears off her face, then gripped each other at her waist, the knuckles white. She faced him, rigid with self-control. "The army will take care of the Indians and the renegades, and then we'll be safe. No more walls or shutters or crosses."

Her voice was thin but steady, and Jesse couldn't help but admire her control even as he wanted to shake her until her stiff neck snapped. "Yes, they will," he conceded, "but don't count on it happening anytime soon. And when it does, what then? This still won't be a good place to live. The land is miserable. It takes three times as many men to run cattle here because the country is so rough and stock has to be spread out too much to find pasturage. You might make it pay in a good year, but one hard winter, one summer of drought, and you'd be selling off stock just to pay wages. A couple of years of that and you'd be broke, with nothing for you or Tommy or Jessa."

"We could make it work, Jesse, you and I together. I know we could."

He heard her quiet desperation, her need to believe in her words and wished with all his heart that he could believe, too. "No, Randy, we couldn't, and I'm not even going to try. Thomas Hart knew silver mining, not cattle. If he had, he would have known that once the silver ran out, there would be nothing left for Tommy to inherit. The Silver Tejo has no future. And neither do we, if we stay."

She blinked away fresh tears, and finally he saw it, the shadows of stark fear in her eyes. Finally he understood. It wasn't just that she was trying to honor a promise to a dead man. She was too sensible not to eventually realize the futility, the *wrongness*, of that. She was terrified of leaving the only home, the only stability and security, she had ever known. How could he make her understand that he would do whatever was within his power to do to make sure she was never without a home, never without the security she so desperately needed, again?

"Miranda." He took her shoulders gently in his hands, his thumbs automatically trying to caress away the stiffness in them. "I can't give you a fine house like this one, but I can give you a home in country so beautiful it takes your breath away just to see it. I can't promise you there won't be hard times, but I can promise you a home with a man who loves you, a home where Tommy and Jessa and the children we'll have together can have a better inheritance: to grow up safe and happy, without walls, free to roam and play the way children should."

Sensing the ultimatum that was coming, her hands clenched in panic in the sweater she had made for him. "I love you, Jesse. Please don't ask me to choose between you and the Silver Tejo," she begged him in an agonized whisper.

Gently he undid her fingers from the soft wool. They wrapped around his with a grip made painful by her despair, and he held them to his heart. "I'm going back to Montana in the spring, Randy. I am hoping, *praying*, that you, Tommy and Jessa will be going with me, but I'm going."

"I can't."

Her tortured whisper was like a scream of agony in the silent room. He looked down into her beautiful eyes as they pleaded with him to stay and felt the coldness encase his heart, freezing it into a solid block of hopelessness and misery. With infinite tenderness he kissed her forehead, then set her away.

Through her tears, Miranda watched him walk to the door. The word that would call him back, the one three-letter word that would stop him before he stepped through it—*yes*—clawed at her throat to get out. But her fear caught it and strangled it into silence. At the door he turned, and she saw his mouth twist in a sad, bitter smile.

"I know you love me, Randy, but love's not enough. You have to trust me, too. You have to trust that I can give you the home you want."

Chapter Seventeen

Her heart was broken, and she knew of no way to repair it. Miranda wanted to believe with every drop of blood in her body that spring would come and he wouldn't ride out of the gate one last time. How could she live if she never talked to him again, never saw him again? How could she exist, knowing that never again would she feel the touch of his hand, his mouth on hers, know the sweet ecstasy of his body, the simple joy of waking up in his arms? Even now, her body still felt the indelible imprint of his.

But she knew he would go. And she would live. She had Tommy and Jessa, and life would continue as if she had never met him, except that it would be as it had been the past three days: the sun would have no brightness, and every color would be another shade of gray. He would take the color and the brightness with him.

It was childish, perhaps, but she avoided him as much as possible, although it wasn't possible as much as she would have liked. She was trying to wean herself from the need to see his smile, to hear his laugh. He continued to occupy a chair at the table each night, and her pride wouldn't allow her to ask him not to come. She tried to maintain the pretense that nothing was wrong between them, chattering through supper, smiling brightly, but Leola kept looking at her with a question in her eyes that she would never ask aloud. Even Tommy had seen through her empty smiles. His little face sad, his forehead knitted with worry, he had just asked her why she was mad at Jesse. She'd had to run from the room, leaving his question unanswered, because she knew that if she had tried, she would have burst into tears. She had seen him dragging out to the barn, where she knew Jesse was, his little shoulders sagging as if he were carrying the weight of their problems on them, and she'd wondered what Jesse would say if Tommy asked him the same question.

Apparently he had, and Jesse had done a better job of answering it than she had, because Tommy was coming back out of the barn now, skipping. She would have given a lot to know what he'd said. She turned away from the window where she'd been watching from behind the curtain. Tommy was going to be heartbroken when Jesse left. Even Jessa would miss him. Already she seemed to listen for the sound of his deep voice or his laugh, brightening when she heard it. As bad as her mother, Miranda thought dispiritedly as she wandered into the kitchen and, out of habit, set the kettle on the stove for tea. She opened the stove door, added lumps of coal to the smoldering cinders and pulled open the damper.

She couldn't even be angry with him because he didn't love her enough to give up his ranch and stay with her, because then she would have to be angry with herself for the same reason. They were two strong people, each believing they were right, standing now at an impasse, with no way for either of them but to go back the way they had come, alone.

The kettle's cheerful whistle made her feel even more depressed, and she snatched it off the stove top, burning her hand in the process. After pumping cold water over her scorched fingers, she reached for the tin of Earl Grey. She knew by its weight that it was empty before she even opened it. A quick search of the pantry revealed that it was empty of any more tea, too, and she remembered now that she had opened the last tin yesterday morning. Disgusted, she tossed the empty tin into the trash pail. She'd been swilling tea like a drunk did whiskey, only the drunk was at least able to forget his troubles for a time.

She opened the front door, checked to see that the yard was clear, then started for the bunkhouse. Maybe, although it wasn't likely, Toppy had some tea.

He didn't. Pausing on the bunkhouse porch, she decided to hunt up someone and send him to town for more tea.

The first person she found was Jesse.

"Oh!" Miranda had started toward the first pair of denim-clad legs she'd seen in the midst of several dozen covered with horse hide and ending in hooves. When he straightened and turned around, she realized too late that it had been his legs she'd seen while he was stooping to doctor one of the horses.

Deliberately Jesse screwed the cap back on the bottle of liniment and set it on top of a corral post. He climbed through the rails and stopped a pace in front of her, his legs spread slightly, his thumbs hooked in his belt. "Did you want something?" he asked mildly.

"Yes," she said stiffly. "I should like someone to go to town and get some tea."

His mustache quivered slightly. "Oh, you should?" he confirmed, still in the same mild tone.

Miranda gave him a narrow look. On top of breaking her heart, would he make fun of her, too? "Yes, I should. Straightaway."

"Straightaway?"

He was making fun of her! She enunciated each syllable. "Straightaway." With an abrupt nod, she turned to go back to her house.

His low voice, lazy and with a thread of laughter, stopped her before she'd gone a foot. "Don't try to play 'Lady of the Manor' with me, Randy. Remember, I'm the man who knows about the mole on your sweet butt."

Her stiff back disappeared around the corner of the barn seconds later, and he turned back to the corral. Instead of climbing back through the rails, he braced the heels of his hands on the top rail and stared across the horses, not seeing them. He shouldn't have teased her, shouldn't have made her think he thought she was just in a "mood" and that, when she got out of it, they'd go off to Montana. Yet if he didn't find something humorous somewhere, he was afraid he was going to kill somebody. The only man who dared to approach him lately was Tyree, and even he looked as if he were half expecting to get shot for saying howdy.

She wasn't in a mood; she was dead serious about staying, as serious as he was about going. Despite her promise to Hart, staying here was wrong, wrong for her, for Tommy, for Jessa, and for himself, yet he wondered if he would find the strength to ride through that gate if she wasn't beside him. He let his head hang down between his arms. He hadn't cried because he was hurting since he was eight years old, but he was hurting now, and just for a few minutes, he wished he could be eight years old again.

"Your leg is doing well, Señor Moreno." Cisco Moreno was young enough to be her son, if she had been so blessed, Leola reminded herself. She did not have to call him "*señor*" even if he was a *hidalgo*, but old habits were hard to break. "Have you been drinking your *oshá*?" she asked him sternly as she straightened from examining the healing wound in his thigh.

"*Sí, señora,*" he lied with the angelic smile that had had many *señoritas* committing sins that guaranteed them admission straight through the gates of Hell.

"Humph." Leola gave him a dry look as she rewrapped the leg with a new strip of linen. The handsome and very spoiled young man had seemed determined to be the worst patient she had ever had. In loud and very obscene Spanish he had announced that he hated staying in bed, hated his medicine, hated the food and most of all, he hated his nurse. Only the fact that Emma Lee spoke no Spanish and Cisco very little English had eased her conscience about asking the girl to care for him. It had only enraged him further that Emma Lee couldn't understand his insults, although Leola was sure she understood the intent, if not the actual words.

But Emma Lee had seemed undisturbed by them, treating Cisco exactly the way he was behaving—like a small boy who was having a temper tantrum and was best ignored until he exhausted himself. Her indifference had had an amazing effect on him, probably, Leola thought sardonically, because no female with less than two feet in the grave had ever ignored him. He became a model patient, and Emma Lee paid more attention to him—the kind of offhand attention she might have given a little brother. That seemed to confound Cisco, too. In fact, he seemed to be fascinated with the thin, homely *gringa*.

"Where is Emma Lee?" he asked fretfully. "Why isn't she changing my bandage?"

"She took some medicine down to the village for me," Leola told him as she covered him with a blanket. "She needed some fresh air. She has been spending all her time here with you."

"Well, she better come back soon. She is teaching me English, and we haven't had our lesson today," he grumbled.

Leola hid a smile as she continued briskly on her way to the door. The English lessons had been her idea, too, and Cisco was proving to be a remarkably apt pupil. "Tomorrow you will begin the exercises to keep the muscles in your legs from getting too weak. Maybe in a few days they will be strong enough so that you can use the crutches." She beamed at him as if she offered him a special treat and got a black scowl in return. She heaved an inward sigh. "I will come in the morning to show you and Emma Lee how to do the exercises. But for now, *señor, adios*."

"*Señora.*"

His voice stopped her in the act of opening the door, and she turned to look back at him, lying in the narrow bed. He no longer looked like a petulant little boy, but a man, mature and sober.

"Will I be able to ride a horse again?" he asked her quietly.

"If God wills it," she said, and he had to be satisfied with that answer.

Outside, she met Emma Lee, who was back from her errand to the village. Taking her arm, Leola steered the girl away from the house. The young *hidalgo* needed to learn patience. "Did you have any trouble finding Señora Álvaro?"

Emma Lee shook her head. "She said to thank you for the medicine and sent six eggs as payment."

Leola nodded absently. "Did you tell her the medicine was a new one?"

"No, I thought perhaps you wanted to see if it worked before you told her anything about it."

Leola nodded her approval. She was trying a cure that Emma Lee had told her about, one that the Apaches had used, a tea made from boiled yucca root for old Señora Álvaro's stiff joints. The girl seemed to have an almost instinctive knowledge of many plants and herbs and their healing properties, as well as a strong desire to know more. Leola was reminded of another young girl, nearly forty years before, who had followed her father's aunt into the hills around their village in Mexico to help her pick what the young girl had always dismissed as weeds. As the old *curandera* had rambled on about the various healing powers of those "weeds," the young girl had become fascinated. Listening to the old woman, it had almost been as if she were listening to a voice calling her, telling her what her lifework would be.

The voice had never weakened over the years, Leola thought. Instead it had strengthened, given force by her faith in God and his power working through her. The voice had given her the courage to heal bodies and spirits when she could and to accept it as God's will when she could not. Her only sorrow was that she had found no one over the years to pass her skills and knowledge on to. She had no daughters of her own, and none of the young women in the village had ever seemed interested. Now she wondered if this thin quiet Anglo girl might not have heard the voice, too. Perhaps Emma Lee would be the daughter of her heart. "Tomorrow I will show you the exercises for Cisco's leg. He is going to hate them, too," she predicted, and Emma Lee's soft laugh agreed with her.

Miranda picked up the tin plate from the ground. The cat hadn't come last night, and she'd finally left the plate for him and gone to bed, hoping it would be empty in the morning. But it hadn't been. Even the bobcat had left, she thought morosely.

She was turning to go back, when she heard a faint sound, similar to a baby crying. She scanned the hillside, hoping to hear the odd cry again. She did, fainter this time, and it seemed to be coming from up near the boulder where the cat always sat. Hitching up her skirt, she scrambled up the steep slope, the slick soles of her shoes slipping on the loose rock. She searched the area on one side of the boulder, finding nothing, then heard the mewling cry again, louder now, and definitely coming from the other side. Quickly she climbed on top of the huge rock and looked down the other side.

The bobcat was lying in a small fissure that had formed when a large flake of rock had split off the boulder. At her feet she saw a smear of blood and another, longer one, halfway down the side of the boulder directly above the fissure. There appeared to be dried blood on the cat's side, as well. She theorized that he had been hurt somehow and slipped or rolled off the side down into the crack.

As she looked down at him, trying to decide if she could get him out by herself, the cat raised his head. For a moment his amber eyes, dulled with pain, looked directly at her. He mewed softly, then his eyes closed and his head flopped down. Miranda climbed up to the highest point of the boulder, noting the drops of blood leading across it. "Tommy! Tommy!" she called. Tommy was out riding around the compound on Sam. The last time she'd seen him, he had been heading toward the back of the house, and she took a chance that he could hear her so she wouldn't have to waste time climbing back down for help. "Tommy!"

She heard the clop of hooves on hard-packed ground; then Tommy, on his small paint pony, appeared around the back corner of the house a few seconds later.

"Tommy, the bobcat has been hurt. Go find somebody to help me get him down, then run and tell Leola I need her," she called to him.

Hearing the urgency in his mother's voice, Tommy didn't ask questions but immediately wheeled his pony around and galloped off.

As soon as Tommy had gone for help, Miranda worked her way down to the injured cat. Crouching at one end of the crack where he was wedged, she cautiously reached out a hand. His eyes were closed, and he showed no sign that he was aware of her presence. Gently she touched his side and felt the rapid rise and fall of his ribs beneath the thick fur.

Miranda sat back on her heels to study how she and whoever came to help could get the cat out without hurting him any more. He was wedged in tightly, and had to weigh at least fifty or sixty pounds.

She heard the sound of someone scrambling up the slope as she had done minutes before. "Down here, on the other side of the boulder," she called.

"What happened?"

She should have realized Tommy would go for Jesse, she thought as he dropped down beside her. "I don't know." She looked up at him anxiously. "Can we get him out?"

He nodded. "We can, but the question is, are we going to get scratched or bitten up doing it?"

"I don't think so. He didn't respond when I touched him a minute ago."

He gave her a mildly exasperated look, then spread out an empty burlap feed sack she hadn't noticed before. "All right. His hind-quarters seem to be wedged tighter than his head and shoulders. Your hands are smaller. See if you can work them under him."

Miranda managed to work her hands beneath the cat, jamming dirt and tiny pebbles under her nails in the process. "All right."

Quickly Jesse slid his hands under the cat's head and shoulders. "Now, let's lift him up. One...two...three!" The uncrossable rift between them temporarily forgotten, they worked together, and the unconscious cat never even twitched as they lifted him out of the fissure and placed him carefully on the makeshift litter. Miranda steadied the cat's body as Jesse balanced the animal in his arms; then they started back down.

Leola and Tommy met them at the back corner of the house.

"Leola, the bobcat's been hurt. Will you take a look at him?" Miranda asked hurriedly.

The *curandera* gave the animal in Jesse's arms a startled glance, then muttered to herself, "Well, I have had many kinds of patients over the years, but this is the first cat!" She entered the house, and the others quickly followed.

"He has been shot," she murmured a few minutes later, examining him on the kitchen table. High on the cat's right shoulder was a ragged tear in his beautiful silver-gray fur. Carefully she probed the wound.

The cat shuddered at the pain, and Miranda and Jesse grabbed his legs, ready to hold him down if he should regain consciousness.

"Here it is." Leola held up the slug, then dropped it on the table. "The bullet grazed the bone, but I think it is not damaged. If he doesn't develop an infection, he should recover."

Miranda watched her clean the wound, then bind it with a strip of linen.

"Where do you want him?"

She looked up at the man standing beside her and resisted the urge to lean her head on his shoulder, just for a moment. "The last bedroom is warm and sunny. That would be a good place for him, I think.''

Jesse picked the bobcat up gently in his arms again and carried him through the house, Miranda hurrying ahead of him to open the last door leading off the hallway. The room was empty except for a bed, its bare mattress covered only by a sheet. Carefully he laid the cat on the bed in a patch of sunshine, then stepped back beside her. His hand reached for hers unconsciously; consciously he pulled it back. ''I think he was trying to get to you,'' he told her softly, ''because he knew you would help him.''

Wordlessly she looked at him, then looked quickly away, nodding.

They both turned at the sound of Leola's voice as she came into the bedroom. ''He will need water, but no food, I think for a day or two. Also, he will need a box of sand.''

Jesse watched Miranda scratching the cat's head, then petting his neck and side. He remembered, too well, the feel of those slim strong fingers in his own hair, petting his body. ''I'll see to the sand,'' he said in a rough voice, and started to move away.

''Don't get attached to him, *señora*,'' Leola warned. ''Remember, you can't keep him. He is a wild animal.''

''Yes. I know I can't keep him.''

He heard Miranda's low whisper as he brushed past her. She glanced up as if against her will, and he knew by the pain in her eyes that she hadn't been talking about the bobcat.

''*¡Ay! ¡Madre de Dios! ¡Basta!* Enough! You are killing me, girl.'' Cisco groaned a little for effect. ''I had to go so far on the crutches. Now this. It is too much.'' He let his head flop back on the pillow and closed his eyes. When nothing happened for several seconds, he slit open one eye to see what she was doing. Calmly folding his pants, he thought in disgust. For days he had been driving himself *loco* trying to think up new ways to get some kind of reaction out of her. At first it had simply been to relieve his boredom, as studying English had been, but after Señora Rivera had told him her story, he'd had another motivation for both pursuits, although he wasn't certain exactly what that was. So far he had been successful only with the English.

He had spent many hours thinking about what the *curandera* had told him about Emma Lee. The ignorant might consider her lower than a whore, but he knew better. She had endured deprivations and degradations few men could have survived, much less triumphed over, and his admiration and respect for her were enormous. It was the first time, he realized, that he had ever felt those emotions for a woman younger than his grandmother. Could that be why, *loco* as it sounded, he was trying to provoke her into showing some kind of feeling for him? Because he had so much for her?

Emma Lee set the pants carefully over the back of a chair. Her heart ached to see his face so white. Sweat plastered the dark curls to his forehead, but she knew he would never walk without a cane or ride a horse again if his leg was not exercised. Without movement, the badly torn muscle in his thigh would shrink and heal in a useless knot. "Most *men*—" she accented the word with a scornful curl of her lip "—would not find anything too much if it meant they could walk and ride again." She saw his hand go unconsciously to his brow to wipe away the dripping sweat. "They would be willing to sweat blood, but—" knowing he was peeking at her, she turned away with a shrug before he could see that she was feeling his pain so acutely "—I can see that I am wasting my time. I will tell Manolo to take you to town." She turned back to face him. "He will get you a tin cup, and you can sit on the street with your useless leg and beg for pennies!" she told him contemptuously.

Eyes popping open, Cisco stared at her, dumbfounded by the reaction he'd wanted and finally gotten. Now he saw through her. All her indifference to him had been a sham. She did have feelings for him. Her wispy hair seemed to crackle around her face like pink-gold lightning. Her eyes glowed with green fire, and her pale thin face suddenly flushed with color. She stood over him, her fists on her narrow hips, her frail body radiating power and strength, demanding that he be a man. He saw not the forlorn waif she was now, but the strong woman she would become, and Cisco fell in love.

He stared at her in wonder. Now he understood why he had never had any real interest in the sloe-eyed *señoritas* his father trotted past him like fillies at a horse sale. He'd been waiting for his feisty *gringa*! He almost laughed with relief and delight, but schooled his features into a scowl even fiercer than hers. She had wounded his pride to the quick and didn't deserve yet to know that the most eligible young bachelor in Sonora had decided upon her. Besides, he admitted candidly to himself, she probably wouldn't be impressed even if she did know. She didn't seem to think too much of him at the moment. He would have to prove himself worthy of her.

"*Bueno, señorita.*" He gritted his teeth at the agony lancing his thigh when he raised his leg. "Since you seem determined to kill me, I will try to please you." He swept the sweat from his forehead, flicking away the drops disdainfully. "Count the drops of blood," he commanded dramatically.

Her small hands slid with gratifying swiftness under his thigh, tenderly supporting it as he began to slowly lower and raise his leg. He felt the sweat spouting again on his forehead at the pain, but he grinned secretly at the emotion her eyes betrayed.

"How is the cat doing?"

Jesse glanced up from the clean straw he was pitching into Lucky's stall to see Tyree leaning against the side. Tyree had only gotten back from Deming an hour ago, after being gone for a few days on some business of his own, and already he'd heard about Miranda's cat. For the past three days the recuperating bobcat had been the main topic of conversation. "Mrs. Rivera thinks he'll be well enough to leave in another week or so."

"Better not tell Cisco that," Tyree advised dryly. He took a cheroot out of his inside coat pocket, glanced around at all the dry straw and put it back.

Jesse laughed shortly. Cisco was grousing to anyone who would listen about the length of time he was having to stay in bed. Since he was also enjoying the devoted attention of Emma Lee, he wasn't getting too much sympathy. "He was trying out a pair of crutches a little while ago. Made it as far as the bedroom door, I understand."

Tyree chuckled, then murmured, "Penny been doing any night riding lately?"

Jesse glanced out of the corner of his eye at the sharp-faced man just coming through the barn door. "The first night you were gone, I trailed him up to the rim of the canyon. He took a couple of shots at something, rode around for a while, then came back. If he was supposed to be meeting somebody, they didn't show. It was the night the bobcat was shot, so I imagine that's what he was shooting at."

"Probably wanted a new hatband," Tyree said in a dry undertone as the subject of their conversation walked by on the way to his horse's stall.

"Boss. Tyree." Frank Penny acknowledged the two men standing by the stall.

"Penny." Jesse returned the man's verbal greeting while Tyree nodded. Both men watched Penny walk past; then, after stabbing the pitchfork into a hay bale, Jesse led the way out of the barn.

The day was clear but cold, even for the last day of the year. As they lounged against a corral, he took out the makings for a cigarette while Tyree found a cigar. "Did you hear any news in town on Leyba's whereabouts?"

Tyree shook out his match. "Nary a word. The gang hasn't been reported here or across the border since they tried to take the silver." He knocked the ash off his cigar. "I did hear something interesting, though," he added, with a thoughtful look at the closed barn door.

Jesse noted the direction of the look as he put the tobacco pouch away. "Penny?"

Tyree nodded, exhaling a thin stream of smoke. "The same time last month that we were in town, two Chinese were found murdered in an alley. One of the men had been shot, probably with a derringer, the other one stomped to death. Apparently there were no witnesses, but an old whore who has a crib in the alley remembered a customer leaving about the time the sheriff thinks the two men were killed. She stays liquored up most of the time, but she remembered this customer because he beat her pretty badly with his belt." Tyree took a drag on his cigar. "She remembered his hatband was a strip of some light-colored fur with a black stripe."

Jesse swore one succinct word. "I'm surprised the sheriff hasn't been out to see him about the murders, to see if he saw anything." He knew the sheriff wouldn't bother himself about the whore Penny had beaten; both he and the woman would consider it a professional hazard.

Tyree smiled faintly as he blew out a curl of smoke. "I got the impression the sheriff is only interested in knowing who to thank. The two dead men were pimps."

"Was the whore he beat one of theirs?"

"Theirs were all Chinese, young girls."

Jesse remembered something suddenly. "Penny looked like he'd been in a fight the next morning, remember? And he wouldn't say anything about what had happened?"

Tyree nodded. "Maybe he used his belt on one of their girls, too, and they didn't take too kindly to it, especially if she couldn't work for a while." He glanced down at the cigar in his hand, then up at Jesse. "The sheriff would probably call it self-defense."

Jesse tossed away the cigarette he'd never gotten around to lighting, his mouth tightening into a thin line of disgust. "You're probably right. I've had a bad feeling about Penny ever since I saw that damned hatband. I'll give the bastard his time tomorrow and tell him to pack his gear." He glanced up at the bloodred flush in the sky. If it wasn't already sundown, he thought, he'd do it right then.

Tyree stared straight ahead, smoking. "The man sure fooled me."

It was as close as Tyree would come to a spoken apology, Jesse knew.

Tyree straightened away from the corral. "I'll be leaving tomorrow, too, Jessie Mack."

Jesse didn't look at Tyree with any surprise. He knew Tyree wasn't leaving because of Penny; it was simply time for him to go. Frankly, he had been surprised that his friend had stayed as long as he had. The trip to Deming had probably been to set up another job. "I suppose you'll be leaving first thing in the morning?"

Tyree's nod confirmed it. Toppy clanged the triangle announcing dinner, and the two men began walking toward the bunkhouse. Several men hurried past them, greeting him and nodding to Tyree with wary respect. Tyree hadn't shared the bunkhouse dormitory; liking his privacy, he'd taken the other small room like Jesse's. The only person he would likely say goodbye to, Jesse thought, was himself.

Tyree paused before stepping up onto the porch running the length of the bunkhouse to grind out his cigar; then his gaze shifted. "I imagine you'll be leaving pretty soon, too."

Jesse looked in the same direction as Tyree, at the auburn-haired woman hurrying toward the barn. "As soon as spring comes," he said neutrally. He'd said nothing about having asked Miranda to go with him, so Tyree's next words were a surprise.

"She'll come around, Jessie Mack," Tyree said softly. He touched the dark green wool scarf at his throat. "Tell her goodbye for me."

"Tommy? Tommy! It's time for supper. Tom—" Miranda's hand flew automatically to her breast when a man suddenly stepped in front of her. "Oh! Mr. Penny! You startled me!" With a shaky laugh she stepped back, putting some distance between them. "Have you seen Tommy anywhere? It's time for supper, and I can't find him."

He wished that she hadn't moved away so fast. For a few seconds he had been able to smell her, sweet, clean, the way a woman should smell, not cheap and dirty, like a whore. "No, ma'am, haven't." Miranda. He would have liked to say her name instead of "ma'am." She had a beautiful name, as beautiful as she was

McClintock called her "Miranda." She shouldn't let him be so familiar, but it didn't matter. After tonight, McClintock wouldn't be around anymore, and *he* would be the one calling her "Miranda." "I can help you look for him," he said, taking a step forward.

"N-no, thank you." Abruptly she was aware of how alone they were in the big empty barn, and the tiny prickle of uneasiness she always felt around Frank Penny became a ripple raising the fine hair on the back of her neck and darting coldly down her spine. She tried to tell herself that the reaction was utterly foolish. He had never done or said anything to provoke it, yet on some deep level, almost below consciousness, the level that she imagined alerted wild creatures to an unseen danger, she felt threatened. Without consciously planning it, she stepped away from him and half turned toward the door. The move put her left hand within reaching distance of a pitchfork stuck in a bale of hay, and she wondered fleetingly if, like one of those wild creatures, she had instinctively been looking not only for a way to escape but for a way to protect herself if she couldn't.

A flicker of movement caught a corner of her attention. She recognized a long beautiful white tail and realized that she was standing by Lucky's stall. Oddly, the solid presence of Jesse's horse reassured her, almost as if he were there himself. "Thank you," she repeated in a stronger voice, and even managed a smile. "But I'm sure I'll find him. I wouldn't want you to miss your supper. I heard Toppy ringing the triangle on my way over here." She nodded briefly to him. "Good evening, Mr. Penny."

She heard his soft response as she started down the center aisle, very aware of his eyes following her. After a couple of steps she stopped and turned around, not smiling this time. "It's been very kind of you, but you needn't bother about milking Bessie any longer and bringing the milk up to the house. I'll take care of it from now on."

"Yes, ma'am." Frank watched her until the door creaked closed; then he turned back to the nondescript dun mare in the stall. After a cursory look at her, he went to the back of the stall and dug around in the straw piled deeply in one corner. After a few seconds he pulled out four bottles of *mescal*, his contribution to the little New Year celebration he had talked up in the bunkhouse last night. The other men had been grumbling because the weather had looked too uncertain to risk a trip to town to celebrate in the saloons, so he'd suggested they have a party of their own. He would have liked them to be able to go, too, because it would have meant fewer guns that Leyba and his gang would have to deal with, but the potent *mescal* should take care of them. He held up one of the bottles of clear, faintly greenish liquor, and the limp body of the white worm at the bottom curled lazily, as if it were still alive. He gave it a look of disgust, then stood. The *mescal* wasn't the fine aged tequila Leyba had had the night they'd met, but he hadn't wanted to waste the money on that. These cowhands wouldn't know the difference anyway, he thought derisively.

It really was going to be a new year for him, he thought with satisfaction as he started toward the door with the bottles. A new life, the one he deserved but had had to wait too long to have. He paused outside the door to roll and light a cigarette, then leaned against the wall of the barn to smoke it. He didn't want dinner tonight; his stomach felt a little queasy.

He wished he could have talked to Leyba one more time, gone over their plans to be sure they hadn't overlooked anything, but, as the 'breed had said, it was simple enough. The attack would come just at midnight, when the hands would be outside, stumbling drunkenly around, firing their guns to welcome the new year. He knew they would be because he planned to be the drunkest, shooting the most, encouraging the others. Just before that he would have slipped out to take care of the guard on the gate and open it. Then, while all the shooting was going on, Leyba and his gang would ride in. Their fire would be covered by the celebration already in progress.

Before McClintock realized something was wrong, he'd be dead, Frank thought, tossing away the cigarette butt. He would take care of McClintock himself. It would be easy enough. The boss wouldn't join the bunkhouse celebration, but he'd be next door, and when the shooting started he'd be sure to come out, to make sure nobody got too rowdy. Frank would shoot McClintock, then head for the house. Leyba and his men could take care of the others. He would convince Miranda to leave with him, tell her that McClintock had sent him to get her to safety. It wouldn't be easy, he knew; she wouldn't want to leave without her brats, so it would probably be best if he took care of them before he went to get her. Then she should be willing to go. They'd slip out, and he'd meet Leyba at the cave for his split of the silver buried under the house and then . . . Mexico. He began walking slowly toward the bunk house. She might not want to go at first, but once she saw how good he was to her, how nice he treated her, she'd be willing, even happy, to go. He knew it.

Miranda moved through the dark, silent house. She was the only one awake. Tommy and Jessa were asleep, the bobcat deep in whatever dreams bobcats dreamed. She had been in bed, too, but, still caught in the strange apprehensive mood that had begun in the barn with Frank Penny, she hadn't been able to sleep, so she'd gotten up, put her robe on over her nightgown and decided to read for a while.

When she reached the parlor, she didn't immediately light the lamp. She'd forgotten to draw the curtains, she realized, and went to the window. Instead of pulling the heavy drapes across the glass, though, she simply stood and gazed out across the dark compound. Everything lay still under the cold winter moon, but she knew that others were awake. There were lights in the bunkhouse. The men were waiting up to greet the new year, she thought absently.

Maybe that was why she was up, too, waiting for the new year, she decided as she turned away from the window, forgetting the curtain. Waiting, she thought with a bitter laugh, to see if, on the stroke of midnight, her irresolvable problem would somehow magically be resolved. If Jesse would come through the door and announce that he would stay and they would make the Silver Tejo into the finest cattle ranch in the territory.

She wandered through the room, warm and faintly lit by the low sputtering glow of the coals in the fireplace. She stopped by the Christmas tree, which was still standing in a corner. It should have been taken down, the ornaments wrapped and packed away until next year, but she couldn't seem to bring herself to do it. Maybe it was because the tree reminded her of the wonderful bright promise her life had suddenly assumed when Jesse had asked her to marry him, a promise that had been broken almost before she said yes. Hardly aware of what she was doing, she found the sulfur matches that they had used to light the candles on the tree that night. One by one, she relit them, pulling a chair over to reach the ones Jesse had reached before, until the green tree was once again glittering and sparkly, bright and wonderful, like the promise her life had so briefly held.

The candle flames glinted off the silver band around her wrist as she touched a match to the last burned wick. Then she stepped back to gaze at the tree, unconsciously rubbing the cool silver, warming it. *I love you.* The words she had spoken that night, the words they had spoken to each other in the miner's cabin, seemed to echo through the room, mingling with the scents of evergreen and candlewax. *I love you.* Those most special of all words should be a magical incantation that made everything perfect, she thought despairingly. Why did telling someone you loved him suddenly become a curse, instead of a blessing?

She sank down onto the carpet, huddling like a little child who had gotten herself lost on a cold dark night. He had said love wasn't enough, that she had to trust him, too. She did trust him. It was herself she didn't trust, her ability to make the right decision—not just for herself, but for Tommy and Jessa, too. Was the promise she had made to Thomas cancelled out by the promises she and Jesse had made to each other with their bodies and their hearts? That seemed so selfish...yet Thomas had never been able to be a father to his son. Tommy might not have Jesse's name, but he now had a father because Jesse was his and his sister's father in every way that mattered. Should she trade their inheritance for the new one he offered? Were a new home and his enduring love worth thousands of acres of land? Just how much was a father worth?

And what about herself? she thought. How much was security worth? She didn't expect him to simply give her a home and take care of her. She expected to build the home with him, and that they would take care of each other, but she didn't trust herself to have the strength to do it—because she was afraid. She had waited so long to have a home, a permanent place that was hers, that she was afraid to lose it. What if she traded the security of the home she had for the opportunity to build a new one with him, then found she didn't have the strength to build it after all?

All she had were questions that demanded answers, and her inability to find them filled her with a kind of panic that seemed to paralyze her, making any kind of decision even more impossible. She buried her face in her hands.

He had said he would stay until spring, hoping of course that she would change her mind, would give him the trust he didn't know he already had. The odd sense of foreboding she'd had all evening grew stronger, and she knew suddenly that he mustn't stay any longer. Twice, because of her, he had only narrowly escaped death. How many more times could he escape? His love for her was like a silver noose around his neck, shining and beautiful, yet still as deadly as any rough hank of hemp. The longer he stayed, the tighter it would draw. It might be a bullet that struck him, but it would be his love for her that killed him. And Miranda knew that somehow she must find the strength to make him go.

Jesse stood alone on the darkened porch, watching the windows of the house across the empty yard. They stared back at him like blind black eyes. There was a poker game and—from the increasing noise level—some serious drinking going on in the bunkhouse behind him. He could join in, swap a few lies, get a little drunk. Or he could mosey on down to the barn, where Tyree was readying his horse and gear for his departure in the morning.

In the parlor window across the way a spark appeared, like a firefly hovering in place. Another firefly appeared, then another and another, until the window glowed with their soft light, a beacon of warmth and hope on a cold and lonely night. Jesse stepped off the porch. He could join the men—or he could be where he wanted to be.

For a moment Miranda wondered if she'd fallen asleep for a few hours and woken up just as midnight had struck.

"Miranda? What's wrong?" he asked in a soft tone as he squatted in front of her and took her hands. The candlelit room was warm, and she was wearing a thick velvet robe over her ruffled nightdress, but her fingers were icy.

The shock of seeing him as if she'd conjured him up robbed her of her voice, and his thick arched eyebrows flattened in a frown when she didn't immediately answer. He was starting to speak again, when she swallowed and managed to say, "Nothing. I...just couldn't sleep."

His eyes searched her face, and a fine tremor traveled through her body as his expression changed. His mouth hardened with intent, and a fierce glitter entered his blue-smoke eyes. His hands released hers, and she watched in silence as he rose, crossed the room and closed the door, then locked it. Returning, he crouched before her again, cupping her shoulders in his big hands, pulling her onto her knees, and she felt the heat of his thighs as they pressed against her hips.

"We shouldn't do this," she whispered.

"Yes, we should." He leaned forward, and his kiss expressed his intent, hard, deep and a little rough.

Her hands clutched at his shoulders as pleasure and need began throbbing through her, but stubbornness, or even more stupid pride, demanded that she make a token objection. She forced her mouth away from his and pulled back. "We should talk," she said in a voice without any strength.

"No, we shouldn't. Neither of us is going to say what the other one wants to hear." His mouth took hers with a stunning power that left no room for argument.

She wouldn't have argued, because she didn't have the strength to send him away tonight. There were no more words, yet still they talked, with deep urgent kisses. Hands spoke with greedy caresses of how much they wanted to touch. Bodies answered with near desperate whispers of how badly they needed to *be* touched.

With his hands still clamped around her shoulders, he stood, dragging her up with him by the sheer force of his grip. His mouth still fused to hers, his hands dropped to her waist and tugged impatiently on the sash of her robe. It loosened, and he jerked the heavy velvet out his way, then slid one hand across her hip and spread his fingers over her bottom. He ground his hips against hers, both of them groaning at the pleasure of it when his hard flesh found the warm cradle it was seeking through the thin fabric of her nightgown.

Her hands made clumsy by need, Miranda fumbled with the buttons of his shirt. Finally it was open, and she laid her palms flat on the smooth hot muscles of his chest. Tearing her mouth free, she kissed the flesh framed by her hands. She felt his fingers pulling at the ribbon tying her gown closed at the throat, then coolness as his hand brushed the ruffled fabric and red velvet aside. Coolness was replaced instantly by the hot rush of his breath as he traced the slope of her shoulder with openmouthed kisses. Her head fell back, and her fingers curled fiercely in his hair as his mouth tracked lower until it latched onto the tender erect bud of her breast. She cried out at the delicious pull and ache as his mouth began working the nipple, sucking, lapping, scraping lightly with his teeth.

Straightening, he gave her a swift hard kiss, then stepped back to tug off his shirt and boots. Her arms limp at her sides, eyes closed, she started to sway, lost in a sensual daze. He caught her, then turned her and pulled her back tightly against him. Splaying his hand over her belly, he laid his other arm across her shoulders. His hand slipped her robe and nightgown off her shoulder, and her head arched back against his shoulder as she knew instinctively what he wanted.

His mouth buried itself in the hollow of her shoulder, and he felt her shudder, then shudder again, at the erotic tickle of his mustache. His hand slipped lower under her gown until his searching fingertips found her breast. She jolted as he brushed his thumb across the stiff hard nipple; then his hand spanned the softer flesh. He squeezed gently, feeling her buck again, and he laughed softly in satisfaction as he swept her up in his arms.

Miranda was hardly aware when he laid her in the middle of her bed, then left her for a few seconds to secure the door. Dimly she understood that her nightgown and robe were gone; then his body was heavy on hers. There was no need for any more petting or stroking. Without conscious thought she drew her knees up, and he positioned himself between them. Her hands raced down to his hard buttocks, urging him closer. Eyes open, she stared into his as she absorbed the bold power of his entry. His eyes widened, then narrowed in intense absorption as he slid his arms beneath her to raise her higher. Finally he began moving with a rhythm that grew steadily harder and deeper and rougher. At last, their bodies unable to endure such pleasure another second, they both convulsed in a shivering, gasping release.

Miranda lay in his arms, small shudders still running through her body. She felt the same quivers rippling through him. Nothing had been solved between them, but she had needed this, needed one more precious memory to store away for the time when she had nothing but memories.

Gradually their bodies settled and cooled, and she reached to pull the quilt over them. As she lay back down, he gathered her closer. Tucking her head under his cheek, she felt him sigh deeply.

"Good night, Randy. I love you."

Gunfire woke her. Automatically, while she was still more asleep than awake, she reached for the body that had felt so right beside hers, but the bed was empty. Sitting up, she pushed her hair back out of her eyes to see him buttoning his pants. "It must be midnight," she said in a husky voice. "The hands are shooting in the new year." Was he leaving so soon? she thought. She knew neither of them would want Tommy to find him in her bed, but surely he could stay another hour or two.

As he fastened the last button, he was already leaving the room at a run. "It's not a New Year's celebration, Miranda. We're under attack." He had been drifting in daydreams, avoiding sleep so he could enjoy watching her, when he'd first heard the shots. He, too, had thought it was just the hands firing off a few rounds to bring in the new year; then the number of different guns he heard told him otherwise.

By the time she had put on her nightgown and was struggling into her robe as she ran out into the parlor, he was fully dressed. "It looks like about a dozen men," he said as he checked the situation from the parlor window. "Some of our men are mounting a defense from the bunkhouse."

"Apaches?" Miranda asked tightly as she jerked two rifles out of the gun case and tossed him one.

"Leyba," he said tersely as he rapidly closed the shutters across the parlor window and dropped the bar into place to secure them. "None of the doors are locked, are they?"

"No." Miranda heard his curse as he sprinted to the front door. She dashed for the kitchen and dropped the bar across the door. The kitchen shutters were closed in seconds, and she was running back down the hall to the bedrooms. Jesse met her coming out of her bedroom.

"I've got the other bedrooms. I want to go out and take a look around. I can't see anything out of those damn gun ports."

She followed him at a run through the house to the kitchen before she was able to grab his arm. "No, Jesse! Stay in the house where it's safe. When it's daylight, we'll be able to see better where they are."

Even as the words were leaving her mouth, he was unbarring the door. "They'll be able to see us, too." He gave her a quick, hard kiss, then opened the door. "I'll knock three times to come in," he said, then slipped through.

"Be careful!" she whispered, but he was already gone. Quickly she closed and barred the door, then ran to the front. A cry from Tommy's room made her detour for the hall. Until now, she hadn't had time to be afraid, but now she was terrified—for Jesse out in the dark. The house was impregnable, she assured herself.

The house was completely dark except for the light from the Christmas tree, and the candles were rapidly burning out, but it was enough to show her Tommy coming down the hall toward her.

"Mama? Mama!" he whimpered.

She grabbed the little boy up in her arms and headed back for the parlor, praying Jessa wouldn't wake up, too. "Shh, Tommy, it's all right. Some men are shooting, but they'll stop, soon." She peered out one of the gun ports. Jesse was right, she thought, frustrated. You couldn't see anything. Quickly she sidestepped to the next one. This one was a little better. She had a fairly good view of the yard and part of the bunkhouse, and the full moon gave her enough light to see clearly. What she saw most clearly were the three bodies sprawled in the dirt. Desperately she wished she could see Jesse, then realized that if she did see him, probably the renegades would, too.

Outside, flattened against the patio wall, Jesse waited for the brief flash of flame that would give away an attacker's position when he fired a shot. A shot and the accompanying flash came from near the barn, and he raised his rifle. He squeezed the trigger, then, keeping low, ran past the open gate to a new position, knowing the muzzle flash from his rifle would give away his position, too.

He heard a faint cry and saw a body fall a split second before a bullet smashed into the adobe wall where his head had been moments earlier. There was another shot, this one from the bunk-house, and he saw another body fall near the first corral. Tyree, he thought, and chuckled grimly to himself. Only Tyree could make a shot like that in the dark at that distance.

It looked like five, maybe six, men were holed up in the bunk-house. Several bodies lay in the compound, but how many were Leyba's men? He didn't know. The gates stood wide open, and he could see a body there, too. Somehow Leyba had lost the element of surprise he'd expected to have, Jesse was sure. He was certain the leader of the renegades had never intended to fight a pitched battle for the Silver Tejo.

He heard a faint creak and saw a bunkhouse door opening, then a man rolling out. Several guns fired, but the man, whoever he was, made it to safety around the corner. Jesse fired at the muzzle blast closest to him, then scrambled back to his original position on the other side of the gate as a bullet whipped past his ear. He saw an-other shadow slip out of the bunkhouse. As he had hoped, his maneuver had occupied the gang's attention long enough for someone else to get out. The two who had made it would be cir-cling around now to get behind the gang, he thought, holding his fire as the men in the bunkhouse kept the gang busy; then they could catch them in a three-way cross fire.

Miranda saw the movement by the gate and let out the breath she'd been unconsciously holding. The brief glimpse had been enough to tell her where Jesse was.

"Mama, where's Jesse? Are the men shooting at him?"

She looked down to see Tommy's white face and wide, fright-ened eyes. She hugged him reassuringly. "There are some bad men out there, Tommy, but Jesse and our men are going to make them go away. It's just going to be noisy for a while until they do." She prayed the little boy did not understand enough to realize how precarious Jesse's and the other men's situations were.

Tommy nodded, then looked at her solemnly. "Maybe I should go stay with Jessa so she won't be scared if she wakes up."

She caressed his small cheek. "I think that's a very good idea, Tommy." She carried him down the hall, then set him in the mid-dle of her bed. A quick check of the cradle proved that Jessa had, amazingly enough, slept through the sounds of the battle, al-though, with the shutters closed across the windows, the gunshots sounded more like muffled pops now. She clasped Tommy's sturdy little hands between hers. "Tommy, I want you to promise me that you'll take care of Jessa, not leave her." Her purpose was two-fold—the baby would have someone with her, and Tommy wouldn't be subjected to the disturbing sight of his mother shooting, and possibly killing, people.

"I promise," he said soberly.

Gunfire suddenly erupted from beyond the bandits' positions, and Jesse knew the two from the bunkhouse had managed to get behind them. At the same time someone began shooting from the direction of the Riveras' house. With the bandits caught in a cross fire, it was time for him to seek a position where he could get a clearer shot. Dropping into a crouch, he started across the compound in a sidewinder run, heading for the near corner of the barn.

Miranda watched with her heart in her throat as Jesse snaked across the empty compound. She heard the popping of bullets and wanted to close her eyes, desperately afraid of what she might see if she didn't. Instead she raised her gun and fired at every flash of muzzle fire aimed in his direction, knowing she was too far away to hit anyone, but she could damn well scare them! Jesse reached the safety of the barn, and she slumped against the shutter. It was when she felt the wetness on her cheeks that she realized she had been crying all the time he had been running and dodging bullets. Wiping her eyes on the back of her hand, she dashed across the room to the gun case for more bullets. Fortunately Jesse was wearing his gun belt, she thought as she reloaded the carbine; both his pistol and his rifle used the same ammunition, so she didn't have to worry about him running out.

By the time she got back to the window, it looked as if the battle was about over. There was only sporadic shooting now, and she suspected that the remaining bandits would be trying to surrender anytime. Feeling suddenly exhausted, she turned away from the shuttered window and started toward the children's bedrooms.

The sudden pounding on the kitchen door startled her. Indecisive, she stood in the hall. It wasn't the three-knock signal Jesse had arranged. Cautiously, gun raised, she approached the kitchen. It could be Leola, though, or Manolo, or one of the other men. As she reached the center of the darkened room, she heard a familiar voice calling to her to open the door, and putting the gun down on the kitchen table, she rushed to open it.

"Mr. Penny! Are you all right? What about the others?"

Frank Penny shut the door behind him. "I'm fine, ma'am." He wasn't fine. Somehow the plan that had seemed so simple hadn't worked. He didn't know what had gone wrong. Maybe the men weren't as drunk as he'd thought they'd be. Maybe Leyba's men had started firing too soon. All he knew was that nothing was working out the way he'd planned, and it suddenly looked as if he was going to be cheated out of what he deserved again. Not this time! This time he was getting what he had coming to him. He saw that she was staring at him oddly and realized that he'd been quiet too long. "McClintock sent me, ma'am," he said quickly. "He wants you to—"

They both turned as the door opened again.

"So, *amigo*, this is the widow. I see why you want her."

The man looked like a snake, Miranda thought; he even sounded like one. For a moment the revulsion she felt was so strong that neither the gun in his hand nor his words registered.

Then a loud gunshot startled her so that she cried out. She was too stunned by the noise and the sudden violence to do more than stare at the two men. One of them had shot the other without warning, but for several seconds neither man moved. Then the snake in the doorway crumpled to the floor, and, slowly, her head turned toward Frank Penny.

"You were the one," she breathed in slow realization. She began to back away from him, her hands behind her, her brain scrambling furiously, trying to remember if she'd left the gun on the table when she'd opened the door. "You told Leyba about the silver shipment. You betrayed us tonight." Her fingers touched the edge of the table, and she cautiously extended one hand behind her. Her knees were shaking so badly that she had to grip the table to keep from falling. Keep him talking, she commanded herself. "Why?"

Through a red haze Penny saw everything he'd dreamed of, everything he'd worked for, slipping away. He raised the gun with which he'd just killed his former partner and pointed it at her stomach. "For the silver, the silver you have buried under the house," he said hoarsely.

"Silver!" She almost laughed; then she saw the gleam of madness in his eyes. "There is no silver." She said it gently, as if explaining to a child. Behind her, her fingers stretched. "I know there's a rumor that there is, but there never was any silver buried under the house." The tip of one finger touched cold steel, and she willed it to reach just half an inch farther.

"You're lying!" He grabbed her, jerking her away from the table, and her fingertips slid off the gun. "I know you're lying. It's here, and you're going to show it to me." A trace of panic crept into his voice as he twisted her arm behind her and jammed her wrist high between her shoulder blades.

Miranda bit down on her lips, tasting blood to keep from crying out at the pain. It felt as if he were pulling her arm out of the socket as he propelled her roughly through the house. Please, God, she prayed desperately, keep Tommy in the bedroom. Don't let him come out.

"Where is it?" Penny hissed in her ear, and she smelled the sour stink of his fear.

"Th-the parlor," she gasped, realizing too late that she should have told him the kitchen to keep him as far away from the children as possible. Penny shoved her through the door, letting go of her arm, and she stumbled, almost falling into the Christmas tree. Only a few candles still burned; the room was almost completely dark, with the shutters still closed.

"Light the lamp," he ordered, holding the gun steady on her.

Her hands shook so badly that it took three attempts before she touched the match head to the rough striker. It flared, and she raised the chimney on the lamp. The wick caught, and the glass chimney slipped out of her sweat-slicked fingers and crashed down, shattering. Penny gave an involuntary start, and Miranda braced herself for a bullet.

He seemed to calm down a little and pointed to the floor. "Where is it buried?" he demanded.

"Under there, where you're pointing, but you'll need a shovel," she said as convincingly as she could.

"Don't lie to me!" he half shouted, waving the gun wildly, and for a brief moment Miranda thought she might be able to dart out of the room, but then the gun steadied on her again. "Your husband would have built a trapdoor." He gestured for her to lift the carpet, and Miranda moved as slowly as she dared toward the edge, knowing with sick certainty what would happen when he saw that there was no trapdoor underneath.

"Drop the gun, Penny."

For a moment the three of them were frozen into a deadly tableau, herself, Penny and Jesse in the doorway; then Miranda saw the madness glaze Penny's eyes completely. She started to shout a warning, diving toward him, but she knew with a sense of utter futility that she would never reach him in time. Before the first sound left her throat, Penny whirled with the speed madness gave him and fired. Suddenly it seemed as if everything around her slowed so that she should miss none of the macabre details. She saw Jesse flinch as the first bullet caught him high in the chest. Blood bloomed like a grotesque flower. His finger squeezed with agonizing slowness, jerking when the second bullet struck his arm. Penny spun in a slow circle, knocking the lamp from the table. The coal oil inside spilled across the carpet, spreading a line of fire across the room.

Her scream was echoing with the last shot, when abruptly everything was moving very fast again. Jesse slumped to the floor, directly in the path of the racing fire. Ignoring Penny, Miranda grabbed Jesse under the arms and, with a superhuman effort, dragged him away from the fire. Glancing back, she was frantic to see that tongues of flames were licking at the heavy drapes. The adobe walls wouldn't burn, but already the smoke from the burning carpet and drapes were making her eyes water and her throat burn.

She was running down the hall toward Tommy and Jessa, when hands suddenly grabbed her from behind and lifted her. She fought furiously against them until she saw that it was Tyree who was carrying her. "The children," she croaked, and saw him nod, but he didn't put her down. She was trying to push herself out of his arms, when Charlie Baxter brushed past them with Tommy and Jessa in his arms. Tyree set her down in the kitchen, Charlie shoved the wailing Jessa into her arms and both men disappeared back toward the parlor. Grabbing Tommy by the hand, Miranda pulled him outside. He cried out, and as she glanced down, it registered instantly that he was barefoot on the cold boards of the back porch. So was she. Bending, she scooped him up, holding him tightly. She wasn't aware of his dry sobbing or Jessa's crying. All her attention was concentrated on the kitchen door. Finally, after what seemed like an eternity but was in reality only seconds, Tyree and Charlie Baxter, carrying Jesse between them, appeared like dark spirits through the thin gray smoke.

Miranda sensed someone behind her and, without seeing who it was, thrust Jessa and Tommy blindly into their arms. Stumbling on the hem of her robe, she ran the short distance to where Tyree and Charlie were setting down their burden. Miranda fell to her knees in the dirt beside him, her hands searching over him frantically for signs of life. He was so still, so white. Had the noose already pulled too tight?

Chapter Eighteen

Jesse would live. The words sang continuously through her heart, a joyous song she would never tire of hearing. Leola had worked over him for several hours. One bullet had passed through the heavy muscle of his upper arm, which was hardly more than a flesh wound, according to Leola. She'd had to probe deep for the bullet in his chest, but it had missed his lungs and his heart. He would spend several months recovering, Leola predicted, but he would live.

Yet as great as her joy was for Jesse, it was bittersweet. There would be two more crosses for Tommy to count, she thought sadly. Shorty had died guarding the gate...and Manolo. As his final act of betrayal, Frank Penny had shot Manolo when he had tried to prevent Frank's escape. She knew Jesse's shot had found its target, but Frank had survived and managed to slip away in the smoke confusion. Miranda grieved for Leola, and she grieved for herself, at the loss of a good and loyal friend.

Still wearing her robe and nightgown, now grown ragged and filthy, she stared around her. In the cold thin light of dawn, the ranch yard looked like a battlefield after the battle. And she felt the way the survivors must feel, she thought absently—dazed, exhausted and just beginning to feel very grateful that she had survived. The brown adobe of her house was smoke blackened, the parlor gutted. The bodies of the renegades were covered with a tarp, awaiting burial. Three of them had surrendered and were securely tied up in the barn, awaiting a trip to Deming and the sheriff. As she had suspected, they had identified the man Penny had killed in the kitchen as Leyba. Several of the gang had escaped, but they were now the sheriff's problem, too, she thought tiredly.

She turned at the sound of a horse behind her. Silent, she watched as Tyree dismounted and covered the short distance between them.

"I'm leaving now, Mrs. Hart."

Miranda found a smile for the tall dark man. "I've appreciated your help, Mr. Tyree. I know Jesse has, too." He gave her what she knew was a polite meaningless nod. "The sheriff will take care of Penny," she said evenly. "He's not your responsibility."

"I vouched for him," he said tonelessly, and Miranda knew any further discussion would be useless.

"Good luck, Tyree," she said softly.

He gave her a sad, peculiarly sweet smile. "Goodbye, Miranda. You and Jesse Mack take care of each other."

Miranda watched him ride out the gate, ready to wave if he turned for a final farewell, but it didn't surprise her when he didn't.

He picked up Penny's trail almost immediately. The man was making no attempt to hide his tracks, Tyree thought as he rode almost due west across the desert, the sun rising behind him. After several miles, the trail angled sharply toward the low foothills of the western Floridas. After dismounting about two hundred yards from the base of the first peak, he followed the trail on foot. He stopped, puzzled, when it looked as if the trail were going to simply dead-end at a solid wall of rock. The only way Penny and his horse could have climbed that was if they had wings, Tyree decided, yet there seemed to be no other explanation for why the tracks just disappeared. Finally, not having a better idea, he followed the tracks right up to the wall, and there he discovered the secret of Penny's seemingly magical disappearance.

He knew he was dying. The spittle that kept collecting at the corner of his mouth had left a pale pink smear on his sleeve two hours ago. Now the sleeve was soaked and bright red from his elbow down, and he could feel the air bubbling in and out of the hole in his chest. A sudden coughing spasm seized him, racking his body with excruciating pain. When it passed, Frank leaned back weakly against the cool slab of rock behind him. Only it wasn't cool now, like it had been an hour ago; it was freezing him, like a giant block of ice. Slowly he realized that the cold wasn't external; it was internal. The cold was spreading from the core of his body out to his arms and legs.

Damn McClintock. He and Miranda would have been across the border by now if not for that son of a bitch. He was glad he had killed him, and Rivera, too. All of them. He was glad....

He couldn't remember what he was supposed to be glad about. Opening his eyes, he looked across the cave toward the entrance. A cloud must be passing over the sun, because there was a shadow across the entrance.

"Hello, Penny."

The shadow was talking to him. Did shadows talk? He couldn't remember. The shadow was walking toward him, crouching in front of him, looking at him. Frank tried to focus his eyes to look back. He felt the shadow take something from him...his... Frank thought hard. Gun, he finally remembered, feeling very pleased with himself. The shadow had green eyes. That reminded him of something....

When he finally remembered, his vision cleared abruptly, and he saw the green-eyed, dark-haired man with perfect clarity. "Tyree?" His voice was hardly a whisper.

"It's me, Penny."

His hand clawed for his gun. It was gone, and then he remembered suddenly that Tyree had taken it.

"You're dying. If there's anything you want to get off your conscience, now's the time," Tyree told him, although he doubted Penny would feel the need to confess his sins.

"McClintock?" Frank heard the rattle in his throat.

"He's alive."

He hadn't done one thing right in his whole life, Frank thought sadly. Then he remembered. Focusing all his strength in his right hand, he groped at his belly. His fingers were so stiff and cold but... finally... he felt the familiar shape in his palm. "Tyree."

The clawlike hand, more than the airless whisper, beckoned Tyree closer. "What is it, Penny?"

The gunshot echoed and reechoed in the cave. Frank Penny slumped, the derringer falling from his hand to the dry dust. "Mother," he whispered with a smile as the coldness became complete.

The impact of the bullet knocked Tyree back against a wall of the cave. Intellectually he knew he had been shot. He had heard the gun discharge, felt agonizing pain in his neck, but now he felt nothing, no pain, just a wet warmth, like tears. He put his hand up—it seemed to take a peculiarly long time to move the short distance—and discovered that the wool scarf around his neck was sodden with his own blood. His green eyes, the brightness gradually dimming, stared unseeing across the cave. If he had a mirror he thought vaguely, he knew he would see the same surprise in his eyes that he had seen in so many others. So this was to be the sum total of his life: nothing to call his own except death—not even the dust that would eventually sift over his bones....

"Tommy says the bobcat left yesterday."

"He did," Miranda confirmed as she plumped a pillow and placed it behind Jesse's back. "He jumped out the window I left open for him. Then last night," she said, laughing, "he was back on the rock again as usual, waiting for his scraps."

"Maybe I ought to try jumping out the window to get out of here," he muttered. He was in the bedroom next to hers, the one where he'd slept after Jessa's birth in case she had needed him. Now he was sleeping there in case he needed her. He'd been in bed a week, and he still felt as weak as Jessa. But, he thought as he watched Miranda bustling around him, it had its compensations.

"You can try jumping next week," she said dryly, handing him a mug. "Drink this."

He looked at it suspiciously. "What is it?"

"One of Leola's potions," she told him. "It's good for you. Now drink up."

He looked at her thoughtfully. "You know, I never realized what bully you are, Randy."

"I am, aren't I?" she asked cheerfully, then looked pointedly at the full mug in his hand.

"All right," he sighed, then gave her a crafty look. "But I want a reward."

He raised the mug, and Miranda giggled at the terrible face he made at the nasty taste. "Aaachh! What the hell is in that?"

"I've never dared ask," she confessed with a laugh, taking the mug and starting to turn away.

He caught her hand and pulled her back to the bed. "I want my reward." He slipped his other hand up her arm and tugged her down. "A kiss, Randy."

She let him pull her down until she was sitting on the bed, her arms braced on either side of him as she took care not to put any pressure on his chest.

Ignoring the pain of his week-old wounds, Jesse reached up for her mouth. He fused his lips with hers, catching them just right so that the fit was perfect. Slowly his tongue explored her mouth, dueled briefly with hers, then set up a slow rhythm, both carnal and deep. If all he could do was kiss her, then he was damn well going to make it count, he decided, fighting the exhaustion that seemed to overwhelm him after even the smallest effort. He felt the brush of her hands through his hair as she kissed him back. Her teeth scraped his tongue lightly, and he knew she was feeling the same frustration he was. "Lie down with me," he murmured against her moist mouth.

"No, I can't," she murmured back regretfully. She slipped free of his grasp and stood quickly. "You're supposed to be resting," she said with mock sternness, noting how pale and tired he looked. She arranged the quilt around him and watched his eyes drift shut almost immediately. Within seconds she knew he was asleep.

Leola's whisper came from the doorway. "*Señora.* Lieutenant Riddle is here to see you."

She found the lieutenant standing in the middle of the ruined parlor. "Señora Rivera told me what happened," he said after his greeting. "I'm sorry, Mrs. Hart. I imagine you're going to make repairs." There was a hint of a question in his voice, as if he were wondering why she hadn't already started.

"I...haven't decided," she said, leading the way to the kitchen. They sat at the table.

"I came to tell you that the Apaches have agreed to surrender," he began without preamble.

Miranda heard the lieutenant's good news and wondered why she felt so little reaction to something that would have pleased her enormously only a week ago.

"Chatto is going to surrender the first of February, but Geronimo won't be coming in until April," the lieutenant continued, accepting a cup of coffee from Leola. "And that may be a problem for you, Mrs. Hart."

Miranda absently stirred the tea Leola had set in front of her. "How so, Lieutenant?"

"The reason Geronimo isn't surrendering with Chatto is that he needs time to steal more cattle to build up the herd he wants to take back with him to the reservation. And because of its location, your ranch will probably be one of his favorite places to raid."

"How many does he want?"

"About three hundred head."

Suddenly Miranda made her decision. "You have met with Geronimo, haven't you, Lieutenant?"

He nodded as he took a sip of his coffee.

"Well, I want to meet with him, too." She smiled faintly, ignoring the choking sounds coming from Lieutenant Riddle. "I have an offer I think he will be interested in."

* * *

"*Señora*, I do not think you should do this *loco* thing."

It was the same opinion Leola had offered at least four times a day since Miranda had convinced Lieutenant Riddle to contact the Apache chieftain for her. Miranda ignored it now as she had all the other times.

"At least tell Señor Jesse," Leola pleaded.

"When I get back," Miranda agreed. "Not before," she added when she saw that Leola was about to argue again. She mounted her gray Arabian mare and leaned down to take the lead ropes of two horses from Cisco Moreno. Cisco was doing very well on his crutches, she thought absently. He had been making rapid progress since the night of the attack, when he had insisted that Emma Lee help him outside to defend the ranch.

He handed the lead ropes of two other horses to Emma Lee, who was mounted beside her. "Are you sure you want to do this?" he asked her quietly.

She gave him a rueful smile. "No, but I will. Miranda may need an interpreter if Geronimo decides that he will not speak Spanish. Lieutenant Riddle says sometimes he chooses to pretend that he doesn't know it. And she needs help with the horses."

He nodded and stepped back as Emma Lee kicked her horse into a trot to follow Miranda's.

They rode for several miles in silence; then Miranda stopped. "I think that must be the trail. It looks as if it leads over the mountains." She pointed to a rough trail that led to a low gap. She sat for a moment longer, looking over the landscape around them. There were a few inches of snow on the ground, and somehow that made the land seem even more desolate than usual. The endless expanse of white under a cloudless turquoise sky stretched unbroken to the darker peaks of the Floridas. The snowcapped mountains looked grimmer, more foreboding, than ever. That anyone survived in this land was a testament to their strength and tenacity—or their stupidity, she thought wryly. She saw the land through Jesse's eyes now, saw it as it really was—a place of many hardships and few satisfactions. It was no wonder the Apaches were so merciless and savage. That was the nature of the land they lived in, and to survive in it, they had to be the same way.

She saw a lot of things through Jesse's eyes now, she thought as she nudged the mare into motion again. She had finally understood as she watched Leola fight Death for his life, that a house was not a haven, security; it was the man. Thomas had wanted the richest legacy possible for Tommy, but there was no way either of them could have known when she had made her promise to him that that legacy would prove to be a man, not the Silver Tejo. Jesse McClintock was the best inheritance Tommy and Jessa could have, and she knew she could now break her promise without guilt. Four walls couldn't love you back. When she thought now of home, she thought of Jesse. If he still wanted her.

As they reached the top of the low pass, two Indians appeared, as if out of thin air. They gestured that the women were to follow them, and Miranda looked at Emma Lee. "You don't have to go any farther. I can manage the horses myself."

"I'll go," the girl said quietly.

They rode into a circle of horses and men a few minutes later. Miranda was surprised that she didn't feel more fear. In truth, she was fascinated. After all the horrifying stories she'd heard, she had expected fierce, ugly giants. Nearly all these men were shorter than she was, and while most of their expressions were fierce, only one, whose face looked as if it had been kicked in, was ugly.

Miranda reined in her mare in front of the man who was clearly the leader, Geronimo. "What do we do now?" she whispered to Emma Lee.

"We get down and wait for him to speak to us," she said, following her own instructions.

Geronimo studied the two women waiting quietly beside their horses. Both were tense, he saw, but neither seemed particularly afraid. And they had brought him a present. Four fine horses, four—his lucky number. None of them was spotted, he noted with a trace of disappointment, but they were fine horses all the same. "The army lieutenant said you wished to see me." He addressed the dark-haired woman in Spanish, which the lieutenant said she spoke, although he was certain she was not a Mexican.

"I wish to give you a present, a token of my respect, and to discuss a matter with you," Miranda replied in Spanish. Walking forward, she and Emma Lee presented the lead ropes of the four horses. Miranda saw a man who did indeed command respect. He was, according to Lieutenant Riddle, in his mid-fifties, yet his hair was still black, and his body under the red calico shirt and pants and breechcloth looked to be hard. He had dark, sharp eyes and the most resolute expression she had ever seen. No wonder the army bargained on his terms, not he on theirs, she decided.

Geronimo gestured to two of his men to take the horses, and they were led away. "What is the matter you wish to discuss?" he asked. The lieutenant had intimated only that it would be to his advantage to listen.

"Lieutenant Riddle tells me that you are going back to the reservation in four months. He tells me that you would like to take some cattle with you. I am leaving my ranch, the Silver Tejo, in two months." She sensed Emma Lee's startled gaze. "I wish to round up my cattle in peace. In return for that peace, I will leave three hundred fine cattle behind."

The woman was bold, and he liked her proposal. "I think you will be able to gather your cattle in peace," he said, giving her a long, considering look.

He gestured toward a woman hovering in the background, and she came forward with two new pairs of knee-high mocassins, presenting a pair to Emma Lee and one to Miranda. "Thank you," Miranda said simply, having been told by Emma Lee in advance that it was poor manners to acknowledge a gift too effusively.

"You are the woman of the dark-haired giant with the spotted horse?" he asked her suddenly.

"Yes," Miranda said, hoping that she still was.

"Tell the giant that I hope you give him many sons, and that they all stay in Mon-Tana." He laughed at his own joke, and Miranda sensed that their meeting was over.

Quietly, she began to carry out the plan that Jesse had outlined the night he had asked her to marry him. She let it be known that the Silver Tejo was for sale, but she didn't anticipate any buyers. Under Charlie Baxter's and Cisco's direction, the men began rounding up the cattle. The day Cisco mounted his horse for the first time everyone on the ranch joyfully shared his triumph over his injury—a triumph that he acknowledged was Emma Lee's as much as his.

Three hundred head of prime cattle, including some of the cows with young calves, were set aside to honor her agreement with the Apache chief. The remaining cows with calves would be sold locally. The rest of the herd was going to much greener pastures near Big Hole, Montana, she hoped—and prayed.

Confined mostly to bed, Jesse couldn't, she was certain, suspect what was happening. She asked Charlie, Cisco and the others to avoid mentioning it when they visited him, using the excuse that he needed to focus all his energies on recuperating and couldn't afford to expend any worrying about a roundup. She didn't mention it, either, because the real truth was that she hadn't quite figured out how to tell him. She didn't know if his offer of marriage was still open and, although she could find the courage to ride into the midst of savage Indians, she couldn't seem to find enough to ask him a simple question.

He gained strength steadily, but at a rate that she knew frustrated him. His only consolation in the enforced inactivity was the lavish amount of time he was able to spend with Tommy and Jessa. He never mentioned his original intention to leave in the spring, which was now only scant weeks away, and return to his home in Montana. In fact, he didn't speak of the future at all. It was as if they were both pretending that spring would never come, she thought, yet each day the air was a little softer, the wind a little warmer, and her subterfuge was only that much more foolish and cowardly, but she didn't know how she would bear it if his answer was no. She was delaying until the roundup was finished, she suspected, so that she could present him with an accomplished fact, a plan already so far along that he couldn't say no. But she knew that nothing and no one would force Jesse McClintock to say yes if he didn't want to. Despite all her machinations and hopes and prayers, he still might very well return to Montana alone.

The last week in February, Charlie Baxter sought her out. "The cattle are all sorted out, Miranda. I thought we'd drive the cows and calves into Deming tomorrow. The rancher who's buying most of them is coming up from Las Cruces, so they won't have to stay in the holding pens long, and a cattle buyer will take the rest."

"Thank you, Charlie. I appreciate how hard you and the other men have worked to get them rounded up so quickly." She paused for a moment, giving him a quick, almost guilty glance. She hadn't told the men why they were rounding up the cattle, but they must have guessed. Cisco had already said that he and his men would be leaving for Sonora once the roundup and sale were completed, and she was gambling that the rest of the hands would have new jobs in Montana if they wanted them. "Calvin Ruebush ordered two new Studebaker wagons for me. Would you see if they've come yet, and bring them back, if they have?" she asked. For weeks she had mentally been sorting the contents of the big house, deciding what to discard and what to pack into those two wagons she'd ordered on hope.

He hoped he was going to need a wagon, too, Charlie thought as he knocked on Celia Kershaw's door. It was too late to come calling, but he didn't have the patience to wait until morning.

"Charlie!" Celia opened the door wide to admit him. "What are you doing here?" she asked when she had closed the door behind him.

She was ready for bed, he realized. She wore a pink wrapper over a white nightdress, and her hair was free of that god-awful tight bun. As he had suspected, it was a mass of blond curls, framing her fresh-scrubbed face and big blue eyes. She looked like a doll, a pretty precious china doll. "I've brought the rest of the money I owe you, Celia." He pulled the paper bills out of his pocket, counted them out and gave them to her.

Celia took them without looking at them, setting them down absently on the small table. "Thank you, Charlie." She waited. He hadn't come so late just to pay her back a few dollars.

He paced the small room, wishing it were larger. "I'm moving on, Celia," he said abruptly. "Miranda Hart has rounded up all her cattle and ordered a couple of wagons, and although she hadn't said so yet, I'm sure she's going to be leaving the Silver Tejo, probably in a couple of weeks." He glanced across the small room to see her still standing by the little table, seemingly frozen to the floor. "I'm going to Wyoming, around Laramie. I've saved a little money, and the government's offering homesteads around there. I was thinking it might be a good place to start up a horse ranch."

"Th-that sounds like a fine idea, Charlie," Celia said in a bright voice. "I know how good you are with horses. I'm sure you'll be very successful. I'll m-miss you," she added softly.

He stopped in front of her. "I don't see how, since you'll be coming with me." Taking her hands, he looked down into her big blue eyes. "You will be coming with me, won't you, Celia? As my wife?" he asked quietly.

For a moment her face lit with joy; then the light died. Carefully she disengaged her hands from his. She moved away a few feet, stopping with her back to him and asked, "You think I'm a virgin, don't you, Charlie?"

She turned around then, and he saw a curiously sad wistfulness in her eyes. "I never really thought about it," he answered honestly. "But, no, I don't. As old as you are, and as beautiful as you are, although—" one corner of his mouth quirked up in a wide grin "—you do your damnedest not to be, there had to be a man somewhere, sometime. I don't c—"

She shook her head, the golden curls bouncing gently around her face and shoulders. "There wasn't a man, Charlie—there were dozens, maybe a hundred, maybe more. I lost count." She corrected herself. "I didn't want to count."

"I come from a small bayou village in Louisiana, Cajun country. The main cash crop was women—girls, really. I was fifteen when I was sold to a whorehouse in New Orleans." Her tone turned self-mocking. "It was the best house in town. Only the wealthiest men could afford it." She wished he would show some reaction—anger, disgust, something. Instead he just stood there, seemingly relaxed, his strong, capable hands tucked into his coat pockets. "After a while, there was just one man, an older man, nice, very kind. He paid for me every night, whether he came or not. But then he died, and I knew I would have to go back to the parlor, back to two or three different men every night, and I couldn't. So—" she gave a small, helpless shrug "—I ran away."

Charlie watched her small, soft hands knotting themselves together, her neat nails digging deep half-moons in her palms. He controlled the urge to take her hands in his to keep them from damaging themselves. He would let her tell it, get it all out; then they would never speak of it again.

"I knew I couldn't go back home, to the bayou. I didn't really know what I was going to do until I saw an advertisement for Harvey Girls. They wanted attractive, intelligent girls of good character." He saw the ghost of a smile. "I met two out of three requirements, so I applied." She finished, her head down, her hands finally settled at her waist.

He said nothing, and finally she raised her head to look at him. Her mouth trembled only slightly, her voice not at all. "Is that what you want by your side in Wyoming, Charlie? A whore? I thought I could deceive you. I thought I could have a chance at a family, a husband, a home, but—" her eyes slowly filled with tears "—I can't do that to you. You deserve so much better," she said with a sad smile, turning away from him.

His hands were gentle on her shoulders as he turned her back to face him. "Do you think I'm a virgin, Celia?" Her blue eyes looked startled. Mutely she shook her head. His hands began kneading the tight muscles under them. "Of course I'm not. I don't care about the young Celia Kershaw, and I hope you don't care too much about the young Charlie Baxter, either, because his life wouldn't bear too much inspection." His arms slipped around her, folding her close against him. "I only care about the Celia Kershaw of today." He smiled at her. "The woman of good character, the one I want by my side in Wyoming, bearing my children, patting my shoulder and telling me things will be better when they're going bad, sharing good times and making them better just because she's there."

She pulled back, tears glistening, making her eyes bottomless blue pools. "You won't throw my past up to me when we fight?" She took a deep breath. "And we'll fight, Charlie, make no mistake about it."

He grinned hugely. "Hell, I'm counting on it. I enjoy fighting with you so much I can't imagine what the loving will be like. We may not survive it."

Celia would have thought it impossible, but she felt herself blushing. She hid her hot face against his shoulder, almost missing his soft vow. "I promise I'll never mention your past, Celia, even in anger. If you ever want to talk about it, I'll listen, but frankly, I don't give a damn about it."

She searched his sober, rugged face for the truth. "I'd be proud to marry you," she said at last. She ducked her head shyly back to his shoulder. "I love you, Charlie," she murmured against his shirt.

He tipped her chin up firmly and locked his eyes on hers, holding them fast. "I love you, Celia." He kissed her softly to seal their promise. Their kisses began to change subtly, deepening, his tongue seeking surely.

Her bed was incredibly soft and comfortable, he decided a little while later. And he had been right; he couldn't have imagined what the loving would be like. They survived it—barely.

"Go to sleep now," Miranda whispered to her tiny termagant of a daughter, patting her back. Jessa was cutting her first tooth and not being stoic about it. Miranda smiled at the baby's faint snore and straightened, glancing around the room, mentally packing the wagons Charlie was going to be bringing back tomorrow.

Within a month the house would be empty, and she couldn't help but feel a little melancholy at the thought. Not for the house, she realized, but for the breakup of the "family" that had grown together over the past months. Cisco and his *vaqueros* would go back home to Sonora, and Emma Lee and Leola would go with him. Cisco and Emma Lee were the most unlikely combination, she thought with an unconscious smile, but their feelings for each other were real. The two had invited Leola to go with them, and she had accepted. She would be able to return to her beloved Mexico, and finally, in Emma Lee, she had found someone with whom to share her knowledge and skill. Charlie had mentioned Wyoming, and she was certain the Harvey House was going to be needing a new dining room manager very soon.

She, Tommy and Jessa were going north with the cattle to Montana, with Jesse. He would just have to take them, she had decided after a long sleepless night. Home for her was not a place, it was a man, and Jesse McClintock was that man.

She turned around to find him lounging in the connecting doorway between her bedroom and his, watching her. He was still pale and much too thin, but he looked wonderful.

He straightened away from the door frame with that loose, casually powerful, supremely masculine grace she so enjoyed watching. "Since you seem to be getting ready to move, don't you think it's about time you let me in on your plans for me, Miranda?" he said mildly. "I am still in your custody, after all," he added with a sardonic twist of his mustache.

"You're going to take us to Montana with you," she said simply. "Tommy, Jessa . . . and me."

One thick dark eyebrow rose. "I don't have any say in the matter?"

"None at all. You made me an offer, and I'm going to hold you to it," she said with a certainty she wasn't feeling, especially when his face revealed nothing of what he was thinking.

"What about the Silver Tejo, the children's inheritance?" he asked in a voice that also revealed nothing.

"The best inheritance they could have is you," she said quietly. She went on, striving for a tone as emotionless as his. "We can do whatever you want about the cattle, but I think we ought to take them. If you still want to have papers drawn up, we can but . . . it isn't necessary for me." He said nothing, and finally she turned away so she wouldn't have to face his expressionless silence, and so he wouldn't see the despair that was beginning to overwhelm her. And before she swallowed the last scraps of her pride and begged. "You aren't in my custody any—anymore." Her words faltered, and she tried to force strength into them. "I wrote to Willis. He commuted your sentence."

"So I'm free to go? To do whatever I want?"

The low, soft question rasped over her nerves, shredding them. Closing her eyes against the pain, she took a long ragged breath that caught in the middle, then opened them and turned slowly to look at him. She swallowed, but was unable to find any strength now to speak, so she shook her head in mute agreement.

Staring down into her depthless twilight eyes, he nodded. "I see." Then, in a lightning move that belied the injury he was still recovering from, he grabbed her, swinging her up into his arms. "You sure took your own damn sweet time making up your mind," he growled, carrying her toward his bedroom.

"Well, I had to be sure you were going to survive first," she sniffed, wrapping her arms around his neck. "I didn't want to get my hopes up and then have you die on me." Suddenly her eyes were bright with tears. "Oh, Jesse, I love you," she whispered, pulling his head down to hers.

"I love you, Randy," he murmured, kicking the door shut behind them, and there was no more conversation that night.

* * *

A week later the Silver Tejo was deserted, alone except for the dry desert wind. Silhouetted against a magnificent sunrise, a man and a woman rode together, beginning their journey home.

Historical Note

Geronimo surrendered in April of 1884. His cattle and horses were immediately confiscated and sold, with the proceeds going to the Mexican government as partial reparation for his many raids. Conditions on the San Carlos Indian Reservation led him to break out again in 1885 at the age of fifty-six. For a year, he and his band of seventeen warriors, fourteen women and six children eluded the five thousand soldiers hunting them until, worn and weary, he surrendered for the final time on September 4, 1886. It had taken an industrialized nation only forty years to finally defeat him.

He was immediately declared a prisoner of war and exiled to Florida, along with Chatto, who had not left the reservation but was deemed dangerous anyway. In Florida, and later at Fort Sill, Oklahoma, where he spent his last days, Geronimo earned money by selling pictures of himself, small bows and arrows inscribed with his name, locks of his hair and an endless supply of buttons from his coat, to tourists. He was the hit of the 1904 Saint Louis World's Fair, regaling visitors with his exploits. He died of pneumonia in 1909 at the age of eighty.

Chatto, who had once ridden four hundred miles on horseback in six days, terrorizing settlers in Arizona and New Mexico, died in an automobile accident in 1934.

* * * * *

Harlequin Historicals

COMING NEXT MONTH

BETWEEN THE THUNDER—Patricia Potter

Ryan Mallory was a survivor. Though she had lost nearly all she held dear, her spirit was the inspiration of her brother's Rebel camp in the last bloody days of the Civil War. Captive Union Colonel Ben Morgan struggled to deny the traitorous love he felt for his enemy's sister. Could Ryan's passion for life conquer the hatred around her to win the prize that mattered most?

PROMISES—Pamela Wallace

Belinda Sutton had lost everything, until Shane Kincaid saved her from starving in the London streets. When he left her, she rose from the gutter to become the sensation of the Edwardian stage and royal society, but she could not forget the consuming passion she'd known with Teddy Roosevelt's most trusted spy. Fate had divided them, and only danger would teach them that certain promises can never be broken....

AVAILABLE NOW:

CHINA STAR
Karen Keast

SILVER NOOSE
Patricia Gardner Evans

Harlequin Superromance

Here are the longer, more involving stories you have been waiting for... Superromance.

Modern, believable novels of love, full of the complex joys and heartaches of real people.

Intriguing conflicts based on today's constantly changing life-styles.

Four new titles every month.
Available wherever paperbacks are sold.

SUPER-1

Harlequin Temptation dares to be different!

Once in a while, we Temptation editors spot a romance that's truly innovative. To make sure *you* don't miss any one of these outstanding selections, we'll mark them for you.

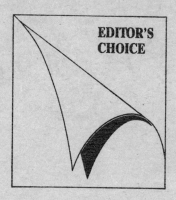

EDITOR'S CHOICE

When the "Editors' Choice" fold-back appears on a Temptation cover, you'll know we've found that extra-special page-turner!

THE

Temptation

EDITORS

Harlequin American Romance

Romances that go one step farther...
American Romance

Realistic stories involving people you can relate to and care about.

Compelling relationships between the mature men and women of today's world.

Romances that capture the core of genuine emotions between a man and a woman.

Join us each month for four new titles wherever paperback books are sold.
Enter the world of American Romance.